Catatonic

ISBN: 9781980859536
Independently published

First Edition

Set in Apple Garamond size 12
Cover Designed by Alyssa DiCarlo

This is a work of fiction. Names, characters, places, and incidents either are the
products of the author's imagination or are used fictitiously. Any resemblance to
actual persons, living or dead, businesses, companies, events, or locales is entirely
coincidental.

For Cassidy

I

Day 722.

A mess of brunette hair concealed an unvaried expression, parted directly down the center as it framed a pair of hollow, sunken cheeks. The oily locks gingerly hugged the woman's chest, several strands fanning outward in an array of split ends as two fingers pried a stray piece from her eyes. Eyelashes briskly batted at the sudden absence of the intrusion, hazel orbs refocusing on the yellowed pages of the written novel held between bony fingers as the hair rotated back into place. She stretched out against the wall, several stiff bones cracking up the length of her back as she brought her knees to her chest. Miniscule pieces of dirt audibly shifted beneath her weight, several microscopic grains easing into the fabric of her sock, courtesy of the hole hovering her big toe.

There were whispers today among the usually timid crowd—whispers of a certain "freak", as they called him. The woman had no knowledge of such a peculiar individual. Although televisions were nonexistent within these walls, word of the outside world traveled fast, courtesy of some of the loud-mouth nurses up on Level 3.

"I heard that Switch is coming today," a beautiful face buried beneath a thick, curly mane confidently announced, dark gaze momentarily flickering in corner-girls direction. The gossiper was known as Nayeli, a twenty-two-year-old with an abundance of naturally curly hair and smooth, olive skin. She apparently plead guilty under the insanity defense and was sentenced to twenty years in the loony-bin. Word on the block was that she beat her brother with a baseball bat after he stole her diary. However, that tale couldn't possibly be true, for she had to have done something dreadfully worse to end up in a place like this.

A place like this a place like this a place like–
"Where'd you hear that from?" Cora interjected, cobalt eyes widened in curiosity as she threaded her fingers through her knotted locks. She leaned forward, the metal feet of her chair noisily sliding against the floor as several onlookers glanced upwards through hooded eyelids.

"Nurse Jackie," Nayeli dryly explained, avoiding the hardened glare of the woman in the corner with a deteriorating copy of *Sense and Sensibility* held tightly in her clutch. Her nails were chipped and uneven, thick mounds of black dirt present beneath the white nail as her hazel gaze lay transfixed on the gossiping women.

"Apparently I've caught the *mutes* attention." Nayeli snickered through half-sealed lips. Cora glanced curiously over her shoulder, chapped lips curling into a devilish smirk as she viewed the woman's stone-cold expression.

"I wonder what he looks like," Cora wondered, reconnecting her gaze with a stiff Nayeli as she attempted to visualize the possible appearance of the notorious villain. "Do you think he's *cute?*"

"Maybe," the olive-skinned girl gloated. "I wonder if they'll make a big deal about his arrival. I mean, he *is* a serial killer and all, or so they say." Nayeli added, chewing mindlessly on her bottom lip as hazel eyes veered away from her rigid frame, returning to the repetitive print imbedded upon the aging pages.

The substantial steel doors opposite the trio swung widely open, revealing a scarlet-cheeked woman in her mid-thirties with precisely dyed platinum blond hair and bright, cobalt eyes. A single nail sat between rows of teeth, widened gaze focusing on the woman with faded brunette locks and holey socks in the left corner of the rec room.

The rec room was decently sized, currently filled with twenty-six-or-so slightly calm and sedated individuals, all of whom were given four hours of socialization time in this very room per day—a decent escape from the confinement of their concrete cells. Matted furniture littered the heavily stained concrete floor—a tri-cushioned couch, matching loveseat, and cracked leather chair, respectively. Most of the material on the sofas lay severely torn, resulting in the insistent picking of the severed fabric by an obsessive man named Lloyd.

Sometimes, Lloyd would be caught tearing the bright white stuffing from the material, rigid fingers delicately slipping the object into his mouth as it disappeared from sight. Until later that night, (or the following morning), of course.

Briar Cunningway has been employed for the asylum's nursing staff for three consecutive years, and she'd taken quite a liking to the mute girl in the furthermost corner. Although she'd known the scraggly-haired woman for nearly two whole years, she didn't have a single clue what her voice actually sounded like.

Simply put, the woman *did not speak.*

Nurse Briar's unpigmented shoes shuffled against the concrete, darting in the direction of the woman clutching her book as she fell to her knees before her.

"Adelaide," Nurse Briar hissed through gritted teeth, her dainty fingers abruptly claiming her clothed knee. Adelaide's emotionless eyes flickered upwards, meeting Nurse Briar's frantic expression as she lowered the book from her hooked nose.

"It's—*uh*," Nurse Briar heavily stuttered, glancing over her shoulder to view the gossiping girls seated several feet away before hastily continuing with, "time for your bath."

A set of nearly nonexistent brows raised in reply, the pages gliding closed on Adelaide's thumb as she observed Nurse Briar's peculiar stance. Typically, Adelaide did not receive her bath until after supper, at the very same time that Nayeli, Cora, and Jasmine received theirs.

"It's an early bath," Nurse Briar added, sensing Adelaide's confusion as she tugged aimlessly at her impossibly skinny forearm. "By yourself, too. You won't have to deal with Jasmine's annoying banters. Come on." She urged, yanking Adelaide into a standing position.

She inaudibly urged Adelaide to slip into her sleek, inky black combat boots—the holed socks disappearing from sight as the silent woman tightly clutched her favorite novel to her chest. The rolled sleeves of her black and white striped trousers eased down the length of her unshaven legs, delicately kissing the leather of her boots as she took Nurse Briar's hand in hers and headed in the direction of the hefty steel doors.

Nayeli and Cora's eyes contorted into tight slits at the sight of the mute promptly exiting the rec room, following closely on Nurse Briar's heel.

"Where's *she* going?" Nayeli murmured, a skeptical expression overcoming her features as Cora merely shrugged. It was best if they didn't pry in regards to Adelaide Lynch. After all, the woman was undoubtedly *psychotic*, (or so it seemed. . .)

The wash room was several doors down from the rec room, complimented with six clawfoot porcelain tubs, nailed firmly into the concrete floors. A trio of tubs claimed either side of the room, respectively. The most interesting aspect of the otherwise bland and colorless room, however, was the shower—if it could even be called that.

Located on the very back wall directly between the rows of tubs laid a broad, open cubicle with zero privacy and faded multi-hued tiles, some cracked and some chipped. Instead of walls, a single pole sat on either side of the "shower", full of grimy fingerprints.

Adelaide glanced in Nurse Briar's direction, pouted bottom lip tugged tightly between her teeth as Briar motioned in the direction of the tub nearest the shower on the right side, her fingers lacing around Adelaide's large top as she motioned for her to remove it.

Why am I the only one taking a bath?

A perplexed expression overcame Adelaide's sullen features, droopy eyes settling upon the vacant tub as she tugged the striped jumpsuit top from her torso. She hadn't worn a bra today, which wasn't necessarily unusual for the woman. The bothersome material nearly suffocated her breasts, and even gave her backaches.

Unlike the typical orange jumpsuits prisoners wore, the patients at Stillwater Sanitarium were supplied with two-piece ensembles, layered with faded blackish/gray and white stripes. Hovering Adelaide's left breast was her patient number, sewn precisely onto the fabric with inky thread.

Patient 4210.

"Adelaide," Nurse Briar urged, trembling fingers lacing around the decorative metal taps as the water obnoxiously emerged from the faucet.

"You need to hurry up and get in the tub, sweetie. I think they're bringing in someone for a cleansing."

Oh. That's why she brought me here.

Adelaide nodded, lips curling into a smirk as she shuffled out of her clothing, discarding them into a heaping pile along with her unlaced boots and worn book at the foot of the half-full tub.

Just as the silent woman settled into the lukewarm water—her bountiful breasts concealed by the deeply filled basin—an influx of slamming doors and loud shouts suddenly emerged. Nurse Briar let out a considerable squeak, falling to her knees behind the tub as she squeezed a bit too much shampoo into her palm. Her pulse quickened beneath her ribcage, thumping thickly in her throat as the commotion increased.

Adelaide's gaze lay glued upon the broad, open doorway, brows cocked in curiosity as Nurse Briar's fingers threaded into her tangled locks, massaging the soap into her skull as she let out a muted sigh of relief at the feel. The woman absolutely adored bath time—in a peculiar, maybe inappropriate and completely morbid way—it reminded her of bath time as a child. Only these baths were given in the presence of others, males and females intermixed. At Stillwater, *nothing* was private.

"Piece of shit." A firm tone announced, voice slightly muffled by the concrete walls as the distinct sonance of heavy-footed steps appeared.

Nurse Briar's nails unintentionally dug into the thin skin of Adelaide's scalp, prompting a petite squeak to emerge from the shy woman's mouth as Briar spluttered a series of apologies immediately following. The woman's heart was beating so rapidly she feared it may burst straight out of her chest.

Suddenly, five-or-so armed men entered the premises, failing to even glance in Briar and Adelaide's direction as they urged their prey into the cleansing chamber.

Nurse Briar audibly gulped, her thick, erratic breaths showering Adelaide's neck as goosebumps instinctively arose at the mixture of the situation and the sensation. Her sopping wet hands emerged from the basin, fingers curling around the circular sides of the tub as she agonizingly squeezed.

Two men ushered a strange individual into the nearly vacant room—a lanky figure with wide, broad-shoulders that lay hunched as he walked. Unkempt, chestnut-hued curls concealed his vision, several ringlets clinging to the sweat present on his glistening neck as the guards spat obscenities in his direction. His sullen expression was pale and oily—deep, dark bags cloaking the supple skin beneath his drooping eyes as a gruesome deformity cloaked half of his complexion. The man, however, remained deathly silent towards the guards heated insults.

Nurse Briar continued to mindlessly massage the shampoo into

Adelaide's sudsy hair, utterly transfixed at the scene as she intently observed the man in red, who was currently being lead in the direction of the shower.

Adelaide painfully gulped, eyelids squeezing shut as she quickly reminisced on her first day at Stillwater and her experience with the shower. The crimson, swollen welts on her arms and legs took fifteen days to eventually dissipate.

The strange man was dressed in an abundance of black and red—a nice pair of inky pinstripe slacks claimed his legs, complimented by a crimson hued dress shirt, accessorized with a profusion of miscellaneous designs. The wrinkled sleeves lay dowdily rolled at the elbows, thick fabric contorted into uneven folds as the material loosely clung to his skin. A sleek black tie claimed his neck, which was currently entangled between the fingers of a considerably pissed-off guard as he hastily tore it off.

Adelaide's knuckles flushed a deathly white due to her death grip on the porcelain, eyes wild with horror as she observed the scene unfold. Nurse Briar still managed to massage her nearly raw scalp with shampoo, drifting into a temporary trance as she, too, couldn't seem to tear her gaze away.

Her lips suddenly met Adelaide's ear, prompting the woman to impulsively flinch at the sudden sensation as the soapy water shifted against her obscene jerk. Several droplets eased over the sides, splattering the floor with varying shapes as Briar whispered a haunting confirmation into Adelaide's ear: "Switch."

An immediate shiver overcame the rigid woman's every limb, her eyes remaining unblinking as she carefully studied the man in red as the guards forcefully thrust him into position. Shallow breaths emerged from an anxious Adelaide as the guards aggressively yanked Switch's arms in the directions of the scuffed silver poles, latching one end of a pair of cuffs around the pole, whereas the other half claimed the man's scarlet tainted wrists. By the looks of it, the guards had applied the cuffs extremely tight, as clear indents appeared upon his flesh. Adelaide winced at the sight, hazel gaze flickering in the direction of her wrists as she squeezed the porcelain between clammy fingers.

The man—Switch, apparently—laced his crimson-riddled fingers around the cool poles, the distinct sonance of the metal cuffs clinking against the surface sent violent shivers down the length of Adelaide's spine as she physically twitched. Nurse Briar realized her blatant reactions, similar shivers overcoming her limbs as she slowly rid the woman's hair of the excess soap.

"Undress him." A beefy guard with hardly any neck barked through gritted teeth, a slimy wooden toothpick buried between his lips.

Adelaide frowned as she watched the guards literally cut the clothing from Switch's body, discarding the ruined material into bulky heaps on the floor as they began to tear open the silky fabric of his decorative dress shirt.

Switch's head lay bowed, shoulders hunched as he clung tightly onto the metal poles. Several oily ringlets lay in his eyes, marred bottom lip tucked harshly between stained teeth as his eyelids screwed agonizingly shut.

The guards sliced the material directly down the center of his back, revealing an essence of pale, muscular skin as they tore the fabric away in several large pieces. Briar's jaw fell agape at the mortifying sight—the muscles beneath Switch's flesh contracting with rage as his shoulders dramatically rose and fell with every deep, staggered breath. A series of dark ink claimed his upper arms, arrays of miscellaneous drawings, which varied in shapes and size—as well as multiple handwritten terms and scripts. His knuckles flushed a ghastly white as his grip tightened, head hung low on his shoulders as the guards tore at his trousers, as well as urging him to step out of his shoes.

Surprisingly, the silent man obliged with their every request, stripping down bare as Briar silently instructed Adelaide to clean her body, a weak attempt to keep them busy.

"Back away." The guard with hardly a neck thickly ordered, voice muffled by the presence of the toothpick.

The others did as they were told, quickly side-stepping as a steady stream of water suddenly erupted from the hose at an appalling speed.

Switch's lids squeezed shut, a heavy wince overcoming his pale, marred features as the water furiously pelted his bare back. The stream felt like a thousand hot knives repeatedly striking his flesh, the scorching temperature nearly boiling his skin raw as he choked back painful shouts. Suddenly, it was nearly impossible to breathe, his lungs neglecting to intake air as he repugnantly gasped.

The balmy water drenched his oily locks, plastering the loose curls to the sore skin of his craned neck as his back heavily heaved with every stagnant breath.

Finally, after what seemed like an eternity, the stream ceased.

Switch dramatically inhaled through parted lips, his tight grip loosening on the metal poles as his glowing skin flushed bright scarlet, still painfully stinging from the intense heat and speed of the water.

"Spin him 'round."

A petite whine got caught in the madman's throat, the guards quickly returning as they unlatched one wrist at a time from the safety of the cuffs. His left hand scooped downward, cradling himself in his palm as he effectively concealed his genitals. Although the duo had remained exceptionally silent, he was well aware of the presence of two *lovely ladies* in the room.

The guards roughly spun him around, aggressively latching his single free hand to the pole once more as his fingers laced around the metal, clinging to the material for dear life as he mentally prepared himself for the pain to return.

Empty, soulless eyes momentarily flickered in Adelaide and Briar's direction, searching the women's faces for any plausible response at all as he prepared for the absolute worst. How *degrading* was this . . .

Switch was being forced into submission, and he did *not* like it.

A miniscule, tight-lipped grin overcame Adelaide's features as she sympathetically smiled in Switch's direction, as if to wordlessly ensure him that it would be over soon enough. The water in the basin had gone cold, her breasts still effectively submerged beneath the soapy liquid as the beefy guard ignited the scarring stream once more.

Switch heavily grimaced as the harsh water met his torso, lips curling into a distasteful scoff as his head lulled backwards. His Adam's apple obscenely shifted beneath the clammy skin of his neck as the water continued to pelt his skin, leaving behind painful sores in its wake as his hold tightened around his extremities.

I promise it'll all be okay. The pain will end soon.

Adelaide's fingers unconsciously glided along her pale skin, a frown overcoming her complexion as she vividly recalled the ghastly sores that once coated her flesh, courtesy of that very same hose, operated by that very same thick-necked guard with a toothpick between his chapped lips.

"Straighten your neck, fucker! I need to clean that hideous face!" The guard shouted, his stern tone ricocheting off the concrete walls as Switch hastily obeyed, his limp neck straightening as his beady, black eyes disappeared from view.

The steady stream suddenly met his complexion, fingers once again tightening around the pole as the madman choked back a hefty shout, a distressed wince riddling his complexion as the water pelted his lacerated features, which glowed a vibrant scarlet beneath the exceedingly hot temperature of the water.

Oddly enough, Adelaide found the sight conflictingly beautiful. The flushed flesh of Switch's toned torso was effortlessly marred by the intrusive liquid, arrays of fraternal, discolored welts coating the exposed flesh of his stomach and legs as the hose left behind physical evidence of its aggravated assault.

Eventually, the strand steered from his bare features, displaying a ghastly group of glowing scars along the left side of his face, scars that Adelaide hadn't even entirely noticed before. Horrifyingly, the left half of his face was nearly mutilated entirely—strutting an abundance of shallow, uneven scars, at least four or five of them. They were all fraternal, completely different in both shape and depth, the woman noticed from this distance. She could only steadily study the most prominent (and the ghastliest) of the bunch—a deep laceration that started at the corner of his frayed mouth and pointed down towards his jaw, taking a sharp hook towards his chin before abruptly stopping, as if unfinished. She'd *never* seen such a morbid, artificial deformity before this very day, and it was evident that whoever had disfigured Switch's face had ultimately failed at their mission, as the right cheek remained completely unscathed. In fact, compared to the left side of his face, the right half was in particularly good shape—entirely free of any artificial markings. An additional, deeply healed cut hugged the underneath of his eye, about an inch-or-so in length as it covered up any evidence of deep, inky bags that would typically claim the supple skin in that particular area. A multitude of additional healed scrapes claimed that very same cheek and temple, prompting Adelaide's stomach to violently churn at the undeniably morbid sight.

This poor man . . .

The guard tossed the inactive hose aside, snatching a bundle of robes from an additional guard as he thrust it in Switch's direction.

"Dress." He simply ordered as they unlatched the criminal from the confinement of his cuffs.

His bare features hastily met Adelaide's blank expression, several soaked ringlets claiming the flushed skin of his cheeks as he ineptly tore his palm away from his goods.

Unlike Briar, Adelaide diverted her stare, respecting the strange man's privacy as she saw him quickly dress from her peripheral vision. She'd seen what lay buried beneath his hold for only a moment, which left a conflicting image burning in the back of her mind. She almost—*almost*—wanted to verbally scold Briar for gawking at his naked form, but she swallowed the statement with difficulty as the voices thoroughly convinced her otherwise.

After all, it was *them* who were in charge.

Once Switch's lanky form was cloaked by the heavy fabric of the mandatory jumpsuit, Adelaide's stare returned—a reassuring expression overcoming her features as the guards cuffed his wrists together once more. Her hazel orbs glided along to his left peck, where the number 4428 lay engraved upon the fabric with thick black thread.

Before Adelaide knew it, the madman was gone, dragged from the room by the irritable group of guards as Nurse Briar began to drain the cold water from the tub.

"I'm sorry," Nurse Briar murmured, assisting a rigid Adelaide as she clambered from the emptying tub. "I'm selfish. I shouldn't have brought you here just so I could be nosy."

Adelaide eased back into the comfort of her jumpsuit, tugging the soiled socks back onto her feet as her palm confidently met Nurse Briar's shoulder, a reassuring, toothy grin tugging at her lips in the place of audible acceptance.

"By the way," Nurse Briar began, threading her fingers through Adelaide's stringy, wet hair in a sloppy attempt to style it. "He's moving into the cell next to yours."

II

"The only thing that I could see
Was a pair of brown eyes that was looking at me."
–The Pogues, "A Pair of Brown Eyes"

Per tradition, new arrivals at Stillwater Sanitarium are required to go without supper for the first night. Although this may seem cruel to an outsider, most new patients either intentionally or unintentionally starve themselves for the first several days regardless. After being admitted to a psych ward, eating is truly the *last* thing on one's mind.

Similar to the rec room, Adelaide Lynch sat secluded in the furthermost corner of the cafeteria, her back plastered against the concrete wall as a vibrantly colored plastic tray lay upon her lap, the compartments precisely filled with an assortment of hardly edible eats.

The cafeteria floor was layered with checkered tiles, some a faded army color, and others a bleak yellow–resembling butterscotch. Three obscenely long rectangular tables covered the floor—creme colored—with disk-shaped seats. The tables gently reminded Adelaide of the tables present in her high school cafeteria.

Times were best back then.

Mindless chatter of thirty-two surprisingly cheerful individuals filled Adelaide's ears, her fingers curling around a soft circular dinner roll as her mind drifted to the scarred-face man from the shower.

They called him Switch. The alias was almost ironic, considering the deep, gruesome scar that lined his left cheek, accompanied by a profusion of dissimilar lacerations—which were most likely created by a dull switchblade. As Adelaide's thoughts momentarily drifted towards Switch's interesting complexion, she couldn't help but wonder—*had he carved his own face?*

Hazel eyes drifted towards the surrounding guards, the pad of her thumb tracing the soft mound of bread in her palm. Three male guards manned the petite cafeteria, typically hovering a corner each, as the fourth corner was always claimed by a tight-lipped and severely stiff Adelaide. The young, baby-faced guards strut navy-hued suits, the ankles of their slacks tucked messily into black laced combat boots, which were identical to the ones present on Adelaide's tiny feet.

The woman audibly gulped, tightening her hold on the roll as all three guards diverted their attention, allowing the shy woman to effortlessly conceal the food into the waistband of her trousers.

"Time's up, Lynch."

Adelaide instantly stilled the moment that dreadful tone emerged from above her petite frame, heart thumping thickly in her throat as the room begun to violently spin.

He's going to hurt you again.

He's going to touch you again.

Exhausted eyelids screwed shut, digits curling into tight fists at her sides as the man snatched the hardly touched tray of food from her lap, his knuckles grazing the slight lump present beneath her pants as a painful breath hitched in her throat.

Today was apparently Elliot Greenwald's first day back from his thirty-day suspension. *If only the suspension could've been infinite . . .*

He was a scrawny fella with biceps full of muscle and thick tan skin, cloaked with an abundance of vibrantly colored tattoos. By the looks of his chicken legs, it was apparent that Elliot focused a bit too much on lifting weights and forgot all about the cardio. His hair was fine and slowly dissipating, crimson in hue and curling around his precisely pierced ears. To an average woman, Elliot was mildly attractive. However—to Adelaide Lynch—Elliot Greenwald was the most hideous individual she'd ever encountered, mainly due to his sickening personality.

Elliot assertively yanked Adelaide into a standing position, her weakened knees wobbling slightly at the sudden shift as her limbs locked up, imitating a statue. His emerald eyes dramatically rolled at the sight, an audible grunt escaping through Chapstick-smeared lips as he laced his ring-clad fingers around her skinny wrists, forcefully yanking her arms into a downward position as he laced a pair of metal cuffs around her scrawny wrists.

"Jesus, Greenwald," a second voice announced, a pair of urgent eyes meeting Adelaide's still form. Soft, cocoa-tinted eyes immediately met her empty orbs, delicate fingers lacing around the secured cuffs as he shoved a tiny silver key into the lock. "Lynch doesn't need cuffs. She's not a threat."

"Just let me do my job, Vern." Elliot Greenwald lowly snipped, his grip faltering on Adelaide's aching arm as he ran a disgruntled hand through his hair.

"Obviously you don't know how to properly *do* it, considering you were on a month's unpaid suspension." Vern countered, locking his fingers around Adelaide's incredibly tiny bicep as he silently urged her to begin walking. "I'll take Lynch back to her cell. Why don't you escort Nayeli instead?"

Greenwald released a prolonged sigh, thrusting a suggestive hand gesture in Vern's unfazed face before twisting on his heel and rapidly approaching a chirpy Nayeli two tables away.

"Sorry 'bout him," Vern whispered dismissively, leading Adelaide out the swinging double doors of the cafeteria as several security guards followed, a single patient held in each of their grasps. "I wish Dr. Evers would've just fired his ass. I've heard about the—*things*—he's done to some of you girls. It's repulsive."

Adelaide's lips transformed into a tight frown as extremely intrusive recollections of Greenwald's grubby hand dipping beneath the waist of her trousers appeared, making her stomach painfully churn and the bile to rise up into her throat.

Vern directed the woman towards a nearby elevator, his bottom lip jutting outward in a sloppy attempt to blow away a loose jet-black curl from his line of sight. Just like Nurse Briar, he'd taken quite a liking to Adelaide Lynch, regardless of her diagnosis. Whether it be due to the fact that the woman was practically a statue—he wasn't quite sure. All in all, she was the most compliant patient currently enrolled in Stillwater Sanitarium.

The duo clambered into the right corner of the elevator, squishing along the back wall to allow several guards and additional patients to enter the tiny compartment. A strangled breath caught in Adelaide's throat at the exceedingly cramped space, her pulse quickening as a sense of extreme claustrophobia began to truly sink in.

Hefty double doors glided closed, sealing the chamber once and for all as widened eyes frantically searched the area for possible escape routes. The air was stale and still, so agonizingly silent that a single pin dropping would surely ripple through the air with gratification.

Get out.

Get out get out get out get out.

A whine vibrated thickly throughout Adelaide's throat, her weight shifting from either foot as Vern's questionable glare refocused on her rigid stance.

"Lynch?" He lowly inquired, tightening his hold on the anxious woman as she squeezed her eyelids tightly shut. Her paling lips slightly parted, an exasperated exhale exiting as her worrisome gaze met Vern's—trembling skull nodding in reassurance as she desperately attempted to ward off the heightened voices.

She shook with rage, firmly ordering the voices to go away as the elevator promptly arrived at the fourth level.

You're stuck with us forever, remember?

"We're almost at your cell, Lynch. Just try and relax. Nurse Briar will bring you your meds soon." Vern assured the woman in a hushed tone, avoiding the piercing gaze of a hunched Cora as a separate guard tugged her from the confinement of the elevator.

Level 4 was poorly lit and smelt of mold and dust. The bland concrete floors were stained with a variety of substances—blood, fecal matter, urine, vomit—the whole nine yards. The eerie halls were illuminated by single light bulbs, which were buried in petite pockets along the ceiling and produced an undeviating buzz at every moment of the day. The presence of windows was absent in all portions of the sanitarium, all except for the rec room and the front foyer, a room which was off-limits to all patients and heavily gated for security measures. Within the deep halls and miserable cells, sunlight was entirely nonexistent. Nobody knew what time of day it was in these areas. To Adelaide, however, time simply did not exist.

Adelaide and Vern shuffled into the familiar cell block, his grip loosening on the thin skin of her arm. This particular block held six cells, three on each side.

The guard and the silent woman rapidly approached the second and middle cell on the right, his free fingers lacing around a rectangular plastic card as he tore the clipped identification badge from his outer shirt pocket. The card slipped elegantly between the indented plastic, gliding in a downwards motion as the tiny circular light present on the pad flushed a vibrant green.

The mahogany, rusted steel door unlatched with a clamorous *click*, swinging open on the hinges as Vern politely applied a fair amount of pressure to Adelaide's shoulder with his palm, urging her to enter the silent abyss of her apparently permanent home.

"Goodnight, Adelaide." He whispered, a weak grin tugging at his full lips as the door snapped shut on his heel, audibly locking once more as the woman let out a strangled sigh.

The cells on this level were decently sized—accented with a single, twin-sized bed with a shiny metal frame. The mattress resembled a pile of rocks and the pillow was as good as a stack of old withered newspapers, but it was better than sleeping on the floor. A metal toilet and matching sink hovered the back wall, pieces of furniture that were always effortlessly freezing. In addition, a single, triple-drawer wooden dresser lay upon the opposite wall, containing several different approved outfits and an additional striped jumpsuit.

The only bars present within these particular cells was a row of six on the steel door, placed neatly inside a broad rectangular box. This box had measured about a foot in length and a half-foot in height, and Adelaide had to stand on her tippy-toes to view the cell block on the opposite side. The surrounding walls were bland, thin concrete, only about an inch or so in width, but cold and dark, nonetheless. Typically, the confinement of these particularly constructed cells disallowed patients from viewing one another. However, the recently deceased patient who resided in Adelaide's neighboring cell had gone on a little rampage before his untimely demise.

Adelaide's back faced the sealed steel door, hazel gaze transfixed on the uneven circular hole present in the direct center of the right concrete wall. The obscene hole was rather large in size, measuring ten-or-so inches in height and the very same in length. Due to Stillwater's irritable budget cuts and differing priorities, the hole had never been patched.

The woman quickly shuffled out of the strict confinement of her unlaced leather combat boots, kicking them sloppily aside as her socked feet met the cold floor. Involuntary shivers engulfed her spine at the sudden sensation, the hole hovering over her big toe gradually widening as the sock tore further open.

Come on, Addy.
Stick your fingers beneath your belt, sweetheart.
You know what to do. You've managed to sneak it in.
Finish the job.

Hesitantly, the rigid woman obeyed, slipping her trembling fingers beneath the waist of her striped jumpsuit as she retrieved the soft dinner roll, which sat snug between the fabric and her recently cleansed skin.

An audible gulp traveled throughout her throat as she dragged her sock-clad feet along the ground, insistent piles of sand and dirt ineptly slipping into the depths of her holed socks as she openly grimaced at the feel.

Maybe it's time for some new socks, love.

Adelaide froze several inches from the hole, free fingers clenching into a furious fist as she mentally spat a phrase back at the bothersome voice: *No! No change!*

Have it your way, the voice snidely countered, a slight hiccup present in its tone. *Whether you like it or not, things are going to change, sweetie. Starting with **him**.*

The woman eventually met the glassless window, which hovered over her concealed belly in height as she slowly fell to her knees. Staggered breaths escaped through cracked lips, knees abruptly colliding with the concrete as a wince overcame her features. Wild eyes observed the now occupied neighboring cell, which laid vacant for many days—up until now.

Trembling fingers met the rough edge of the concrete, placing the food onto the petite ledge as she choked back a mouthful of bile. The wall separating the duo was incredibly thin, so thin that the roll took up the entirety of the inch-thick surface.

A pair of uncommonly dark eyes flickered in Adelaide's direction, conflicting hazel orbs widening at the sight as greasy brunette curls audibly shifted against the scratchy pillowcase present beneath his skull.

Nothing could've possibly prepared Adelaide for the astonishing melodic sound that would momentarily emerge. The tone was dark, undoubtedly calamitous and oddly gravely and thick. The sonance rippled keenly through the stale air, bouncing elegantly among the nearly paper-thin concrete walls as involuntary shivers cloaked Adelaide's every limb, her jaw parting in deep fascination as patches of persistent goosebumps arose underneath the jumpsuit that clothed her torso.

"What's *that*? Some kind'a-*uh*, *peace* offering?" He boldly inquired, a snicker falling off of his tainted lips as he thrust himself into a sitting position upon the rickety bed.

Adelaide intently observed as the man's legs tugged away from the bed, the thin, unpigmented blanket hooking around his boot-clad ankle as he hastily kicked it off. The soles of his shoes efficiently met the ground, the dry, cracking skin of his elbows colliding with a set of knees as an array of scarlet, circular burns appeared on his uncovered forearms. The sleeves of his top had been messily rolled, hooked behind the prominent skin of his elbows as the woman carefully studied the dark ink imbedded upon his flesh.

For starters, his left wrist was encircled by several inky lines, arranged in the form of a bracelet, it appeared. Adelaide used to wear bracelets similar to that odd tattoo as a child. Nonetheless, she was slightly stunned that a man would get something so—*odd*—permanently engraved upon his flesh. By the looks of it—from this angle, at least—the woman was also able to see some type of extremely dark flower coating several inches of skin along that very same forearm, her nearly invisible brows knitting together in bewilderment as she studied the abundance of designs present on his exposed lower arms.

"Not much of a talker, *hm*?" He teased, cautiously studying Adelaide's appalled expression as a suggestive, toothy grin claimed his scarred lips. It was then that she'd noticed the clear discoloration present around his left eye. The dainty skin was flushed a violent violet hue, accented with a slight yellowish tint as he mindlessly picked at the excess skin present on his fingernails. The black eye seemed to further intensify the gaudy, uneven scar that lay directly beneath, which was swollen and red, as if fresh.

Once his gaze had curiously met hers once more, he'd noticed that she was pointing to her own eye. A snort emerged through his nostrils at the innocent gesture, her index finger circling her skin as she wordlessly urged him to spill some kind of explanation.

"Green *somethin'*," he grunted, clearly referencing the idiotic Elliot Greenwald, who apparently took the liberty to punch Switch while he was already down.

Adelaide simply nodded, stomach contorting into thick knots at the mere thought of Greenwald's hideous face as she tapped the dinner roll with a single finger, urging Switch to come and collect the item of food.

"You could've-*uh*, gotten in trouble for nickin' that, y'know." He mused, shuffling into a standing position as he slowly approached the hole present in the wall.

The air stiffened as he fell to his knees before it, mimicking Adelaide's frozen stance as she held her breath. He was within inches of her face, a healed, faded scar vertically lining the left side of his cheek as his marred lips amusingly twitched. His mouth slightly parted, allowing a soft pink tongue to sliver out from the depths, the tip poking and prodding at the deep lacerations present upon his flesh as dirt-riddled fingers laced around the soft object. Several extremely lengthy bothersome curls framed his face, drifting into his eyes as he studied the item.

Switch took the dinner roll into his grasp, eyeing the food questioningly before meeting Adelaide's skeptical glare once more.

"What's your *name*, princess?" The man softly cooed, shifting the bread between calloused fingers as his unblinking eyes bore deeply into hers.

Adelaide frowned, forehead heavily crinkling as she argued with the irritating voices in her skull.

Let me tell him, she begged.

No. Not yet.

Adelaide audibly sighed, her fingers dancing along the wall as they inched further up towards the hole. *Please. He's really sweet.*

He's a psychopathic killer. Why else would he be locked up here?

Because he's like me, she thought. The voice did not counter her argument.

Cautiously, her fingers cradled the choppy edges of the hole, inching closer towards Switch's unwavering expression as he eyed the woman curiously. Just as she'd managed to thrust her hand through, the very tips of her fingers just *barely* grazing his lacerated cheek, a heavy knock erupted on her door.

Fearfully, she yanked her hand back onto her side of the wall, a heightened gasp escaping her lips as Nurse Briar's muffled voice emerged, saying: "I'm coming in with your medication, Adelaide!"

"Ade-*laide*," Switch growled, lips curling into a devilish smirk as he twirled the roll between his fingers. "You'll-*uh*, hafta *tell* me about this little hole here." His fingers collided with the uneven edges of the concrete, curious, chocolate-tinted eyes scanning the oblong shape as he twisted on his heel and abandoned the glassless window.

Adelaide quickly strut across the room, easing onto the bed that hovered the opposite wall as she claimed the thin duvet between strangled fingers.

The rusted, mahogany door swung elegantly open, revealing a grinning Nurse Briar with two decorative paper cups in her hold.

"Hey, Ad," she whispered, closing the door tightly on her heel to prevent any means of escape as she sunk to her knees before the colorless bed. "Interesting day, huh?"

Adelaide snatched the cup of three multi-hued pills from Nurse Briar's palm, bringing the soft paper to her parted lips as she tossed the circular objects into her gaping mouth before chasing them down with a swig full of water.

Nurse Briar glanced fleetingly over her shoulder, eyeing a lax Switch laid upon his bed, boot-clad ankles precisely crossed as he nibbled away at a piece of bread from supper. Her brows perplexedly raised, gaze reconnecting with a skittish Adelaide as her palm met her jumpsuit-cloaked knee.

"Don't worry," Briar whispered, squeezing the skin slightly beneath her hold. "I didn't see anything."

III

It happened on day 688.

Oliver Quinten had lived in Switch's current cell for six and a half years. He was a fairly quiet individual, with a messy mane of brown hair and identically colored eyes. Freckles littered his features like constellations, dipping between the innermost creases of his pointed nose and even onto his thin upper lip.

He was fairly nice to Adelaide, always greeting her in the mornings, asking her how she slept even though her response was always a simplistic nod. And yet, he'd still ask every single morning without fail.

Oliver was a social butterfly in the rec room, always poking his nose in others business as he offered to teach several patients how to play chess. Several took him up on the offer, and eventually, Lloyd became his permanent partner for some solid two-hundred days on the dot.

On that two-hundredth day, also known as Adelaide's six-hundred and eighty-eighth day at Stillwater, Oliver was catapulted into a raging downward spiral after receiving news of his wife's sudden death, an unfortunate result of a tragic motor vehicle accident.

Things began to go south following the news. Within the next fourteen hours, Oliver Quinten had banished himself to his cell, muttering strands of obscenities underneath his breath as Adelaide listened through a curious ear, which sat pressed firmly up against the concrete wall. His low tone was muffled by the obstruction, but the woman was clearly able to hear the diabolical phrases that slipped off his silver tongue. Just before Adelaide's evening bath, an obscene, muffled ruckus emerged from Oliver's half of the wall, the distinct sound of the bed frame violently scraping against the concrete floor prompted a heavy wince to overcome the woman's features as she curled into a petite, fearful ball atop her thin mattress.

Somehow, in some super-human strength type of way—Oliver managed to plunge a miniscule hole through the thin concrete separating their cells, only about two-and-a-half inches in diameter as a horrified shriek tumbled off Adelaide's parted lips.

Her trembling fingers had laced tightly around the thin duvet, tugging the fabric up to her face as she concealed her gaping mouth, hazel orbs wide with fright as Oliver continued to repeatedly strike the wall with the metal frame of the bed.

The rotting concrete began to peel away like butter, revealing a wild, untamed expression as the man attempted to crawl his way through the wall, bloodied fingers digging into the harsh, uneven material as heightened cries escaped Adelaide's lips. His usually tamed hair had gone awry, sticking obscenely up in sporadic places as bloodshot eyes glared deeply into hers as he attempted to crawl his way through. After several excruciating minutes of quivering violently in her spot, Nurse Briar came to the rescue, yanking the woman's door open with glee as she cheerfully announced the arrival of her bath. However, once her stare had settled upon an irate Oliver literally crawling his way through the wall, she too had let out a horrified shout, her slender digits lacing around Adelaide's bicep as she practically tore her from the bed.

"F-Fuck! Holy shit—*Addy*! Hurry up!" The artificial blond ushered in a hoarse tone, dragging the woman from the confinement of her cell as Nurse Briar obnoxiously called for help, her fingers laced tightly in Adelaide's as they scurried down the dingy cell block.

Oliver's cell remained unoccupied for thirty-four days. That was, until the infamous Switch had arrived. Nobody knows exactly how Oliver died, but Adelaide was almost certain that Greenwald had planted a bullet between his eyes.

"Why doesn't Miss Lynch speak?" The unfamiliar woman thickly inquired, vibrant blue eyes magnified by the thick lenses of her oval-rimmed spectacles as she eyed a stiff Nurse Briar.

"She's a catatonic schizophrenic," the nurse uneasily explained, smoothing her clammy palms along the fabric of her lilac scrubs as she avoided Mrs. Blake's placid expression.

"*Catatonia?*" Mrs. Blake gawked, purple painted lips parting in awe as she claimed the hefty manila folder in her grasp, manicured finger curling around the edge of the thick paper as Adelaide's files riddled her vision. "Kind of rare in this day and age, isn't it? Especially for such long periods of time?"

"Perhaps," Nurse Briar slyly replied, dainty fingertips fiddling with the back of an old, ripped plush chair. "One thing I've learned from working in an *asylum* is that nothing is impossible, ma'am."

Mrs. Blake's sturdy gaze lay transfixed on the abundance of papers neatly clipped into the folder, the pad of her index finger grazing Adelaide's mugshot.

"Adelaide Rhea Lynch," she murmured, a series of inaudible mumbles immediately following the patient's name as she scanned the basic information printed in fine ink. "Age twenty-four, one sibling, parents divorced, *yadda–yadda–yadda...*"

Nurse Briar uncomfortably shifted her weight from each foot, timid gaze carefully studying a mumbling, middle-aged woman opposite her as she intently scanned Adelaide's files.

"Why are there no recent sessions?" Mrs. Blake boldly pried, magnetized glare meeting an indifferent Briar once more.

"How could she have sessions if she doesn't speak?" The woman countered.

"Touché, I suppose. However, every patient requires at least one monthly session, at least under my personal preference. Tell me, Miss—er—"

"Cunningway." Nurse Briar spat.

"Right. Miss Cunningway," the woman breathed. "It appears you've spent nearly every day with this woman since her arrival. Tell me, when is that last time she's spoken?"

"Mrs. Blake," Nurse Briar stammered, mouth instantly running dry as skeptical eyes met hers. "Adelaide has never spoken here."

It was around three in the morning on day 723 when Adelaide Lynch abruptly woke from her deep slumber to the sound of a menacing cackle.

The sonance began as a low rumble, creating arrays of goosebumps along her exposed flesh as the frantic woman tore her frizzy hair from the static-riddled pillowcase. The bleak duvet shifted beneath her weight, blanket tangling tightly around her bony ankle as the sound managed to crescendo into a full-fledge laugh.

An abundance of air instantly eluded her lungs at the foreign sound, the miniscule hairs present on her skin standing tall as her stomach painfully churned. The laugh was a mixture of peculiar sounds: insistent giggles that transformed into obnoxious cackles, and vice-versa. It was a haunting noise, one that she'd never heard in the twenty-four years she'd been alive. It was one of those sounds that made the blood instantaneously curdle inside her veins—the type of sound that made her skin agonizingly crawl and toes uneasily curl.

Make it stop.

Make it stop make it stop make it stop.

A strangled whine slipped through her ajar lips, socked feet meeting the frigid floor as she slunk from the safety of her bed. Unfortunately, the sudden shift in weight prompted the metal frame to obnoxiously creak, generating a sound that cleanly ricocheted off the thin walls and dipped swiftly through the blatant hole present in the wall.

It was then that the laughter ceased.

Adelaide halted in place, her palms gently cradling her biceps as she shivered from the shift in temperature. Her torso was currently cloaked by a simplistic white tank top, leaving very little to the imagination as her nipples promptly hardened in response to the cool floor beneath the soles of her feet.

The habitual striped jumpsuit bottoms claimed her legs, laying low on her hips as a slight strip of her midriff lay completely exposed, prominent hip bones shifting with every miniscule movement as she inched closer and closer to the gaping hole that revealed Switch's now very silent cell.

She fell to her knees, peering curiously through the ten-inch wide hole to view the madman that lay within. However, due to the severe lack of light, nothing but a deep, black abyss greeted her eyesight, a thick swallow traveling through her throat as she clambered back to her feet.

During lights off, the only light present in the drastically small compartments were those of the hallway, which were a low, blue hue, one that reminded the woman of the old screen savers on desktop computers.

The dainty lights barely illuminated the cells, flooding in through the rectangular box (complimented with those six metal bars) present on the hefty steel doors.

Oddly enough, the low hue was slightly comforting to most. It resembled the type of moonlight that would bleed in through the cracked blinds present on the windows. To most, the simplistic lights brought a sense of comfort within these wretched walls.

Adelaide hesitantly eased back onto the rock-hard mattress, her legs ineptly curling beneath the drastically thin sheet as her hair fanned out in diverse directions upon the measly pillow.

You should've talked to him.

You should've. You should've. You should've.

Adelaide's eyelids squeezed tightly shut, several stars littering her vision as she countered the voices' compelling argument. *Why would I do that? Did you hear that laugh? He's absolutely mad!*

And absolutely handsome.

Her features contorted into a grimace, Switch's complex expression raiding her thoughts as those compelling scars absolutely tortured her soul. Oh—how the voices were *always* right! He was exotic, unlike any man Adelaide had ever encountered. He struts a head full of obscenely long hair— a comforting, brunette hue and presumably unwashed for prolonged periods of time. The strands were exceptionally wavy, curling heavily in particular places, especially around his ears, she'd noticed. Those eyes—like endless cases of cocoa. Her father worked at a candy factory during her youth, and she'd always loved viewing the massive amounts of finely shredded cocoa, which created a fascinating color, drastically similar to the irises that claimed Switch's confident, lively orbs. Fingers—much like her own, as they were surprisingly slender, yet masculine and calloused all at the same time. The irregular ink etched upon his flesh, creating morbid pictures along his skin— each of them told a story, whether or not that was his intention—to Adelaide, each individual piece of artwork had a true tale to tell. Plus, his muscular arms looked oh so *ravishing* with the complimentary ink upon them . . .

The *scars*. Oh, how she so heavily *craved* the feeling of those mysterious lacerations etched upon his flawless features. He must've been a handsome chap before his disfigurement—tremendously handsome, by the looks of it. Such a charming, toothy grin, accented with deep smile lines, the way his cheeks elegantly folded several times as his lips curled into a toothy, genuine grin—one that she'd seen for a split second, but the image had permanently embedded itself into the depths of her mind. All (*four? five?*) of them were jagged, uneven, gruesome, horrifying and morbid and just—*perfect*. A perfect batch of miscellaneous mismatched scars to compliment a dashing face.

All of those scars would feel marvelous between your legs, eh? Especially that one by his mouth.

Stop. Adelaide spat, uncomfortably shifting against the mattress as she buried her hooked nose into the questionably smelly pillowcase.

You can't deny it, sweet heart. You're obsessed.

I hardly know him, Adelaide thickly countered, eyes screwing tightly shut in a weakened attempt to drift off into a dreamless sleep. *There's nothing for me to be obsessed with.*

The 'not knowing him' is an easy fix. Plus, there's many things to be obsessed with. I mean, just look at him for Heaven's sake.

The exhausted woman released an exaggerated sigh, exhaling brashly through her nostrils as she tossed and turned uncomfortably upon the mattress. For some reason, the bed felt unusually hard beneath her spine tonight.

I bet he's more comfortable to sleep on than this sorry excuse for a bed. His heartbeat will put you right to sleep.

Adelaide audibly snickered at the amusing comment, her gaze glued to the gaping hole in the wall as the familiar click of her steel door unlatching prompted fearful trembles to arise.

"Random cell check," a hauntingly familiar voice announced, tall frame slinking into the room as Adelaide immediately shuffled into a sitting position.

No no no no no no–

The slight blue hue from the hallway poorly illuminated half of Elliot Greenwald's expression, the door snapping closed behind him as his lips curled into a broad grin. Widened gaze settled upon Adelaide's frantic form, the left strap of her tank top slipping down the slope of her shoulder as he blatantly stared at her exposed skin.

"I've missed you," he mused, earning a distasteful whine from the woman as she flattened herself against the wall, violent trembles enveloping her spine as the guard rapidly approached her. "I've missed *all* of you."

Before Adelaide could properly react, Greenwald had managed to pin her frail frame flat against the mattress, a considerable yelp falling from her horrified expression as his palm claimed her chest.

"You *knooow*," a sudden voice appeared, prompting a plethora of relieving goosebumps to appear on Adelaide's skin as Greenwald instantly froze above her. "Consent is *key*, pal."

Greenwald immediately shuffled off of Adelaide, plopping his round bottom against the foot of her bed as she brought her trembling knees to her chest, cowering against the cool concrete wall as he fished a sleek, inky flashlight from his utility belt. The pad of his thumb applied pressure to the plastic button, igniting a harsh stream of light as he pointed it in the direction of the late Oliver's sloppily made hole.

Switch heavily blinked at the sudden intrusion, the discoloration present upon his left eye sticking out like a sore thumb as he rest his forearm against the bottom half of the hole, marred left cheek laying against the skin as he lazily lounged.

"Ge-*zuuuus*," the madman nasally drawled. "Can you point that thing somewhere *else*?"

Greenwald let out an irate grumble as he hastily diverted the strand of light, creating a warm glow over Switch's features as a wild grin tugged at his lips.

"Much better," he cooed. "Now, where *were* we?"

"Fuck off, freak." Greenwald spat. "Or I'll come in there and make your eyes match."

"*Ooo*," Switch giggled, lips curling into an enthusiastic "*o*" shape as he lifted his chin from the firm skin of his arm. "Feisty little *fucker*, aren't we? Say, why don't you leave little Miss Adelaide alone, *hmm*?"

"This is none of your business. Go to bed." Greenwald countered, inching towards a frozen Adelaide as she let out a heightened squeak at his abrupt touch.

"Ah," Switch called, amusingly shifting his weight against the destroyed wall. "That-*uh*, doesn't *sound* like consent. How would your boss feel if he knew you were sticking yourself in places you *don't belong*?"

"And who's gonna tell him? Hm?" Greenwald seethed, running a palm through his crimson mane. "*You*?"

"May-*beeee*." Switch giggled, chocolate-tinted eyes momentarily flickering in Adelaide's direction. "Don't be afraid, princess. Don't let this *mean man* frighten you."

"D'you really think they'll listen to anything you say, psychopath? It's your word against mine. They'd never believe you." The guard argued, his fingers slipping beneath the fabric of Adelaide's top as he aggressively yanked it down. The woman gasped as her breast tumbled from the fabric, falling into Greenwald's greedy palm as Switch's glare instantly diverted from the sight.

"Maybe they won't take my *wooord*, but you do realize that they can swab some'a your *dee-en-aye* off of little missus lady bits, hm?" Switch boldly stated, gaze momentarily flickering over her exposed chest. Greenwald's greedy palm instantly froze, eyes contorting into slits as he observed a giddy Switch.

"So-*uh*, I *highly* suggest that you refrain from sticking your lil tic-tac in places where it doesn't *belong*."

Greenwald's fingers curled into furious fists, his beady eyes refocusing on a routinely mute Adelaide as she stuffed her breast back into the fabric of her shirt.

"You seem to know quite a bit about sexual assault, pal. Something you do in your free time?" The guard mocked, a deep chuckle resonating through his chest at the weak insult.

"Greenie, Greenie, Greenie," Switch giddily sang, running a hand through his oily locks. "I'm a *lotta* things, but a rapist ain't one'a them. Y'see, the best part about sex is the emotion, *hmm*? The little noises they make when you finally *touch* 'em—the sighs 'n begs, the open-mouthed *kisses*—"

"Who would ever want to sleep with *you*?" Greenwald interjected, thrusting Adelaide out of her temporary trance as Switch's words worked wonders on her mind.

"I could say the same for you, bud." Switch snipped, stepping away from the gaping hole in the concrete as the sporadic piles of dirt crunched beneath the soles of his heavy boots.

Greenwald killed the steady stream of light from his flashlight, dark eyes flickering in Adelaide's direction once more as he intently wet his lips.

"You're lucky you have a nice rack, because with a face like that, no man would ever want you." He spat, rising from the creaky bed as Adelaide's heart instantly plummeted in her chest. "Ugly bitch." The guard added, twisting on his heel as he headed in the direction of the sealed cell door.

"Hey, hey, *heeeey*," Switch's distant voice called. "That's no way to talk to a lady."

"I suggest you shut your mouth, freak. Otherwise I'll beat your ass and toss you in max." Greenwald dryly threatened, sliding his card between the deep grooves of the keypad as the door unlocked with a distinct *click*.

"Try me." Switch lowly muttered, but Greenwald hadn't heard him, his stiff frame slipping from the cell without another word as Adelaide violently flinched at the abrupt slamming of the door.

A stale silence littered the air as Adelaide swallowed a thick lump in her throat, the persistent glow of the hallway lights dully illuminating Switch's scarred face as he sympathetically stared through the substantial hole in the wall.

"Dollface," he cooed, resting his forehead against the concrete. "C'mere."

Adelaide thickly swallowed, her hazel eyes significantly widening as Switch laced his arm through the hole, dainty fingers parting as he playfully wiggled them in a determined attempt to call her over.

Go on, love.

Sock-clad feet shifted against the mattress, heart erratically thumping beneath her ribcage as she shuffled from the safety of her drastically uncomfortable bed. The sorry excuse for a sheet slipped from the frame, fluttering to the floor as Switch intently eyed her every move.

Her hazel gaze lay transfixed on his fingers, nails untrimmed and slightly uneven—the flesh of his digits riddled with dirt and grime, as if they hadn't been washed in weeks, even though he'd received a forceful cleansing less than twenty-four hours prior. Partially scarred lips parted in awe, dark eyes glued to Adelaide's uneasy form as she fell to her knees before the hole, his outstretched hand just barely grazing the blemish-ridden skin of her chin.

Uneasily, the woman raised her palm, the very tips of her equally uneven nails grazing the hair surrounding his tattooed wrist as she sucked in a sharp breath. Skin collided firmly with skin—an equal unison exhale filling the void as the pads of her quivering fingers precisely traced the permanent lines imprinted upon his flesh. Switch's tongue darted outward, caressing the seared skin of his lower lip as he silently observed the curious woman, her fingers prancing lightly along his skin as if he were a valuable trinket that absolutely shouldn't be meddled with.

Her fingers cupped his frozen palm, the rough flesh of her thumb steadily outlining his remarkably long fingers. The flesh of her palm buzzed with satisfaction—digits turbulently tingling as blatant sparks marred her flesh. His skin resembled an open flame; gorgeous in appearance and a hazard to touch, but oh-so-compelling to feel. She craved the warmth of his skin against hers, whether it be just as simple as fingers laced together, just like this . . .

Adelaide wedged her slender digits tightly between his, firmly holding his hand in hers as an audible sigh of relief slipped off of her chapped lips. Instinctively, her eyelids fluttered closed, a pleasurable warmth filling her rigid limbs as she went lax at his touch. A still Switch observed the woman in wonder, the pad of his thumb gently caressing her palm as she apparently drifted off into a euphoric state—all because of a simple hand hold.

"You don't know who I am, do you?" He murmured, hazel eyes swiftly reconnecting with his as her touch abruptly vanished.

Stiffly, the woman shook her head from side to side, pressing her vacant fingers against her full lips. Switch keenly watched through the hole in the wall as she caressed the cracked skin, smearing the feel of his fingers against her mouth as she openly shuddered.

Boldly, his thumb met her chin, gliding up ever so slightly to meet her mouth as the rough skin met her lip, promptly replacing her fingers as she openly sighed at the sudden feel. His hands were obscenely rough, marred by an abundance of calluses and healed scars.

Where have those hands been?

What have those hands done?

"Goodnight, Adelaide." He whispered, tearing his touch away from her pleading lips as his arm disappeared from her side of the wall, the distinct sound of boots scratching against the concrete sending violent shivers down the woman's spine.

Goodnight, Switch.

IV

*"In my life there's been heartache and pain
I don't know if I can face it again."*
–Foreigner, "I Want to Know What Love Is"

before

"I think this'll be good for you, Adelaide. Quit mucking about and accept that things have to change." The middle-aged woman sternly spoke, jabbing her index finger harshly against the center of her thick-rimmed glasses as she slipped them back up the greasy slope of her nose. Her salt-and-pepper littered hair was strung into a picture-perfect bun atop her skull, a single stray strand tucked behind a tri-holed ear, accented with faux jewelry from a consignment shop in the slums.

Adelaide did not reply, her arms firmly laced across her chest as she clambered from the idle vehicle, hazel-hued orbs glaring skeptically in the direction of the vast building before her.

"Plus," her mother slyly added, slinging her army green leather purse strap along her bony shoulder. "It was either Stillwater or Hoyer. Which would you prefer?"

Neither, Adelaide hastily thought, glaring at her rigid mother through hooded eyes as they carefully climbed the cracked concrete steps.

"Beautiful building, innit? Lucky you, you're going to call this place home." The woman rambled, the toe of her sandal colliding sloppily with the top step as a wince instantly overcame her features. An exasperated "*shit*" slipped off her crooked lips, wide eyes glancing downward at the throbbing toes as Adelaide held back a sarcastic snicker.

Karma.

Dude, Adelaide thickly countered, continuing with: *don't speak of her that way. She's my mother.*

Hardly.

"Hold my hand, Adelaide." She sternly spoke, beady-black eyes glaring in her daughters' direction as determined, wrinkly fingers latched onto

Adelaide's. Her daughter audibly scoffed at the peculiar gesture, her hand roughly ripping from her mother's hold as she shot her a perplexed glance.

"Addy," the irritable woman hissed, penciled-in brows knitting together in angst as her daughter defiantly stuffed her palms into the depths of her single sweatshirt pocket.

"I can walk on my own, thanks." Adelaide thickly spat, frigid digits curling into tight fists within the fabric of her worn sweater.

The duo silently approached the hefty steel front doors of the building, which were nearly ten feet in height and stained a rustic maroon tint. Several patches of paint obnoxiously peeled away from the doors, revealing a charcoal gray hue beneath as Adelaide's gaze lay glued to the modish metal numbers, which clung to the brick wall directly beside the right door. She intently studied the numbers that lay plastered upon the building—88688— the final eight resembling that of a crooked infinity sign due to the absence of several screws. Her mother laced several ring-clad fingers around the circular door handle, roughly yanking the broad door open as Adelaide sucked in a sharp breath.

The front foyer of the building was rather elegant, accessorized with a clearly expensive chandelier, which hovered over the very center of the room. A weakly stained oak desk lay directly beneath, the surface littered with stacks of papers, manila folders, a broad desktop computer, and an inky, corded phone. Bright blue eyes flickered upwards at the sudden intrusion, a forced smile enveloping the young woman's lips as she abruptly stood from her seat.

"Hello!" She cheerfully chirped, rounding the cluttered desk as her obscenely tall stilettos clicked against the tile floor, the obnoxious sonance prancing along the thick walls as an involuntary shiver overcame Adelaide's every limb.

"Alice Lynch," Adelaide's mother boldly introduced, thrusting her arm outward to claim the receptionists palm. "This is my daughter, Adelaide."

"Oh my!" The woman cheered, eyes significantly widening at the sound of Alice Lynch's voice. "You're Australian!" She cheered, reaching out to shake Adelaide's hand. The woman, however, failed to comply, earning a rather stiff reply from the receptionist as her palm met her hip.

"Yes," Alice awkwardly grinned, shooting Adelaide a scolding glare.

"Born'n bred in the down under. Hubby and I brought the girls over to America on their tenth birthday, we've resided in Chicago ever since."

"Wonderful! I hope you've had a decent experience with Chicago," the jolly woman exclaimed, shifting her bright gaze to an extremely silent Adelaide. "I know it can be a little rough here with all of the crime and all, but that's what we're here for!"

Great. So, they're locking you up with a load of criminals.

Adelaide tore her clammy palm from the confinement of her sweatshirt, fingers lacing tightly around the sleeve of Alice's sweater as she aimlessly tugged.

"Mum," she murmured, digging her nails into the fabric as Alice irritably shoved her off.

"Jeez, Addy!" The woman hissed, earning a blatant wince from the frozen receptionist as Alice's cheeks flushed bright scarlet. "This is a brand-new jumper! Piss off! Haven't you any manners?"

Alice released a dramatic sigh, soulless eyes rolling within their sockets as she diverted her attention to the stunned receptionist.

"I have a meeting with Dr. Evers about Adelaide's enrollment?" She spat. The wild-eyed receptionist nimbly nodded, scurrying back to the desk as she shuffled through an abundance of severely disorganized paperwork.

"M-Mr. Evers is currently ill, but Nurse Briar Cunningway would be more than happy to give you a tour of the facility, Mrs. Lynch." She stammered, audibly gulping as Alice let out an irate huff.

"I guess that'll do," she dismissed, eyeing a stiff Adelaide as she hastily continued. "Dr. Evers and I did come to an agreement, however. Would that still be honored in his absence?"

"Certainly, ma'am." The receptionist awkwardly gulped, sympathetically eyeing a glassy-eyed Adelaide, fingers curled around her clothed biceps as she avoided the awkward glare.

Adelaide shifted her weight against the balls of her feet, gaze raking the impossibly tall ceilings as Alice stood silently beside her, painted lip strung tightly between rows of teeth as the receptionist summoned Nurse Briar over the phone in a hushed tone.

The trio sat in an uncomfortable silence for six agonizing minutes, the silent void eventually broken by a flustered woman who burst through a nearby door. Her hair was precisely dyed a platinum blond color, azure-tinted eyes outlined by a thick layer of inky, liquid eyeliner as her evenly-applied lipstick coated lips curled into a toothy grin at the sight of both Adelaide and Alice.

"Hi," she breathlessly greeted, taking Alice's stiff hand in hers. "I'm Briar Cunningway, a nurse here at Stillwater. You are?"

"I'm Alice, and this is my daughter, Adelaide." Alice blandly replied, her tone low and monotone as she glared fleetingly in Briar's overwhelmed direction. Her limbs were cloaked with a periwinkle hued set of scrubs, the sleeves dowdily rolled past her bony elbows as she ushered the rigid women into the depths of the facility.

"Hello, Adelaide." Nurse Briar politely greeted, taking the young girls' hand in hers. "How are you?"

Before Adelaide could even attempt to formulate a reply, her mother had spat out a forced and rushed statement, "she's shy. She doesn't speak."

A slight frown overcame Briar's sullen features, hand dropping from Adelaide's hold as she murmured a simple: "Oh."

"On with the tour?" Alice forcibly urged, disregarding her daughters blank stare as Briar promptly nodded.

"Right. Of course. As I'm sure Dr. Evers explained, Stillwater has a lot to offer for those seeking professional help," the winded woman confidently began, twinkling eyes connecting with a wary Adelaide as the trio strut down a dingy, dimly lit hallway. "For those who qualify, several hours of socialization in the rec room occur daily. This gives our patients the opportunities to socialize and even make friends during their stay at Stillwater."

Nurse Briar's carefully rehearsed tour blended into a stagnant blur, her giddy tone agonizingly ringing in Adelaide's ears as she showed both her and Alice the best bits the facility had to offer. Although everything seemed fine-and-dandy from an outsider's view, Adelaide knew better than to expect sunshine and daisies while committed to such a facility.

Once the slightly short tour had ended, the women returned to the front foyer, a stupid smile slapped upon Nurse Briar's face as she politely requested Alice's preferred point of action.

"With all due respect, Miss," Alice stated in a hushed tone. "I did not intend on leaving today with Adelaide."

"Oh?" Nurse Briar mutely inquired, her worrisome gaze instantly connecting with an extremely stiff Adelaide, who hadn't said a single word during the entire tour. "And this is something Dr. Evers approved?"

"Check your files if you don't believe me, or simply give him a bell." Alice clipped, crossing her arms as Nurse Briar audibly gulped. Typically, parents of patients weren't so adamant about locking up their offspring . . .

"With all due respect—Mrs. Lynch—Unless we perceive your daughter as an immediate threat to your wellbeing, I don't see why you're so eager to admit her right this instant. I can assure you that we could get her in within the next fourteen days—"

"Listen here, *bitch*." Alice promptly interrupted, her slender index finger jabbing the tip of Nurse Briar's nose as she instantly stilled under her touch.

"This little *freak* tried to stab me three times last week. I'm telling you, I wouldn't be here if I wasn't fearful of my life. I don't want her in my house anymore. Please—for the love of *God*—take her off my hands, will you? For my family's sake? We just aren't safe."

She's lying straight through her teeth!

Do you hear the bullshit spewing from her mouth? When have you ever put a blade to her neck?

Speak up for yourself! Defend yourself!

No. Adelaide defeatedly countered, thick tears clouding her vision as Nurse Briar glanced warily in her direction. *Maybe this is for the best. You guys might have convinced me to stab her sooner or later anyways. Now I'll never be tempted.*

"Is this true, Miss Lynch?" Nurse Briar collectively questioned, her quivering fingers meeting Adelaide's. The young woman jerked out of her hold, lips parted in angst as the words failed to emerge.

We should've had you kill her while you had the chance.

She's always played favorites. She prefers Westlynn over you. It'll always be that way.

"Her sister Westlynn refuses to sleep in the same room anymore," Alice added, lying straight through her crooked teeth as Adelaide physically shook in rage. "Adelaide may seem shy, but I promise you, she's the devil reincarnated."

WENCH!

Westlynn is your best friend! Defend yourself!

Adelaide let out a heightened shriek, her knobby knees wobbling as they eventually gave out completely—sending her rigid frame tumbling to the tile floor as horrified shouts slipped through her parted lips. Blinding tears concealed her vision, stomach achingly churning as she forcefully swallowed the obscene amount of bile that threatened to spew. This wasn't happening . . . this couldn't happen . . .

"She's having an episode! She's going to kill me!" Alice feigned fear, her palms clamping over her gaping mouth as she scurried in the opposite direction of Adelaide's convulsing form, exaggerated shouts emerging through cracked lips as she lost all sense of reality.

Nurse Briar fell to her knees, steady palms colliding with Adelaide's jerking form as she loudly sobbed beneath her hold. Strands of unkempt pale brown hair cloaked her complexion, the locks lodged between her lips as irregular cries continued to frantically emerge. The woman held her knees securely to her chest, arms locked tightly around her slender legs as several guards rushed to her aide, the distinct sonance of metal keys clinking together echoing in Adelaide's ears.

It was the voices. They were yelling—screaming—shouting and pleading— literally *begging* her to wrap her fingers around her mother's throat and squeeze the life completely out.

For years, Adelaide was expected not to speak. Dad left shortly after their drastic move to Chicago, leaving herself and her sister Westlynn in the care of their deranged mother—the completely monstrous Alice Lynch. For some unexplained reason, she'd favored Westlynn over Adelaide—whether it be due to the sheer fact that Westlynn was a natural overachiever at everything she'd ever attempted, she wasn't quite sure.

On multiple occasions, Alice had simply told Adelaide that she wasn't wanted. Her and Dad wanted one single child, and instead, they were stuck with two. One wanted, and one drastically unwelcome.

The young woman's limbs harshly stiffened, chest sorely heaving as the polite nurse whispered reassuring phrases into her ringing ears, the sound of Alice's faux cries filling the frantic void as Adelaide clearly witnessed the guards escorting her from the premises.

"Don't worry, Adelaide," Nurse Briar cooed, the pad of her thumb gently wiping away a fallen tear as the woman lay in a frozen heap on the floor, her limbs contorted at dreadfully uncomfortable angles as the overwhelming choir of voices finally ceased. "We're going to help you."

But there's nothing wrong with you!

Tell her. Tell her there's nothing wrong with you!

Adelaide chewed on her bottom lip, the brash, metallic taste of blood immediately filling her senses as her blurred vision eventually focused on the gorgeous features of Nurse Briar, who steadily hovered over her.

No. Adelaide hissed, angering the voices once more as her eyelids fluttered shut. *Mum told me not to speak.*

Your mother is gone! You're free to speak! To finally be yourself!

A strangled sigh escaped her oozing lip, Briar's fingers delicately pulling the bloodied strands of hair away from her mouth as hazel eyes met a sea of blue once more.

"C'mon, sweet pea. Let's get you situated." Nurse Briar cooed, attempting to tug Adelaide's severely locked limbs into a standing position. Involuntarily, her body obeyed, forming into the exact shape Nurse Briar had formed her into as she directed her through the nearby door.

Speak, Adelaide Rhea.

Adelaide sighed, knees wobbling with each individual step as Nurse Briar held her close. With one final burst of bravery, she spat back: *I have nothing to say.*

V

"My body aches to breathe your breath /
Nothing stands between us here"
—Sarah McLachlan, "Possession"

Day 723.

Adelaide sat stuffed in the very same corner of the rec room, her gaze glued to the deteriorating pages of an old copy of *Sense and Sensibility*. The woman has read the very same line thirteen times now, her mind constantly veering away from the comfort of the story as Switch's complexion riddled her thoughts.

The hole hovering her big toe had grown substantially, traveling over to an additional toe as a plethora of sand entered through the gaping wound in the fabric, the flesh of her foot irritably itching from the sudden intrusion as her fingers met her lips.

She swore that she could still feel Switch's touch upon her flesh—the perfectly imperfect callouses that littered his bony fingers, a profusion of cicatrices lining his palm as her untrimmed nails met his—dipping down and between every single inch and crevice of his fine flesh. By the whispers that interrupted her daily trance, the soft, comforting touch of the scarred-face man was apparently completely and utterly unforgivable—as if one single taste of the devil's flesh would ultimately propel her into an eternal damnation. An eternity in the fiery pits of hell for one single night with the devilishly handsome Switch—*would it be worth it?*

Adelaide's stomach fluttered at the mere thought of the man who she hardly knew—the man who she only met a whopping twenty-four hours prior. For some perplexing reason, the timid woman craved his touch—not even in a necessarily sexual sort of way, but just a simple, innocent touch. She wanted to feel his fingers along her flushed flesh, his fingertips tickling her goose bump-riddled skin as she reveled in the extraordinary feel.

Adelaide refocused on the yellowed pages of her novel, breaths emerging in short pants as she shifted from her frozen stance, her extremities tingling as a nearby Nayeli shot her a puzzled glance.

"You okay, mute?" The olive-toned woman snipped. Her sudden outburst caught a sleepy Cora's attention, her glare glued to a rigid Adelaide as she audibly gulped in reply.

Hesitantly, she nodded her head, inching the book higher to completely conceal her flushed features as a skeptical Nayeli and a nosy Cora disappeared from sight.

Time ticked leisurely by, Adelaide's jumbled thoughts solely fixated on a greasy-haired man with a permanent set of selcouth scars as supper rapidly approached. There had been no sight of the madman in the rec room today, the woman's heart plummeting at the thought of him isolated in his cell for the entire day. Maybe he had an appointment with the psychiatrist, or a check-up with medical. Deep down, the silent woman secretly hoped that he was able to at least stretch his legs outside of the confinement of those lonely four walls.

Several hours later during her evening bath, Nayeli's irritating voice had managed to interrupt the bothersome voices, Adelaide's attention instantly diverting to the curly-haired girl as an unrecognizable nurse thoroughly cleansed her scalp.

"Why haven't any of us seen the Switch? Does he not get supper?" The woman boldly inquired, shifting her weight beneath the soapy water as the basin nearly swallowed her petite frame whole.

Adelaide abruptly tugged out of Nurse Briar's embrace, the blond woman's manicured nails catching on a loose strand of sopping wet hair as the mute woman winced in retaliation. Her wet palms met the curled edges of the porcelain tub, hazel gaze fixated on a chattery Nayeli as she continued to spit out an abundance of queries.

"Is he in maximum security, or something?" She wondered, meeting Adelaide's piercing gaze.

"Or something." A nearby nurse grumbled, digging her fingers against Cora's scalp as the woman outwardly cried.

"Why do you care so much about him, Nayeli? He's a monster. He killed many people this summer, and probably even more before then that even we don't know about quite yet." Nayeli's nurse stated, eyes contorted into tight slits as her bottom lip extended, hastily blowing away a loose curl from her eyes.

Killed? Many?

Adelaide's brows perplexedly raised, nails digging into the harsh material of the tub as Nurse Briar quietly rid her straggly hair of the abundance of foaming soap. Her lips remained tightly sealed, vivid visuals of Switch's recent cleansing tainting her mind as Nayeli countered her nurse's argument.

"So? That's what makes him so interesting, Nurse Lora." She spat, craning her neck to view the blatant scoff on Nurse Lora's face.

Nayeli and Nurse Lora continued their insistent banter, an uncomfortable twinge arising in Adelaide's lower belly as a grimace overcame her exhausted features. Her fingers unraveled from the sides of the basin, slipping back into the depths of the warm, soapy water as her hand slowly drifted to the discomfort present between her legs.

Nurse Briar felt Adelaide's sudden stiffness, brows raising in curiosity as she whispered a simple question beside her ear, "what's wrong, Addy?"

Adelaide's dainty fingertips grazed the in-between of her legs, instantly becoming slick with thick blood beneath the water as she raised her crimson palm from the basin. Nurse Briar's eyes immediately widened at the sight, lips parting in concern as she rang the excess water out of Adelaide's hair.

"Are you early? You always let me know when you're on your period, especially since your flow is so heavy." Nurse Briar inquired through a hushed tone, her lips knitting into a tight frown as a bewildered expression overcame Adelaide's features. She'd been thinking so much about the Switch that she'd forgotten all about the arrival of her period.

The young woman's lips parted in angst, sopping wet strands sticking to the features of her face as she merely shook her head. Hazel gaze lay transfixed on the fluorescent liquid that currently coated her fingers, brows knitting together in uncertainty as Nurse Briar's palms lodged beneath her armpits, yanking her frozen frame from the vacant tub as Nayeli's strained tone propelled Adelaide from her momentary trance.

"Ew!" The olive-skinned girl yelped. "Adelaide's bleeding all down her legs! Don't you know you're not supposed to take baths without a tampon? Jesus, mute! You've been here long enough to know that!"

"Hush it, Nayeli!" Nurse Lora scolded, fingers lacing in the irate woman's curls as she forcefully tugged.

"It's okay, Addy." Nurse Briar cooed, collecting an armful of towels in her grasp as she laced her free arm around a timid Adelaide, her gaze still solely glued to the substance present on her fingers as Nurse Briar cleaned the skin between her legs with several towels. The rapidly drying blood slipped between the miniscule creases of her fingerprints, creating morbid pictures against her flesh as Nurse Briar effectively rid the skin of any and all evidence.

The remaining five concrete cells were occupied when Adelaide and Nurse Briar eventually trekked up to Level 4 a bit past curfew. Adelaide's palms claimed her lower stomach as she walked, a heavy wince overcoming her flushed features as she practically dragged her boot-clad feet along the concrete floor, Nurse Briar's arm securely laced around her shoulders as she whispered reassuring phrases into her ear. Nayeli's inappropriate outburst at the sight of Adelaide's situation had embarrassed her beyond belief, her ears heating up a bright scarlet as thick tears clouded her vision. The absolute last thing Adelaide ever wanted to be was the laughing stock of Stillwater. In fact, she preferred to stay completely invisible. The less attention, the better.

By the time Nurse Briar had unlocked Adelaide's vacant cell, the lights had promptly extinguished, leaving behind the warm, blue glow of the night time lights as a stiff Adelaide shuffled into her cold, lonely cell.

"Goodnight, Addy." Nurse Briar whispered, lacing her fingers around the handle of the hefty steel door as she sympathetically smiled. "I'll see you tomorrow."

Adelaide routinely stepped out of her unlaced boots, socked feet colliding with the frigid floor as she collapsed onto her intolerable mattress in an exasperated heap. A sigh escaped through parted lips, fingers tugging at the hem of her jumpsuit as she tore it from her torso, a grimace overcoming her features as her palm unintentionally collided with her tender breast.

Once she'd managed to rid her sticky skin of the jumpsuit—remaining only in a pair of jet black cotton underwear—the woman let out a vexed groan, her hooked nose burying in the pitiful excuse for a pillow as her slender limbs curled up beneath the thin duvet. The pain in her lower abdomen was nearly unbearable, obnoxious tears clouding her vision as several slipped from her eyelids, gliding down the slopes of her flushed cheeks as she quietly sobbed upon her mattress.

C'mon, Addy. You know what'll make the pain go away.

Go ahead, sweetheart. Don't be shy.

Adelaide scoffed, appalled at the provocative suggestion as she swiftly countered with: *No! What if he sees?*

So? Let him watch.

A petite whine escaped Adelaide's lips as her abdomen seized up once again. With a disgruntled grimace, the woman's fingers slipped beneath the measly sheet, traveling south towards the main source of extreme discomfort as she hastily gave in.

A scarred-faced Switch sat hunched on his identical mattress, head held in his hands as pointy elbows claimed his knobby knees. A shirt was absent, swirls of oddly shaped ink claiming his arms as slender digits latched tightly onto his unwashed curls. Several insistent patches of hair littered his cheeks, dipping between the tiniest crevices of his lacerated skin as his left leg expeditiously bounced. Within the past several moments, the madman had found it quite difficult to breathe within these four walls.

It was as if he had an itch that couldn't be scratched. His mouth was dreadfully parched, his tongue nearly begging for the comforting taste of a warm cigarette as his lips struggled to remember how to function without the cancer stick lodged between them. It was a nasty habit he'd had for several years, one that he couldn't quite kick for some inconceivable reason.

His calloused fingers irritably buzzed, desperately craving the marvelous feeling of a freshly sharpened blade. To be able to run the pad of his thumb along the keen tip, to physically feel the glorious metal that had taken so many lives with such ease . . . *and by his hand!*

It was as if knives were his lifeline—they made him feel truly *complete.*

And yet, beneath the blur of blended, bothersome voices that currently cloaked his mind—he'd managed to catch wind of a muffled grunt. Brows intently raised at the sound, the voices dissipating as his tired features left the safety of his palms.

Switch rose from his spot, the metal bed frame creaking slightly from the sudden shift in weight as his bare feet glided across the dirt-riddled floor, several grains of sand and dirt slipping between his toes as he openly grimaced at the feel.

The man cautiously approached the gaping hole present in the wall— which was about the size of a standard picture frame—as he slowly lowered to his knees. Dark eyes rolled at the sonance of his knees inexplicably cracking with every sudden movement, his fingers meeting the coarse concrete as his gaze struggled to adjust to the poor lighting present in the neighboring cell.

A low blue hue partially illuminated Adelaide's form, courtesy of the rectangular hole cut out of the steel door as he observed her dreadfully skinny frame, which currently writhed beneath the sheets. The woman's eyes were screwed tightly shut, evenly parted hair draped over the pitiful pillow as her dainty fingertips kneaded desperate circles between her parted legs. The exceptionally thin white sheet left very little to the imagination—gaunt limbs trembling as the woman concealed her presumably bare chest with the blanket, the fingers of her opposite hand curled shut around the fabric in the shape of a tight fist as several heightened squeaks threatened to escape her firmly sealed lips.

"What the—" Switch lowly murmured, twisting around on his heel as he lowered himself to the ground, ankles tempestuously cracking with every miniscule movement as several vivid visuals raided his mind.

Instead of taking another lengthy peek, his eyelids had fluttered elegantly closed, Adelaide's muffled sighs enveloping the otherwise stale void as vivid visuals continued to consume his tainted thoughts—beautiful images of the peculiar woman beneath him, releasing those very same gasps as his fingers laced securely around the silken skin of her throat. Blood rapidly rushing beneath her thin flesh, heart thumping thickly in her throat as the evidence of her life drummed against the skin of his fingertips. *Oh*, what a glorious feel—to hold her life in his hands—to firmly grasp her every sorrow, every memory, every hardship and heartbreak and emotion—to hold it within his clutch and effortlessly *take* it.

Switch's eyes rotated blissfully back, a shudder overcoming his every limb as he imagined a frantic Adelaide beneath his sturdy hips, fingers frantically clawing at his arms as his hold gradually tightened around her throat. Eyes bulging—heart racing and lips pleading—crying—*begging* for him to stop—begging for the end to finally come. Her uneven nails persistently latching onto his tattooed arms, digging deeply into the flesh as beads of blood arose on the tainted skin, pleasurable bolts of electricity shooting up his spine at sight of the crimson liquid as it arose.

The vivid visuals became extremely overwhelming, Adelaide's very real moans and groans prompting him to involuntarily twitch beneath his trousers as a hasty palm met the tented fabric.

Finally, Switch succumbed to his violent fantasies, eyes screwing tightly shut as he went lax against the wall. The sloppily made hole hovered above his disheveled curls as his fingers slipped beneath the waist of his trousers, a strangled sigh of relief intermixing with Adelaide's muffled moans as the duo drifted into equally tranquil states, both completely unaware of the absolutely morbid situation at hand, as well as the incredibly intimate moment that they unintentionally shared.

VI

"Tell me what do they see when they look at me?
Do they see my many personalities?"
–P!nk, "Split Personality"

A sleek ball-point pen lay in the tight grasp of Dr. Lyra Blake's elegantly manicured fingers, the butt of the pen held between rows of artificially whitened teeth as her spectacle-coated gaze lay transfixed upon an abundance of documents.

The infamous Switch's paperwork lay upon the square steel table before her, her pointy elbows resting sturdily against the cool surface as her widened gaze intently studied the nearly bare files. A photograph of his recent mugshot clung loosely to a paperclip, a pair of dark, haunting eyes boring deeply into hers as she curiously stared. Although he was absolutely horrifying to look at, something about him was morbidly exhilarating. She wanted to know *more*.

"Dr. Blake?" The thick, beefy guard with hardly any neck inquired, fingers laced into a tight fist hovering his lap as the middle-aged woman's magnified eyes met his. "We have 4428 just outside. Are you ready for him?"

"Bring him in." Dr. Blake lazily instructed, curling her fingers beneath the front flap of the manila folder as she hastily flipped it closed, Switch's menacing mugshot disappearing from view.

The thick-necked guard simply grunt in reply, his broad frame slithering out of the room as Dr. Blake rigorously tapped the sole of her heel against the multi-hued tile floor. Her electric blue almond-shaped nails tediously tore at her pouty bottom lip, pulse quickening beneath her ribcage as the hefty steel door opened once more.

The woman didn't dare turn around to view the sudden intrusion, her breaths emerging as staggered pants as the distinct sonance of metal chains clashing together sent violent quivers down the length of her spine.

A pair of weighty, loosely-laced inky combat boots drug across the cracked tile floor, the ankles of his striped jumpsuit were carelessly bunched at the tip, slipping from the confinement of the boots with every staggered step as he rounded the petite table, the beefy-neck guards fingers laced agonizingly tight around his bicep.

The madman eased himself into the drastically uncomfortable metal chair, the legs obnoxiously scraping against the tile to emit a horrific screech as Dr. Blake impulsively flinched at the sound.

The abrasive guard yanked Switch's wrists forward, latching the cuffs attached to the table by short metal chains around each of his wrists, the pale skin heavily irritated by the harsh metal as the guard latched each cuff on excruciatingly tight.

"Easy," the psychiatrist scolded, eyes contorting into worrisome slits as the guard retracted his hold, shuffling from the dainty room without a single word as he abandoned Dr. Blake with the most dangerous man in Chicago.

Her widened eyes trailed upwards, curiously observing the bits of permanent ink that littered his exposed skin as she met a cold, blank stare. Several greasy brown ringlets interrupted his line of sight, beady black eyes boring into hers through hooded lids as he toyed with the inside of his left cheek, extending the marred flesh outward with his tongue. If the man wasn't such a raging lunatic, Lyra could possibly consider him to be quite handsome—minus the hideous lacerations imbedded upon the left half of his face, of course. By far, those scars were the ugliest facial deformity she'd ever laid eyes on.

Long, slender fingers rubbed intently together at a vigorous speed, the pads of his thumb intently tracing miscellaneous shapes against the palm of his hand as his broad frame lay severely hunched. His left shoulder inexplicably raised, stiff neck craning sideways to meet the raised shoulder as he irritably brushed it against his apparently itchy ear.

Dr. Blake audibly gulped, a stale silence littering the air. She pried open a vibrant orange journal, an essence of blank, college-ruled lines filling her vision as her lips parted to speak.

"I can taste your fear." Switch darkly drawled, tapping his foot expeditiously against the tile floor. His mouth curled upwards into a grin.

"I'm not afraid," Dr. Blake countered, her tone surprisingly confident and bold as she laced the pen between her fingers. "There's nothing to be afraid of."

"Oh," Switch mused, his tone shifting to a higher-pitched octave as an amused giggle slipped through his parted lips. "That's where you're wrong, doc. You *should* be afraid."

Dr. Blake let out an irate sigh, the pen abruptly colliding with the blank page as an abundance of ink involuntarily bled through the thin paper, emerging on the opposite side as a thick, obnoxious dot.

"Let's start with names, shall we?" The middle-aged woman slyly suggested. "I'll start. My name is Dr. Blake. And yours is?"

"Switch." He simply grunts, picking aimlessly at his nails as he avoided the woman's scolding glare.

"No," the woman grunted through gritted teeth. "Your real name. Birth name. The one your parents gave you."

"That *is* my real name. Wanna see my birth certificate?" Switch collectively dismissed, his rigid frame instantly going lax as his back collapsed against the frigid metal chair.

"Right," she hissed, scribbling down an irate sentence into the journal. "Age?"

"Twenty-nine." He confidently answered, a devilish grin overcoming his features as he continued with, "and *you* are?"

"We are not here to discuss me." Dr. Blake countered, completely disregarding his nosy query as she scribbled his age onto the page. Switch smacked his lips in reply, dark eyes completely avoiding the woman's hardened expression as she desperately attempted to decipher his blank complexion.

"What are you thinking about right now?" She softly inquired, crossing her legs tightly beneath the table as his piercing gaze instantly reconnected with hers. Her stomach painfully churned at the harsh glare, pulse quickening once more as he let out a simple snicker.

"The truth?" He spat, tracing the top row of his teeth with the tip of his tongue.

"Nothing but." Dr. Blake stated, a faux smile enveloping her features.

"Truthfully," Switch confidently began, inching forward in his seat as knobby elbows met the harsh surface of the table. "I'm thinking about *you*."

"What *about* me?" Dr. Blake nosily wondered, her voice slightly wavering as a low chuckle slipped off his lips.

"About your blood," he thickly began, eyes rolling sideways in his skull as he blatantly toyed with the deep lacerations imbedded upon his flesh. "How marvelous it must feel. All warm 'n *silky*. I want to play in it."

Dr. Blake thickly swallowed, trembling fingers tightening around the pen as she sloppily etched the vile information he provided upon the blank pages of the journal.

"Do you have a deep fascination with blood?" She dumbly inquired, chewing anxiously on her bottom lip as Switch shifted his weight against the uncomfortable chair.

"I have a deep fascination with *you*, precious." He drawled, left eyelid flickering closed momentarily as he winked in her direction. A violent shudder overcame her every limb at the sight, mouth instantly running dry as she struggled to formulate a proper response.

"Don't call me those inappropriate pet names," the woman interjected. "I'm your doctor, you are my patient."

"You know," he drawled, uncontrollably giggling as his index finger and thumb met his bottom lip, aimlessly tugging at the skin as Dr. Blake uncomfortably stirred in her seat. "I've always-*uh*, *fantasized* about scenarios like this. The whole doctor/patient combo. Say, why don't you help bring my little fantasy to life, hmm? Maybe *you* can wear these cuffs while *I* bend you over this table–"

"Enough!" Dr. Blake exploded, her cheeks flushing a bright scarlet as low, insistent giggles emerged from a hunched Switch opposite her, his fingers capturing his lip once more as he toyed with the mutilated skin.

"Am I making you *uncomfortable*, doctor?" Switch taunted, clearly enjoying the way Dr. Blake squirmed in her seat.

"If you want, I can share my other fantasy, *hmm*?" He confidently added, pointer finger tapping against his chin to imitate his possible thought process. "How 'bout I share the one where my fingers are wrapped around your pretty little neck, hm? D'you like being choked, doc-*tooor*? I can choke you *real* good. . ."

"This session is over." Dr. Blake snipped, snapping the cover of the nearly vacant journal closed as she abruptly stood from her seat.

"Oh, but we're just getting started, baby." Switch teased, winking once again in the woman's direction as she openly scoffed at his infelicitous physique. "C'mon, don't be shy. Daddy'll make you feel *real good*."

Dr. Blake wordlessly excused herself from the stale room, instructing the irritable guard to quickly enter and drag Switch out of her sight. After all, the discomfort present in her belly had become borderline overwhelming, and if she remained around the psychotic freak for even another moment, she wasn't quite sure what would happen. Although he was chained to the table, she irrationally feared that he'd find a way to wrap his fingers around her throat, just as he'd promised . . .

Once the giggling mess of a man had finally abandoned the room, Dr. Blake released a staggered exhale, a breath she hadn't even realized she was holding as she flipped the journal open once again and scribbled a blatant, bold word upon the page: *sociopath*.

The woman's palm cradled her throbbing forehead, Switch's menacing cackles still taunting her thoughts as the guard returned much too soon, informing her that her second patient of the day—4210—was waiting just outside.

Dr. Blake awkwardly cleared her throat, forcefully shoving away the gruesome visuals of Switch's fantasies as she requested the presence of her other patient.

A dreadfully skinny girl entered, her uncuffed hands held up towards her face, fingers laced tightly around the collar of her jumpsuit as she tugged the heavy material away from her neck. Long, stringy light brown hair cradled her heart-shaped face, several strands dangling in her widened eyes as she slowly approached the table, easing into the particularly warm chair where Switch only just sat.

"Want me to cuff her?" The guard grumbled, earning a puzzled glance from the silent girl as she tugged her chapped bottom lip between severely stained teeth.

"No," the doctor stated, smiling sympathetically in 4210's direction. "She's not a threat to my life like 4428 is. Thank you, you may be excused."

The guard nodded curtly, strutting from the miniscule compartment as the broad steel door obnoxiously slammed, prompting an involuntary jerk to overcome Adelaide's limbs as she avoided Dr. Blake's stare. Her hands met her face, untrimmed nails tugging at the blemish-ridden skin surrounding her mouth as the doctor viewed her files.

"Adelaide Rhea Lynch?" Dr. Blake inquired, ball-point pen held in clutch.

Adelaide mutely nodded, wild eyes observing a skeptical middle-aged woman as her magnified gaze returned to the manila folder, which contained all of Adelaide's information.

"My name is Dr. Blake, I'm going to be your new psychiatrist. You're going to be twenty-five in January, correct?" Dr. Blake questioned.

Another silent nod.

"You have a sister named Westlynn?" Another bland inquiry, followed by an additional nod. Adelaide's lips, however, remained firmly sealed.

"Can you tell me about yourself, Adelaide?" Dr. Blake politely urged, a toothy grin overcoming her lips as she silently begged Adelaide to speak. However, the younger woman failed to comply. Instead, her mind drifted to that of Switch. They'd passed one another in the hallway only moments prior, dark, beady eyes colliding with a mess of a chocolate and cobalt hued mixture, which instantly widened at the sight of his broad frame beyond the miniscule hole in the wall. She'd wanted to reach out and grab him—to touch him and hold him and breathe in his intoxicating scent.

A distinct frown overcame Dr. Blake's features at the lack of reply, the pen audibly scratching against the paper as she jotted down several notes in regards to Adelaide's extremely bland session.

"Would it help if you wrote things down instead of speaking them?" The doctor politely suggested, tearing a single page from her journal as she thrust it in Adelaide's direction.

The young woman's wide eyes collided with the sloppily torn page, tongue toying with the torn skin of her lip as she argued with the irritable voices present in her mind.

Finally, she caved, outstretching a slender arm as the dowdily rolled sleeve of her jumpsuit slipped down the length of her skin, concealing her bony wrist as Dr. Blake handed over the inky pen.

Adelaide claimed the foreign object in her clutch, her fingers momentarily forgetting how to properly hold the pen due to her lack of writing within the past seven-hundred days. Once her slender, quivering fingers had remembered how to properly grip the object, the tip met the paper, gliding inelegantly along the page as she etched her answer onto the surface.

Once she'd finished—her messy penmanship littering the page, dipping beneath and above the picture-perfect lines provided—she thrust it back across the shiny metallic table, easing the paper into Dr. Blake's prying clutch as she snatched it from the surface.

Magnified gaze focused on the sloppy writing, brows raised in bewilderment as she observed the statement imprinted on the page: *I have nothing to say.*

An exasperated sigh slipped off Dr. Blake's painted lips, the measly page colliding once more with the table as she glared questionably in Adelaide's direction. From what Nurse Briar had told her, Adelaide followed a strict routine daily—she sat in the very same corner of the rec room, heavy combat boots discarded off to the side as she strut a holey pair of socks, the very same pair she wore every single day. Apparently, Nurse Briar was able to convince the woman to remove them every three days, allowing the artificially blond woman to wash them so that they didn't smell absolutely horrid. Adelaide read the very same book, which strut obscene creases along the spine from the overactive wear and tear on the paperback novel. *Sense and Sensibility*—it was—one of Lyra's least favorite classic novels. In fact, she absolutely despised the story entirely, and the fact that Adelaide has read the very same book every single day for nearly two whole years brought an involuntary scoff upon Dr. Blake's features.

It was now evident that Nurse Briar was, in fact, absolutely correct. Adelaide Lynch showed clear signs of Catatonia.

"Thank you for your time, Miss Lynch." Dr. Blake cooed, a forced smile tugging at her lips as she beckoned the guard into the room once more, who hastily escorted a dreadfully silent Adelaide from the room as Lyra settled back into her dreadfully stiff seat.

Her gaze lay glued upon the blank page, rotating harshly to meet Adelaide's chicken scratch upon the torn paper.

I have nothing to say.

Suddenly, an idea dawned upon the woman, her fingers instantly lacing around the pen once more as she dug through her briefcase in search of a particular pad of parchment. An enthusiastic *"ah-ha!"* slipped through her lips when she eventually located the hefty pad of printed paper, which collided audibly with the metal table as she urgently scribbled two clear orders upon the prescription order form.

Lorazepam, high dosage — Electroconvulsive therapy once every two weeks until results occur.

She admired the neat penmanship imprinted upon the page, suddenly shuffling from her seat and made a beeline towards the pharmacy.

If all goes well, Dr. Blake would be the one to finally cure Adelaide Lynch's bizarre case of catatonia.

VII

"Listen, I can't fake an attraction to it
Magnetic, it pulls so hard
When two powerful forces collide and break down"
–Anthrax, "Cadillac Rock Box"

Day 727.

The same corner. The same book. The same holey pair of socks.

An unkempt fingernail sat wedged between her teeth, eyes solely fixated on the printed word of a classic Jane Austen novel as she chewed on the excessively long nail.

Surprisingly, Nayeli's irritable presence was absent today. Apparently, she'd clawed at Vern's face this morning after he'd woken her up from a nightmare. Unfortunately for Nayeli, she was thrown in max for assaulting a guard. The poor man had obscene scratches all down the length of his jaw, his bottom lip promptly scabbing as she'd torn the skin clean open.

Due to Nayeli's absence, Cora was unusually quiet, her gaze glued to an old copy of *Wuthering Heights* as she, too, chewed aimlessly on her fingernails, slender legs curled beneath her bottom as she lounged on the worn sofa. On the opposite end, an irritable, wide-eyed Lloyd intently picked at the torn cushion, extracting several handfuls of stuffing as he stashed them in the waistline of his trousers for later.

Adelaide's curious gaze returned to her novel, tongue poking and prodding at the innermost corner of her chapped lips as the hefty double doors opened widely, revealing a scarlet-cheeked Nurse Briar. The blond woman scurried in Adelaide's direction, her manicured fingers tugging aimlessly at her bottom lip as she rapidly approached the silent woman.

"Addy," she lowly cooed, sinking to her knees before the mute woman as a set of brows perplexedly raised. "You have a visitor."

Who the–

"Westlynn? Your twin sister?" Nurse Briar anxiously added, eyes sparkling reassuringly as Adelaide's face fell.

Adelaide *never* had any visitors. In fact, she wasn't even sure how the visiting procedure went, as no one ever took the time to come see her.

"Visitors meet privately with you in the same room that you have your therapy sessions," the woman explained, lacing her palms around Adelaide's biceps as she lifted her frail frame from the floor. "Typically, the patients are to be cuffed to the table while outside visitors are present, but I trust that you'll remain calm at all times, per usual. Dr. Blake will be monitoring the meeting—"

Adelaide's jaw fell, her eyes wild as she vigorously shook her head. She'd only met Dr. Blake once before a day prior during their very first session, and something about the blue-eyed, middle-aged woman rubbed Adelaide completely the wrong way.

"I know, I know," Nurse Briar murmured, palms meeting Adelaide's stiff shoulders as she reassuringly squeezed. "I tried to convince her otherwise—to convince her to let me sit in instead, but she wouldn't budge. She has higher authority than I do, Addy. I'm sorry."

Before Adelaide knew it, the pair stood outside the tightly sealed door of the miniscule meeting room, her heart obscenely racing beneath her heaving chest as wide, watery eyes met a sympathetic grin plastered on Briar's face.

"It'll be okay, Addy," she whispered, her cool touch cradling the girl's sullen features as the pad of her thumb wiped away a fallen tear. "It's just your twin sister in there. She's here to see *you*."

Adelaide audibly gulped, her head nodding curtly as Nurse Briar's slender fingers laced around the circular knob, twisting clockwise as the door promptly unlatched with a noisy click. Her palm met the small of Addy's back, urging the petite woman into the obscenely bright room as she hastily entered.

A set of ocean blue magnified eyes instantaneously focused on Adelaide's rigid form, a faux smile enveloping her brightly painted crimson lips as Dr. Blake welcomed her into the tiny room, her thin stilettos vociferously clicking against the tile floor as she directed her towards the unoccupied chair.

Identical hazel-hued orbs met Adelaide's empty gaze, pupils enlarging at the sight of the scraggy woman as she eased into the frigid metal chair opposite her.

"Would you like the patient to be cuffed, ma'am?" Dr. Blake politely inquired, her tone unusually high-pitched and nasally as Westlynn immediately shook her head in reply.

"No need," the woman stated, lips curling into a toothy grin as her stare fixated once more on the carbon copy sat directly across from her.

Dr. Blake bleakly grinned in reply, slinking towards the furthermost corner of the drastically tiny room as she collapsed against a rickety metal folding chair, the legs shifting obnoxiously against the tile floor as Adelaide impulsively flinched.

Westlynn and Adelaide were a true example of legitimate identical twins—identical hazel-hued orbs, oval shaped eyes that were wide ninety-percent of the time. Impossibly long and full eyelashes, which framed their obscenely large eyes quite nicely. Westlynn's lashes contained a heavy layer of inky mascara, unlike Adelaide's bald lashes that were beginning to thin out due to her insistent picking. Stringy, ashy brown hair, naturally straight and thin as it draped past each of their busty chests. Unlike Addy's sloppy do, Westlynn's hair was properly brushed, half of it tugged into a messy bun at the top of her skull, whereas the remainder lay draped over her bony shoulders.

Westlynn's droopy gaze intently studied a silent Adelaide, her taffy-tinted bottom lip tucked tightly between her artificially whitened teeth. Perfectly manicured fingers met her jaw, the pad of her thumb tracing oblong circles against the foundation-caked skin as her lips parted in preparation to speak.

"Addy," she breathed, tearing her hand away from her face as her lips tugged into a tight frown. "I've missed you so much."

Several stale minutes ticked by, Westlynn's expression faltering with every aching moment as a strictly stiff Adelaide watched her, her fingers drumming against the cool metal table. The heavy weight of her skin generating a generous, low-volume tune as Dr. Blake noisily rummaged through her briefcase.

Westlynn's stare momentarily flickered in the direction of the intrusion, darkened brows knitting together in vexation as Adelaide's jaw fell ajar, the tip of her tongue anxiously prodding at the torn skin of her lip as the words struggled to emerge.

Please, she sternly begged. *Let me talk to her.*

No. She's never visited you before now. She must want something.

No, Adelaide defeatedly countered, growing irritated with the strict voices. *She probably was busy. She's my twin sister. I love her.*

She doesn't love you. If she did, she would've come to see you ages ago.

Adelaide's chest blatantly ached at the counter argument, her heart plummeting at the sheer fact that the voice had provided.

They were always right.

The disheveled woman thrust an arm outward, indicating for Westlynn to speak as she shifted uncomfortably in her chair.

"I'm sorry it's taken me so long to visit," her sister spoke, slender arms snaking their way across the table as her cold fingers met Adelaide's warm digits. The woman flinched at the sudden contact, the muscles slightly spasming in her cheeks as her form went rigid. Westlynn instantly noticed her reaction, her features falling as she tugged her hold away once and for all.

"I miss you," Westlynn boldly added, avoiding Dr. Blake's unblinking stare in her peripheral vision. "My twin sister."

She wants something from you.

What could she possibly want? Adelaide thickly argued, forehead crinkling in detest as she desperately attempted to ward off the conflicting voices.

Just wait and see. I promise you—she wants something.

"Mum's moving back to Australia," the woman revealed, prompting a painful bubble to emerge in Adelaide's chest at the mere thought of the wretched Alice Lynch. "She's been talking about the big move for months now. Tried to convince me to go, but I've got bigger plans. Chicago's my home, and plus—" she lazily trailed off, maneuvering her left hand into Adelaide's line of vision as a glimmer of something silver caught her eye.

Adelaide stared blankly at the expensive piece of jewelry, which sat snug around Westlynn's ring finger. Several bold diamonds sparkled beneath the obscene artificial lighting of the room, her fingers rotating ever-so-slightly to reveal several additional angles of the gorgeous ring to her twin sister.

"Jasper finally worked up the courage to ask me," Westlynn revealed, a slight giggle present in her tone. "We were only together six years, y'know. Thought he'd never ask. I would have invited you to the wedding, if it weren't for your current—uh—*predicament.*"

Jasper Harris was an exemplary human being—Adelaide knew that much from the moment she'd met him nearly seven years prior. He was a straight-A student throughout high school, and even graduated in the top four percent of his class. Rest assured, the man was nothing short of an absolute genius, and he treated Westlynn as if she were royalty. Although Adelaide wanted to be happy for her twin sister—her womb mate—her absolute best friend, she just couldn't bring herself to smile. After all, she hadn't even known about the engagement, let alone the apparent wedding.

It was as if Adelaide no longer existed beyond these thick, concrete walls.

"Dad walked me down the aisle," Westlynn gloated, blinking away an array of tears as vivid visuals of her special day littered her mind. "Mum was surprisingly modest around him, regardless of how they'd left things off. Everyone asked about you."

What did you tell them? She bitterly thought, her jaw painfully tightening as she clenched her teeth.

"Mum told them you were off studying abroad in Ireland and couldn't get the time off to attend. Don't worry, nobody asked beyond that, darling." Westlynn weakly assured her, her palm patting the bruised knuckles of Adelaide's frozen hand as she remained unfazed.

"I really miss you, Adelaide. Things are so different without you 'round. I bloody hate it sometimes. Can hardly stand it." She confidently revealed, a single tear slipping beyond her cautiously lined eyelid as it slipped down the slope of her scarlet tinted cheek.

Westlynn's fingers laced around Adelaide's, her index finger rubbing miscellaneous shapes along the sullen woman's skin as she sat expressionless across from her, a blank stare meeting Westlynn's worrisome expression as she glanced questionably in Dr. Blake's direction.

"How d'you get her to speak?" She croaked, bottom lip quivering as she held Adelaide's unmoving hands in her own.

The middle-aged woman immediately thrust herself into a standing position, her free palm gliding along her cat hair littered pencil skirt as she smoothed down the fabric. Her magnified gaze widened, a piece of parchment and a single ball-point pen held tightly in her clutch as she rapidly approached the table.

"I don't," the woman replied, setting down the materials before a stiff Adelaide as her stilettos gaudily collided with the tile floor with every miniscule step. "I've had her write down her thoughts, though. Maybe she'll do the same for you?"

I didn't reveal my thoughts to you, you lying bitch. Adelaide angrily thought, fingers curling into fists beneath Westlynn's hold as her sister raised a curious brow.

"Good idea!" Westlynn chirped, unraveling her fingers from Adelaide's unmoving hands as she slid the blank page across the table, urging her sister to write something down for her.

"Please talk to me, Addy." She lowly begged, snatching the uncapped pen from the surface as she slipped it between Adelaide's frozen fingers. "Please?"

Adelaide let out an irate sigh, her fingers tightly lacing around the thin plastic of the pen as her sister's expression immediately brightened, her lips tugging upward into a toothy grin as Adelaide's sloppy penmanship instantly appeared on the page.

Westlynn's hands clamped together enthusiastically, a forced squeal slipping through her parted lips as her twin sister thrust the paper across the table and into her prying grasp. Hazel hued gaze focused solely on the messy writing embedded onto the page, expression faltering almost instantly as she read and reread Adelaide's statement.

Why are you here

The woman audibly gulped, her weakened gaze reconnecting with a skeptical Adelaide as Dr. Blake sat stunned in the corner, cobalt stare fixated on a heartbroken Westlynn as she desperately wondered what Adelaide had written upon the piece of paper.

"What d'you mean?" Westlynn murmured. "I'm here to see you. To see my sister, of course."

Two of Adelaide's fingers reconnected with the top of the page, harshly tugging it from Westlynn's lazy hold as the tip of the pen met the page once more, her fingers tightening around the slender pen as she angrily jotted down a snarky reply. Once she was finished, she routinely shoved the paper back across the table, slipping the page between her sisters manicured hold as she defeatedly viewed the query.

Why now

"I know, I know. I shouldn't have waited so long. But I'm here now, that's all that matters, right?" Westlynn replied, picking aimlessly at the skin surrounding her nails as Adelaide impatiently tapped her foot, confident gaze glancing over her shoulder to view a nosy Dr. Blake seated in the corner.

"Mum and I heard the news," her sister added, earning a puzzled glare from Adelaide as she inaudibly requested more information. "About the Switch'n all. Heard he's been locked up here. Have you seen him at all, Addy? He's an interesting fella, he is. Murdered lots'a people over the summer, started loads of ruckus. H-He put a bunch'a bombs in a shopping mall downtown, and tried to kill the Senator, but just ended up slaughtering his wife and kids…"

Adelaide's expression hardened, Switch's haunting complexion instantly bombarding her thoughts as his genuine, toothy grin riddled her mind.

She's lying she's lying she's lying she's lying!

Adelaide's hold tightened around the pen once more, a short burst of air emerging from her nostrils as she snatched the paper once more from Westlynn's hold and irritably scribbled down a third statement. The letters were sloppy and slanted, courtesy of her rough hold on the pen and her slightly shaking form. Once again, the moment she'd finished, the paper met Westlynn's curious touch, the pen arduously colliding with the metal table as Adelaide's feet firmly met the ground, her weight thrusting against the chair as she abruptly rose into a standing position.

Westlynn's eyes immediately widened at her peculiar actions, diverting to meet the page as Adelaide's chicken scratch raided her vision.

GET OUT GET OUT GET OUT GET OUT GET OUT GET OUT GET OUT

Westlynn vehemently gasped, her palm flattening against her chest as she, too, abruptly stood from the table, her widened gaze focusing on the tight fists at Adelaide's sides as Dr. Blake jumped up from her seat.

"What is it?" She pried, her fingers lacing around Adelaide's biceps as her eyes met the page. "Westlynn, I think it's best if you leave."

"B-But—"

Suddenly, an aberrant sound filled the room, prompting the tiny hairs present on the back of Westlynn's neck to stand tall as she instinctively covered her ears in response. Dr. Blake's hold tightened on the irate woman, an obscene cry emerging from her parted lips as she let out a series of strangled cries and shouts, audibly begging—*pleading* for Westlynn to leave the room.

Make her leave!

Get her out!

Adelaide continued to obnoxiously shout, her knobby knees buckling as she tumbled to the floor, a strand of obscenities escaping Dr. Blake's lips as she signaled for a nearby guard to come in and assist her.

A thick-necked guard entered the premises, sloppily shoving his way past a horrified Westlynn. Several fat tears slipped down the slopes of her cheeks, her chest aching at the sight of her identical twin sister in shambles upon the floor. She'd never seen Adelaide like this—not ever—and to say that she was mortified was a severe understatement.

"I'm sorry, Addy!" Westlynn cried, her tone cracking with every separate syllable as Nurse Briar suddenly entered the room, her palms clamping down onto Westlynn's shoulders as she urged her to promptly depart.

"I love you, Ad." The woman pressed, eventually shuffling from the room as Adelaide's strangled cries lowered into a series of vehement sobs, cheeks coated with salty tears as she lay broken in Dr. Blake's embrace. The neatly-kept doctor lay cross-legged on the floor, her skirt hiking up the length of her legs as Adelaide lay in a defeated heap upon her lap, almond-shaped fingers threading through her mangled locks as petite coos slipped through her painted lips.

"It'll be all right, Adelaide." Dr. Blake lowly assured her, wiping away the fallen tears with the pad of her thumb as she held the younger woman close to her chest. "I'll take you back to the rec room. You'll be safe there. Nobody will bother you."

Red-rimmed eyes collided with a dashing sea of blue, painful hiccups traveling through her chest as her arm slowly rose to meet the agonizingly soft flesh of Dr. Blake's pointed chin. Adelaide's fingers pranced along the prominent flesh, her heart thudding painfully beneath her ribcage as Dr. Blake's wild stare bored into hers.

"C'mon, sweet pea." The aging woman urged, assisting a weakened Adelaide from the depths of the frigid tile floor as she laced her fingers tightly between hers.

Once they'd exited in the room hand-in-hand, a frantic Nurse Briar reappeared, her wide gaze colliding with the interlaced hands as a visible pout consumed her features.

"What's going on?" She pried, chest heaving from her recent influx of physical activity.

"Just taking Adelaide back to the rec room." Dr. Blake replied, tugging the frail woman forward as they started down the hallway.

"I can take her back!" Nurse Briar spat, following closely on Adelaide's heel as she gawked at the sight of her holding hands with the wretched Dr. Blake. Briar knew quite well that the middle-aged woman didn't give a damn about

Adelaide's wellbeing, and for some unforeseen circumstance, she was desperately attempting to earn the mute woman's trust.

"I insist, Briar. Go back to Level 3 and catch up on whatever it is that nurses do." Dr. Blake dryly countered, a faux smile tugging at her lips as she directed Adelaide in the direction of the rec room.

Nurse Briar halted in place, her off-white Keds squeaking against the dirt-riddled concrete floor as she intently observed a rigid Adelaide and an overly-confident Dr. Blake as they eventually disappeared from sight.

"Bitch." Briar hissed beneath her breath, twisting sharply on her heel as she headed in the direction of a nearby elevator.

The rec room was just as quiet as Adelaide had left it.

Cora was still in the very same position, her crooked nose buried in the yellowed pages of her borrowed novel as Lloyd sat opposite her on the sofa, his unwashed fingers kneading at the cushion as he extracted several clumps of stuffing, per usual.

Several additional patients littered the floor, mostly keeping to themselves and keeping busy with miscellaneous board games and novels they'd borrowed from the library.

Adelaide's focus, however, wasn't on the typical setting of the room. No—her gaze immediately settled upon the corner reserved for herself, which was currently occupied by an unfamiliar face to this room.

The air immediately eluded her lungs at the sight of him, wrists confined by a set of metal cuffs as they lay upon his cross-legged lap. Per usual, the sleeves of his striped jumpsuit were negligently rolled, the bunched material sat snug behind the bulging skin of his elbows. Lazy, almond gaze instantaneously brightened at the sight of a bewildered Adelaide frozen at the entrance of the room, the healed lacerations present upon his cheek tugging upward into an amused half-smirk as she shuffled into the depths of the room.

Her boot-clad feet slackly trailed along the floor, the overwhelming abundance of dirt audibly shifting beneath the soles of her shoes as she rapidly approached a grinning Switch seated against the wall.

"Hiya, doll." He thickly mused, eyes glimmering beneath the mixture of the artificial and natural lighting of the room as Adelaide eased onto the floor beside him, her back abruptly colliding with the stiff concrete as a wince overcame her features.

She softly smiled, a tight-lipped expression plastered upon her features as she claimed the discarded withered copy of *Sense and Sensibility* in her clutch.

"I know what you're thinking," he began, his fingers tugging at a loose strand present on his jumpsuit trousers. "They've finally let the dog out of the crate. They've all-*uh*, been gawking at me since I got in *here*."

Adelaide glanced upward, her amused glare meeting a sea of wide eyes as they instantly diverted at her stare. A snort emerged from her nostrils at the sight, a chuckle tumbling from Switch's scarred lips as he shuffled in place against the wall, tugging his knees to his chest as his skull collided with the cement.

"S'better than being in that cell all day." He added, tugging at the agonizingly tight cuffs laced around his wrists. Suddenly, Westlynn's influx of information bombarded her mind.

He bombed a shopping mall.

He murdered lots of people.

He murdered Senator Wilson's wife and children.

There was simply no way that this beautiful man beside her was capable of such atrocities. However—if he was, Adelaide wasn't so sure if she'd even mind it at all.

Adelaide simply nodded in reply, slipping her fingers between the pages of her novel as she flipped it open, revealing an essence of repetitive printed ink.

"Wha's *that*?" Switch drawled, thrusting his thumb in the aging books direction as Adelaide stiffened against the wall. She slapped the book closed, displaying the cover to the curious man as he raised a set of curious brows.

"Ah," he throatily drawled, conjoined hands slithering in her direction as he snatched the book from her hold. "Y'like to *read*?"

Adelaide's forefinger collided with the cover, tapping it several times as she wordlessly replied to his inquiry.

"Oh, you only like to read *this* one, hm?" He whispered, handing the book back into Adelaide's greedy hold as she nodded, overjoyed at the fact that he'd understood her inaudible speech.

"Maybe we can read it together one time?" He boldly suggested, his left leg drifting sideways to collide with hers. Their knees harshly collided, several bolts of electricity enveloping her spine at the innocent action as her heart leapt into her throat.

Adelaide's jaw parted, her eyes meeting the familiar, comforting sight of cocoa as she melted into liquid putty at the close contact. For once, they were actually touching—although it wasn't skin to skin, their knees were resting against one another's, bare elbows colliding ever-so-slightly, heart thumping thickly in her throat as she reveled in the simplistic touch. For once, a holey wall didn't separate them—in fact, there was absolutely no separation at all. There was no barrier—no barricade or divider.

Adelaide's breaths emerged in shallow pants, the book tumbling to her lap as her arm extended sideways, crawling up the length of Switch's clothed torso as he instantly stilled beneath her touch. He was oh-so-close, his marred complexion mere inches apart from hers as she practically forgot how to breathe entirely at the situation at hand. If it were even remotely possible, the man was even more attractive beyond the obstruction of the unevenly punctured wall, the deep crevices of his scars twitching slightly as her fingers innocently and confidently collided with the skin.

Bliss.

Pure, euphoric bliss enveloped her every fiber as the pads of her fingers grazed along the obscene folds of his face, dipping between the harsh curves of his facial scars as she marveled in the feel. They were unlike anything she'd ever felt—ever experienced or admired. He was entirely divergent, a rare species that she'd come to admire in such a drastically short amount of time.

And thus, in that very moment, as her fingers gently caressed his marred flesh—his welcoming gaze glaring deeply into hers, eyes unblinking as her mouth ran painfully dry—Adelaide found herself spiraling into the deepest pits of admiration.

There was no going back.

VIII

"Voices are calling from inside my head
I can hear them, I can hear them
Vanishing memories of things that were said"
–Ozzy Osbourne, "Shot in The Dark"

"Fucking peas *again?*" Cora groaned, lifting her tri-colored tray upwards to meet the glass as the irritable lunch lady slapped a spoonful of mushy peas onto the surface.

The natural blond scoffed at the sight, eyes contorting into slits as she shuffled towards the second station to receive her main course as Adelaide approached the particularly round lunch lady, an additional spoonful of peas held in her clutch.

Adelaide hesitantly raised her vibrantly stained tray, the sudden weight of the mound of peas prompted the thick plastic to shift beneath her weak hold as she weakly smiled in the lunch lady's direction.

Once she had filled up her tray with an abundance of hardly edible food, she twisted sharply on her heel, heading towards the comforting corner in which she sat every single day. However, halfway there, her vision caught hold of a mess of comforting brunette curls nearby.

Her neck craned sideways, snapping at a slightly bothersome angle as she viewed the hunched-shouldered man, who sat seated at the very end of the rectangular table. Several chairs both beside and across from him lay vacant, courtesy of the absolutely terrified surrounding patients who took refuge at completely opposite tables, avoiding any and all chances of socialization with the madman.

A sudden smile smeared across Adelaide's lips, her ankles twisting slightly to allow her legs to strut in Switch's lonely direction. The petite woman rounded the corner of the table, her bottom colliding with the circular stool directly across from his as the plastic tray collided obnoxiously with the table.

Several heads turned at the abrupt noise, eyes significantly widening at the sight of Adelaide Lynch seated anywhere but her typical corner.

Switch's empty gaze met hers, several oily ringlets concealing his vision as the skin beneath his eyes were flushed stygian. It was apparent that the man hadn't slept in several days, if even. The deep lacerations imbedded upon his cheek twitched slightly at the sight of her cheerful form, jaw falling lax as he let out a disgruntled sigh.

"Hey," he murmured, twirling several lonesome peas around his tray with a cream-hued plastic spoon. Patients at Stillwater were never supplied with anything other, mainly due to the fact that several individuals attempted to snatch the plastic knives and forks and use them for self-harm.

Adelaide had been one of those individuals on day 30.

The woman weakly smiled, her sealed lips tugging up the slopes of her cheeks as she irritably stirred the pile of mushy peas slapped upon her tray. She openly grimaced at the sight, nose crinkling in disgust as Switch let out an audible chuckle through a mouthful of food.

"Not a fan'a peas, I'm guessing?" He mused, running several dirty digits through his unwashed hair.

Not particularly, she thought, eyeing the man kindly as she lifted her shoulders in a shrugging fashion.

"Me neither." He lightly added, thrusting the circular edge of his spoon in the direction of the pile of untouched peas as a forced burst of air emerged from Adelaide's nose.

The duo finished their lunch in a comforting silence, Adelaide's hazel gaze glued to Switch's haunting complexion as he studied her intently.

She was unlike any woman he'd ever encountered. For starters, she was the only patient at Stillwater who wasn't absolutely terrified of him, nor did she gawk at the hideous facial deformity present upon his once attractive face. In fact, she seemed quite mesmerized by the healed wounds, and the man swore that he could still feel the soft, feathery touch of her fingers prancing along his marred skin. It took every fiber of his being to allow such a rash instance to occur—he'd voluntarily allowed her to caress his face, and without consequence. The last time a woman touched his scars, they found her remains scattered behind Lu's Bakery deep within South Side. Simply put, *no one* touched Switch's scars. However, when Adelaide's unkempt fingernails traced the odd shaped lacerations, something peculiar had stirred deep within him. Although he hated to admit it—the feeling of

Adelaide's fingers upon his ruined flesh was nearly orgasmic. It was as if she'd found a particular kink that he wasn't even sure that he had—whereas most men preferred a specific touch or a harsh kiss in a certain area, it was now evident that Switch enjoyed having his cheeks caressed. Plus, hair pulling was a definite kink as well. But the two together—Oh boy, oh *boy*.

Adelaide wasn't beautiful, not even remotely so. Her hair was never brushed, always stringy and frizzy and concealing her sullen, sunken features. She was dreadfully skinny and extremely malnourished, courtesy of the scarce amounts of food she consumed on a daily basis. Suddenly, the madman's mind began to drift towards the thought of her bony hips.

Her slender form prompted the bones of her hips to stick out rather obnoxiously, and the man was actually quite surprised that the trousers of her jumpsuit were able to stay up without the assistance of a belt.

Oh God, he wished he had his belt.

Lord have *mercy*—the remote thought of the leather slipping between his grasp was enough to make him hard beneath the thin fabric of his pants. Switch shifted in his seat, the palm of his hand irritably taming the growing bulge beneath his trousers as Adelaide raised a curious brow from across the table.

Suddenly, vivid visuals raided his tainted mind—visuals of an itty bitty Adelaide beneath his hips, squirming from a mixture of pain and pleasure as he gripped tightly onto the belt, contemplating where to strike—oh, what to do, what to *do—oh!*—Maybe she'll look pretty with it 'round her *neck* . . .

"Time's up, bitch." Greenwald spat, snatching Switch's nearly vacant tray from the surface of the table as he tossed it onto the floor.

The insistent murmurs that once littered the room suddenly ceased, the air becoming silent and stale as the plastic tray collided loudly against the tile floor, prompting a reflexive flinch to overcome Adelaide's limbs as her eyes grew wide.

Dozens of eyes focused on Switch's rigid form, lids wild with wonder as several amused snickers slipped off of Greenwald's parted lips.

"Clean it up." The guard thickly ordered, crossing his ink-littered arms across his chest as Switch's fingers curled into agonizingly tight fists upon the surface of the table.

The tips of Switch's uneven nails dug achingly against the calloused skin of his palms, nearly drawing blood to the surface as wrathful trembles enveloped his spine. Warm, cocoa-hued orbs expeditiously vanished, immediately replaced by a crimson tint as Greenwald's boastful laughter filled the silent premises.

Adelaide's pulse quickened, mouth running dry as she observed Switch's infuriated frame, his shoulders hunched incredibly high as his jaw twitched with extreme vexation.

Touch him.

Calm him down.

Hold him, Addy!

Adelaide let out a shrill squeak at the voices commandments, the plastic spoon toppling from her hold as her right hand instantly jutted outward, cool digits lacing tightly around his balled fist as his bold gaze swiftly connected with hers.

The furious man went somewhat lax beneath her surprisingly comforting touch, the angry trembles significantly calming as his tongue darted out from the depths of his mouth, intently tracing his marred bottom lip with ease as he aggressively exhaled.

"S'okay." He lowly assured the woman, climbing to his feet abruptly as he tore his trembling fist from her desperate hold.

The curly-haired man towered over Greenwald's confident stance, thin lips curling into an amused smirk as he awaited Switch's next possible move.

"If I were you, I'd think twice about what you do next, buddy." Greenwald teased, shifting his weight from either foot as Switch's jaw visibly clenched.

One punch. That's all it would take to knock this douchebag dead.

One. Damn. Punch.

"Clean it up!" Greenwald pressed through gritted teeth, becoming quite irritable with Switch's hesitation as he thrust an arm in the direction of the spilled peas scattered across the floor.

Adelaide sat idly by, a sweat breaking out over her brow as her chest painfully heaved. Greenwald was really pushing his limits, and she wasn't sure how long Switch would put up with the bullshit. However, one swing at the guy would surely land the madman in maximum security for a solid week—or more.

Can't have that, the voice interjected. *Can't let them take away your beau. Not after he's just been granted socialization time in the rec room.*

You're right, Adelaide replied, planting her palms flatly against the surface as she stood to her feet. *You guys are always right.*

To Greenwald's absolute horror, Adelaide fell to her knees beside the edge of the table, cradling her palms into cupped half-fists as she scooped the mushy peas into her grasp at an alarming rate.

"What the shit—*Lynch!* Get up!" Greenwald fumed, approaching the woman quickly as he laced his fingers around her bicep, abruptly yanking her petite frame from the ground as her shoulder suddenly shifted out of place from his rough hold.

The peas slipped through her parted fingers, a vociferous cry escaping her lips as thick tears pooled in her eyes. The pain in her shoulder was borderline excruciating, and she just couldn't seem to help the horrific cries of pain that managed to emerge from her chapped lips.

"You've gotta be *joking.*" Switch hissed, curling his arm around Greenwald's neck as he harshly tore him from Adelaide's timid form, slick, warm tears coating her flushed cheeks as she tumbled defeatedly to the floor.

"Get Nurse Briar!" A nearby guard shouted, falling to Adelaide's aide as he observed the dislodged joint. The surrounding guards scurried to Greenwald's side, tugging an irate Switch off of his neck as several shouts and Adelaide's persistent sobs filled the room.

Absolute chaos erupted, an abundance of nearby patients cheering Switch on as several beefy guards attempted to pry his hold away from Greenwald's reddened neck, but to no avail. Simply put, Switch was an *extremely* strong man . . .

"Adelaide! What happened?" A frantic Nurse Briar shrilly exclaimed, her cool touch meeting Adelaide's flushed skin as she observed the painful kink present in the young woman's shoulder.

"Greenwald knocked her shoulder outta place," the guard explained, handing Adelaide's heaving form over to a worrisome Nurse Briar as she cradled the woman in her arms.

"Shh," she cooed, running a perfectly manicured set of fingers through Adelaide's knotted locks. "Breathe, Ad. You're okay. I'm going to bring you up to Level 3 and get your shoulder straightened out."

"Fuck you, you piece of shit!" Greenwald exploded, shoving Switch's hunched frame off of him entirely as his fingers met the irritated skin of his neck.

Several guards held a fuming Switch back, several strands of oily ringlets concealing his widened, wild eyes as Adelaide's stare promptly met his. Batches of butterflies littered her belly at the sight of him, her pulse quickening beneath her ribcage as she viewed his timid form. He'd attacked Greenwald—*for her.*

A shaking set of fingers met her chin, applying a faint amount of pressure to the surface before extracting her hold and thrusting her arm slightly outward, signing a blatant thank you in Switch's direction as Nurse Briar practically carried her from the dining hall.

Switch nodded curtly, jaw clenched as the woman caught one single glance of Greenwald's horrific assault on the man as he delivered a stern blow to his stomach with a knotted fist.

The scene disappeared from view as the duo rounded the corner, several cries of protests emerging from Adelaide's parted lips as she inaudibly begged Briar to turn around.

Then, *it* emerged. Just as horrific and bone-chilling as it was the very first time she'd heard it.

A bold, exuberant burst of laughter instantly filled the void, ricocheting off the thin cement walls as patches of goosebumps arose on both Adelaide and Briar's skin. The low sonance rescinded into a high-pitched, menacing cackle, reverberating throughout the premises with ease as Greenwald presumably delivered several additional blows to Switch's sternum in a weak attempt to silence him. However, it seemed as if the harder he'd hit him, the louder Switch laughed, as if he were mocking him.

"I think he might be a masochist," Briar lowly observed, a snort emerging from her nostrils as Adelaide shot her a perplexed glance, eyes widening at the sudden sharp pain that originated in her misplaced shoulder once more as they approached the third level of the asylum.

Oooo, a MASOCHIST!

Fucking hell, Adelaide groaned, wincing at the severe discomfort present in her shoulder. *Can we not? I'm injured.*

Not too injured to think about how hard Switch's dick probably is right now. Y'know, it would make sense that he's a sucker for pain—he loves it. Maybe you can smack him around a little while you screw?

"Addy, I have something to tell you." Nurse Briar chirped, interrupting the bothersome voices as they strut into the Hospital Wing.

Adelaide raised a curious brow, her feet shuffling over towards an olive

-hued hospital bed, her bottom colliding with the drastically uncomfortable plastic mattress as Nurse Briar tugged the fabric from her shoulder.

"Per Dr. Blake's requests, the pharmacy has approved some new medical procedures for you," Nurse Briar uneasily began, her frigid digits cautiously gliding across the sore skin as Adelaide impulsively flinched.

"Tonight, you'll start a new round of medication. It'll replace one of your old ones, and this one has some annoying side effects, Ad. You'll probably be extremely exhausted a lot for the first several weeks, okay?"

Adelaide nodded, inhaling sharply as a searing pain shot through her shoulder.

"Sorry," Briar mumbled, thoroughly inspecting the dislodged joint. "This is going to hurt, but for only a minute. Okay? Just take a really deep breath, I'll count to three."

Adelaide blinked away several thick tears, a sharp breath hitching in her throat as she nodded in reply.

"One," she whispered, positioning her fingers in the proper placement against Adelaide's shoulder.

"Two," Adelaide inhaled deeply, eyelids flickering closed.

"Three." Briar mumbled, applying an overwhelming amount of pressure to Adelaide's shoulder as she effectively popped it back into place, earning an exasperated yelp from the young woman as she cried outward in pain.

"I have some other news in relation to your medical procedures, sweet pea. I don't think you'll like this one very much, though. In fact, I tried to fight it—I really did, Addy." Nurse Briar lowly rambled, massaging the tender skin of Adelaide's shoulder as she shot her an anxious glance.

"Starting tonight, they're going to administer electroconvulsive therapy to you. I'm not sure how long they'll do it for, as they stated it was until results occur." The woman spilled, several tears slipping down the slopes of her cheeks as Adelaide's jaw fell slack.

"It's okay," she assured her, running a hand through Adelaide's hair in an odd attempt to soothe her nerves. "I'll be there the entire time. You'll be safe."

"Nurse Briar," Dr. Blake snipped, fiddling with a filled syringe as she eventually thrust it in Briar's uneasy direction. "I trust you will be able to properly administer the anesthetic to patient 4210 prior to the procedure."

"Of course," Nurse Briar stammered, snatching the syringe from Dr. Blake's bony fingers as she turned it over in her palm. A breath emerged through slightly parted lips, her gaze eventually focusing on a fidgeting Adelaide laid upon the operating table, hazel-hued orbs widened in absolute fear as she observed the abundance of doctors and nurses that currently surrounded her bed.

Although Dr. Blake had insisted that Adelaide be strapped down before her anesthetic, Nurse Briar heavily disagreed, countering with the fact that it was cruel and pointless to worry the poor woman further whilst she was still conscious. After much debate, Dr. Blake finally agreed to Briar's terms.

"All right, Ad." Briar softly began, crouching beside Adelaide's bed as wide cobalt eyes met a pair of wild, tri-colored orbs. "I'm going to put you under so you won't feel or remember anything, okay? I won't let them hurt you. I'll always protect you."

A particularly large lump currently occupied Adelaide's throat, her hair fanned out against the paper-thin pillow as she hastily nodded. After all, she truly trusted Briar Cunningway with her entire life.

"Count backwards from ten, sweetie. You'll be asleep before you hit zero." Nurse Briar collectively instructed, tying a fluorescent orange tourniquet around Adelaide's slender arm as she tugged it tight. Her cool touch prompted arrays of goosebumps to arise on Adelaide's flesh, her stomach doing painful somersaults as Briar searched for the proper vein.

"Ready?" She cooed, applying pressure to a particularly prominent vein with the pad of her thumb.

Adelaide bleakly nodded, her gaze locking on a tight-lipped Dr. Blake, who stood cross-armed across the room, magnified stare unblinking and jaw tightening.

Just as Nurse Briar plunged the needle into Adelaide's skin—a harsh wince overcoming her strained features as her eyelids snapped tightly shut—Switch's tainted features instantly raided her mind. He was smiling, an arm outstretched, the sleeve of his striped jumpsuit inattentively rolled above his elbows as they almost always were. Fingers parted—begging—*pleading* for her to take hold of them, for her to lace her grimy digits between his and hold on tight for an eternity and furthermore. Just as the unmarred flesh of his face inched upwards into a lovely smirk, the vision faded to black, and Adelaide drifted into the depths of a dreamless pit.

Adelaide's audible heartbeat severely slowed upon the monitor, the consistent beeps trickling into a steady rhythm as Dr. Blake summoned the nearby doctors.

"All right, she's out. I'll say we have about thirty minutes, so let's try and get things done quickly and efficiently, okay?" Lyra Blake snidely snapped. "I'll connect the electrodes, Nurse Briar, you can administer the Succinylcholine through the IV."

"Yes, ma'am." Nurse Briar lowly spoke, claiming a clean syringe from a nearby metal operating table as she filled it to the brim with Succinylcholine, a drug that would relax Adelaide's muscles and prevent the possibility of broken bones and a cracked vertebra from the harsh procedure. Unfortunately, she'd done this once before with a different patient, and it was, by far, one of the most sickening things to witness. In fact, the bile had already begun to creep up her esophagus . . .

As the artificially blond woman began to insert the drug into Adelaide's bloodstream, Dr. Blake shoved her sharp nails into the unconscious patient's mouth, prying her frozen lips open with difficulty as she shoved a matte, navy-hued rubber block between her yellowing teeth. Nurse Briar visibly frowned at the sight, her fingers daintily retracting the empty syringe from Adelaide's arm as she promptly sealed the wound with a periwinkle pink bandage.

"Step away, Nurse Briar." Dr. Blake ordered, the tone of her voice strictly monotone as she placed a mask over Adelaide's parted lips, whereas a thin-lipped doctor by the name of Chadwick applied the conducting jelly to the unconscious woman's temples.

Briar's pulse quickened, her fingers curled into a firm fist as she held it close to her chest. She'd never wanted to see Adelaide like this—she never wanted it to be like this. However, the woman simply had no say in the matter.

Dr. Blake was the one in charge.

Dr. Chadwick brushed away several brunette strands out of his watering eyes, the pad of his index finger colliding with the power button on the machine as it sprung audibly to life. Briar's chest clenched at the sonance, choking back fat, blinding tears as Dr. Blake sarcastically grinned in her direction.

"Ready to cure Miss Lynch, Cummingway?" Lyra announced, a confident giggle emerging as she claimed the electrodes in her greedy palms.

"It's Cunningway, cunt." Briar shakily spat beneath her breath, a sharp breath hitching in her throat as Dr. Blake efficiently placed the electrodes on either temple.

"Go." Lyra lowly ordered, Chadwick's finger colliding with the crimson circular button as a wave of electricity fluently entered Adelaide's brain.

Her once unmoving, frail frame suddenly sprung to life, her limbs involuntarily convulsing as Nurse Briar released a horrific, strained cry at the sight. Adelaide's body seized for all of twenty-or-so seconds, a severe seizure wracking through her brain as Chadwick killed the power.

Finally, the seizure ceased—her limbs flattening against the bleak mattress once more as her heart rate slowed to a steady pace upon the monitor once again. Beads of sweat occupied Briar's brows, heart racing beneath her ribcage as she frantically tugged at her bottom lip with her fingers.

"Take her to her cell." Dr. Blake dryly requested, placing the electrodes on a nearby table as she wordlessly excused herself from the hospital wing.

Nurse Briar weakly nodded, her hand still firmly clutched to her chest as she slowly crept towards a still Adelaide, her chest rising and falling with every staggered breath as she Briar shakily tugged the adhesive electrode pads from the woman's busty chest, leaving behind an irritable circle of sticky residue as she recovered her momentarily exposed chest.

"It's okay, Addy." Nurse Briar defeatedly whispered, thrusting an arm beneath Adelaide's knees, whereas the other claimed her rigid neck.

Chadwick assisted the woman with placing a limp Adelaide in a wheelchair, his sultry complexion contorting into a look of sympathy as Briar excused herself and an unconscious Adelaide from the wing.

The low blue hue of the night time lights on Level 4 sent shivers down Briar's spine as she shakily unlocked Adelaide's cold, vacant cell. The cell block was eerily silent, all except for Cora's obnoxious snoring on the opposite end, the irritable sound whisking through the rectangular hole present in the mahogany steel door as the nurse choked back hefty sobs. Adelaide was still fully unconscious, resembling a pitiful ragdoll in Briar's arms as she lifted her frail form from the chair and elegantly placed her upon the sorry excuse for a mattress.

The cheap metal frame audibly shifted beneath Adelaide's abrupt weight, several tears slipping from the comfort of Briar's eyes as they sloppily collided with Adelaide's exposed flesh. She was still dressed in a bleak, unpigmented hospital gown, accessorized with evenly spaced baby blue polka dots the size of dimes as Briar admired her sleeping form.

Somehow, the woman looked rather youthful in her sleep. Her eyelids twitched slightly, eyeballs rolling instinctively beneath her tightly sealed lids as she presumably dreamt about something rather pleasant. Her flushed cheeks twitched sporadically, chapped lips parting to allow a heavy inhale to enter as she murmured inaudibly beneath her breath.

"Sweet dreams, Addy." Nurse Briar whispered, falling to her knees beside the bed as she ran a shaking hand through Adelaide's knotted locks. The comatose woman stirred beneath her warm touch, fingers twitching against the creme-hued duvet as she released a dramatic exhale.

"What'd they *do* to her?" A sudden voice intruded, ricocheting off the paper-thin cement walls with proficiency as Briar flinched.

She spun around on her heel, eyes contorting into tight slits as her vision struggled to adjust to the dim lighting of the cell.

"S'only *me*," the man thickly mused, a slight giggle immediately following his proclamation as Briar's gaze eventually settled upon a pair of dark, haunting eyes beyond the sloppily built hole.

"If yah wan-*t*," Switch added, forcing a bit of emphasis on the latter letter of the word as he swayed in place against the wall. "I can give you another show. You seemed to like it before."

Vivid visuals of Switch's cleansing immediately raided Briar's mind, her blood running cold beneath her veins as she climbed to her feet beside Adelaide's bed.

"I didn't mean to be so nosy," she lightly spoke, insinuating a nonverbal apology as Switch's scarred lips curled into a blatant smirk.

"Oh, don't you worry your pretty little head, missus. I'm *more* than happy to provide a *generous* encore, hm?" The man lazily drawled, tongue lapping out to meet the frayed corners of his scar as he winked suggestively in Briar's direction.

"That won't be necessary, sir." She whispered, glancing over her shoulder to view a sleeping Adelaide as her stomach twisted into tight knots.

"*Sir?*" Switch yelped, fingers fiddling with the cracked concrete of the hole. "*Wha-ha-ha!* Oh—my oh *my!* You'd never guess I was a prisoner with *that* kinda language! Oh, *baby!*"

"Well, what would you prefer me to call you?" Briar inappropriately countered. She knew quite well that this type of banter was strictly prohibited, but she had to admit—it was just too damn fun. Plus, she needed someone to speak to, besides that wretched Lyra Blake . . .

Switch's gaze darkened, several determined fingers knotting in his greasy locks as he intently traced the deep scar imprinted upon his lower lip.

"Well well well," he announced, tugging at the strands as he let out a vehement groan. "If we're playing games like *that*, you can-*uh*, call me *daddy*, sugar plum."

Heat immediately rose to Briar's cheeks at his wildly provocative statement, her chest tightening as she inched towards the sealed door.

"Goodnight, Switch." She uneasily dismissed, snatching her badge from the depths of her scrubs pocket.

"Mmm, that's *daddy* to you, baby girl." Switch pressed, his tone low and husky as he cautiously observed Nurse Briar's rigid frame. "Hey, what's your name again?"

"Nurse Briar." She shamelessly revealed, the hefty steel door audibly unlocking with a harsh *click.*

"Baby Briar," Switch giggled, swiping his thumb against the skin of his lip as he hardly blinked. "When you're-*uh, touching* yourself tonight, I want you to think of *me*, mkay?"

Nurse Briar's fingers laced around the handle of the mahogany door, her stomach doing somersaults as she struggled to maintain steady breaths. *Was Switch actually saying all of this to her right now? Was she hallucinating?*

"Just so yah *know*," he confidently continued, fingers latching around his bottom lip as he hastily tugged it outward, releasing it an inch away from his face so that it would noisily snap back into place. Briar's heart fluttered at the peculiar action, her heart thumping thickly in her throat as she shifted her weight from either foot.

"I'll be touching myself to the thought of *you*, pumpkin."

With that, Nurse Briar hurriedly vacated the cell, flattening her back against the frigid steel as it sealed shut once and for all.

The distinct sound of Switch's cackles emerged from the neighboring cell, the miniscule hairs present on the back of her neck standing tall as she violently shivered.

Briar Cunningway involuntarily trembled the entire drive home, her fingers laced extremely tight around the rubber steering wheel as her knuckles flushed bright white. For some odd reason, she just couldn't seem to kick the thought of Switch's statements out of her mind.

He was a cunning mastermind, she knew that much. Manipulative as hell—Simply put, the man would go to any extent to get what he wanted. And yet, as the exhausted woman trudged into her exceedingly small apartment, a wisp of jet black fur nudging at her toes as persistent meows filled her ears—she just couldn't stop thinking about him . . . which was *exactly* what he had wanted.

"Calm down, Styx." Briar scolded as the miniscule ball of fur nipped hungrily at her ankles, audibly begging for a bowl full of food as she willingly complied.

Once the kitten was happy and fed, Briar collapsed in an exasperated heap upon her squishy mattress, using her toes to rid her aching feet of the withering shoes as they tumbled to the carpet at the foot of her bed.

Unwillingly, Briar's mind reiterated Switch's wildly grotesque remarks, the mere thought of his jumpsuit trousers around his ankles made something strange stir deep within her.

As if on cue—just as he'd predicted—Briar's reluctant fingers slipped beneath the waist of her scrubs, slipping into the depths of her panties as her fingers finally collided with her aching place of want and a harsh realization suddenly struck: She was undoubtedly and unbelievably turned on by the mere thought of the infamous and malevolent Switch.

IX

"But you touched my hand
I loved this new sensation / So call on me, my hearts on fire"
–Foreigner, "I Need You"

"Does it hurt?" Switch cooed, threading his fingers through Adelaide's stringy, unwashed hair as she lay in a heap against the cement wall. Her knees were pressed against her chest, slender arms laced around her legs as she locked them in place.

Empty, soulless eyes met an abundance of warm, comforting cocoa, her lips tugging into a weak, half-assed grin as her fingers toyed with the loose strand present on her jumpsuit trousers.

The woman was utterly exhausted, courtesy of her new medication and the two excruciating electroconvulsive therapy treatments she'd received within the course of a week. Although she didn't remember any of them, she could clearly recall waking up intensely dazed and confused after every single time, her head throbbing and the room expeditiously spinning, as if she'd downed too many shots of Fireball.

Adelaide drifted into a blissful state at the innocent gesture of Switch's fingers in her overgrown hair. They'd spent days upon days together in the rec room, seated hip-to-hip as he'd spill the utmost random things to her, keeping her company whilst she read and reread the same paragraphs of her aging novel.

"Hey," Switch began, detaching his digits from her locks as she let out an irate huff at the absence of his fingers. "Gimme that book, will yah?"

Adelaide audibly gulped, her fingers lacing around the dilapidated novel as she lifted it from the dusty ground, her palm swiping against the cover repeatedly to rid it of the sand and dirt as she eventually thrust it into Switch's outstretched palms.

A pair of shiny, silver cuffs routinely claimed his wrists, the inky set of tattooed lines present on his left wrist slightly peeking through the material as he turned the book over in his grasp with a heightened sense of curiosity.

"Ready?" He mused, dipping his pointer finger beneath the soft flap of the paperback cover as he pried the book open, revealing the inside cover and title page as his chocolate-tinted gaze instantly widened at the sight of considerably neat handwriting etched upon the inside cover.

My dearest Adelaide,
Now you can carry Elinor and Marianne around with you always.
Whenever you look at these pages, I hope you'll always think of me and the
countless times we spent reading this together. Also, I hope you'll stop
stealing my copy, since you now have your own. My heart is forever yours.
-E. xo

Switch raised a questionable brow, his gaze locking on a stiff and distracted Adelaide sat directly beside him as she curiously observed the gossiping duo of Nayeli and Cora on the opposite side of the room.

The scarred-face man garishly cleared his throat, earning a wide-eyed Adelaide's attention as he began to read the story aloud.

"The family of Dashwood had been long settled in Sussex," he boldly began, taking a brief, momentary pause to caress the obscene scars that littered his cheek. At this, she simply smiled, her joyful expression catching his eye. Thus, a smirk replaced his bland complexion as he let out a throaty statement, "ah, *there's* my girl."

A scarlet tint overcame the woman's features, her palms clamping over the lower half of her face in a pitiful attempt to conceal her broad, toothy grin. With that, Switch redirected his attention, his stare settling upon the printed word once more as he confidently continued.

"Their estate was large, and their residence was at Norland Park, in the centre of their property, where, for many generations, they had lived in so respectable a manner, as to engage the general good opinion of their surrounding acquaintance."

Adelaide laid lax against the dreadfully uncomfortable wall, her bottom going numb from sitting in one specific spot for such a long period of time as her eyelids fluttered elegantly closed. She'd managed to drift into a euphorically blissful state at the mere sonance of Switch's voice, which read aloud the printed words of her absolute favorite novel as she practically fell in love.

No–it wasn't love. No, not entirely–not even remotely–not that she could even fathom. Adelaide hadn't been in love with another human being in years, and she honestly couldn't imagine falling in love with anyone but that specific individual that she'd once (and still) loved. However, if the man beside her continued with this utterly romantic façade, she'd absolutely crumble in his embrace within a moment's time. In fact, she may even actually–genuinely–*truly* fall in love with him.

The pair continued on like this for several days, so much so that it actually became some type of routine. She adored the unique, melodic sound of his voice–the way he carefully enunciated certain syllables, as if certain parts of specific words served some type of significance in his mind. It was absolutely unique, the way he spoke. The tone of his voice would gradually shift depending on the topic, merging from a cheerful tone full of giggling undertones, to a darker, more sinister sound, laced with menace and depth as the words cut through the skin like hot knives.

Switch was truly something else, and Adelaide Lynch wanted to know absolutely everything about him.

You know what they say—Curiosity killed the cat.

"How've you been feeling, Adelaide?" Dr. Blake blandly inquired, shoving her index finger against the thick rims of her spectacles as she shoved them back up the slope of her sweaty nose.

The therapy room was unusually warm today, and Adelaide had found herself having to roll both the arm and leg sleeves of her jumpsuit up to prevent herself from beginning to sweat beneath the harsh glow of the fluorescent lights.

The thin woman toyed with the perfectly sharpened wooden pencil, the pad of her thumb grazing slightly along the serrated edge as she glanced at the clean sheet of lined paper.

"Don't be shy, Adelaide." Dr. Blake impatiently urged, slipping the paper into Adelaide's space as she inaudibly begged for her to begin writing. "Tell me, are the voices still present?"

Are you guys still with me? Adelaide requested, knowing quite well that she wouldn't receive a response. Ever since her second electroconvulsive therapy session and the recent influx of different medication, the comforting set of voices that usually claimed her mind had apparently gone into hibernation.

Shakily, the woman positioned the pencil between skeptical fingers, applying pressure to the page as a sloppy word emerged from the tip of the pencil.

Dr. Blake snatched the parchment from her weak hold, magnified eyes grazing over the simplistic response as she simply nodded, scribbling a bit of information into her therapy journal as she sympathetically smiled.

"This is positive progress, Adelaide. The voices are gone—you're one step closer to becoming normal again, sweetie."

What about me isn't normal?

"You may be dismissed, Miss Lynch." Dr. Blake stated, snapping her journal closed as she waved her hand.

The guard named Vern entered the room, a genuine grin enveloping his lips as he lifted a stiff Adelaide from her chair and excused her from the area. The moment the duo slipped through the open doorway, however, the woman's heart nearly burst out of her chest.

A cuffed Switch stood opposite her, a toothy grin plastered up on his features as he shifted his weight from either foot. The laces of his jet-black boots were untidy and unlaced, the aglets scraping against the bland concrete floor as Greenwald's fingers applied an ample amount of pressure to Switch's particularly large bicep.

"Lighten up, Greenie." Switch spat, attempting to yank his arm from Greenwald's impossibly tight hold as the crimson-haired guard shot Adelaide a stern glare. He hadn't dared to enter the woman's cell following that very first encounter with a smart-mouthed Switch beyond the sloppily made hole, and Cora hadn't exactly been putting out like she used to . . .

Simply put, the man was starting to get antsy. He needed a quick shag, and he needed it with someone easy—someone who'd let him have his way with her without any protest.

Vern urged Adelaide forward, the flat of his palm pressed between her shoulders as she offered Switch a sympathetic smile, as if to wish him good luck. Greenwald, however, had assumed that the smile was aimed towards him, which ultimately sealed the deal for tonight's events in his mind.

"Get in there, freak." Greenwald spat through gritted teeth, his palm rotating to Switch's lower back as he expeditiously shoved the madman through the open doorway. The soles of Switch's boots loudly squeaked against the tile, leaving behind deep, dark scuffs upon the surface as he glared menacingly over his hunched shoulder.

Dr. Blake craned her neck at the sudden intrusion, her purple painted lips tugged into a tight smirk as she observed a heavily restrained Switch and a giddy Officer Greenwald.

"Officer," she greeted, artificially whitened teeth flashing in the attractive man's direction as he forced a timid Switch into the harsh metal chair.

"Lyra," Greenwald grinned, eyelid flickering closed momentarily as he delivered a wink in her direction. He knew quite well that Dr. Blake was married—hence the shiny, bland gold band that circled her ring finger. However, the man simply knew no boundaries.

Greenwald latched the table cuffs around Switch's highly irritated wrists, the once pale skin forever tainted a dark scarlet due to the overuse of uncomfortable metal restraints. Per usual, the officer latched the cuffs around agonizingly tight, practically limiting the circulation made available to Switch's slender fingers as Dr. Blake audibly scolded him for his actions.

"If you keep this up, he'll lose his hands." She scolded, rising from her chair to snatch Switch's wrists out of Greenwald's greedy hold. The thin fabric of her baby blue blouse got caught onto the edge of the frigid metal table, revealing a bit too much of her cleavage to both of the men as she outwardly gasped.

"Out." She pressed, jabbing a thumb in the direction of the ajar door as Greenwald unhappily obliged, strutting from the room as he abandoned a giddy Switch and a flustered Dr. Blake.

"Nice tits," Switch boldly announced, taking his bottom lip tightly between his teeth as he aggressively bit down. A familiar metallic flavor filled his senses, a thick strand of crimson liquid smearing along the irritated skin as the lip popped audibly back into place.

Dr. Blake's brows knit together in vexation at the sight of his bleeding lip, her fingers fumbling with the inky ballpoint pen as she thrust open her therapy journal.

"You seem to be in a good mood today," she observed, adjusting her top with dainty fingers as Switch's tongue intently traced the thick scarlet liquid upon his lip. "How are you feeling?"

"Ecstatic," Switch beamed, fiddling his fingers together atop the table as the metal chains collided with the identical surface, emitting a harsh *clink*. "S'pecially since I got a little *peep* at your boobies."

"You sound like a middle school boy." She sternly observed, scribbling unnecessary oblong circles against the blank page of her journal as her chest involuntarily heaved.

"Oh baby," Switch huskily began, shifting his weight against the drastically uncomfortable chair. "I *feel* like a middle school boy right now."

"Have you been taking the medication provided for you every night?" Dr. Blake inquired, completely disregarding his wildly inappropriate banter as she scribbled down crucial information about the session into her journal.

"No." He spat, lips curling into an enthusiastic "o" shape as he heavily enunciated the simplistic word.

"Why's that?" The woman partially scolded, heavily-filled in brows knitting together as her thick-rimmed spectacles slipped down the slope of her greasy nose.

"Be-*cause*," Switch mused, a slight giggle present in his tone. "I'm afraid if I take 'em, my dick won't work. Meds can do that, y'know."

"Yes, I am fully aware of the possible side effects evolving from specific types of medication. However, you still need to take them, Switch. It's not like you're—*uh*," the woman paused, instantly biting her tongue as she struggled not to spill the following statement, which was *highly* unprofessional . . .

"Not like I'm *what*?" Switch pressed, curiously picking at his fingernail as he arched a brow. "*Using* it?"

Dr. Blake swallowed thickly, her mouth running dry as she eyed a skeptical Switch opposite her. His shoulders were dramatically hunched, eyes wild in curiosity as he awaited a plausible response.

"Do you *want* me to use it, Doc-*tooor*?" He lowly questioned, shackled wrist arching upward so that the pad of this thumb could meet his blood-smeared lip. Dr. Blake intently observed as he harshly wiped the substance away from his skin, allowing the crimson hue to transfer to the flesh of his fingers as she stirred in her seat.

"Can we just have one normal session?" She croaked, the tone of her voice ultimately defeating her as the Switch released a considerably deep chuckle, one which resembled that of a growl.

"Nothing about me is normal, toots. The sooner you learn that, the better."

"Oh, I'm fully aware of that." The woman sarcastically replied, jotting down and additional round of notes as she eyed Switch through her peripheral vision. He was blatantly staring at her, gaze remaining unblinking as he studied her somewhat calm physique. However, he knew for a fact that if he continued to push her buttons *juuust* right, she'd eventually snap directly in two.

"You're staring." She pointed out the obvious, manicured fingers toying with her lip as a devious grin enveloped his marred mouth. "What are you thinking about?"

"The truth?" Switch drawled, reminding the woman of their very first session. She audibly gulped in response.

"Nothing but." She whispered, tapping the cap of her pen against her pointed chin. Switch went lax in his seat, his back collapsing against the stiff material as glorious fantasies invaded his mind.

"Truthfully? I'm thinking about *you*, dollface. About you beneath my hips, those perky tits on display as I revel in their glorious appeal. You've got a *niiiice* rack—so round'n perky and inviting, practically begging for me. However, my main focus ain't on those beautiful breasts—no sir-*reeee*—God, all I can *think* about is my fingers 'round your perfect little neck—"

"Switch—" Dr. Blake pressed, fearful of what was to come as a considerably large lump took refuge in her throat.

"I'm not *finished*, cupcake." Switch sternly spat, curling his digits into a tight fist as it shrilly collided with the table, sending violent shivers down the length of Lyra Blake's spine as her eyes significantly widened.

"Do you like choking, love? Because I can choke you real good. Y'know, they say that the female orgasm is a *bajillion* times better with a restricted airflow . . ."

"What do you want from me, Switch?" Dr. Blake demanded, snapping her journal closed as she dismissively tossed it onto the table. A devilish smirk overcoming the man's features at the sight of her extremely flustered form, the color completely draining from his once bright eyes as a menacing dark hue promptly replaced his orbs.

"I want you," he purred, tugging at the restraints circling his wrists as she boldly shook her head. "I want to bend you over this table and show you who's *really* in charge."

"Christ," Dr. Blake scoffed, crossing her arms irritably as she took in Switch's amused glare. "You're repulsive. You truly don't have any filter, do you?"

"No-*pe*. I just can't help myself—you're gorgeous, sweet cheeks." Switch fluently lied. *This was way too easy*. "Y'know what I do at night, princess?"

Dr. Blake simply shrugged, inaudibly urging him to continue his erotic spiel as her lips tugged into a tight frown. This was getting completely out of hand.

"I think about you. I think about those pretty painted lips—" he trailed off, eyes sarcastically rolling to the back of his skull as his mind wandered to the familiar, somewhat comforting complexion of Adelaide's face. Plus, if he was going to make this whole scene convincing, he just had to bust out a bit of a stiffy, and the mere thought of that bitch Lyra Blake was enough to make his balls take refuge inside of his damn body.

"You'd look so *purdy* between my legs, darlin'. Those big ole eyes begging for me to have my way with you." Suddenly, the stern expression plastered upon Dr. Blake's ugly mug rapidly transformed. The wide, magnetized set of bright blue eyes quickly vanished, molding into a familiar hazel hue as the spectacles disappeared into thin air. Stringy, ashy brown hair draped past her bony shoulders, hovering over her busty breasts as a thin, toothy smile replaced her disapproving frown. Switch practically gawked at the sudden sight of Adelaide—of *his* Adelaide, sat cleanly across from him as the blood rapidly rushed from his complexion.

Then, just as quickly as she'd appeared—she vanished. Replaced yet again by the mean mug of Dr. Blake's heavily painted face as she abruptly stood from her chair and excused herself from the room.

Switch released an irate sigh, eyelids fluttering closed as Adelaide's features bombarded his tainted mind once more. For the first time in a very, very long time, he found himself craving the touch of another human being.

He needed her, just as much as she needed him.

X

Adelaide spent the majority of night 759 with her upper half hunched over the frigid metal of the u-bend.

The woman was mostly dry-heaving, mainly due to the fact that she'd thrown up virtually everything in her stomach within the course of an hour.

"You okay, toots?" Switch pried, his voice somewhat muffled by the obstruction of the cement wall as several greasy strands tumbled into Adelaide's eyes. The woman heavily heaved, her fingers gliding along her sweat-riddled complexion as she let out a vociferous sob.

He knew quite well that she was, in fact, *not* okay—nor was he. The soft, silky skin surrounding his left eye was achingly pulsating, as if the flesh contained a second separate heartbeat. His ribs were undoubtedly bruised, a piercing pain enveloping his every limb with every staggered breath as he leant against the sturdy wall. Greasy, unkempt locks clung to the moist skin of his neck, slow, steady streams of crimson oozing from his cracked knuckles as several beads of blood stained his jumpsuit trousers.

Vivid visuals of a scene from only an hour prior raided his mind—visuals of the wretched Greenwald and his thick-skulled ego. Switch could clearly see the scarlet-haired man's fingers cupped around Adelaide's parted lips, wide eyes locked in Switch's direction as she silently begged for the end to come. He couldn't bear to watch it—*no*—it was beyond screwed up. He couldn't bear to watch the atrocity unfold—although, Adelaide's muffled pleads and cries were enough to turn his stomach into agonizingly tight knots and prompt the blood to thickly curdle in his veins.

The only one who could hurt Adelaide was *him*.

The man sharply twisted his ankles, rising to his feet as the bones in his knees indecently creaked and cracked with every staggered movement, his neck craning so that he could properly view the woman who currently lay in a sobbing heap over the metallic toilet bowl.

"Hey," Switch huskily cooed, threading his fingers through the unevenly punctured wall as he snuck his arm through the hole. "C'mere, princess."

Adelaide let out an additional heightened cry, the pads of her thumbs roughly wiping away the abundance of fallen tears that littered her sunken cheeks as she lazily twisted on her heel. A pair of empty, broken eyes met Switch's surprisingly sympathetic gaze, his marred lips threading into a blatant frown as she crawled on all fours in the direction of the hole.

Her jumpsuit clung lowly to her bony hips, the straps of her bleak, crème-hued tank top slipping down the slopes of her shoulders as she propped herself up on trembling knees, her fingers encircling Switch's extended wrist. She buried her hooked nose into the warm, comforting embrace of his palm, her salty tears coating his cracked skin as she went lax under his touch.

The scarred-face man gently caressed her cheek with his thumb, slightly stroking the chapped flesh of her upper lip as he tugged the skin sideways, fingers becoming slick with salty tears as she nuzzled her face further into his grasp. It stunned the madman that he was able to be so gentle with the frail woman. If only she'd known what these hands had done . . .

"I'm going to kill him," he boldly announced, studying Adelaide's sullen features as her eyelids instantly fluttered open, hazel hue colliding with a sea of cocoa as her heart instinctively fluttered. "I swear it, pumpkin. I'll fuckin' kill him for what he's done. To the both of us."

In the place of a verbal reply, Adelaide simply craned her neck, brushing her lips against Switch's palm as she pressed a dainty, short-lived kiss to the surface.

The action, in itself, spoke greater volumes than physical words ever could.

"Briar," Officer Harrington gruffly called, his tone muffled by the obstruction of a lit cigarette as a steady strand of smoke emerged.

"Yes, sir?" Nurse Briar anxiously squeaked, smoothing down the raised flap on the hem of her scrubs with her palms as she abruptly stood from her swivel chair and entered the office.

"I'm assigning you a second patient," Harrington announced, his beady, black eyes swiftly colliding with Briar's conflicting blue orbs as her lips parted in bewilderment.

"O-Okay?" She breathlessly replied, shifting her weight from either foot as Officer Harrington thrust a manila folder into her wary grasp.

"It'll be easy, considering he's your original patient's neighbor." The thick-necked man monotonically explained, beefy fingers threading around the cancer stick as he tore it from the safety of his round lips.

The air instantaneously eluded Briar's lungs at Officer Harrington's revelation, a shaking finger hooking around the flap of the folder as she tore open the file, revealing a mess of gruesome, jagged scars and dark, menacing eyes.

"H-How will t-this—"

"You'll bathe them together. Feed them together. All that jazz. Think of it like a package deal." The man dryly explained. "I have faith that you can handle this one, Briar. You're the best that we've got."

"I-I'm honored, sir." The woman whispered, swallowing a significant mouthful of bile as her stare reconnected with Switch's amused mugshot. He was *smiling*, as if getting caught was the best thing that had ever happened to him.

"He's to remain cuffed in the rec room until further notice, since he's—" Officer Harrington momentarily paused, a deep grumble resonating within his throat as he obnoxiously cleared it, his arms raising as his fingers generated a set of air quotes as he hastily finished with, "*high risk.*"

"Understood, sir. Anything else I need to know?" Briar breathlessly inquired, forcefully tearing her desperate gaze away from his marred face as she reconnected with Officer Harrington's skeptical glare.

"Everything you need to know about that piece of shit is in that file, Cunningway." He gruffly spat, thrusting the burning object between his lips once more as he shuffled through an abundance of files upon his large oak desk.

When Briar overstayed her welcome, she was met by a pair of skeptical eyes, followed by a grim, "you're excused."

A petite squeal emerged through the woman's slightly parted lips, her ankles acutely twisting as she shuffled from the room, Switch's file clutched to her chest.

The woman reentered the nearly vacant hospital wing, collapsing defeatedly into her inky black swivel chair as the furniture shifted beneath her weight. She released a considerably long exhale, her fingers toying with several loose strands that had tumbled from the confinement of her rubber hair tie as she pried the folder open once again.

His complexion riddled her sight once more, stomach painfully churning as she hastily shoved away the horrifically embarrassing memories of her—*fondling*—her lady bits at the mere thought of the crude man. Briar's cheeks flushed a bright scarlet hue, her face tumbling into her palms as she dug her nails against her scalp.

Admittedly, the woman hadn't quit after one single time. In fact, she'd rubbed one off to the thought of the Switch a solid four times, give or take a few. She was absolutely disgusted by the fact, thick tears clouding her vision as she let out a hefty sigh.

Now, unfortunately for her—*and her defiant body*—she'd be seeing the man nude every single night during his bath.

The thought alone was enough to make her stomach obnoxiously flutter.

"Miss Dashwood had a delicate complexion, regular features and a remarkably pretty figure." Switch routinely read, his amused gaze straying away from the page as it collided with a giddy Adelaide sat directly beside him. Her lips curled into an enthusiastic grin at the sight of his cheerful expression, her fingers fiddling with the obscene hole present in the wilting fabric of her sock as she studied his heavily bruised eye.

"You know," he slurred, irritable tongue interrupting his line of speech as he caressed the lining of his severed lower lip. "She almost sounds as pretty as you."

Adelaide's expression instantly brightened, her lips tugging into a toothy grin as she curled her arm around Switch's, threading her fingers along the miniscule hairs present on his exposed arm. For once, the woman was actually thankful that the voices were currently absent, due to the fact that they would've found some type of way to absolutely demolish this glorious moment.

Switch's gaze returned to the printed page, his chest aching at the incredibly intimate gesture as the woman tightly clung to his side. It took an unbelievable amount of self-control to not shove her off and slit her throat with the metal cuffs encircling his wrists . . .

"Marianne was still handsomer," he continued, raising a curious brow as he quickly reread the term several times over.

"*Handsomer*? Is that even a word?" He taunted, earning a profuse giggle from the tiny woman as she unraveled her arm from his. A tremendous weight instantly lifted the moment her touch left his, an involuntary exhale emerging from his nostrils as he was finally able to efficiently ward off the violent tendencies.

God, he wanted her *so* bad. However, he wasn't quite sure which way he wanted her more . . .

"Her form, though not so correct as her sisters, in having the advantage of height, was more striking; and her face was so lovely, that when in the common cant of praise she was called a beautiful girl, truth was less violently outraged than usually happens."

Thus, the duo continued like this for the next seventy-two minutes. Adelaide was surely wrapped up in a blissful nirvana, the gorgeous word of Jane Austen slipping keenly off Switch's tainted lips as he effortlessly read the text aloud. She adored him with every fiber of her being, and even though they currently sat hip-to-hip, she wanted more. She *craved* more. The woman dreamt of straddling his waist, lacing her slender arms around his neck as the loose, overgrown curls that claimed his scalp would tickle the fine hairs of her forearms. She'd felt the glorious feel of his partially marred mouth, the complex crevices and folds of his torn skin and how they overlapped and gaudily parted—how they so effortlessly slipped between her curious touch as she felt the effects of the keen blade that had destroyed his complexion for an eternity. She wasn't quite sure which artificial marking was worse—the one that nearly carved his mouth open entirely on one side, or the one below his eye, which causes the skin to slightly bulge and overlap. Maybe even the vertical gash that claimed nearly the entirety of the edge of his face . . .

Adelaide also shamefully found herself glaring at the scar that hovered his bottom lip—so gaudy and choppy and harsh, as if the attacker had attempted to slice the skin directly in two. She wondered what it would feel like against her lips . . .

"Adelaide," Nurse Briar keenly interrupted the woman's trance, Switch's slits for eyes connecting with a wide cobalt gaze as she awkwardly cleared her throat.

"We're busy." Switch harshly dismissed, tugging at the shackles binding his wrists as Briar fell to her knees beside the pair, a hesitant smile plastered upon her lips as she disregarded his comment entirely.

"I have some news," the woman shyly began, avoiding the man's harsh glare as Adelaide softly smiled, as if to urge the woman on.

"I've just been assigned as Switch's primary caretaker as well. Tonight, will be your first round of baths—*uh*," the woman fumbled her words, Switch's features brightening as a devious smirk overcame his lips. He knew *exactly* where this was going.

"You'll be bathing together. Not in the same tub—of course—but I'll be trading off between the two of you, and uh, yeah." Nurse Briar stammered, avoiding Switch's piercing gaze as Adelaide's face fell. Suddenly, she felt extremely awkward about the fact that she'd be sitting in a porcelain bowl of her own filth in an hour's time—directly beside a fully naked Switch.

"It's time for supper, anyways. I'll escort the both of you." The woman stuttered, rising to her feet as Switch snapped the partially read paperback book closed, his giddy expression meeting a timid Adelaide as she avoided him entirely.

Supper was awkward.

For the first time in days, Adelaide avoided her newly found spot opposite Switch. Instead, her ass currently claimed the multi-colored corner of the tiled floor, trembling fingers timidly tugging at a soft dinner roll as Switch glanced fleetingly over his shoulder to view her.

She could spot him from her peripheral vision, but she purposely chose not to acknowledge him. Something about their combined bath tonight made her drastically uncomfortable. Although he'd surely seen her changing into her jumpsuit every morning from her matted pajamas, suddenly the thought of them nude beside each other was rather—*intimate.*

Adelaide was not pretty, she knew this much. Her nails were dirty, uneven and unkempt, littered with an essence of dirt and grime. The hair that clung to her skull was dead and riddled with split-ends, faded in color and parted directly down the center, which managed to flatten it to her skull even further. The pale complexion upon her hollow cheeks was drastically uninviting, and her miraculously beauteous eyes were slowly sinking into her decrepit skull. And suddenly, the woman become very aware of the fact that her legs haven't been shaven in quite some time, let alone her *coochie* . . .

She would never be worthy of anyone, not even the allegedly nefarious Switch.

The diffident woman's appetite promptly vanished, her stomach contorting into tight knots as her wary gaze connected with the hunched-shouldered man several yards away. His left leg was tapping against the floor at an alarming rate, fingers toying with the mess of mashed potatoes upon his tray as the woman raised a curious brow.

His physique was oddly riveting—so enthralling and inviting and beyond it all—beneath the horrific scars that marred the left portion of his complexion—he was effortlessly gorgeous. So much so that Adelaide's heart fluttered beneath her ribcage at the mere sight of him. He was absolutely gorgeous, and he *knew* it.

Just as the woman had managed to drift off into dreamville, a haunting expression forcefully tore her from her trance, the apparent ache between her legs arising as he appeared by her side.

"Hey, dolly." Greenwald grinned, falling to his knees beside the rigid woman as he admired her horrified expression. "Sorry if it was hard for you to walk yesterday, I know I can be a little rough."

Adelaide immediately grimaced at his statement, vivid visuals of their encounter raiding her mind as she choked back a mouthful of bile. He'd never gone as far as he had the other night . . . No—this time he did something absolutely unforgivable. He wasn't even remotely gentle, as if the act itself was done out of spite for everything she'd done to counter his inappropriate advances. Switch had attempted to stop him, and he probably even watched, Adelaide wasn't quite sure. Besides, it was difficult to clearly see through the bothersome tears that had overcome her vision.

That night wasn't about sex for Greenwald.

It was about power.

"Piss off, Greenie." Switch harshly spat, hovering over Adelaide's trembling form as her eyes raked up his confident figure. An instant rush of relief washed over her at his close proximity, her eyes reconnecting with a timid Greenwald as he blatantly scoffed in response.

"If she didn't want me, she'd tell me herself. Don't even attempt to speak for her." The guard countered, eyeing Adelaide skeptically as she audibly swallowed, her fingers tugging at the torn skin of her bottom lip.

"You know damn well she doesn't speak." Switch hissed, glancing cautiously in Adelaide's direction as she sunk lower to the floor.

"Greenwald!" Vern exclaimed, marching over to the bickering duo as Adelaide breathed out a staggered sigh of relief. "Quit it, will you? Haven't you done enough? Look at Switch's eye!"

"Should see my ribs." Switch lazily slurred, his tone resembling that of a younger sibling who's finally gotten the attention of their mother.

Vern's eyes contorted into tight slits, his finger jabbing against Greenwald's chest as he spat out: "So help me God, I'll get your ass fired one day."

"Good luck." Greenwald giggled, swiping the man's hand away with his palm as he started in the opposite direction towards Cora and Nayeli's table.

"You guys okay?" Vern breathed, his chest dramatically heaving as he exchanged wary glances between both Switch and Adelaide.

"Fuckin' *peachy*." Switch snarled, abruptly bumping shoulders with the guard as he strolled back in the direction of his vacant seat. Vern tumbled backwards several steps, his brows quizzically raising as he viewed a shy Adelaide below him in a heap on the floor.

"I know what he did," Vern stated, fingers tugging at his utility belt as he anxiously licked his lips. "It's inexcusable. I promise I'll bring you justice."

Don't worry about it, she thought, offering him a small smile as he turned on his heel and abandoned the woman against the wall.

Twenty-three minutes later, Switch and Adelaide found themselves face to face in the bath room, violent shivers running up the length of Adelaide's spine as Nurse Briar prepared the tubs.

The porcelain basins were about a yard apart, both filled nearly to the brim with lukewarm water. Briar dipped her fingers into each of the basins, testing the temperature of the liquid before nodding curtly in their direction.

"The baths are ready," she acutely explained, tenderly rolling the sleeves of her scrubs as she motioned for both of them to disrobe.

Adelaide's lips parted in angst, her hazel orbs widened in objection as she clutched her crossed arms firmly to her chest, fingers prying at the bunched material as Switch let out a vociferous sigh.

"Addy," Briar cooed. "Don't be shy. I can have him close his eyes, if it makes you uncomfortable."

Adelaide shook her head from side to side, fingers dipping down to the hem of her jumpsuit top as she glanced warily in Switch's direction. A gasp nearly escaped her lips at the sudden sight of him, nude from the waist up, his top discarded in an unfolded heap upon the cement floor. A cheeky, tight-lipped grin tugged at his scars, several ringlets tumbling into his line of vision as he curled his fingers around the stretchy waist of his trousers.

Fuck, this was so fucking awkward. Fuck.

Adelaide chewed aggressively upon her lip, slowly peeling the fabric from her torso as her gaze immediately diverted, arms instinctively covering her exceedingly large chest as an innocent giggle filled the void.

"Quit it," Briar darkly scolded. "Close your eyes, Switch."

The man threw his arms up in surrender, eyelids fluttering closed as he blindly shrugged out of his slacks, the material bunching obnoxiously at his ankles as Nurse Briar awkwardly diverted her gaze from his naked form.

"Can I open?" He mused, giddily chewing on his lip as Nurse Briar let out an exasperated: *"No!"*

Once a timid Adelaide had eased herself into the tub, her vision shielded from a very naked Switch only mere feet away from her—Nurse Briar finally granted the man permission to open his eyes, a sullen expression plastered on his features as he, too, climbed into the warm abyss of the basin beside Adelaide's.

The woman avoided his stare, gaze solely fixated on the shifting water that currently engulfed her straggly features as Nurse Briar quickly washed her outgrown hair.

How do I ask her to shave my legs?

Once the nurse had migrated to the opposite tub, her fingers threading through Switch's knotted locks as he released a sarcastic groan—Adelaide finally managed to divert her attention to the nude man.

The skin surrounding his swollen eye had flushed a delicate yellow, accented by a mixture of intermixing purple hues as Nurse Briar delicately massaged the man's scalp, her tongue determinedly poking at the innermost corner of her lips as she did so.

And suddenly, Adelaide's nerves instantaneously calmed. For some peculiar reason, the situation at hand no longer seemed wildly inappropriate. Now, if she could just slither into that basin with him . . .

Lord have mercy.

"Little had Mrs. Dashwood or her daughters imagined when they first came into Devonshire, that so many engagements would arise to occupy their time as shortly presented themselves, or that they should have such frequent invitations and such constant visitors as to leave them little leisure for serious employment." Switch fluently read, pausing momentarily to dramatically regain his breath as Adelaide let out a satisfied snort.

"Yet such was the case. When Marianne was recovered, the schemes of amusement at home and abroad, which Sir John had been previously forming, were put into execution."

Switch's right hand had currently claimed the flimsy book, his fingers thoroughly spread to allow himself a good, firm grip as his opposite hand lay airborne, wrists still heavily confined by the thick, metal handcuffs as the pads of his free fingers eloquently rubbed together.

Adelaide intently stared, her gaze locked upon the flawless features of the man beside her as his lips contorted into varying shapes, differing words slipping off of his tainted mouth as she reveled in the sight.

"When he was present she had no eyes for anyone else." Switch breathed, efficiently spilling Marianne's innermost thoughts on her darling Willoughby as Adelaide promptly found herself heavily relating to the fictitious woman. Just like Marianne, she too had no eyes for anyone else—Only Switch. The abundance of warm, chocolate curly locks and striking brown eyes were all that she ever needed, and ever wanted.

Routinely, the sleeves of his striped jumpsuit were attentively rolled, hooked around the protuberant skin of his intensely dry elbows, displaying an array of miscellaneous tattoos imbedded upon his flesh.

Upon his right arm, lay a rather peculiar image, one that reminded Adelaide of the fruity lollipops her mother used to gift her and Westlynn on their birthday, along with an abundance of fizzy drinks and chocolate candies. The dark, permanent ink claimed the inner flesh of his forearm, accented with two oddly drawn figures—lollipops, by the looks of it. Or maybe a duo of dandelions, Adelaide wasn't quite sure.

"What?" Switch wheezed, his attention diverted from the printed word as Adelaide's eyes immediately widened. She hadn't realized how hard she was staring at the ink imprinted upon his arm.

The woman's lips instinctively parted, a verbal reply effortlessly failing her as the pages glided shut against his thumb, which he used as a temporary placeholder in order to fully divert his attention to the curious girl.

"You're truly something else . . ." the man whispered, his left wrist darting outward to meet her jaw as the right unintentionally followed, courtesy of the bothersome cuffs. The pads of his fingers daintily traced her protruding chin, her pulse drastically quickening as she forgot how to breathe entirely. He was dreadfully close, cocoa-hued orbs fixated on the thin skin of her agape lips as she searched his expression for any plausible explanation . . .

His touch was morbidly fascinating, igniting a fire deep within the desperate woman as her breaths slowed and her heart rapidly pounded. She was entirely certain that he could actually hear how loudly her heart was thumping beneath her chest, but in this very moment, she couldn't quite bring herself to care.

Suddenly, the surrounding crowd dissipated, fading to black as the room nearly concave on them entirely. She could blatantly hear his accelerated breaths, his gaze shifting between her wide eyes and pleading lips as he debated on what to do next.

What to do, what to do . . .

Oh, and she just wanted to *grab* him—to lace her fingers around the collar of his jumper and yank his face to hers—to smash their pleading lips together and breathe life into him—breathe love and happiness and triumph and *lust*. Oh—*God*, she wanted to taste him *oh* so bad, so much so that the urge was entirely overwhelming . . .

So, she did.

The woman caved, feeding into her demons as she sloppily laced her fingers around the bleak fabric of his collar, squeezing so agonizingly tight as she tugged his rigid form forward, her determined lips crashing onto his with absolute boldness as she finally—truly—*tasted* him.

The scar hovering the left edge of his lips was rugged and harsh against her skin, unlike anything she'd ever felt before. Like a jagged pockmark—skin so rough and full of patches and creases and crevices that her tongue so effortlessly explored. There were particular spots where it was evident that the blade had cut rather deep, and she tasted and felt those spots with absolute glee and curiosity. The jarred skin of his bottom lip–which strut a single lined scar–felt particularly great along her chapped skin, oh-so-different and oddly enticing all at the same time . . .

The paperback novel immediately tumbled from his weakened embrace, lips parting to allow the needy woman access to his welcoming mouth as a sharp breath hitched in his throat. Although her lips were undoubtedly chapped and overwhelmingly dry, he found pleasure in the simplistic feel. She tasted just as he'd expected: warm and cozy and comforting. As if her lips had been awaiting his for all of an eternity. His restricted hands met her sunken cheeks, fingers tugging aimlessly at the flushed skin as he desperately pulled, teeth obscenely clattering together as she forcefully parted his lips, pridefully dominating the weakened man as she tasted every corner–every inch and every crevice of his lovely mouth.

Knobby knees collided, breathless sighs spilling between the miniscule cracks present in their conjoined mouths as they molded into one blissful state–an absolute nirvana.

Switch's head fleetingly swam, his toes curling within the confinement of his thick boots as his nails impulsively dug into the flesh of her face, his touch literally itching to sink downward and cradle her throat–to apply *juuust* the right amount of pressure to her windpipe so that he could finally take away all of her pain–so that he could breathe in her life as it slowly whittled away from her gaping mouth.

Then, she tugged away. The vibrant colors ceased–the aching itch to drain her life promptly vanished as a set of wide, hazel eyes met his.

"Addy," the man croaked, his tone cracked and disheveled as he struggled to formulate a proper reply to–well–*that.*

A genuine, toothy grin claimed her swollen lips, her palm meeting the destroyed flesh of his left cheek as she gently caressed his face.

Just as his lips parted once more in preparation to speak, an unfamiliar sonance emerged. In fact, it took several seconds for the madman to realize that the sound had actually come from Adelaide's mouth.

"W-*What?*" He gasped, unable to retain the information as the words blurred together inside his jumbled brain.

Adelaide simply giggled, her hold slipping from his cheek as it met the cool cuffs encircling his wrists.

"I like the lollies on your arm." She confidently repeated, the pad of her thumb colliding with the peculiar ink imbedded upon his flesh as she showed him exactly what she was referring to.

Switch let out a rigid chuckle, perplexedly stunned at the situation as he met Adelaide's gaze once more.

She fucking spoke.

"Talk again." He requested, palm meeting her cheek as she openly blushed.

"Your mouth tastes good." She said, her voice thick and raspy as the words flowed effortlessly off her tongue. She sounded as if she'd smoked several packs of cigarettes, most likely due to the fact that she hadn't talked in such a drastic amount of time. Regardless of the fact, he was absolutely entranced by the sound of her voice, and it was entirely–*unexpected*.

"You're Australian." He dumbly observed, eliciting a giggle from the woman as she playfully rolled her eyes.

"And *you're* going to shut up, now." Adelaide countered, threading her fingers between his as she leaned forward once more and captured his stunned lips in a short-lived, simplistic peck.

Oh–the present was so very, very good.

XI

before

"D'you need anything before I go, Laide?" Victoria lightly wondered, lacing her fingers around the beaten leather strap of her tan-hued purse. Her crimson-tinted bottom lip jutted outward, a forced burst of air emerging as she lazily blew away a stray strand of hair from her eyes.

"Nope, you're all set, babe." Adelaide grinned, nodding curtly in the olive-skinned girl's direction as Victoria simply nodded, bidding the younger woman a simple goodbye as she eased out of the front door of the vinyl shop, the petite bell atop the door chiming as the woman abandoned the premises.

Adelaide threaded her fingers through an abundance of new deliveries, her hazel-hued orbs brightening at the sight of her favorite Black Sabbath record.

"Hello beautiful," she mused, turning the object over to view the artwork as a hearty grin tugged at her lips. The soft sonance of Led Zeppelin's greatest hits ricocheted off the walls, courtesy of the playlist from her MP3 player—which was currently connected to the store speakers.

She'd been employed for Redd's Records since her Junior year of high school, courtesy of a boy named Cody who offered her the job (his father owned the joint). Adelaide's wretched mother, Alice Lynch, had been on her case for months following her sixteenth birthday about getting a job, so the girl just couldn't seem to turn the offer down. Plus, she absolutely adored the art of music—there was just something so magical about a set of notes and rhythms and beats, all intermixed to create varying tunes. Adelaide was truly happy with a good book and whilst listening to a great tune.

The shop was rather petite, crammed to the max with an abundance of shelves that reminded the girl of an old-school library. Although to the naked eye, the store seemed to be a complete and utter mess—there was a method to Redd's madness, and the vinyls were organized in a peculiar type of way. The old man claimed that he never discriminated, but the least popular and total trash vinyl copies were always shoved to the back of the shelves.

An amplitude of multi-hued string lights—more commonly referred to as Christmas lights—littered the ceiling, bolted into the surface by a profusion of tacks as the varying colors created a lovely aesthetic within the store. These particular lights were the only source of illumination after the sun had set every night.

The woman cradled an armful of albums in her grasp, twisting on her heel to head in the direction of the varying oak shelves as she nearly ran smack-dab into a tall, lanky boy with deep, chestnut curls.

An abundance of records slipped from her grasp, a heightened gasp slipping off her parted lips as the brand-new merchandise littered the standard wood floors, coating her matted Chuck Taylor's as the boy fell to his knees before her.

"Shit," he dramatically exclaimed, lacing his slim digits around the vinyl's as he snatched them from the floor at an alarmingly quick pace. "My apologies, I didn't mean to scare you."

Adelaide slowly sunk to her knees, curious eyes glaring at the mysterious boy as he claimed the merchandise in his grasp. His eyes were an extraordinary shade of blue, complimented with vibrant green and gold specks as his perky pink lips tugged into a toothy smirk, displaying a clear set of dimples. The varying hues of the string lights above them created a multitude of colors along his complexion, mimicking a gorgeous rainbow as his eyes dramatically twinkled beneath the artificial lighting.

"Emmett DuPré." He boldly introduced, thrusting a hand outward as several records messily tumbled from his diverted grasp, a groan slipping off his lips as Adelaide merely giggled. The shy woman tugged a loose strand of stringy, ashy brown hair from her vision, tucking it neatly behind a pierced ear as her warm palm met his.

"Adelaide Lynch."

"Oh!" Emmett cheered, vibrant eyes brightening. "You're a—Brit?"

"Close," she giggled, again. "Aussie."

"Damn," Emmett sighed, handing the neatly stacked vinyl's back into her clutch. "I'm trash at identifying accents."

"S'all right," she cooed, climbing to her feet once more as she rearranged the stack of records in her clutch. "They sound similar anyways."

The pair stood in an awkward silence, bottom lips tugged between rows of teeth as Emmett obnoxiously cleared his throat, his clammy palms shoved deeply into the pockets of his denim jeans as he scanned Adelaide's features.

"Anyways, I actually needed some help finding a particular vinyl," he rambled, chest inordinately heaving as the woman let out a petite giggle.

"Of course. What's the album name?" She politely asked, setting down the stack of albums onto a nearby rickety shelf as Emmett ran a broad hand through his disheveled hair.

"I can't remember the name of the album, but it's Nirvana—and, uh—"

"You're looking for the one with the naked baby on the cover, I'm assuming?" Adelaide cheerily interjected, lips tugged into an amused grin as Emmett's cheeks flushed bright scarlet.

"Yes, actually." He awkwardly breathed, twirling a particular strand of chestnut-hued hair around his index finger. "Do you have it in stock?"

"I have several in stock, actually." Adelaide gleamed, directing the strange boy down a nearby aisle as she scanned the jam-packed shelves. Her slender digits twiddled in mid-air, curious tones slipping off her parted lips as her eyes swiftly searched the shelves.

"A-ha!" The woman exclaimed, standing on her tippy-toes to retrieve the album, which was stacked on the fifth shelf of the bookcase. The thick, cotton fabric of her Black Sabbath tee tugged upwards, displaying a smooth, silky surface of pale skin. Emmett awkwardly diverted his attention.

Adelaide claimed the vinyl between two determined fingers, tearing it from the shelf with ease as she settled back onto the balls of her feet.

"Here you go," she mused, thrusting the object into Emmett's outstretched hands as he offered her a gentle grin.

"Thanks," the boy monotonically stated, turning the theatrical album over in his hands as he silently admired it. "I grew up on Nirvana. Mom was devastated when Kurt Cobain died."

Adelaide simply smiled, scurrying around the frozen boy as she shuffled in the direction of the register.

"If you're done shopping, I can check you out back here!" She lively chirped, threading her fingers through her precisely curled locks as she rounded the oblong counter. Several boxes littered the surface, filled nearly to the brim with newly purchased merchandise awaiting placement on the already cramped shelves.

"Is that some type of cheesy pick-up line?" Emmett teased, rapidly approaching the counter as he placed the precisely wrapped vinyl onto the surface. Adelaide's cheeks flushed at his bold statement, eyeballs rolling dramatically in their sockets as she quickly scanned the single item.

"Only if you'd like it to be," she confidently countered. "That'll be nineteen ninety-four."

Emmett released a heightened grunt, shoving the entirety of his flattened palm into the depths of his front pocket as he attempted to fish out his mangled leather wallet. Adelaide raised a curious brow at the sight of his struggle, choking back a giggle as he eventually tore the object from his trousers.

"Jesus," he slurred, slipping his pointer finger beneath the flap as he thrust open the meaty wallet. "Thought I'd never get that out." He retrieved a twenty-dollar bill, handing it into Adelaide's open palm as he seductively grinned. "Keep the change."

"Oh, *wow*," Adelaide sarcastically remarked, tugging open the cash drawer as she mindlessly counted the change. "Five whole cents! An entire nickel!"

Emmett heartily chuckled as she shoved the change into her back pocket, her brows amusingly rising as she observed his giddy stance.

"D'you guys have a record player?" He suddenly requested, precisely tearing the thin plastic wrapping from the brand-new album.

"Well, I'd hope so," Adelaide remarked. "Considering we're a vinyl shop'n all."

"You bleed sarcasm, dollface." Emmett gingerly pressed, handing over the vinyl. "Let's have a listen."

"The turntable is in the back office. Let me lock up really quick and I'll take you back there." Adelaide politely explained, falling to her knees behind the register to claim a shiny, silver key looped onto a circular ring.

"Oh, are you closing?" Emmett innocently wondered, feeling a bit guilty for overstaying his welcome as Adelaide scurried in the direction of the front door several yards behind.

"Yeah, it's nearly nine!" She called over her shoulder, voice slightly muffled by the low murmur of the stereo overhead as Emmett awkwardly twiddled his thumbs, leaning his frame against the register counter as his eyes scanned the store.

The girl before him—Adelaide Lynch, as she'd introduced herself—was unlike anyone he had ever met before. He had known her a total of five minutes, give or take, and he was already completely entranced by her. She looked youthful, but not any younger than sixteen, at the least. Her eyes were bright and wild, round and wide as the multi-colored lights strung along the ceiling frolicked about upon her hazel tint. Her lips were substantially sized, but borderline chapped and exceedingly dry, as if she'd ran out of Chapstick the night prior and spent nearly the entire day licking them moist. She struts a simplistic tee, adorned with a peculiar graphic and the name of the band Black Sabbath. He wondered if she was a fan, or if she simply wore the shirt. Her shoes were matted and outdated, an old style of torn gray Converse with a significant hole dug into the side of the fabric. Torn, holey jeans clung nicely to her hips, pale, knobby knees peeking out from the substantial tears as she approached the man with glee.

"C'mon, let's go have a listen." She gleamed.

Adelaide's back unceremoniously collided with the surface of an old, wilting wooden desk, an abundance of papers scattering beneath her abrupt weight as a pair of urgent lips latched onto hers.

Desperate fingers tangled into unkempt curly locks, overgrown nails digging into the skin of his skull as a satisfied groan slipped off Emmett's lips, seeping into Adelaide's gaping mouth as she swallowed it with glee.

Palms clamped down onto her tiny hips, holding her writhing frame in place against the surface as Emmett's lips peppered soft, feather-like kisses along her exposed jaw, eventually dipping down onto the thin flesh of her neck as she openly gasped.

The woman lowly sighed, massaging Emmett's scalp as he painted invisible pictures along her exposed flesh, marking his territory with elation as Kurt Cobain's voice elegantly filled the void.

Needy fingers tugged at the hem of Adelaide's t-shirt, her clammy palms meeting Emmett's trembling grasp as she assisted the man in removing her top. Their lips parted momentarily, the skin swollen and pulsating, courtesy of their aggressive needs, wants, and desires.

"How did we come to this?" Adelaide breathlessly queried, discarding her tee onto the cluttered carpet floor as Emmett eyes wondrously twinkled.

"Need a refresher?" He teased, nipping along the fragile skin of her jugular as Adelaide's back arched in immediate pleasure.

"Maybe later," she murmured, craning her neck to meet his lips once more in a rushed peck.

Articles of clothing were hurriedly removed, the melodic masterpiece of Nirvana's album resonating throughout Adelaide's chest as the bare skin of a complete stranger met hers, lips sloppily colliding—teeth clattering and fingers prying—wanting—needing—*craving* some type of release . . .

"Emmett," Adelaide whined, latching her fingers into a particularly large chunk of his hair as she effortlessly tugged his face away from her neck.

"Yes?" He croaked, pupils dilated as the pads of his fingers delicately swiped along her perky breast. She impulsively squirmed beneath his touch, bottom lip tucked tightly between teeth as she choked back an audible groan.

Don't tell him! Don't ruin this moment!

I hardly know him! Adelaide countered, desperately wishing to spill the truth to Emmett DuPré, whose exasperated expression slackened, lips dipping downward to meet her flesh as his mouth pranced along her prominent collarbones.

Addy, a single voice spat. *Do not tell him that you are a virgin. Enjoy this while it lasts.*

Okay, Adelaide eventually caved, Emmett's swollen mouth wrapping around her breast as she let out a heightened squeal, hips bucking upward to meet his bare body as a groan vibrated against her skin.

This was it. Eighteen-year-old Adelaide Lynch was going to lose her virginity to a random paying customer—whose age she did not know—whilst listening to the blissful lyrics of a Nirvana vinyl at an obscenely high volume. The office was exceedingly cramped, complimented with a single desk in the center of the room, the very same desk that the woman currently laid upon. A multitude of boxes scattered the blemished carpet, articles of clothing strewn along the floor as Emmett abruptly tore his clammy frame from hers.

"What is it?" She wondered, eyes wild with anticipation as Emmett fell to his knees, digging through the pocket of his discarded trousers as Adelaide brought herself up on her elbows.

"Protection." He announced, digging a wrapped condom out from his wallet as his slender frame met hers once more.

The rest—as they say, was history.

"I told you, I get off at three." Adelaide pressed, stifling a giggle as she twirled the crinkled phone cord around several fingers, pink tongue poking and prodding at the corners of her lips as they tugged into a hearty grin.

"But I *miss* you." Emmett's voice emerged through the receiver, his tone low and husky as Adelaide's stomach fluttered.

"I miss you too, Emmett. I promise I'll be right over as soon as I'm off, baby." The woman boldly promised, digging the toe of her tennis shoe into the cracked wooden floor.

"Okay, okay . . ." he sarcastically sighed.

The bell atop the front door obnoxiously rang, thrusting Adelaide out of her temporary trance as she muttered a rushed, "I gotta go" before hanging up.

She'd been seeing twenty-year-old Emmett DuPré exclusively for the past six months. Things were absolutely blissful—he was everything she could've ever wanted and more, which was peculiar considering they'd shagged the very first night they'd met atop the desk that belonged to her boss.

Several hours later, the woman found herself curled into a miniscule ball atop Emmett's navy duvet, insistent giggles slipping off of her lips as he told her several amusing stories.

"Did you like growing up as an only child?" The woman wondered, the tips of her fingers dancing along the flesh of Emmett's bicep. He intently observed her innocent gestures, lips curled into an amused smirk as his glorious dimples appeared.

"It got lonely," he revealed, rubbing his thumb along her index finger as he slowly threaded his fingers between hers. "But my parents spoiled me rotten from it. Guess it was nice in the end, it got me this nice apartment so I can't complain."

"You're so lucky," Adelaide muttered, burying her hooked nose into the crease of his neck as he held her close. "I love Westlynn, don't get me wrong, but I've always gotten the shit end of the stick. Mum never liked me. Dad left when I was young. Typical sob story."

"Adelaide," Emmett pressed, curling his finger beneath her chin as he forced her to look at him. Bright, hazel eyes met a stunning sea of blue as her stomach heavily churned. "You're so much more than that."

"It just sucks sometimes," Adelaide confessed, thick tears pricking her vision as she hastily blinked them away. "Being the unwanted child'n all. Being the ugly twin."

"You're beautiful," Emmett immediately interjected, silencing the woman's rambles as he pressed a soft kiss to her mouth. "And you're definitely wanted."

"By you," she dismissed, a single tear slipping from the confinement of her lid as it glided down the slope of her flushed cheek. Emmett's thumb collided with her skin, wiping the tear away as he flatly frowned.

"Ad," he scolded. "I hate it when you talk like this. You think so lowly of yourself."

"Always have." She confessed, collapsing into a heap of sobs as Emmett's sturdy arms encircled her petite form, pulling her agonizingly close as she cried.

"Adelaide Rhea," the man cooed, pressing a kiss atop her hair. "I love you. That's all that should matter."

"I love you too, Emmett." She breathed through steady sobs, her tone cracking as she drenched the fabric of his shirt with salty tears.

Stop being such a baby, a stern voice scolded. *He just told you he loves you. He doesn't say that often, so quit your whining and reward him for the kind gesture.*

He isn't like that, Adelaide spat. *He doesn't expect anything in return for saying it. He truly means it.*

He'll mean it more if you get on your knees.

Adelaide's fingers curled into bold fists, claiming chunks of Emmett's tee in her hold as she attempted to force the voices out of her mind. They've been there for as long as she could coherently remember, but within the past several years, they've grown particularly noisy . . .

For the most part, the voices were negative and wildly inappropriate, serving as an invisible devil upon each shoulder. From what she could gather, there were three distinct voices—all female, and all incredibly snippy. Sometimes, Adelaide felt as if she wasn't even in control of her very own mind.

"Hey," Emmett cooed, caressing Adelaide's sunken cheeks with his fingers. "I have an idea. You said you like Jane Austen's work, right?"

"I've only read *Emma*." Adelaide lowly spoke, her voice muffled by the cotton of his shirt as he shrugged from her tight hold.

"Perfect!" The giddy man cheered, enthusiastically clapping his palms together as he rummaged through a dresser drawer full of miscellaneous junk. Within several moments of rustling, he eventually located a specific novel, one which was severely beaten and aged what appeared to be a million years.

"C'mon, lovebug." He whispered, easing against the headrest as he urged the woman to join him.

Adelaide shuffled up the length of the bed, tugging the measly sheet along with her as the left corner of the fitted fabric messily unhooked from the mattress. She eventually joined the man, burying her chin into the crook of his neck as a withered copy of *Sense and Sensibility* sat upon his lap.

"I'll read it to you." He whispered, claiming the book in his grasp as he effortlessly pried it open. "My mom used to read this to me as a child. I loved it, I think you will too."

Adelaide laced her arm around his, peppering kisses along the prominent skin of his clothed shoulder as he began to read the printed word aloud.

I love you, Emmett James DuPré.

"You hang up first." Adelaide murmured, balancing the corded phone between her shoulder and ear as she flipped open the flimsy cover of Emmett's novel. Her socked feet claimed the old, ripped mahogany swivel chair, the low sonance of a classic Foreigner album filling the otherwise stale void.

"No," Emmett chuckled through the line. "*You* hang up first."

"God, you're such a child." Adelaide teased, flipping open the book to reveal a triangular folded page halfway through. The pads of her fingers elegantly smoothed down the yellowing page, toes tapping against the surface of the chair as Emmett suddenly shifted the subject.

"By the way, have you seen my copy of *Sense and Sensibility*? I can't find it anywhere, I'm starting to panic." He revealed, his tone wary and full of worry as Adelaide's eyes widened at the sight of the book sat currently on her lap.

"About that . . ." she murmured, earning a considerable sigh from the other end as she profusely giggled.

"*Addy–*"

"I'm sorry, Emmett! I couldn't wait, I needed to read more!" She exclaimed, eyes fixated on the center of the page as he let out an exasperated huff.

"You're lucky I love you, gorgeous." He mused. "Also, don't forget about dinner with my parents tonight."

Adelaide frowned, the pages gliding closed against her thumb as she tore the desk phone from her shoulder.

"That's tonight? Shit–"

"*Adelaide–*"

"I didn't forget! I promise I'll be there. Just nervous, s'all. Jittery'n such." The woman shyly revealed, tearing her feet from the comfort of the chair as she stuffed them back into the depths of her high-top Chuck Taylor's.

"Don't be nervous, sweetie. They'll love you. You've been mine for half a year, they're actually starting to get a bit impatient." Emmett dryly joked, the petite bell ringing as the book tumbled from Adelaide's lap, slipping onto the floor in an exasperated heap as her widened gaze met an elderly man in the doorway.

"Shit, Emmett. I have a customer. I've gotta go." She urged. "I love you."

"I love you more." He said, her lips curling into a satisfied grin as she hung up the phone, determined fingers prying the novel from the ground as she smoothed out the folded pages.

"Welcome to Redd's Records, how may I help you?"

"We should do it." Emmett announced, his voice muffled by the obstruction between his lips as a steady stream of smoke emerged.

"Do what?" Adelaide wondered, picking at the excess skin around her nails as her ass began to fall numb from the oddly shaped concrete beneath her. The duo was currently seated on a curb outside of a McDonald's in the outskirts of Chicago. The woman heavily shivered from the extreme cold, her breath visible as it slipped through frozen lips.

Emmett's gloved fingers encircled the lit cigarette, delicately tugging it from his lips as he ran a hand through his outgrown curls. Several strands dangled in his vibrantly hued eyes, which diverted to meet Adelaide's. At this, he genuinely smiled.

"Get married." He breathed.

A snort emerged from her scarlet-tinted nose, eyes slightly watering from the cold as she merely giggled in reply.

"I'm serious," he pressed, shoving the cigarette back between his lips as Adelaide inched closer to the man, the dirt and grime audibly shifting beneath the pockets of her jeans as she slid across the cement. "We should do it."

Adelaide's leather gloved fingers circled the lit object stuffed between his nearly blue lips, yanking it from the safety of his mouth as she tossed it onto the ground, the sole of her boot meeting the stick as she extinguished the flame.

"Cigs are bad for you." She lightly murmured. "They can kill you."

"Says that girl who smokes too," he chuckled. "I live in the moment, darling. You should know that by now. Why look to the future, when the present is so very important? People always talk about planning out your future, but I want to live in the now."

Adelaide audibly gulped, fingers lacing with his as she softly smiled.

"I don't want to postpone all the good things," he explained, delicately licking his chapped lips as Adelaide's chest painfully heaved. "You're a very, very good thing, Adelaide."

"Emmett—"

"I love you." He boldly confessed, the same statement he's uttered nearly every day for over a year. "I knew you were the one the day I met you in Redd's Records sixteen months ago, baby. Please, Addy. Please marry me."

"Emmett—"

"Ad." He sternly argued, twisting on his heel as he climbed from his position on the curb. Adelaide's eyes significantly widened as he fell to one knee before her seated frame, the pad of his thumb delicately tracing her palm as he blinked away tears.

"I love you more than words will ever describe, sweetie. You're truly the best thing that's ever happened to me. I know we're young, but—hell—I want to live every single day with you. I want to make babies with you, to grow old with you." Emmett rambled, his tone firm and confident as Adelaide audibly gasped, attempting to conceal her arising sobs as the man she truly loved confessed his innermost feelings for her. Everything about this moment was absolutely extraordinary, regardless of the scenery. In this moment, she couldn't give a damn if they were in the parking lot of a crusty McDonald's in twenty-two-degree weather. She couldn't care less that she couldn't feel her face, hands or toes—all she cared about was him.

"Adelaide Rhea Lynch," Emmett announced, his voice wavering as his gloved palm rummaged through the deep pocket of his coat. Adelaide gawked at the sudden sight, a petite black box engulfed in his palm as he pried it open, revealing an elegant diamond ring surrounded by crimson silk.

"Oh my God, Emmett!" She squealed, palms clamping over her mouth as he held the ring in his grasp. A toothy grin tugged heartily at his lips, his pulse painfully quickening beneath his ribcage as hazel-hued eyes admired the gorgeous ring.

"Will you marry me?" He asked, choking on the final word as Adelaide propelled upwards from the curb, jumping up and down with pure glee as she loudly sobbed.

"Yes!" She screeched, bending her knees to wrap her arms around his neck as she cried into his hefty jacket. "Yes! Yes! Yes!"

Emmett pressed enthusiastic kisses to the woman's face, his lips painting pictures along her numb skin as she held him close.

They were unstoppable. The world was theirs.

"Addy!" Westlynn shouted, shaking her twin sister awake as Adelaide awoke with a disgruntled grimace.

"Jesus Christ, Westie! What is it?" The woman groggily croaked, fingers curling into fists as she vigorously rubbed the sleep from her eyes.

"Someone keeps calling for you, bud." Westlynn irritably pressed. "Phone's been ringing off the hook. Shocked you haven't heard the bloody thing."

"Heavy sleeper, y'know that." Adelaide murmured, tearing the thick duvet from her frail frame as she crawled from the twin-sized bed.

Adelaide blindly scurried across the room, tumbling through the open doorway as her vision struggled to adjust to the dim lighting of the hallway.

The corded phone lay upon a petite table, which hugged the hallway wall and was littered with an assortment of trinkets.

The woman pressed the olive-hued phone against her ear, obnoxiously clearing her throat as she answered with a groggy: "Hello?"

"Adelaide?" A familiar voice bombarded, an immense sense of worry present in her tone as Adelaide's heart instantly plummeted.

"Mrs. DuPré?" Adelaide croaked, her fingers lacing tightly around the phone. "What time is it?"

"I-I don't know, four in the morning, I think?" Emmett's mother uneasily muttered. "That's not the point. Are you busy? Can you get a ride to the hospital?"

"The h-hospital? For what?" Adelaide gasped, the bile immediately rising to her throat as she shifted her weight from either foot.

"Emmett's been in a wreck," Mrs. DuPré revealed. "He was coming home from work at midnight. I'm sorry I'm telling you so late, I've been a bit preoccupied—"

"S-Shit!" Adelaide exclaimed, palm clamping over her mouth in a weak attempt to conceal her obnoxious sobs. "Is he okay?"

"Just—get here. As quickly as you can."

Adelaide profusely vomited in the passenger seat of Westlynn's car, a plastic Walmart bag laced in her fingers as she repeatedly emptied the contents of her stomach into the material. Her identical twin sister grimaced at the sound, her window rolled all the way down as she violently shivered from the cold gusts of wind that whipped through the gap.

"Jeez, Addy. Breathe." Westlynn clipped, blinking away sleep as she directed the vehicle in the direction of the Emergency Room parking lot of the nearest hospital. "We're here."

Adelaide practically fell from the vehicle, discarding the bag onto the side of the car park as she darted in the direction of the glass double doors. Her feet were beyond freezing, toes completely numb as she nearly tripped over her unlaced sneakers several times on the way towards the doors.

"Addy! Wait up!" Westlynn irately called from several yards behind, the set of metal keys jingling in her frozen grasp as she struggled to keep up with Adelaide's pace.

Adelaide disregarded Westlynn's pleas, the double doors sliding open as a forced gust of wind sent her hair astray, thick tears cloaking her sunken cheeks as the obscenely bright lights of the hospital momentarily blinded her.

Carla DuPré sat slouched in a nearby baby blue plastic chair, her broken nails held between her teeth as she aimlessly chewed. The moment her emerald gaze settled upon a frantic Adelaide, she immediately shot up from her position, flip flops snapping against the tile floor as she rapidly approached the broken girl.

"I-Is he okay?" Adelaide sobbed, collapsing into Carla's arms as her chest heavily ached.

"Emmett was driving home from a late shift when a tractor trailer struck him head-on. He's lucky to be alive." His mother revealed. Adelaide let out a horrific shriek at Carla's revelation, possible scenarios of the event flooding her mind as she imagined her Emmett—*her baby–*

"He's in a coma." His mother revealed. "They don't know when he'll wake up. You're welcome to go see him, if you'd like. Before you go, though, I have something to give you. They found it in the passenger seat of his car. It was remarkably unscathed."

Adelaide raised a curious brow, her heart rapidly accelerating as Carla retrieved an aged paperback novel from the depths of her purse. The aging woman placed it into Adelaide's uneasy touch, sliding the book into her hands as a vociferous sob slipped off Adelaide's lips.

A copy of *Sense and Sensibility* lay in her trembling grasp, heightened cries escaping her parted lips as she turned the book over in her clutch. It was gently used, the pages tinted a mute yellow hue as her index finger curled beneath the flimsy front cover, tearing open the book as Emmett's familiar penmanship filled her vision.

My dearest Adelaide,
Now you can carry Elinor and Marianne around with you always.
Whenever you look at these pages, I hope you'll always think of me and the
countless times we spent reading this together. Also, I hope you'll stop
stealing my copy, since you now have your own. My heart is forever yours.
-E. xo

Adelaide mutely nodded, inaudibly thanking the woman for the book as her top teeth dug into the skin of her lip, the metallic flavor of blood instantly filling her senses as her heart rapidly thumped as she headed in the direction of Emmett's current room. She efficiently followed Carla's verbal instructions as she quickly navigated the premises, the book held tightly to her chest as she continually choked back hefty cries.

She'd always heavily despised hospitals. Whether it be the overwhelming sanitary scent or the overall essence of death—she wasn't quite sure the reason.

"Emmett!" The woman exasperatedly cried, approaching the bed as she fell to her knees before her fiancé's unmoving form. The insistent beeping of a heart monitor filled her senses, her fingers threading through Emmett's messy ringlets as she choked back several additional sobs. The flimsy book slipping from her diverted grasp, colliding with the man's chest as she took in his disheveled appearance.

The frail, fragile skin of his face was heavily cut and bruised, displaying an array of varying colors, primarily a harsh purple hue, especially around his sealed eyelids. His mouth and nostrils were obstructed by a mask, providing oxygen to his deprived lungs as his chest routinely rose and fell with every stagnant breath.

"Baby," Adelaide cried, caressing his mangled face with the pads of her thumbs as she fell apart completely. "I'm here. It's okay now. It'll all be okay."

Adelaide hadn't slept for forty-three hours.

Carla attempted on many accounts to drag her from the room, trying to convince her to get a bit of fresh air or even to eat something substantial. However, Adelaide couldn't seem to tear herself away. Her entire world was lying in a lifeless heap upon a sterile mattress, the heart monitor constantly reminding her that he was alive, but only just.

Sometimes, she'd find herself curled up in a petite ball upon the foot of the bed, her head resting between Emmett's unmoving legs as she spoke mindless chatter to the mute boy, audibly revisiting their fondest memories as she openly chuckled at the lovely thoughts.

By day three, Westlynn was finally able to convince Adelaide to go home and rest. The task proved to be quite difficult, and Adelaide verbally begged to have one more minute alone with him before she left for the day.

"Emmett James," the woman whispered, running her fingers along his features as she admired his slack frame.

"I can't wait to marry you. You need to pull through, baby. We have our whole lives ahead of us. This is just a small bump in the road, but we're going to make it through this." She ranted, pressing a soft kiss to his bruised temple. "I love you."

With that, the woman left, clutching the customized novel to her chest, Emmett's inscription etched upon the inner cover.

Six weeks later, Adelaide entered the front doors of the hospital, her stringy, ashy brown hair tugged into a pristine ponytail as several wisps of fallen strands obscured her vision.

Her very own copy of *Sense and Sensibility* sat firmly in her grasp, fingers mindlessly toying with the cover as the soles of her sneakers scuffed against the tile floor. Today, she would reach both hers and Emmett's favorite part in the novel, and she could hardly wait. Although he was still thoroughly unconscious, she knew that he could hear her. She knew that he appreciated the gesture of her reading their favorite novel aloud as they lay in a tangled heap upon the hospital bed.

"Hello," she happily chirped, approaching the front desk as she repositioned the strap of her purse along her bony shoulder. "I'm here to see Emmett DuPré. My name is Adelaide Lynch, and here is my ID." She routinely stated, handing the identification card across the counter and into the unfamiliar receptionist's grasp as she typed aimlessly away at her desktop.

"DuPré, you said?" The woman inquired, chestnut-tinted eyes glaring up at Adelaide through the thin rims of her glasses.

"Yes, ma'am." Adelaide stated, growing wary at the peculiar query as she shifted her weight against the counter.

"Ma'am," the receptionist uneasily began. "Can I speak with you privately?"

"What for?" Adelaide pressed, brows knitting together in vexation as she placed the novel onto the counter, her pulse quickening as the bile began to rise into her throat.

"Follow me." The woman flatly stated, rising from her seat as she directed Adelaide towards a nearby vacant conference room.

The timid woman emerged ten minutes later, the book clutched firmly to her chest as thick, red rings encircled her hazel orbs. The moment she'd stepped out of the room, her knees promptly lost all feeling, sending her rigid form to the floor as a horrific cry instantly emerged.

Several nearby nurses immediately came to her aide, attempting to calm the hysterical woman as she crumbled completely upon the tile floor, pleading shouts emerging as staggered sobs followed. She didn't want to believe the news—she couldn't believe the news. Within the past ten minutes, her entire world had come crashing down.

A significant chunk of Adelaide Lynch died along with Emmett DuPré that day.

XII

"Lady from the moment I
saw you standing all alone
You gave all the love that I needed
She's so shy like a child who has grown /
Lady turn me on when I'm lonely"
-Styx, "Lady"

The first of the month was quite a vexatious day.

Per regulation, nurses were required to conduct physical examinations of their patients on this very day every single month. Although, Dr. Evers was not exactly strict when it came to the health and well-being of the inmates, therefore, many only received their physicals once or twice a year.

Nurse Briar, however, strictly followed this standard, unlike her lazy coworkers. On the first of October, she awoke in a cold-sweat, the vivid visuals of her recent dream bombarding her mind as Switch's taunting complexion littered her thoughts.

A little ball of inky fluff collided with her heaving chest, persistent meows emerging from the kitten's parted lips as Briar released an exasperated sigh, running her palm along the incredibly smooth coat of Styx's fur as she urged the animal off of her.

"I'm up, I'm up." She grunted, swinging her legs off the side of the mattress as she ran a trembling set of fingers through her matted blond locks. Switch's complexion raided her strained thoughts, mouth running impossibly dry as realization promptly set in: She'd be giving him his first physical today.

Shit.

Styx irately chirped at her feet, audibly begging for breakfast as Briar released an irate: "It's coming, Styx! Relax!"

Once the chirpy black kitten was happy and fed, Briar climbed into the warm abyss of the shower, her greasy strands smoothing down the slopes of her cheeks as she hastily shoved away the bothersome visuals of her dream.

They were undeniably gruesome and utterly horrific—a plethora of rage coursing through Switch's veins as he'd managed to overpower the frail woman during his physical. Within mere moments, he'd had her pinned against the frigid tile floor, blinding tears cloaking her vision as the keen blade of a mysterious object pierced her lower back . . .

A petite whine slipped off Briar's lips at the mere thought, balmy water coating her sullen features as she effectively cleansed her sore muscles. To say that she was anxious about today's scheduled events was entirely an understatement . . .

Nurse Briar strut through the front doors of Stillwater Sanitarium a solid four-and-a-half minutes late, a half-consumed cup of coffee held in her clutch as she shuffled along the multi-hued tiled floor. She bid the janitor a lively greeting, eyeliner slightly smudged as she took an additional hefty sip from her heavily creamed coffee.

"Briar! It's four-past-seven," Nurse Penelope chirped, dull eyes fixated on her inexpensive watch as she raised a scolding brow in Briar's direction. "What held you up?"

"Traffic." Nurse Briar tightly dismissed, shoving past Nurse Penelope with an irate sigh as she made a beeline towards the hospital wing. Lucky for her, a majority of her fellow nurses were frolicking about in the halls, oozing gossip and releasing fits of sarcastic giggles like the pestilential women they were. Sometimes Briar wondered why she hadn't any friends within the asylum, but then she recalled how absolutely foul the employees were, and for once, the woman was quite thankful to only be friends with her mute patient.

The woman slipped into the confined space of the nurse's lounge, the air musky and thick with a strong scent of aged cigarettes as she openly scoffed at the revolting flavor, one that was so potent that she could actually taste it on her tongue. Her manicured fingers daintily curled around the cool metal of her vibrant green lock, tearing it from the holster as she untidily shoved her personal items into the depths of her assigned locker. The zipper of her withered purse obnoxiously scraped along the locker, emitting a drastically irritating sonance as Briar's skull promptly pulsated, courtesy of her lack of sleep.

"Shit," the woman lowly murmured, her fingers assertively digging through the scattered items at the base of her purse as she eventually located a particular pill bottle, a satisfied grunt slipping off her hardly parted lips as she poured two circular pills into the palm of her hand.

"Morning, Briar!" A cheerful voice emerged, startling the timid woman as she nearly swallowed the painkillers down the wrong pipe. A slight stream of water slipped from the corners of the blond woman's lips, persistent hacks resonating deep within her chest as a chirpy Nurse Jackie raised a questionable brow.

"Swallow your water wrong?" She thickly inquired, an amused tone present in her high-pitched voice as Briar hastily wiped away the excess water with the back of her palm, chest inordinately heaving as she struggled to regulate her breathing.

"Y-Yeah," Briar stammered, screwing the cap back onto her water bottle as she precisely locked her locker, azure gaze meeting an amused set of perky, brown orbs as Jackie merely smiled.

"You still conducting those physicals every month?" The woman wondered, threading her excessively chewed fingernails through her matted brunette locks as Briar inaudibly nodded.

"Always do. It's regulation." Briar murmured, shifting her weight from either foot as Jackie released an amused giggle.

"Dr. Evers doesn't even care. He said we don't have to follow regulations, you know that." She said, collapsing onto a nearby metal folding chair, which audibly shifted beneath her slender form, the legs loudly scraping against the tile as Briar impulsively flinched. Jackie raised a perplexed brow.

"You're jumpy today." She observed, picking at the active acne upon her skin as Briar let out an irate huff.

"I have to conduct Switch's physical." Briar blandly explained, fingers laced tightly around her water bottle as the measly plastic cracked beneath her fingers.

Nurse Jackie's eyes instantaneously widened, an audible gulp filling Briar's ears as a sympathetic grin immediately overcame her blemished features.

"Oh, wow," Jackie murmured. "I forgot Harrington assigned you Switch. Good luck, Bri. You'll do fine. Just cuff him if you need to."

"Him strangling me is the least of my worries, Jackie." Briar whispered, haunting visuals of Switch stripping down nude before her instantly raiding her mind. Her pulse quickened, a lump forming in her throat as her palms began to profusely sweat.

With that, Briar promptly abandoned the quarters, her breaths emerging as short staggers as she headed in the direction of the cell block on Level 4. She decided to take the stairs to the story directly above the hospital wing, her heart thumping erratically in her throat as she hastily climbed the significantly spaced steps, her toes nearly colliding with the harsh concrete as she almost tumbled face-first into the steps.

"Fucking hell, Briar." The woman lowly scolded, clutching her bottled water close to her chest as she slowly ascended. "Relax."

Much too soon, the anxious woman arrived at the dingy cell block, her widened gaze colliding with Vern's cheery expression as he offered her a lax greeting.

"Morning, Nurse Briar." He politely spoke, nodding curtly in her direction as he headed towards Cora's sealed cell. "Physical examination day, I assume?"

"Correct." Briar muttered. Suddenly, an idea dawned upon her. "Hey, Vern?"

"Yeah?" He breathlessly countered, pausing right before Cora's door as he raised a curious brow.

"Can you help transport Switch to the hospital wing for me?" Nurse Briar uneasily squeaked, unceremoniously chewing on the frail skin of her lower lip as Vern's lips curled into a considerable grin.

"Of course, Briar. I forgot you were assigned as his personal caretaker. He's quite a handful, isn't he?" Vern rambled, threading his fingers through his unruly locks as he approached Switch's sealed cell, the mahogany steel door taunting Briar's rigid frame as the guard quickly unlocked it with a simple swipe of his ID.

The hefty steel door glided open with a simplistic *click*, revealing Switch's lonely, confined space as Briar audibly gulped.

She nearly jumped out of her skin at the sight of him—dressed cleanly in a fresh jumpsuit, sleeves routinely rolled behind the hooks of his elbows as he stood dreadfully close, boot-clad feet spaced evenly apart as he raised a considerable brow.

He was waiting for them.

"Back up, Switch." Vern scolded, lacing his fingers around the metal cuffs as he tore them from his belt. Involuntary shivers enveloped Briar's spine, her heart agonizingly racing as Switch's menacing glare collided keenly with hers.

The theatrical man tossed his hands up in mock surrender, bowing his head as a profusion of brunette curls slipped into his line of vision, feet shuffling backwards several steps as the dirt and grime audibly shifted beneath the soles of his laced boots.

"Morning, Missus Briar." The man huskily mused, willingly latching his wrists behind his back as Vern applied the sturdy restraints, careful not to apply the cuffs too tight (like Greenwald always did) as he urged Switch forward.

"Morning, sir." Nurse Briar uneasily spat, immediately regretting her choice of nickname as Switch's cocoa-hued orbs brightened, lips curling into a devious grin as he reveled in the name.

"*Wha-ha-ha!* We're back to *this*, hmm? Sir Switch, I like the sound of that!" He heavily mused, earning a dissatisfied shove from the irate guard as he forced him from the confinement of the concrete walls, the duo strutting from the cell as Briar anxiously swallowed.

The trio traveled in an uneasy silence to the hospital wing, a rigid Vern glancing in Briar's direction several times as she blatantly ignored his glare, her mind occupied by the gruesome thoughts of her wild imagination as they rapidly approached the nearly abandoned wing.

"We need to go into one of the examination rooms," Briar announced, directing Vern towards one of the nearby isolated rooms that hovered the back of the surprisingly large hospital wing as Switch remained deathly silent. Briar noticed his tiny pink tongue, which currently traced the innards of his scar tissue—but she chose not to pry. It was some type of peculiar tick, she'd come to realize.

Briar's fingers uneasily laced around the frigid circular handle of the petite room, thrusting the door open with ease as the fluorescent lights sprung to life, a persistent buzzing sound filling the void as Vern directed Switch towards a nearby table, accented with a simplistic white paper sheet.

"I'll leave the key to the cuffs with you," Vern dryly explained. "If he tries anything, don't hesitate to press the panic button on the wall. Got it?"

"Savvy," Briar dismissed, tearing the tiny key from Vern's hold as Switch took his place on the low table, wiggling his bum backwards to scoot into the middle as the paper messily shifted beneath his weight.

The door clipped Vern's heel as he abandoned the wildly intimate sized room, Briar's fingers quickly twisting the lock as the door latched closed.

"Ohoho," Switch growled, rolling his neck to rid it of an apparent kink as Briar shifted through his medical file. "Why'd you lock the *door,* baby? Want some alone time with *daddy?*"

The miniscule hairs on the back of Briar's neck instantly stood tall, violent trembles claiming her fingers as she jotted down several hardly legible notes in his files.

"Strip." She simply said, beady gaze meeting his overjoyed expression as he sat frozen upon the bench.

"Kinda hard to do with these-*uh, restraints*, love bug." Switch thickly mocked, tugging aimlessly at his locked cuffs at Briar's eyes meticulously rolled in their sockets. Much to Switch's utter surprise, the woman took the petite silver key in her clutch, inching towards him with determination as she motioned for him to twist around on the table.

Switch happily obliged, inching around on the paper as Briar dug the key into the lock, releasing his irritated wrists of the strict bonds as she dismissively tossed the cuffs onto the nearby counter.

"Thanks, babe." Switch sneered, curling his fingers around the angry flesh of his wrists as he intently rubbed the skin.

"I'm going to thoroughly check your skin first, and then we'll take care of your vitals and such afterwards." Nurse Briar gently explained, motioning for Switch to disrobe as he raised an amused brow.

"Are you sure you're not just tryna get me *naked*, baby?" He suggestively winked, shrugging his shoulders out of the thick confinement of his suit as pale skin promptly appeared.

"It's protocol, Switch. Please, keep the inappropriate banter to a minimum so we can get through this check-up quickly and efficiently." The woman professionally stated, tugging a pair of latex gloves onto her clammy fingers with extreme difficulty as the pile of clothes on the floor continued to grow.

"Switch? What happened to *sir?*" He playfully mocked, fingers tugging at the waist of his suit as he tugged it down the length of his legs, jumping upward into a standing position as he swiftly undressed.

Nurse Briar blatantly avoided his inquiry, her fingers cloaked by the crème-hued gloves as she intently observed Switch's stance, pulse routinely quickening as he stepped out of his shoes, allowing the legs of his suit to slip onto the floor.

"Like what'cha *see?*" Switch confidently teased, dropping his boxers as

Briar shifted her weight from either foot, growing more uncomfortable by the second.

"I'm your nurse, Switch. Please do not speak this way with me." She irritably pressed, approaching the man warily as her gloved fingers met the skin of his chest.

Switch stilled beneath her abrupt touch, a sharp breath hitching in his throat as he closely observed her precise actions, her fingers trailing along his lacerated skin as she inspected the abundance of cicatrices that littered the surface of his flesh.

"You have a lot of scars," she dumbly observed, brows raising at the sight of a considerably large circular mark, which was etched an inch-or-so above his left hip. The skin was raised and tinted a soft pink, freshly healed within the past year, by the looks of it.

"It's a tough business, dollface." He simply replied, overgrown curls draping over his eyes as his gaze lay glued upon the artificially blond woman, who had officially fallen to her knees before him.

"I'm going to need to touch you," she hastily croaked, eyeing his flaccid self as an impulsive smirk enveloped his scarred cheeks. "It's part of the procedure. I just need to make sure that everything's okay—*down there*."

"Be my *guest*." Switch smirked.

The woman rolled her eyes once more, gloved touch hesitantly meeting his privates as she thoroughly inspected the flesh. Much to her disdain, the man let out a heightened giggle the moment she'd cradled his balls, an immediate sense of discomfort rising in her belly as she simply followed procedure, checking to see if there was anything out of the ordinary.

"Cough for me, please." She instructed, claiming his dangling goods in her palm as her skeptical gaze met his. Switch did as he was told, passing the next round of the examination as she continued onto the next part.

"You're so sexy on your *kneeees*." Switch mused, his tone resembling that of a low-volume growl as Briar aggressively bit her lip, his goods twitching beneath her touch as she gently inspected the skin.

Ugh.

"Switch—" she sharply warned, rushing through the procedure as she quickly rolled back his foreskin, closely eyeing the flesh beneath as he blatantly pushed into her touch.

With that, the woman released her prying touch, climbing to her feet as she tore the gloves from her hands, diverting her gaze from Switch's half-hard self as he mockingly released a series of grunts and groans.

"Oh c'mon, Briar. We were just getting to the *good part*." He drawled, darkened gaze meeting hers as she shook her head.

"Put your clothes back on," she ordered. "So, we can finish this physical examination."

"Yes *ma'am*." Switch spat through a fit of giggles, tucking his stiffened length into the depths of his boxers once more as Briar scribbled down an abundance of information onto the blank files.

Multiple healed bullet and stab wounds to the chest and torso area

Once she'd finished filling several lines with her chicken scratch, the woman spun around on her heel, meeting a cleanly dressed freak seated back onto the examination table. Her lips curled into a tight grin, fingers lacing around a nearby stethoscope as she tore it from the hook on the wall.

The rest of the procedure went surprisingly well—Switch complied with her simplistic requests, and Briar was able to record all of the information with ease as the man thoroughly behaved himself. However, the woman couldn't help but notice that something felt a bit—*off*. There was a mysterious tension in the air, a type so thick that it could slice through human skin like butter.

"Okay, I think I have everything I need." She said, index finger curling around the front of the manila folder as she snapped it closed.

"Sweet pea," Switch cooed, palms meeting the table behind him as he leaned backwards, form going lax upon the surface. Briar's brows perplexedly raised, arms firmly crossing as she observed his questionable stance. "I just have a few *questions* for you."

"Okay?" She countered, gaze intently following his determined tongue as it poked and prodded at the deepest creases of his lacerated skin.

"Tell me—*Bri-Bri*—did you think of me when you *touched* yourself, hm?"

Briar immediately stiffened, her breaths growing rigid as Switch's partially scarred lips tugged up the length of his cheeks. He still lay in the same exact position—balancing his weight on his palms as his legs slowly spread, bottom lip tucked between rows of significantly stained teeth as the woman practically quivered in her shoes.

"Am I-*uh*, every girls' *wet dream*, hm? Or just a select *few*?" The man thickly taunted, gaze unblinking as his stare met hers.

"You're *not—*"

"Don't lie, princess. I see *riiiight* through you." He pressed, roughly popping his knuckles as Briar anxiously flinched at the sudden sonance. "How many times, baby?"

"I—"

"*How. Many. Times?*" Switch deeply growled, his voice shifting down several octaves as the volume gradually increased. Briar feared she may suffer a heart attack on the spot, and yet—the fluttering discomfort present in her lower belly was painfully increasing by the moment . . .

"Four." She shamefully revealed.

"What exactly happens in these—*er—fantasies*, baby girl? Feel free to ex-*paaaand*." Switch huskily urged, a sinister smirk enveloping his features as Briar intently studied the gaudy deformity upon his left cheek.

"I-I c-can't—" she cried, stomach painfully churning as she struggled to tear her desperate gaze away.

"It's *okay*," he encouraged, releasing a substantial groan as his eyes rolled back in ecstasy. "C'mon, toots. Don't be so *shy,* I promise I'm not picky."

Briar threw up her arms in angst, muttering an exasperated *fuck it* as she rapidly approached the wildly giggling man, falling to her knees as perfectly manicured fingers curled around the elastic waistband of his trousers as his eyes instantaneously widened.

Before Switch could utter a single word, Briar had done the unthinkable; her head massively swimming as her conscious obscenely shouted—*no! Stop! This is wrong!*—and yet, she ignored every pleading attempt to halt her actions as she effortlessly painted arrays of miscellaneous portraits upon him with her tongue. An immediate groan slipped through his lips as his eyelids fluttered elegantly closed, neck falling limp on his shoulders as the Adam's apple beneath the fragile flesh of his throat shifted with every obscene sound.

Although he'd purposely attempted to make the woman squirm, Switch had to admit—he didn't even remotely expect his manipulative banter to actually *work*. And yet, as Briar's tongue torturously teased him—he couldn't help but nearly combust entirely, and in more ways than one.

Thus, Adelaide Lynch's complexion littered his mind as he desperately attempted to push her sullen features away—*holy hell holy hell just enjoy this moment!*—but apparently, his mind needed—*wanted*—literally *craved* the shy

Australian girl, who kissed him on the mouth just yesterday afternoon, and *spoke real words!*

A familiar warmth suddenly appeared in his lower abdomen, right palm tearing away from the table as the damp paper irritably clung to his palm, eventually peeling away with the simple wiggle of his fingers as his trembling digits met Briar's hair.

"S-Shit," he grunted, staggered breaths emerging in the form of pants as his chest heavily heaved, dirty digits still firmly laced in Briar's locks as he sharply tugged, his high prolonging as an amused giggle slipped off her lips as his hold eventually loosened on her hair.

"It's been awhile for you, I'm assuming?" She shyly stated, the pad of her thumb delicately swiping along the flushed skin of her bottom lip as Switch's lazy gaze met hers.

"That *was*–"

"Never speak of it." Briar swiftly interjected, her expression hardening. "I can get fired. That shouldn't have happened–"

"Quit it, baby girl. My lips are sealed. Yours, *however . . .*" he trailed off, tugging his trousers back up as he hopped off of the examination table, two fingers swiping beneath her chin as her cheeks flushed scarlet.

Her gaze locked on his parted lips, every fiber of her being begging her to lurch forward–to slam her lips to his and taste his glorious mouth, to let him taste himself . . .

Suddenly, Briar felt herself slowly leaning in, Switch's curious gaze widening as he took a step backwards, a deep rumble erupting from his throat as he blatantly cleared it. His index finger met her puckered lips, a scolding expression plastered on his features as he released a defeated sigh.

"Those are reserved for someone *else*, sweetie." He simply dismissed.

Briar's jaw fell slack, head nodding as she tucked a stray strand of hair behind her ear.

"S-Sorry," she murmured. "Too far. Let's get you cuffed again so you can get to breakfast."

"Your vitals all look good," Briar started, scribbling a bit of information onto Adelaide's file as the cheery nurse hummed an unidentifiable tune beneath her breath. "Any pain anywhere?"

Adelaide shook her head.

"All right, sweetie. I think I have everything! You're all set." Briar exclaimed, a broad, toothy-grin enveloping her lips as she snapped Adelaide's medical folder shut.

"N-Nurse Briar," Adelaide uneasily whispered, the tone of her voice hoarse and thick as the words struggled to emerge. However, it appeared that the blond woman hadn't even heard her.

"Let's get you back to the rec room." Briar stated, curling her fingers around Adelaide's bicep as the younger woman hastily tugged away from her hold. Briar's brows raised at the peculiar action, lips forming into a straight line as she shot Adelaide a puzzled glare.

"Nurse Briar," Adelaide thickly spoke, her tone confident and significantly louder in volume as Briar's throat immediately ran dry. The folder slipped through her weakened grasp, tumbling to the tile floor with an unceremonious slap as several pages spewed outward, coating the stunned woman's feet as she stared wildly in Adelaide's direction.

"*Adelaide?*" She gawked, dainty fingers meeting the shy girls' sullen features as she audibly gulped. "Did you just—"

"Yes." Adelaide breathed, a genuine grin slapped upon her lips as the nurse laced her arms tightly around Adelaide's shoulders, tugging the frail woman close to her chest as an array of joyful expressions slipped off Briar's lips.

"Oh my god! It worked! You're *speaking*! My Addy-bear—*speaking*! Lord, it's an actual *miracle*!" Nurse Briar exclaimed, her vision temporarily obstructed by thick, cloudy tears as she cupped Adelaide's cheeks in her palms.

"Briar, it's not that big of a deal." Adelaide simply dismissed, stumbling over several of the words as her mouth struggled to form particular letters. It almost felt unnatural to speak again, but at the same time—it felt *right*.

"*Not a big deal?*" Briar spat, a horrified expression plastered on her face as she aimlessly shook her head. "Adelaide, you've never said a single word to me! I actually forgot you were Australian! Holy—"

"Can you shave my legs? And my—uh—coochie?" Adelaide innocently inquired, anxiously rubbing her fingers together as Briar's jaw fell.

"W-What for—?"

"I just feel ugly." Adelaide immediately spat, Switch's complexion riddling her mind as the haunting set of scars teased her. She wanted him—she *needed* him. She'd gotten a small taste of him and now she desperately needed to explore . . .

"Oh, Addy," Briar cooed. "Of course. Go ahead and take off your pants, sweetie. I'll clean you up."

Adelaide simply smiled, following Briar's orders as she shed herself of the clothing, tugging the loose trousers down the length of her hairy legs as she discarded them onto the floor.

"I'm so happy you're comfortable speaking, sweetheart. I can't even explain how amazing this is. D'you think it's the medication? The shock therapies?" Briar rambled, readying a cheap drug-store razor as she wet Adelaide's legs.

"It's because of a boy." The younger woman revealed, her accent thick and musky as Briar rid her legs of the unwanted hair.

Briar raised a curious brow, her heart stilling in her chest as she cautiously shaved Adelaide's legs, careful not to prick the woman as she could still clearly taste Switch on her tongue . . .

"Oh?" Nurse Briar breathed. "Who?"

"I can't tell you," Adelaide murmured, picking at her nails as she avoided her nurses desperate gaze. "You'll throw me into max. Or separate us."

"Addy," Briar pressed, climbing to her feet as she met Adelaide's weak glare. "I would never. He obviously means a whole lot to you. I mean, you're *talking!*"

A forced burst of air emerged from Adelaide's nostrils, hazel-hued orbs reconnecting with a dashing sea of blue as her lips slowly parted.

"It's Switch."

XIII

"Just open the door, and you will see
This passion burns inside of me
Don't say to me, you'll never tell
Touch me there, make the move
Cast the spell"
–Michael Jackson, "In the Closet"

"We need to talk about it, sweetheart." Switch pressed, threading his fingers through the choppy concrete of the mangled wall as Adelaide's dainty digits met his. Her nearly nonexistent brows mockingly raised, as if to inaudibly counter his inquiry as the pads of her calloused fingers gradually caressed his.

"C'mon," the man thickly begged, tugging his lip between determined teeth as he irritably bit down. "Talk again. I-*uh, like* the sound of your voice."

An instant, scarlet-tinted blush enveloped Adelaide's playful expression, her fingers interlacing with his between the blatant hole as the uneven cement pricked her outer palm.

"Why do we need to talk about it? It happened nearly a week ago," she whispered, her tone hoarse and uneven as Switch's scar tugged up the length of his cheek, a toothy grin overcoming his features as Adelaide continued to obscenely blush.

"Because," he mused. "You *kissed* me, dollface. That's gotta *mean* something."

"And?" Adelaide murmured, avoiding his steady gaze as she recalled the magnificent memory. It had been six long days since their intimate encounter, and she swore that she could still taste the sweetness of his tongue on hers.

Switch perplexedly raised his brows, running a free hand through his matted curls as Adelaide admired the lovely hue.

"I love your hair," she whispered, unlatching her fingers from his as she thrust her slender arm into the depths of the hole, curious digits claiming the disheveled locks as a stagnant breath caught in Switch's throat.

Oh, how badly he wanted to lace his fingers around her wrist—she made it *so* damn easy. The frail woman was so incredibly skinny that the madman swore he could tug her entire frame through the petite hole with one determined tug, and then—it was game over. She'd be wholly and unreservedly his. His to touch, his to kiss, his to *choke* . . .

"Can we kiss again?" She softly wondered, twisting a particularly lengthy curl between the slopes of her parted fingers as Switch's eyelids squeezed agonizingly shut, vivid visuals of Adelaide squirming beneath his sturdy hips involuntarily riddling his mind.

"Go to sleep, Adelaide." Switch drawled, craning his neck to meet her palm as his lips gently grazed the surface. An immediate shiver overcame her spine at the feeling of his scars against her skin, her fingers dipping between the uneven surfaces, slipping along the rigid folds of his flesh. She was so undeniably curious of their origin.

"Goodnight, Switch." The woman whispered, withdrawing her touch as the lights promptly extinguished—as if on cue—and the persistent, low buzzing of the blue-hued nighttime lights arose.

Adelaide managed to slip into a dreamless slumber within the hour, whereas Switch lay wide awake, fingers consistently raveling and unraveling as he tempestuously tapped his foot against the grimy ground. His calloused fingers physically ached, practically crying for the familiar sensation of a keen blade between them. The skin atop his fingertips blatantly buzzed, physically begging for the simplistic touch of warm, oozing blood between them.

Blood—Sweet, sweet blood—oh, how he absolutely *adored* the thick, crimson liquid with every fiber of his being. His limbs ached for the feel of it, and a part of him wanted to *play* in it—to be able to penetrate the soft, dainty flesh of Adelaide's beautiful neck with a serrated edge and drain her dry . . . perhaps he could create pretty paintings with the liquid form of her life?

Switch's eyeballs rolled to the back of his head in pure ecstasy at the undeniably morbid fantasy, his fingers curling into constricted fists as the featherweight sheet slipped between his clenched digits. Savage shudders claimed his spine, a petite groan slipping through his chapped, parted lips as the visuals became borderline overwhelming—visuals of a very real Adelaide, his dirty digits tangled in her straggly hair as he uncomplicatedly yanked, emitting a heightened cry from the feeble woman as she sobbed beneath his hips. Her trembling palms met his thighs, weak grasp applying pressure as she desperately attempted to shove him off—but no, oh no *no!*—he had her so tightly wrapped around his finger that it was truly shocking that she could still properly breathe.

The madman ripped himself from the confinement of his measly mattress, fierce trembles wracking through his hunched shoulders as his fingers curled into taut fists once again, a strangled grunt emerging as he delivered a sturdy punch directly to the center of the cement wall beside his sorry excuse for a bed.

White-hot pain instantly claimed his throbbing knuckles, the collision generating a second heartbeat beneath the skin as he swung once again, striking the cement with extreme gaiety as the thick skin of his knuckles fleetly cracked and tore, smearing a morbid crimson hue along the vertical surface as Switch released a disgruntled shout.

"*Fuck!*" The man boorishly exclaimed, tight fist colliding several times over with the wall as the erratic shouts began to decrescendo into mute whines, noises that weakly resembled those of an injured puppy. In fact, to the untrained ear—it sounded as if Switch was actually *crying*.

Steady tracks of blood oozed between the crevices of his fingertips, daintily dripping onto the floor as the wide-eyed man observed the dimly lit smear of scarlet present on the wall. His pulse thumped erratically beneath his ribcage, chest arduously heaving as curious fingers met the tainted surface, the pads of his digits swiping along the warm liquid as he reveled in the touch.

Heatedly, the man scribbled a bold, broad obscenity onto the wall with the blood of his knuckles, bottom lip pulled between rows of teeth in intense concentration as the taunt liquid stained his flesh. Once he'd finished, his dark orbs lay transfixed upon the smeared surface—heightened giggles slipping off his lips as his head dipped to the side, vision struggling to focus on the gorgeous color of the drying liquid beneath the bland blue lighting.

Adelaide was considerably lucky that Switch couldn't fit through that damn hole.

"Wanna see a magic trick?" The madman mused, shuffling a profusion of aged playing cards between his bandaged grasp. Adelaide's brows raised.

Her cautious touch met his cloaked knuckles, gently grazing the concealed skin as she murmured: "What happened?"

"Er—" Switch stammered, side-eyeing the bandages as he clearly remembered a distraught Nurse Briar entering his cell just this morning, cobalt gaze significantly widening at the horrific sight of an abundance of dried blood atop his skin and smeared along the crème sheet of his mattress. She'd attempted to rid the concrete of the substance, but instead, she managed to create a sloppy blob of blood among the surface. Briar and Switch had not spoken—her dainty fingertips cautiously lacing the bandages around his distraught knuckles as she quickly and efficiently sterilized his wounds. He'd wanted to remind her of their wildly intimate moment only days prior, but for some peculiar reason, he hadn't been able to spit the words out.

"I punched the wall." He openly admitted, the cards slipping elegantly through his grasp as the metal cuffs boldly collided with every miniscule movement.

In the place of a verbal reply, Adelaide simply offered a tight-lipped grin, her palm placing a reassuring pat atop his knobby knee as she retrieved the disheveled copy of *Sense and Sensibility* from beside her.

"Hey," Nayeli hissed, a single strand of violently curly hair tucked between her teeth as she aimlessly chewed. "Y'think there's something between them? They're abnormally close."

Cora's expression grew lax as she shifted her weight against the worn sofa, curious gaze settling upon the duo laid against the back wall as a grimace overcame her features.

"Gross. Why *her*?" Cora snidely snipped, her voice slightly muffled due to the angle she currently sat at as Nayeli simply shrugged.

Adelaide and Switch sat in nearly identical positions, their backs pressed firmly against the concrete wall as their slender legs lay crossed Indian style (or, according to Nayeli—crisscross applesauce). Adelaide routinely clutched her deteriorating novel between sturdy fingers, gaze glued upon the printed word as the infamous Switch sat hip-to-hip with the odd woman, wrists still confined by the harsh metal of his handcuffs as the madman threaded a deck of cards through his bandaged fingers.

Several greasy strands of brown, curly hair dangled in his dark vision, one particularly long piece occasionally tickling the tip of his nose. The man, however, didn't seem to take notice to the bothersome intrusion, as he continued to thoroughly shuffle through the old deck of playing cards, slender fingers curling around each individually separated stack as he efficiently shuffled the bunch.

"He's truly something else, isn't he?" Nayeli confidently added, irritably biting on her overgrown index fingernail as Cora redirected her attention to the olive-skinned girl.

"He's a serial killer," she simply said. "And a freak."

"Aren't we all, Cora?" Nayeli slurred, gaze still solely fixated on the monster several yards away. "Don't try and act all innocent on me now, everyone knows you set your Math teacher on fire and then proceeded to have a nervous breakdown."

Cora visibly frowned, her dirty digits lacing around a copy of *Wuthering Heights* as she shifted her weight against the beaten sofa.

"He had it coming," she lowly defended, dipping her thumb into the center of the novel as she hastily tore it open.

"Exactly my point," Nayeli pressed. "Maybe that's just it, Cora. Maybe Chicago had it coming."

Time seemed to tick idly by.

Although Adelaide and Switch had managed to share a wildly intimate moment in the presence of many others an astounding two weeks ago—things hadn't really changed since then.

Switch seemed to take a liking to the previously forgotten card deck in the rec room. It was as if he needed something to be lodged within the slopes of his grimy fingers, Adelaide noticed. He was quite jittery, always fiddling with some type of object—whether it be a stray string on the trousers of his jumpsuit, or the metal casing of his cuffs. Lucky for him, it seemed that he'd found a bit of a hobby to occupy his raging tick.

The audible reading of *Sense and Sensibility* continued, but they'd managed to chop their reading time in half. It was almost as if the woman was attempting to savor every last bit of the novel—as if she were fearful that they'd reach the end much too soon, although reaching the end, in fact, was inevitable. There would always be an end, as there always was with everything in life. However, ending this very book would mean that Emmett DuPré was truly and utterly gone.

Adelaide had never finished the book without him. In fact, she wasn't quite sure if she was prepared for that type of closure just yet.

Switch hummed an unidentifiable tune beneath his breath, thick paper cards colliding with the calloused flesh of his fingers. The bandages had vanished several days prior, the skin of his knuckles flushed a soft pink as brand new flesh replaced the old, beaten skin.

Slap slap slap.

Adelaide claimed her bottom lip between two unruly fingernails, brows raising in vexation as the madman beside her hip continued to obscenely shuffle the cards within his grasp.

Slap slap slap.

Three cards slipped between his index finger and middle, exuberantly gliding along the skin as he turned them over, revealing a vibrant set of fluorescent red hearts, along with a sleek black "K" in each corner. A heightened giggle slipped through his lacerated lips at the sight, cuffed wrists arching in Adelaide's dainty direction as he tossed the card onto her lap.

The remarkably silent woman curiously eyed the object, slender fingers curling around the laminated paper as she tore it from the depths of her lap.

"Why don't-cha stick him in your pocket," Switch dryly suggested, glancing sideways at the curious woman as she strut a measly grin. "That way I can always be with you."

"King of hearts?" She giggled, turning the object over in her palm as she glanced in his direction.

"King of *your* heart, sugar plum."

An scarlet tint claimed Adelaide's cheeks at Switch's statement, her fingers curling around the card as she stuffed the object into the deepest part of her jumpsuit pocket, hazel gaze glued upon the curly-haired chap beside her as he resumed his insistent shuffling.

"Y'know," Adelaide lowly began, eyeing a rigid Switch as he slipped the precisely organized cards between his constricted grasp. "You're not as vile as they all say."

The man instantly halted his movements, several cards tumbling from the safety of his fingers as they fluttered choppily to the floor. Adelaide's pulse drastically quickened as the familiar, warm cocoa hue of Switch's eyes immediately shifted, displaying a haunting coal color as a menacing grin tugged at his mutilated features. Switch shifted slightly sideways, lips tickling the flesh of Adelaide's ear as she immediately stiffened beneath the foreign feel.

"Oh–*baby*," the man purred, several stray curls tickling the flesh of her flushed cheek as she intently held her breath. "You have no *idea* what I'm capable of."

"Then show me," she softly clipped, keenly twisting her neck to view his amused features. Their noses nimbly collided, Switch's hot breaths fanning over her lips as patches of goosebumps arose on the exposed flesh of her frail neck.

"*Mmm*," Switch purred, the remainder of the cards elegantly slipping from his temporarily weakened grasp as they collapsed into a sloppy heap atop his lap. Adelaide's chest heaved as his cuffed grasp rapidly approached her scarlet-tinted cheeks, the pad of his thumb grazing along her pouted bottom lip as his darkened gaze met her parted mouth. "Once I get *going*, I don't think I'll be able to stop."

"You don't have to be gentle with me," Adelaide murmured, her dainty fingertips meeting his complexion as a perplexed expression overcame his features.

"I can take it." She assured him, caressing his destroyed bottom lip with her thumb as their foreheads arduously collided, a staggered breath slipping off her lips as the duo continued to gently caress one another's skin.

"Don't make promises you can't *keep*, dollface." Switch darkly murmured, tugging his bottom lip between rows of teeth as Adelaide's blurred features softened.

"I always keep my promises." The woman stated, growing agitated by their extremely close proximity as she sealed the torturous gap.

An immediate sigh of relief slipped into the depths of Adelaide's mouth upon impact, her fingers latching onto the lengthy, greasy curls atop his skull as she harshly tugged, forcing his face forward as their noses achingly flattened against one another's cheeks.

Breathless gasps danced along Adelaide's tongue, spilling into Switch's gaping mouth as his tongue promptly invaded the sweet gap between her partially parted lips. Rows of teeth bitterly collided, occasionally nipping and tugging at the swollen flesh of one another's lips as his grasp rotated to the dainty flesh of Adelaide's neck. The pad of his forefinger collided with the thin skin directly beneath her ear, her pulse actively thumping beneath the flesh as his stomach agonizingly churned.

Oh *God*—just the feeling of her heart erratically thumping beneath his fingers alone was enough to send him into a wild frenzy. Although her tongue currently raided every single inch of his gaping mouth; all the madman could truly focus on was the persistent thumping beneath his fingertips—the physical evidence that the woman was living and breathing beside him. Instinctively, the psychopath cautiously laced his fingers around the skin of her throat, prompting an involuntary groan to emerge from the petite woman as she attempted to tug him even closer, their knees colliding as her fingers worked wonders on the deepest grooves of the scar that claimed the left corner of his mouth.

Thus, the shy woman managed to propel the man out of his temporary trance, her simplistic touch instantly diverting his homicidal thoughts as his palms cradled her flushed cheeks, the pads of his thumbs tracing miscellaneous portraits along her flesh as she reveled in the complex feel of his drastic deformity.

"Adelaide." A distant voice pressed, the sound slipping immediately over the woman's head as she continued to attack Switch's lips with hers, nails dipping beneath the raised flesh of his gruesome scar as his tongue swiped along her bottom lip, savoring the taste of her skin.

Nurse Briar fell to her knees before the duo, a tight-lipped frown tugging at her mouth as she anxiously glanced over her shoulder. Luckily, the remaining patients in the rec room didn't seem to notice Adelaide and Switch's wildly inappropriate episode.

"Switch! Addy!" The woman thickly pressed, manicured fingers latching around the ankle of Adelaide's jumpsuit as she harshly tugged.

Adelaide bitterly detached her lips from Switch's, wild-eyes colliding with a rigid Nurse Briar sat before her as the madman refused to cease his actions. Instead, his lips simply traveled to the hollow of her throat, right palm cupping her jaw as he forced her chin upwards, allowing him clear access to the softest parts of her neck.

"Switch! Stop it!" Briar scolded, swatting at his knee as he continued his gentle assault upon Adelaide's neck, tugging batches of skin between his teeth as the woman released a satisfied groan, her palms flattening against his chest in a weak attempt to pry him off of her tiny frame.

"Don't make me send you two to max." Briar muttered, yanking a heaving Adelaide from Switch's desperate hold as a pair of menacing, inky-orbs instantaneously collided with a shaken sea of blue.

"Don't give me that look," the blond-haired woman snipped, tugging Adelaide into a standing position as Switch still sat in an exasperated heap upon the dirt-riddled floor. "You're lucky it was me that saw you guys and not Dr. Blake or Greenwald. Either one of them would've chucked you into solitary without supper or a bath."

"So, I'm not allowed to kiss Adelaide, but Green-*fuck* can stick his little *pecker* in her whenever he pleases?" Switch darkly pressed, rising to his feet as Briar's eyes instantly widened. Adelaide's heart plummeted at the man's words, her lazy gaze meeting a horrified Nurse Briar as she latched her fingers around Adelaide's drastically skinny elbow.

"Addy? What's he talking about?" Nurse Briar defeatedly breathed, bottom lip quivering in angst as the eyeliner upon her left eye lay severely smudged.

"I-It only happened once," Adelaide softly revealed, her voice low and hoarse as she shifted her weight from either foot. "It wasn't consensual. I-I–"

"He's going to regret ever being born." Briar hissed through gritted teeth, lacing her free fingers around Switch's bicep as she tugged the pair of them from the rec room.

"Absolute trash. I've always hated the guy." She lowly murmured, directing the duo from the nearly vacant premises as they glanced fleetingly in one another's direction, the evidence of their intimate encounter still present among their slightly swollen lips as Briar led them towards the dining hall.

Their evening baths were unbelievably awkward that day.

Typically, Briar reserved the wash room for a specific time slot, that way only Adelaide and Switch would have their baths and no other patients would be present. Unfortunately, there appeared to be some kind of mix-up, and an olive-skinned Nayeli nearly screeched when Switch and Adelaide stumbled into the warm room.

"Oh my *God!*" Nayeli exclaimed, lacing her fingers around the circular edge of the porcelain basin as her personal nurse craned her neck to view the sudden intrusion. "Switch is bathing with us?"

"Briar," Nurse Jackie clipped, her fingers tangled in a mess of brunette hair as her patient—Schizophrenic Sarah—stirred beneath the lukewarm water. "I thought you had a certain time slot to bathe—*him*."

"Sometimes things don't work out that way, Jackie." Briar irritably clipped, tucking a bothersome strand of stray hair behind her ear as she beckoned both Adelaide and Switch forward and towards the vacant baths. Per usual, Switch's wrists were tightly cuffed, a perplexed set of brows raising as he viewed a giddy Nayeli in the bath beside his.

"I'm Nayeli," she boldly exclaimed, a fit of giggles immediately following her outburst as Nurse Briar unlatched his handcuffs.

Much to the curly-haired woman's dismay, the man avoided her entirely, dirty digits lacing around the hem of his jumpsuit top as he effortlessly tugged it from his torso. Although Briar's bathed both him and Adelaide simultaneously for quite some time now, the pair still respected one another's privacy, and Switch's eyelids fluttered tightly shut as Adelaide quickly disrobed.

"Stop staring, Nayeli." Nurse Briar irritably scolded, efficiently filling Switch's basin as Adelaide's nude form settled into the depths of her own, the comforting temperature of the water instantly soothing her tense muscles as the liquid sloshed around her sudden weight.

"No." Nayeli flatly replied, curious gaze transfixed on a very nude Switch as he shot her a questionable glare.

The theatrical man eased into the porcelain tub, gaze consistently locked with Nayeli's as her heart blatantly fluttered. He was staring right at her—*was that some type of invitation?*

"Looky *here*, toots." Switch drawled, inching sideways to lean against the tub as his elbow met the curled side, eyes darkening as Nayeli's features brightened.

"If you don't learn to *mind* your own business, I'll sneak into your cell tonight and chop you up into itty-*bitty* pieces. Kapeesh?" The man monotonically threatened, wiggling his fingers obnoxiously to enunciate his speech as the woman's eyes significantly widened.

"Are you *threatening* me?" She scoffed, a hefty grimace overcoming her features as sarcastic chuckles slipped off Switch's lips.

"Switch—" Nurse Briar warned, her sudsy fingers encased in a mop of drenched strands as Adelaide stirred beneath her touch.

"Y'look like a screamer, Yeli. Tell me, will you be that *cocky* when my *knife* slices through your face?" The man darkly pressed, eyes mockingly rolling to the back of his skull as he forcefully shuddered.

"Briar! Control your patient!" Nurse Lora yelped, lips parted in horror as Nayeli's heart instantly plummeted, her beady gaze connecting with an amused Adelaide as she struggled to stifle a giggle.

"Switch, that's enough!" Briar clipped, lacing her fingers tightly around his greasy curls as she yanked his skull backwards. The man merely giggled at the slightly painful sensation, his tongue prancing along the deepest grooves of his mangled flesh as Briar scrubbed shampoo into his curls.

What're you getting yourself into, Addy? A voice suddenly appeared, prompting Adelaide's toes to instinctively curl as she released a heightened gasp.

You guys are back? She countered, pulse quickening beneath her ribcage as her palms began to profusely sweat. The woman had to admit, the silence was nice while it lasted . . .

The uneasy woman waited several agonizing moments for a reply—a reply that she'd never receive.

"You need to take your medication, Switch. You haven't taken a single dose since you were admitted." Dr. Blake snipped, magnetized gaze glued upon the lax man as he lay idle on the drastically uncomfortable mattress.

"I *told* you," he boldly began, expeditiously tapping his foot against the metal frame as it obscenely shifted beneath his differing weight. "I'm afraid my *dick* won't work properly if I do."

Nurse Briar audibly gulped at his proclamation, palms instantly clamming up as she clutched the softened paper cup filled with different colored pills in her sturdy grasp.

Dr. Blake irritably crossed her arms, an irate sigh spilling from her vibrantly painted lips as she observed the gruesome, smeared blood stain present on Switch's wall.

"My husband would strangle you if he found out how you spoke around me." The middle-aged woman unprofessionally spat, diverting her gaze to meet a rigid Briar near the sealed cell door as she warily shrugged.

"*Ohoho,*" Switch giggled, brightened gaze meeting a stiff Lyra Blake as he slung his legs over the side of the bed, the soles of his inky, unlaced boots colliding with the floor as his palms met the edge of the mattress. "So why don't you bring him in, *hmm?* I could use a little roughin' *up*, I'm gettin' bit *antsy* in here, you know. I never know what to do with my *hands.*"

His gaze shifted to meet a wary Briar, who was attempting to hide behind an overly-confident Dr. Blake. Switch's stomach fluttered at the mere memory of Briar's luscious lips wrapped tightly around him, the way she seductively batted her eyelashes when he completely came undone . . .

The madman winked in her direction, a satisfied smirk tugging at his features as Dr. Blake glanced curiously over her shoulder, gaze darkening as it collided with an anxious Briar in the corner.

"If you don't take the medication, we'll have to start sedating you at night so we can administer it through a needle." The doctor explained, running a hand through her unkempt locks as she twisted on her heel.

"Get him to take them, will you?" She spat in Briar's mute direction, fingers lacing around her ID as she swiped it along the keypad, unlatching the steel mahogany door as she slipped out of the cold, concrete cell.

"I need you to take these pills, Switch." Nurse Briar pitifully begged, her heart painfully accelerating as the curly-haired man suddenly rose from his seat.

"Make me." He lazily drawled, rapidly approaching the worried woman as she backed up against the frigid wall, violent trembles claiming her spine as she clutched the tiny paper cup close to her chest.

Switch was impossibly close to her, several recently washed curls concealing his amused expression as the cell block lights abruptly extinguished, his menacing features drastically darkening as the low blue hue pranced along his partially lacerated mouth.

He looked absolutely mortifying in this type of lighting, half of his amused expression blandly illuminated whilst the other half—the *unscathed* half—remained entirely invisible, determined fingers lacing around the waist of Briar's scrubs as he tugged her close.

"Baby Briiiii-*ar*," the man drawled, hot breath tickling the flesh of her ear as his teeth nipped at the extended skin. He kept his tone drastically low, careful not to draw the attention of a curious Adelaide next door as his fingers laced around the loose strands of Briar's hair.

"I can't stop *thinking* about you," he huskily spoke, placing sloppy, wet kisses along the supple skin of her neck. "About our *time* together." His hand claimed hers, palm flattening against the back of her clammy grasp as he flattened her touch against the impending arousal within his trousers.

"Take your pills." She stammered, thrusting the paper cup into Switch's free hand as she yanked out of his desperate hold, a whine of dissatisfaction slipping off his lips as he bitterly snagged the cup from her grasp.

The man tore his aroused frame fully from hers, the soles of his boots clamorously scraping against the floor as he approached the metal sink opposite the door. With one fluid movement, he tossed his head back, taking the pills into his mouth as he promptly filled the cup with a bit of water to swallow them down. By the time he'd turned around, Briar had managed to slip from his cell.

"You finally took your pills?" A tiny voice inquired, slightly muffled by the inch-thick wall as Switch merely grumbled.

"They won't even have the chance to get into my system." He blandly explained, falling to his knees before the chilly toilet bowl as his fingers brushed against his parted lips.

"What d'you–" Adelaide began, but her inquiry was instantly answered when the obvious sound of Switch emptying the contents of his stomach into the u-bend arose.

Oh.

He really didn't want to take those pills.

"You know what tonight is?" Switch queried, flipping through the deteriorating pages of Adelaide's novel in search of where they'd left off.

"The thirtieth of October?" Adelaide whispered, brows curiously raised as the madman released a heightened giggle. "*Oh*—I know! We do this every year, actually. They host a movie night the night before Halloween. It gives us a bit of freedom, it's really nice." The typically silent woman rambled, her tone low and hoarse as she picked at the spare skin around her overgrown nails.

"*Neat.* But no," Switch snipped, discovering a tiny triangular fold upon a specific page near the end of the novel as he smoothed out the kink with his fingers. "It's *Devil's Night.* Can you believe it? A *whole night* dedicated to *meeee.*"

Adelaide shot him a puzzled glare, fingers prancing along the scarlet skin of his wrists as she hooked a single finger beneath one of the metal shackles, irritably yanking at the obstruction as she released an irate sigh.

"I don't think you're the devil. Hopefully they'll take these off during movie night," she murmured, her breaths emerging as staggered pants as Switch's fingers lightly brushed against hers.

"*Mmm*, I'm not sure if that's such a good *idea*," Switch muttered, gaze transfixed on her wandering fingers as she elegantly traced the tattooed skin of his wrist, the pad of her finger cautiously circling the profusion of permanent lines as his breaths thinned.

"Why's that?" She bluntly countered.

"Be-*cause*," the man began. "I don't think I'll be able to keep my hands *off* of you, dollface."

Their stares promptly interlocked, a mischievous grin plastered on Adelaide's features as she tugged his wrists onto her lap.

"There's only one guard on duty on movie night," she quietly explained, glancing in a curious Cora's direction as she observed the tight-knit couple with wide eyes. "And he always falls asleep halfway through . . ."

"What're you saying, sweet pea?" Switch huskily questioned, his tone low and dark as his stomach instinctively churned.

"I'm *saying*–" Adelaide confidently began. "You can finally have your way with me."

Switch's heart nearly burst out of his chest at her statement, wide-eyes admiring the cheery woman as a toothy grin enveloped her chapped lips. For once, the man was actually–truly–*speechless*.

You can finally have your way with me—ohoho! The *possibilities*!—What would he do first–what to do, what to *do–God*, his fingers were already agonizingly buzzing, physically *begging* him to wrap them so tightly around her throat that her eyes would pop straight out of her skull. *No no no no*–he needed to be semi-gentle with the woman, he couldn't scare her off *quite* yet . . . The mere thought of Adelaide as a panting mess beneath him was enough to make his head spin, and other things twitch . . .

Several hours later during supper, an unfamiliar individual strut into the dining hall—a mess of dark, unruly hair and bright, beady eyes admiring the silent crowd as Switch toyed with an old slice of bread.

"Who's *that*?" He murmured, tearing off a considerable chunk as he tossed it into his mouth.

Adelaide glanced over her shoulder, gaze darkening at the sight of a sharply dressed Dr. Evers as he adjusted his crooked tie.

"Dr. Evers. He owns the place." She croaked, stirring several pieces of corn around on her scarlet-hued tray as Switch thickly swallowed.

"Attention guests of Stillwater," the lively man cheered, extending his arms outward. "As I'm sure you already know, tonight is the Eve of Halloween. Per tradition, we will put on a movie for you all in the rec room at seven sharp. Personal caretakers will judge their high-risk patients and make the call whether or not they will be cuffed or uncuffed during tonight's event. As usual, Mister Jordan will authorize the event—Mister Jordan, say hello,"

An elderly guard took a single step forward, waving in the crowds' direction as a wisp of silver hair littered his skull.

"Two hours. *Hocus Pocus* will be the film for tonight. Thank you." With that, Dr. Evers abandoned the deathly silent room, a low buzz filling the agonizingly quiet void as Adelaide stuffed a spoonful of corn into her mouth.

"Oh, *Adelaide*," Switch hummed, digging his fingers into the soft flesh of the bread. He harshly tapped his foot against the tile floor. The woman raised a single brow, as if to in verbally answer as the madman merely chuckled. "You're a *lucky* girl."

"How so?" She whispered.

"Because," Switch drawled, tauntingly wetting his lips. "Tonight, you get to *dance* with the *devil*."

Adelaide ran her fingers through her drenched locks, following closely on Briar's heel as she eyed an uncuffed Switch beside her, his hands buried in the depths of his jumpsuit trouser pockets as he shot her a wicked grin.

"So," Nurse Briar began, her voice slightly muffled by a periwinkle pink nail lodged between her teeth as she stumbled into the rec room. "No funny business tonight, all right? Adelaide, you've been here long enough to know how these movie nights go. I expect you'll behave, and I want to assume you will too, Switch—"

"When *ain't* I on my best behavior, Bri-Bri?" Switch teased, earning a dissatisfied grunt from the exhausted nurse as she swung the double doors open.

The rec room was dimly lit, cluttered with an abundance of metal folding chairs in the center of the room as a bright white sheet cloaked the back wall, a weak image displayed on the screen as the movie consistently flickered.

"Let's sit in the *back*." Switch suggested, strutting towards the unoccupied chairs in the very last row as he collapsed onto the seat, his uncuffed hands folding atop his lap as Adelaide softly sunk into the chair beside him.

"Night, guys." Nurse Briar weakly dismissed, excusing herself from the rec room as she bid an already sleepy Mr. Jordan goodbye.

Mindless chatter filled the void as Nayeli and Cora obnoxiously giggled up near the front, the back row remaining absolutely obsolete as everyone avoided the infamous Switch and his loyal, mute sidekick.

"A'right," Mr. Jordan's hoarse voice croaked from the right left corner. "Let's begin the movie. Kill the lights."

The low glow of the lightbulbs instantly vanished, enveloping the room in complete darkness as several paranoid patients cried outward in fear, only to be silenced by several irate individuals who also spat out obscene terms in their direction.

The children's movie slowly began, several cheers erupting from the crowd as Switch's boot-clad feet claimed the metal chair directly in front of him, the ankles of his trousers messily tucked into the lips of his shoes as his fingers expeditiously tapped against his knobby knees. It was wildly peculiar to see him without the metal shackles upon his wrists, and something strange stirred deep within the woman as she inched her chair closer to his. The legs sonorously dragged along the floor, prompting several curious heads to inexplicably turn at the sudden sound.

Switch released a heightened giggle at Adelaide's uneasy stance, the fingers of her right hand meeting his vacant palm as she interlaced their digits with ease. An immediate sense of relief instantaneously washed over the woman, a hearty grin tugging at her lips as she effortlessly squeezed his palm, heart thickly thudding beneath her ribcage as she admired his cheery features.

The flickering images of the film danced along his mangled complexion, differing hues illuminating his features as a pair of dark, menacing eyes swiftly met hers.

"You're *staring*, doll." He thickly pressed, dragging his thumb along the top of her palm as she instinctively shivered. *Was he seriously holding her hand?*

Nearly as quickly as they'd come together, the man irritably dropped her palm, running his clammy hand against the fabric of his jumpsuit as he stirred in his seat. The film lacked any type of blood and gore, and to be entirely frank, he was growing quite bored.

Frigid fingers raked through the damp curls upon his skull, tugging several stray strands from his eyes as he glanced fleetingly in the elderly guards' direction. The old man was already slumped over in his seat, obnoxious snores emerging through parted lips as his heart nearly burst from his chest at the sight.

"He's *out*." Switch pressed, thrusting a pointed finger in the sleeping guards' direction as Adelaide audibly gulped.

"Y-Yeah," she murmured, anxiously tugging at the hem of her jumpsuit as she avoided Switch's piercing gaze. "I'm going to go to the loo."

The woman nearly jumped from her seat, slithering between the tight-knit chairs as she skipped in the direction of the open double doors at the back of the rec room.

Switch raised a perplexed brow, palms flattening against his thighs as he, too, rose from the rickety metal chair, slipping from the vacant row with ease as he retraced Adelaide's steps and abandoned the particularly large room.

Directly across the hall from the rec room lay a single bathroom, dull and bland like the rest of the pitiful place as Adelaide laced her fingers around the circular handle, forcing the object sideways as she stumbled into the petite cubicle. Just as she was about to latch the door behind her, a sudden weight emerged, thrusting the door widely open as a strangled shout caught in her throat.

"*Shh*," Switch pressed, clamping a sturdy palm over her parted lips as the door clipped closed on his heel. "S'only *me*."

"What're you doing?" Adelaide rambled, fingers tugging at the bunched wrists of her shirt as Switch efficiently locked the door, blinking several times to adjust to the harsh lighting of the immensely small bathroom as he took in their surroundings.

A single, porcelain toilet cradled the left wall. Unlike their cells, the sink in this bathroom was actually built into a counter, which was dull and grey in hue, the corners chipped and cracked as the madman observed the wall directly behind it where a mirror used to lay, according to the discoloration present on the surface.

"Switch," Adelaide pressed. "I have to—"

Before the woman could finish, Switch had laced his fingers around her wrists, tugging her frail form forward with ease as their lips sloppily collided, teeth clattering upon impact as his uncuffed hands cupped her sunken cheeks. Adelaide's head instantly cleared the moment his lips met hers, eyelids slowly fluttering closed as she became immersed in all things Switch— all things *them*.

"Switch—" she gasped, releasing a petite squeak when the man managed to efficiently tug her tiny frame sideways, her lower back colliding with the low counter of the sink as his lips feverishly attacked hers. His uneven scars were rough and rugged against her swollen flesh, leaving behind pleasant burns in its wake as his lips strayed from her mouth and explored her face—peppering hot, open-mouthed kisses along her cheeks and dipping downward onto her jaw.

Everything was happening so quickly that the woman didn't even have a single moment to think. Her mind was cluttered by a profusion of him—his lips, his hands (*which were finally uncuffed and unrestrained . . .*) God—did it feel oh so *good* . . .

His palms traveled down towards her bum, physically urging her to leap up onto the counter as he aggressively bit downward onto her bottom lip, a strangled cry slipping from her mouth as he swallowed the glorious sonance with glee—assisting her frozen frame onto the sink as she rapidly rid her feet of her bothersome boots.

A sudden metallic taste filled Adelaide's senses, her eyes darting open as her fingers met the soiled flesh of her lip, digits becoming slick with fresh blood as she openly gasped at the sight.

"*Wha—?*" She perplexedly murmured, ogling the streaks of crimson that littered her skin as Switch hungrily eyed her oozing lip, his calloused thumb colliding with the sensitive skin as she outwardly gasped.

The pair sat in a strange silence for several agonizing moments, Switch's thumb intently tracing circles against Adelaide's bleeding lip as he reveled in the touch of her warm blood. *Shit*—it felt so good, and boy oh *boy* did he just want to rip her chest open and bathe in the magnificent substance . . .

Just as Adelaide was about to speak once more, the criminal applied an ample amount of pressure to her lip, a slight whine slipping off her parted mouth at the painful sensation as his wet, determined tongue replacing his thumb as he truly tasted her.

The harsh flavor was borderline overwhelming—the type that made his toes curl and the miniscule hairs on the back of his neck stand nice and tall. She tasted absolutely glorious—and Switch just couldn't get enough. He needed more. He *craved* more.

Switch's lips trailed once more from her mouth, smearing scarlet along her jaw as his nose teased her flesh, rough fingers grabbing hold of her jaw as he forced her skull backwards—just as he had the day they'd feverishly snogged in the rec room. Adelaide released a considerable number of moans and groans at the sensation of her skin tucked between his teeth, eyes rolling backwards in ecstasy as his fingers trailed lower and lower on her abdomen. Trembling digits clawed at the fabric cloaking his back, simplistic sighs oozing from her bloody lips as his fingers suddenly dipped below the waist of her trousers.

Adelaide's eyes fluttered elegantly closed, a taunt grin tugging at her chapped lips as an amusing thought immediately bombarded her mind: *Oh, Mummy would beat my ass if she found out I was screwing the infamous Switch.*

XIV

"I come take all your pain away /
Asylums of lost insane /
Want to kill your pretty face"
–W.A.S.P., "Kill Your Pretty Face"

"If they find out you're throwing up your pills, they'll start pricking you with a needle." Adelaide flatly stated, aimlessly picking at a loose fray of cement upon the damaged wall as Switch dry heaved into the metal u-bend.

The muscles beneath the pale skin of his back vigorously contracted with every harsh hack, a profusion of recently shampooed, cocoa-hued ringlets coating his lazy gaze as several slender fingers curled agonizingly tight around the bowl, knuckles flushed a ghastly white complexion. His knurled knees were beginning to fall numb from the ground, staggered gasps escaping through paling lips as his left hand detached from the bowl. Adelaide intently observed as his fingers laced around the handle, efficiently flushing the remainder of his medication as he released an exasperated sigh.

"Switch–" the woman boldly pressed, knotting her fingers through her unbrushed locks as a pair of dark, beady eyes met hers. The drastic deformity imbedded upon his sullen features appeared even more morbid than usual beneath the low glow of the nighttime lights, prompting Adelaide's stomach to involuntarily churn as she weakly admired the exhausted man.

"No *needles*," Switch thickly pressed, his voice rigorously damaged by the obscene hacks and gags that had recently emerged from the madman as he slunk back into the confinement of his measly mattress. His nearly nude form curled up beneath the paper-thin sheet, sweat glistening upon the flesh of his pale back as Adelaide bit harshly down on her bottom lip. A pair of fluorescent orange boxers loosely claimed his prominent hip bones, complimented with miscellaneous shapes along the fabric as she openly gawked at his rigid form.

"Is my *big bad boy* afraid of needles?" The woman thickly teased, her voice hoarse and deep as a heightened giggle slipped off her parted lips. Switch, however, did not seem to find the humor in her statement.

The mans hunched shoulders visibly clenched—slender digits curling into exasperated fists as he shuffled into a sitting position upon the drastically thin mattress. A quirky Adelaide still hovered over the hole, a dainty grin tugging at her features as Switch's stygian stare met hers.

"Fuck off." Switch spat, the nearly nude man's face falling into his hands as his elbows claimed his knees. His left foot expeditiously tapped against the frigid floor, something Adelaide noticed that he'd done during times of immense stress.

"Ooooh, *c'mon*, mate. Stop being such a grumpy butt—" Adelaide mockingly teased, sporadic giggles slipping off her lips as she balanced the weight of her upper half against the cement.

Every single muscle in Switch's hunched frame tightened at the hauntingly familiar statement that had bled through the lacerated wall. Adelaide's phrase had frolicked about the cold cell with simplicity, prompting Switch's heart to thump thickly in his throat as an unwanted voice bombarded his scrambled mind.

Don't be such a grumpy butt, sweetie.
Grumpy butt.
Grumpy butt.
Grumpy butt.
"Swi–"

"I said *fuck off*, Ken!" Switch raspily exclaimed, fingers lacing into the depths of his mangled curls as realization suddenly dawned upon him. *No no no no no no no–*

Adelaide observed—mouth agape—as the man gradually lifted his features from the confinement of his palms, eyes wide with worry as the woman uttered a defeated, "Ken?"

"Forget it." Switch irritably spat, tugging aimlessly at the curls atop his skull as Adelaide fell deathly silent.

Who was Ken?

"I'm sorry if–" Adelaide uneasily began, but nearly jumped straight out of her skin at Switch's sudden tone as he abruptly stood to his feet.

"Go to *sleep!*" The man exploded, fists arduously clenched at his sides as Adelaide impulsively squeaked, eyelids blinking away heavy tears as she swallowed a mouthful of bile and climbed to her feet.

Defeatedly, the woman trudged back into the depths of her rickety mattress, lanky digits curling around the messy heap of sheets as she shakily coated her frigid limbs. She could distinctly hear Switch incoherently muttering about in the opposite cell, but instead of nosily prying, the woman chose to tune him out.

Two nights ago, Switch had touched her for the very first time. The mere memory of the absolutely glorious event prompted arrays of gleeful butterflies to erupt in Adelaide's belly, a peculiar tingle present in her lady-bits as she clearly recollected the stupendous event. Although it had taken place in the unkempt rec room bathroom atop the grimy sink—the woman, quite frankly, couldn't care less. There was just something about the way he'd kissed her—the way their lips effortlessly molded together like a pair of undifferentiated puzzle pieces, crafted from the source to pair nicely together in the end result. Her and Switch weren't made for one another, that fact was absolutely certain. No—her true soulmate, her true other half would forever and always be the late Emmett James DuPré. Nobody—not even a deranged criminal with sparkling cocoa eyes and a handsome, marred smile—could ever replace her Emmett. *Never.*

Although, Switch was *quite* a lovely distraction . . .

Sporadic bolts of electricity consumed the dainty woman's spine as she thoroughly recollected the scenario, a hearty grin tugging at her lips as she envisioned a handsome and breathless Switch before her. The woman was suddenly propelled from her momentary trance at the sudden sonance of a disgruntled shout, followed by a profusion of obscenities as Switch completely fell apart in the neighboring cell.

Adelaide's pulse drastically quickened, wide eyes glancing curiously in the direction of the dark hole as her legs practically begged her to abandon the measly mattress—to crawl on all fours in the direction of the obscene opening, her fingers buzzing as they physically sobbed for the feeling of the disheveled concrete beneath him. A part of her truly wanted to drag the metal frame of her bed across the grimy ground—to repeatedly strike the concrete wall and open up the hole even further, just enough to allow her a clear passage into the opposite cell. He needed to be held, this much was evident.

However, after much internal debate and a clear continuation of Switch's audible breakdown; the woman eventually decided to ease back onto the mattress, heart thumping thickly in her throat as she buried her skull into the depths of her agonizingly thin pillow.

Within a moment's time, the woman would drift into a heavy, dreamless sleep—Whereas the irritable and restless Switch would spend the remaining hours of the night pacing the confined space of his cubicle, muttering ineptly beneath his breath as the daunting features of Kennedy Carter raided his mind.

"Any concerns?" Nurse Briar inquired, tugging a bothersome strand of blond from her eyes as she monotonically instructed Switch to disrobe. The dainty woman currently wore an interesting ensemble of scrubs today; the pale pink fabric was coated with sloppily etched drawings of cartoon characters such as Winnie the Pooh and Scooby-Doo. To an outsider, the woman appeared as if she worked in pediatrics, not a hospital for the criminally insane.

"Yeah, actually," Switch lazily enunciated, thumbs hooking around the elastic waist of his jumpsuit as the material slid down the length of his legs, bunching up at his boot-clad ankles as his fingers met his flaccid extremities.

Briar raised a curious brow, clammy hands sliding into a pair of crème-hued latex gloves as she cautiously eyed the flesh held in his grasp.

"I've got a weird blemish *riiiiight* here," he said, pointer finger hovering over a specific portion of his shaft as the nurse hesitantly fell to her knees before him, clothed knee unintentionally colliding with the toe of his boot as she winced.

Her greedy touch promptly replaced his, staggered exhales escaping her partially parted lips as the madman failed to remove his touch entirely. Briar's pulse drastically accelerated as his warm palms cupped hers, a deep, raspy groan emerging from the man above her as she inspected the apparent "blemish" present on his privates.

"I-I don't see anything out of the ordinary. If anything, it looks like a birth mark–" Briar thickly stammered, gliding the pad of her gloved thumb along him. Her azure gaze inspected the skin, a considerable gulp easing down the length of her throat as she attempted to pry her simplistic touch away, but to no avail.

"Switch–" Nurse Briar skeptically warned, brows raising as she assertively yanked out of his grasp, heart racing beneath her ribcage as she took several considerably lengthy steps backwards and away from the tempestuous man.

"Oh *c'mon*, baby Briiiiar," he teased, scarred expression stretching up the length of his scarlet cheeks as his eyelid flickered closed, delivering a sultry wink in her direction. "It's *all right.*"

"Did you behave yourself the other night?" Nurse Briar switched the subject, tugging the gloves off of her immensely sweaty palms as she discarded them into a nearby waste bin. The woman deftly rotated on her heel, gaze diverting to Switch's printed files upon the nearby counter as a pair of greedy palms suddenly met her hips.

A heightened gasp slipped off Briar's ajar lips, eyes significantly widening as her palms uneasily met the surface of the royal blue counter, her prominent hip bones achingly colliding with the edge of the oblong surface as Switch's nose wedged into the crook of her exposed neck. Her breaths were heavy and erratic, chest arduously heaving as the man flattened his entire frame against her backside, hot, breathy chuckles littering her flesh as patches of prickly goosebumps rapidly arose.

"I was a *baaad* boy, Briar." Switch drawled, his dark tone generating a series of violent spasms to emerge throughout Briar's trapped frame as she began to profusely shake. She absolutely *hated* herself for it, but she just couldn't stop dreaming of the calamitous criminal whose face was partially and permanently disfigured.

"Did you have sex with Adelaide?" Nurse Briar thickly questioned, her heart drastically sinking at the thought of a cheery Adelaide seated in the corner of the rec room, her oily nose buried in the depths of her novel as she patiently awaited the return of her darling beau.

"*Mmm,*" Switch hummed, transferring his weight from either foot as he intentionally flattened himself against Briar's backside, which elicited a violent shiver from the petite woman as he widely grinned. "That's-*uh*, none'a your *business*, sweetheart. That stays between Adelaide and I. *How-ev-er. . .*"

"Switch—" Briar pressed, but the madman refused to let her intervene.

"What happens between *us*," he purred, digging his fingers against her sore hips as she impulsively squirmed. "Now *that's* a different story, lovebug."

"That shouldn't have happened last month." Briar stated as a matter-of-fact, her neck craning to view the manipulative man as her nose unintentionally brushed against his. Her blurred vision dipped downward, hastily colliding with his rosy-red lips as she openly admired the deep lacerations present upon his handsome features.

"Tell me about them." She boldly spoke, palm detaching from the safety of the counter as her fingertips inched upwards, extended nails just barely grazing the mutilated skin as Switch's fingers latched tightly around her wrist, tugging her curious palm away as a painful yelp emerged from the woman.

"Slow *down*, princess." Switch lightly scolded, several stray ringlets tickling the skin of Briar's forehead as he buried his nose against the back of her jaw. "Those are *off limits.*"

Briar released a husky exhale. Simultaneously, Switch slightly released his death grip on her bony wrist, her fearful eyes focused on his touch. Curiously, she found herself studying the tattooed set of lines permanently embedded into the flesh of his left wrist. She'd never questioned the tattoos that littered his arms—in fact, she hadn't even noticed them until now.

"Please let go of me, Switch." Nurse Briar shyly pressed, tugging her hand from his weakened fingers as she attempted to wriggle out of his constricting hold.

"Your mouth says one thing, but your body says *another*, toots." He giddily mused, lips just barely grazing her ear as she openly shuddered.

"I can't say you aren't convincing," Nurse Briar awkwardly murmured, craning her neck to view the man once again as he laced his arms loosely around her torso. "But I love and respect Addy. I see how she looks at you."

With that, the woman managed to effectively pull away from Switch's slightly comforting embrace, heart still thickly thumping in her throat as she aimlessly tugged at her bottom lip with two fingers.

Switch hastily tugged his trousers back up as he raised a curious brow. Brunette tinted overgrown curls elegantly framed his sullen features, several stray strands tickling the flesh of his flushed cheeks. A pair of comforting chocolate-colored orbs appeared to somewhat glimmer beneath the harsh fluorescent lighting of the tiny room, scarred bottom lip tucked between rows of yellowing teeth as Nurse Briar anxiously twiddled her thumbs.

"What are your intentions with her?" The woman pressed, snapping the manila folder filled with his paperwork tightly shut as he eyed her skeptically.

"What'cha *mean?*" Switch murmured, side-stepping towards the examination table as he stood on his tippy-toes, a shirt still absent as his bottom collided with the crinkled paper upon the surface. The theatrical man sat incredibly slouched, the flesh of his stomach curling into a profusion of rolls as Briar nearly giggled at the sight. It was quite easy to forget that the Switch was—in fact—human.

"I *mean*," she sternly pressed, pacing the petite room. Switch keenly watched as she snatched the pair of handcuffs from the metal hook adjacent to the sealed door. "What are your plans? Are you just using her for sex? Because she doesn't deserve that, Switch. She's a nice girl who likes you–"

"*Likes* me?" Switch scoffed, lips transforming into a scowl as he shifted his weight against the table, prompting the measly paper to audibly tear beneath his wiggling form. "Don't even *pretend* to know what she's thinking."

"I don't need to pretend," Briar countered, her tone gradually darkening as her eyes contorted into slits. "I know Addy. I've never seen her this way. Hell—she's *speaking*, Switch! You don't know how–how *monumental* this is! And because of *you*!"

"She doesn't know anything about me." He murmured, awkwardly picking at the spare skin surrounding his nails as Briar's palms claimed her bruising hips. The woman swore that she could still feel his firm touch upon her clothed skin.

"Maybe it's best if she never learns. Try to control yourself for the time being. I know how—*violent*—you can be."

At this, Switch's glare instantaneously darkened, his twitching scars tugging into a devilish half-smirk as he audibly smacked his lips. Nurse Briar swayed from side to side, an extreme discomfort pooling in her belly as she observed the overly-confident man, his palms meeting the frail paper upon the examination table as his head rolled sideways on his neck, left ear just barely grazing the smooth skin of his shoulder.

"*Oh*," he lazily slurred, intently wetting his marred lips as Nurse Briar swallowed a mouthful of bile. "You seem to have me *allll* figured out, don't cha, *baby*?"

"Knock it off with this cocky façade. You're not fooling me." Briar snipped, rapidly approaching the incredibly lax man as she looped her manicured fingers between the grooves of the harsh metal cuffs.

"Hey, hey, *beeey*," Switch thickly teased, wildly smirking at Briar's astonishingly close proximity as her fingers threaded around the discarded fabric of his jumpsuit top. "Somebody grew some *big balls*."

"Bigger than yours," Briar unprofessionally muttered, thrusting the black and white striped material into Switch's hasty clutch. "Dress, so I can cuff you."

"You seem to *forget* who's in charge, pumpkin." Switch dramatically oozed, tossing the top aside as Briar's lips parted in protest. However, the artificially blond woman hadn't even had the time to utter a single sound.

Switch's arm curled around her backside, fingers clamping down on a significant chunk of her recently washed locks as he maneuvered his broad frame from the table, opposite palm applying an ample amount of pressure to Briar's lower back as he forced her weakened frame forwards. The woman's pointy nose plaintively collided with the stiff surface of the table, an immediate grunt of discomfort slipping through parted lips as the cuffs slipped from her grasp.

Switch's palm detached from her back, fingers lacing around the discarded cuffs as he tore them from the surface of the table, insistent giggles slipping off his tainted lips as his hold on Briar's hair significantly tightened, emitting a vexatious cry to emerge from the woman beneath his hold.

Briar's breaths emerged in strangled pants, the hot exhales ricocheting from the surface of the table and coating her flushed features as several beads of sweat consumed her upper brow. Switch's hold on her hair was unbelievably tight, and the woman was almost certain that he'd managed to tear a hearty chunk directly from her skull.

"P-Please l-let me g-go!" Briar obscenely sobbed, voice somewhat muffled by the obstruction of the table as Switch flattened his broad frame against her squirming self, a profusion of heightened giggles filling her ears as her life began to meticulously flash before her eyes.

"You're *weak*, Briar." Switch huskily drawled, toying with the metal set of cuffs as he precisely held her squirming face against the harsh surface. "You *loooved* having your way with me, didn't you? Oh, how *riveting* it must be to taste a wanted criminal, *hmm*? Say, what would your *mommy* say if she knew about your little fantasies? Or is your mommy a desperate little *whore* like yourself—"

"Piss off!" Briar shrieked, arms bending at an incredibly awkward angle as she attempted to pry Switch's hold off of her. However, the madman merely laughed, fingernails digging into her scalp as she sobbed beneath him.

"With a mouth like that, you should-*uh*, be re-*strained*." Switch obscenely purred, precisely capturing her wrists with a single wide hand as his hold refused to let up from her hair. He'd managed to yank her arms upward, emitting painful cries from the woman as he twisted and bent her arms at horrifically gruesome angles, slender digits latching the cuffs around her bony wrists as a series of incoherent murmurs emerged from his amused grin.

After several moments of zero reply from the rigid woman, Switch heartily continued his playful banter. "Whassa *matter*, dollface? Was this not one'a your fantasies? Don't be shy now, pumpkin. S'only *me*."

"You're a monster." Briar lowly spat, weakened form going slack beneath Switch's profusely giggling frame as his nose suddenly flattened against her soaked cheek.

"Monsters live under your bed and inside your head, toots. I'm not a monster. *However*," he confidently purred, his breath hot against her flushed cheek as she openly grimaced. "I'm your worst *nightmare*, baby."

Nurse Briar did not reply. Instead, she tightly squeezed her eyelids shut, inaudible murmurs slipping off her lips as she begged and prayed for him to just get this over with.

"Just do it." She defeatedly whispered, crumbling beneath Switch's gleeful embrace as the tip of his tongue intently traced the deepest grooves of his scar.

"Do *what*?" He thickly urged, daintily massaging her scalp in a mocking manner as she gingerly yanked at the confinement of the metal cuffs.

"If you're going to kill me, just do it." Briar exclaimed, an extreme wave of nausea overcoming her as Switch tossed his head back, audibly releasing a round of exuberant laughter—the very type that immediately prompted patches of goosebumps to raid the exposed flesh of Briar's arms.

"*Wha-ha-ha*! Nurse Briar! Oh, what a *statement*!" Switch sarcastically giggled, continually shifting his weight from either foot as his fingers threaded between her oily locks, his grasp roughly tugging her skull sideways so that they could make firm eye contact.

"Look at me, toots." Switch grumbled, rotating her skull further as an immediate wince overcame Briar's distressed features. Her painted eyelids darted open, displaying a pair of red-rimmed, cobalt orbs.

"I don't wanna kill you! Oh, no no *no*! God, with a mouth like *that*, Lord have *mercy*–I could never! I think I'll actually keep you around for a bit." Switch spat through a profusion of giggles, his hold letting up on her greasy strands as Briar hesitantly lifted her skull from the flat surface. The madman's hips, however, were still firmly pressed against her backside, isolating her tiny frame between himself and the examination table.

"Please just let me go," Briar pitifully sobbed, lifting her moist cheek from the sticky surface of the softened paper as she glanced warily in his direction. "Please, Switch. I'll do anything–"

"*Ohoho!*" The criminal boasted, a single palm claiming her scarlet-tinted cheek as he rid the fallen tears from her flesh with the pad of his thumb. "Go *oooon.*"

Nurse Briar fell somewhat lax beneath his sudden soft hold, widened eyes scanning his conflicting features as she truly admired his marred complexion. The laceration etched upon the majority of his left cheek was deep and vastly complex, cutting partially into the corner of his equally marred mouth. It was as if someone—quite possibly himself—had carved the skin with a sloppily sharpened knife, paying absolutely no mind to the details of the bold cuts as they etched a crooked, half-frown onto Switch's features. The woman tried to imagine the madman without the hideous deformities, but she found it quite difficult to do so. However, if she already found him quite handsome already, she could only imagine how utterly gorgeous he was beneath the severed skin of his left cheek . . .

"D-Do you want me t-to do it again?" Briar weakly spoke, a slight hiccup present in her tone as she blatantly glanced downward in the direction of Switch's concealed privates.

A menacing grin overcame the man's lips at her query, irises drastically darkening as he choked back several sarcastic giggles.

"No *need*, princess." He spoke. "How 'bout we just not speak of this little *sce-nar-i-o*, hm?"

"Deal." Nurse Briar countered, tugging against her metal restraints once more as she visibly pouted. "Please uncuff me."

"Where're the *keys*?" Switch flatly grumbled, taking a single step backwards to allow the blond woman substantial freedom. Her prominent hip bones achingly throbbed from the edge of the table as her head fleetingly swam, lips parting in angst as she struggled to recall the location of the dainty silver key.

"Shit," Briar murmured, brows worriedly raising as she became thoroughly aware of the keys lodged deeply within her front pant pocket. "They're in my front right pocket."

Switch's expression instantaneously brightened, a cheeky smirk enveloping his features as he took his bottom lip between his teeth. "Oh?"

"Just get it for me, will you? I can't with these cuffs on." Nurse Briar spat, yanking at the harsh metal. The flesh upon her wrists flushed a bright scarlet in extreme irritation.

Switch happily obliged, approaching the woman with a slight skip in his step as her eyes inexplicably scanned the abundance of cicatrices that littered the flesh of his chest. Nurse Briar's breaths markedly thinned as his broad chest met her quivering form, a distinct, wanton glare present in her curious orbs as the tip of his nose grazed hers.

"Mmm," Switch lustfully purred, his features dipping down to meet the supple skin of her neck as the beaten flesh of his face just barely scraped the sensitive skin. Several stray curls tickled her collarbones, petite whines slipping through Briar's cracked lips as the man's hand suddenly invaded the pocket of her scrubs. "You *smell* good."

"T-Thanks?" Briar shortly stammered, eyelids squeezing tightly shut as the raised flesh of his face agonizingly teased her neck. Curious digits sank further into the fabric of her theatrical trousers, digging deeply in search of the petite pair of keys. The warmth of his fingers against the shy fabric coating her thighs sent arrays of shivers down Briar's spine, her breaths dramatically thinning as the pad of his thumb eventually hovered over the tiny silver object.

"*Bingo.*"

Switch tore his hunched frame from hers, miniscule keys held tightly in his clutch.

How was it possible that such a violent and careless man could be so damn attractive?

Inaudibly, the madman unlatched Briar's restricted wrists, claiming the metal cuffs in his grasp as he turned the circular objects over in his palms. The blond woman immediately sighed at the sudden release, fingers daintily curling around the angry flesh of her wrists as she vigorously rubbed.

"Thanks, I suppose." Briar murmured. "Finish getting dressed so I can take you back to the rec room."

"Dr. Blake?" Nurse Briar uneasily called, the tone of her voice drastically shifting as a pair of beady, dark eyes rapidly collided with hers.

Lyra Blake jabbed a single thumb against the center of her periwinkle glasses, slipping the spectacles back up the slope of her greasy, crooked nose as she murmured a simplistic, "yes?"

"I'd–uh," Briar stammered, stepping further into the dingy office where the wretched woman spent her free time. "Like to discuss the Switch's medications."

A hefty manila folder tumbled from Dr. Blake's clutch, colliding with the sloppily stained wood of the old oak desk as she raised a considerable brow. "He hasn't been taking them, has he?"

"No." Briar lied, fidgety fingers toying with the hem of her scrubs as she avoided eye contact with the middle-aged woman.

"Ugh," Dr. Blake irritably sighed, slowly rising from her jet-black swivel chair as she adjusted the nape of her top. "Get the syringes, I'll get Vern. We'll need some muscles to help sedate him."

"How'd your physical go today?" Adelaide curiously pried, fingers laced through Switch's disheveled curls. The amused woman found joy in playing with his overgrown hair—a distinct smile overcoming her features as she threaded her index finger through a particularly loopy strand.

Switch's back lay flat against the frigid concrete wall, sat directly beneath the gaping hole present between his and Adelaide's lonely cells as the shy woman massaged his scalp with her fingers.

"All right," he gruffly dismissed, lazy gaze settling upon a sudden sonance present in the cell block. The blinding fluorescent lights were still brightly blazing, a persistent buzzing present throughout the premises as the steel mahogany door of his cell unexpectedly opened.

Dr. Blake, Nurse Briar, and some guard named Vern quietly strut into the confined space, Blake's magnified stare hardening at the sight of Adelaide's fingers in Switch's hair.

"Get up," the woman thickly ordered. "It's time for your medication."

Adelaide tugged her arm back into the depths of her assigned space, eyes significantly widening at the sight of a rigid Dr. Blake as her pulse immediately quickened. She immediately knew that something wasn't right.

"What's with the-*uh, audience?*" Switch dryly chuckled, obediently rising to his feet as the left sleeve of his sloppily rolled jumpsuit suddenly slipped beyond the extended skin of his elbow.

"I warned you about this, 4428. Unfortunately, I have no choice. Lay down and let us administer the medication through a syringe, please. I don't want to have to sedate you." Dr. Blake monotonically explained, manicured fingers concealed by a pair of thick, latex gloves as she clutched several filled syringes.

"No *fucking* needles. I'll take the pills." Switch grumbled, brows knit together in uncertainty. He flashed Briar a skeptical glare.

"No can do, 4428. Pills aren't working for you. Lay down, please." Dr. Blake sternly instructed, wordlessly demanding Vern to grab hold of Switch.

"Fuck *off*–" Switch spat, arm dramatically yanking from Vern's greedy fingers as Nurse Briar's bottom lip sheepishly trembled.

"Relax, Switch–" Vern stated, threading his fingers around Switch's biceps once more as he attempted to keep the man still. However, Switch thoroughly refused to comply.

The curly-haired man effectively spun around on his heel, curling his sturdy digits into a firm fist as he delivered a confident punch directly to Vern's nose.

The distressed guard released an exasperated yelp, palm instantly cupping his broken nose as a profusion of thick, scarlet liquid rapidly oozed from his flared nostrils.

"Switch!" Dr. Blake exclaimed, shoving several of the needles into Briar's unwelcome grasp as the Switch delivered an additional punch to a weakened Vern, which managed to knock the guard flat on his ass. Vern audibly shrieked as Switch continued to aggressively strike him, an abundance of obscenities slipping through the madman's scarred lips as Vern lay in a bleeding heap upon the frigid floor.

"*Do you know who you're dealing with?*" Switch darkly spat, his tone low and hoarse as he threatened to punch a wary Vern one last time. "*Huh! Do yah!*"

Dr. Blake swiftly approached the madman, fingers curling tightly around the filled syringe within her grasp as she confidently plunged the needle into the softest flesh of Switch's veiny neck, a strangled yelp slipping off her lips as she injected the furious man with the mysterious liquid.

Switch's palm slapped against his throbbing neck, forehead immensely crinkling in bewilderment as his head begun to expeditiously spin.

"Wha'didya *do*–" the theatrical man slurred, eyes rolling to the back of his skull as his lanky frame collapsed into a messy heap upon the floor.

Adelaide choked back a verbal cry, blinding tears concealing her vision as she clearly witnessed the entire scene. It almost appeared as if it were happening in slow motion—several guards entered the premises, assisting a bleeding Vern from the area as the thick-necked guard with a toothpick lodged between his teeth hurled a limp Switch over his broad shoulder.

"Toss the bitch in max for two weeks. Trash."

XV

before

Thick beads of sweat consumed Kennedy Carter's forehead, nuzzling deeply within the thick hairs of her naturally dark brows as she insistently picked at the skin surrounding her nails. She continually swallowed mouthfuls of bile, left foot expeditiously tapping against the freshly swept wooden floor as she glanced warily in the direction of the front door.

Time ticked idly by, the woman's pulse heavily thumping beneath her ribcage as a pair of slender digits irritably yanked at the fallen strap of her spaghetti strap tank top, which had managed to slip down the slope of her creased shoulder. It wasn't necessarily warm inside the dingy apartment, but the woman couldn't help but feel immensely hot, her palms excessively sweating as she intently eyed a nearby syringe discarded atop the rotting wooden coffee table several feet away.

The measly table was vastly deteriorated, littered with an abundance of empty, multi-hued beer bottles and abandoned needles, as well as several half-full packs of Camel brand cigarettes. The air smelled musty and of apples and cinnamon, courtesy of the inexpensive candle burning in the miniscule kitchen as the vibrant orange flame painted exuberant pictures along the unpigmented walls.

She'd been meaning to splash a bit of color onto the bland walls, but truth be told, she could hardly find the time or the energy to do so. When she wasn't working agonizingly long shifts at the grimy gas station on the corner of Walnut Street, she spent a majority of her time laid upon the couch, a used needle threaded between her fingers as she drifted into artificial euphoria.

They'd lived in Midtown Chicago for nearly a year, residing in a particularly small apartment complex with vastly poor ventilation and cheap hardwood floors.

"Shit," Kennedy grumbled, her sullen features collapsing into her moist palms as she released a strangled sigh. "Where *are* you?"

An additional half-hour passed by exceedingly slow, prompting the woman to climb from her jittery position as she anxiously paced the floor, the too-long sleeves of her bright white pajama pants scraping diligently along the wood. The worrisome woman jabbed a distressed thumb nail into the depths of her mouth, chewing mindlessly on the severed skin as she consistently glanced in the direction of several discarded needles.

A vast sensation of discomfort suddenly arose in her belly, the extreme urge to profusely vomit overriding her senses as the olive-tinted front door clicked open, revealing a droopy-eyed man with a messy mop of deep, brunette curls.

Kennedy's heart sank at the sight of him, thin lips tugged into a distressed frown as she rapidly approached the slouched man in the doorway, his cocoa-hued gaze illuminating at the sight of her.

"Hey," he thickly croaked, pink plump lips curling into a toothy grin as the door snapped shut on his heel, his navy Chuck Taylors sloppily unlaced as he promptly rid his feet of his aging sneakers.

"Where the hell have you been?" Kennedy boorishly exclaimed, arms tightly crossed across her dainty chest as she eyed a suddenly rigid man standing before her. An oversized, muted grey sweater claimed his upper half, the slender sleeves bunched around his wrists as he insistently tugged them upwards and away from his fingers. A pair of bland, black slacks cloaked his legs, hugging his bum nicely as he strolled into the dingy apartment that smelled somewhat nice.

"Got caught up," he lazily replied, avoiding Kennedy's glare as he approached the abandoned sofa, left wrist raising to his sullen complexion as he ran the sleeve along his nostrils, ridding them of the abundance of oozing snot as it transferred onto the thick fabric. It was mid-January in Chicago, and he'd managed to come down with the sniffles as a result of the harsh weather outside.

"You shot up with Jimmy, didn't you?" Kennedy thickly scolded, furious trembles overcoming her spine as her arm rapidly extended, fingers curling around the fabric of his top as she yanked him backwards. "Look at me, Drew!"

"Fuck!" He raspily exclaimed, tossing his hands up in defeat as he spun around on his heel to view the aggravated woman before him. "Why're you bombarding me, Ken? What's your problem?"

Kennedy's brows knit tightly together, jaw parting in angst as she glared menacingly in her significantly younger husband's direction. Several stray strands of curly brown hair temporarily concealed his red-rimmed eyes, his eyelids drooping as he heavily blinked. He was high as a *kite*.

"Holy hell, Andrew!" Kennedy pressed, palm claiming Andrew's flushed features as she positioned a single finger above his brow and one beneath his eye, yanking the skin apart as she pried it open. "How big of a hit did you take?"

Andrew hastily slapped her greedy palm away from his face, an incoherent strand of mumbles slipping off his lips as he collapsed into an irritated heap upon the living room couch.

"You promised you wouldn't do this shit without me, Drew. What if Jimmy gives you too much? He's irresponsible—"

"I'm a grown ass man, Ken." Andrew bitterly snipped, collapsing against the back cushion as he hastily brushed several loose curls from his eyes. "I can take care of myself."

"You're only twenty-two, Andrew!" Kennedy countered, diligently pacing the petite space as she ran an anxious set of hands through her oily locks. "You're—*hell*—you're only still a child! At least in comparison to my twenty-eight-year-old self—"

"Does this conversation have a *point?*" Andrew snidely snipped, toying with the bunched sleeves of his sweater as he assertively tore the left sleeve upward, revealing a freshly tattooed set of lines upon the skin. The ink was only aged a solid fourteen days, and sometimes, he forgot he even had it.

"The *point*—" Kennedy spat, the soles of her bare feet skidding along the floor as she came to an abrupt halt before his lax frame. "—is that I've been living this lifestyle for ten years, Drew, whereas you've only scraped the surface of being a junkie. What's it been for you, a year? It was around our year of marriage anniversary when you finally succumbed to my nasty habit, wasn't it?"

"Don't do this, Ken." Andrew grumbled, eyelids heavily squinting as he threaded several fingers through his messy locks. "I'm tired, can we talk after I nap?"

"Shit," Kennedy weakly cried, palms colliding with her flushed features as she dug her palm into the depths of her pajama pant pocket, retrieving a foreign object from the material as she confidently tossed it into Andrew's empty lap.

Andrew curiously glanced downward, brows slightly raising as his fingers curled around the white and pink colored stick upon his lap. His jaw fell incredibly lax at the sight of the peculiar object, tongue darting outward to wet his dry lips. He spat out a vexed, "the fuck is this?"

"There's four more in the bathroom," Kennedy uneasily replied, arms tightly cradling her stomach as she diligently paced the floor, worrisome gaze colliding with a timid Andrew upon the sofa. The man turned the test over in his hands, eyes significantly widening at the sight of a distinct set of lines within the circular window of the stick.

"W-What does this—" he croaked, blinking several times to ensure that he was—in fact—*not* imagining the positive pregnancy test held within his weak hold.

"I'm pregnant," Kennedy weakly murmured, blinking back an array of tears as she hastily swallowed an additional mouthful of bile. "I have no clue how, but I am. I haven't had my period in years because my body is so screwed up from this hell I've been living in for so long. I honestly thought I was infertile—"

"You're pregnant," Andrew breathed, a blank expression plastered upon his features as he sat upwards on the sofa, elbows claiming his knees as he held the test tightly in his clutch. "We're having a baby . . ."

"No," Kennedy countered. "We're not. I have to get rid of it, Andrew. I've already made an appointment for tomorrow morning."

"*What?*" Andrew exclaimed, immediately climbing to his feet as the test toppled to the floor, colliding with the wood with a light *smack*. "Why the hell—"

"Do you want a baby that's born addicted to heroin, Andrew?" Kennedy immediately countered, steady streams of tears coating her scarlet-tinted cheeks as her fingers anxiously tore at the hem of her top. "A junkie baby?"

"Ken," Andrew pressed, cautiously approaching the distressed woman as he laced his fingers around her dainty biceps, softened orbs boring deeply into her blackened gaze. "That's not going to happen. If we just stop using–"

"*Stop using?*" Kennedy exploded, tearing her trembling arms from Andrew's comforting hold as she aimlessly yanked at her artificially auburn locks. "Andrew, I've been using for an entire decade. I can't just *stop*–"

"You *can*," Andrew pressed, tugging Kennedy's sobbing frame into the warmth of his chest as he held her close. "*We* can. We're going to do this for us—for our baby."

"A-Andrew," Kennedy profusely sobbed, her tone slightly muffled by the fabric of Andrew's top as she fisted the material between her palms. "We're barely making ends meet as it is. You haven't been able to hold a job since you dropped out of med school."

"Dollface," Andrew purred, lacing his fingers between her darkly dyed locks as he gently massaged her scalp. "We can make this work. It'll be hell for a little bit, but we can do it. I'll get back into the medical field once I'm healthy again—I'll find some minimum wage job and we'll make things *work*."

Kennedy openly cried into Andrew's shirt, words ultimately failing her as the man craned his neck, creating an illusion of several additional chins as his lips peppered reassuring kisses to the top of her hair.

"Shh," he cooed, chest harshly aching as realization ultimately struck: *What had his life come to?* "It's going to be okay, pumpkin. We'll get through this *together*."

"W-What have I d-done?" Kennedy hiccupped through an exuberant series of sobs, soaking the warm fabric of Andrew's sweater as she hastily pulled her clammy cheek away, glistening orbs colliding with his worried gaze.

"What d'you *mean*, toots?" He lightly purred, palms meeting her sunken cheeks as he rigorously rid her skin of the fallen tears with the calloused pads of his thumbs.

"I've *ruined* you," Kennedy whined, admiring Andrew's incredibly handsome physique as his lips tugged into a thin frown. "What happened to that perfect, eighteen-year-old boy? The one just starting medical school and striving towards becoming a licensed physician? You were so bright and lively and happy and healthy. Drew—I've destroyed you. You can't go more than nine hours without a hit, otherwise you'll get all antsy and fidgety and anxious. I've drug you into this dark, endless pit and it isn't fair–"

"Ken," Andrew firmly pressed, palms cupping her cheeks as he forcefully yanked her skull upwards, wordlessly instructing her to look him in the eye. "It was *my choice.* I knew exactly what I was getting into when I married the twenty-six-year-old junkie from South Side. I might've been a young, naïve twenty-year-old at the time, but *trust* me, I *knew* what I was doing, princess. I don't regret a single thing."

"I should've never given you that needle. I should've never allowed this to happen." Kennedy cried, chewing arduously on her bottom lip as she suddenly drew blood. The metallic flavor instantly filled her senses, prompting an immediate scoff to overcome her features as Andrew's eyes significantly widened.

"Sweet heart," Drew lowly muttered, the pad of his thumb colliding with her swollen lip as her warm blood instantly coated his flesh. A violent, pleasurable shudder overcame his every nerve, mouth running impossibly dry as he smeared the scarlet liquid along her cracked skin.

"M'fine." Kennedy uneasily dismissed, shoving his desperate touch away from her bleeding lip as she tugged the skin between her teeth, concealing the oozing liquid from his sight. He'd always had a rather odd fascination with the bold liquid, she'd noticed.

"I *promise*," Andrew dryly explained, vision refocusing on Kennedy's strained features as he shifted his weight from either foot. "We're going to do it this time. Really do it. It'll be *so* worth it, pumpkin."

"I l-love you, Drew." The woman defeatedly murmured, fingers prancing along his aching digits as a hearty, tight-lipped grin tugged at his features, the skin of his face elegantly folding as a clear, distinct set of smile lines appeared. Andrew Carter, by far, had the broadest and brightest smile Kennedy had ever seen.

"I love you too, dollface. *C'mere*," he urged, tugging the frail woman forward as he strolled in the direction of the worn sofa several feet away. Kennedy happily obliged, latching her fingers into the material of his top as he collapsed into a heap against the arm of the sofa, lanky limbs laying lax against the surface as a pair of warm, cocoa-hued orbs settled upon the discarded cigarette pack on the nearby coffee table.

"Cigar-*ette*," he lazily rasped, thrusting a single index finger in the direction of the measly pack as Kennedy warily rolled her eyes, chewed fingernails lacing around the soft paper pack as she tossed it onto Andrew's limp lap.

Kennedy settled between Andrew's partially parted legs, her cheek colliding with his steadily rising chest as she nuzzled into the moist material of his sweater, meticulously chewed fingernails tugging at the surface as his broad frame shifted beneath her.

"Lay still," she lowly scolded, burying her nose in his warm sweater as Andrew's hand thrust deeply into the constricted pocket of his trousers, desperate fingers digging around for a dainty lighter as a single, unlit cigarette lay lodged between his lips.

"Sorry *toots*," Andrew sighed, his husky tone significantly muffled by the obstruction between his lips as he finally retrieved a vibrant yellow lighter. Kennedy's pointed chin met the hardened surface of his chest, curious gaze settling upon the father of her unborn child as he meticulously brought the lighter to his lips. She intently observed as he precisely rotated the cancer stick with the simple wiggle of his full lips, teeth softly clamping down on the object in order to truly solidify its presence as his thumb applied an ample amount of pressure to the lighter, igniting a bold, fluorescent flame.

The woman drifted into a temporary trance, completely enthralled by the man's simplistic actions as he lit the cigarette with ease, beautiful eyes solely fixated on the blazing flame of the lighter as he effectively extinguished the light. He dismissively tossed the unwanted object onto the nearby table once he was finished, a steady strand of smoke emerging from his flared nostrils as his stare refocused on a nosy Kennedy laid upon his chest.

"What?" He rasped, a cheeky smirk tugging at his features as his chin met his chest, creating the illusion of multiple chins as Kennedy openly giggled at the sight, curious touch meeting Andrew's lips as she tore the lit cigarette from his mouth.

Simply put, the man looked utterly exhausted. Ever since he began using, his general appearance had vastly deteriorated, leaving him a greasy, tired mess nearly ninety-percent of the time. His eyelids were always droopy, threatening to permanently seal shut with every slow blink as his vision struggled to clearly focus on the woman before him. Kennedy had gone through a similar phase when she'd just started using as well, but at this point—an entire decade in—the one thing that surprisingly kept her normal was the heroin. Without it, however, she precisely mirrored Andrew's exact physique—exhausted, sickly; almost like a walking skeleton.

Kennedy rotated the lit cancer stick between her grasp, Andrew's lazy gaze solely glued upon her peculiar stance as she eventually eased the object between her chapped lips, eyelids elegantly fluttering closed as she deeply inhaled the warm nicotine into her lungs.

"Ken," Andrew softly cooed, fingers lacing between the frayed strands of her messy mop of greasy hair as he tugged several pieces away from her flushed face. "You'll have to quit that, *too*."

"Don't remind me," the woman grumbled, tearing the cigarette from her lips as she released a hefty puff of smoke, eyes rotating to the back of her skull in euphoria as she thrusted the object back into Andrew's desperate grasp. "I think I'll have to take some vacation time off work when we decide to do this."

"Whatever you need, princess." Andrew muttered, burying the lit object back into the depths of his mouth as he deeply inhaled. The beautiful set of cocoa orbs suddenly disappeared, masked by a heavy set of lids as Kennedy inched upwards, shy lips peppering feather-like kisses along the prominent bone of Andrew's jaw as he physically stirred beneath her warm touch.

"M'sorry I went behind your *back*," Andrew rasped, hips involuntarily bucking upwards the moment Kennedy latched her mouth onto his particularly sweet spot along the back of his jaw. The cigarette clung loosely to his fingers, arm outstretched sideways and off of the sofa as Kennedy's fingers threaded through his oily curls.

"Won't—happen—*again* . . ." he heavily slurred, writhing beneath Kennedy's fierce form as she aggressively attacked his neck with her lips, tugging a considerable amount of flesh between her teeth as she harshly bit down.

"You're forgiven." She mused, blind fingers latching around the lit cigarette as she blatantly tore it from his weakened grasp, detaching her lips momentarily as she rotated her body towards the coffee table, allowing her electrified frame to properly extinguish the lit flame against the wooden table.

"Ken—" Andrew groaned, eyes still tightly sealed as his hands desperately wandered, slender digits curling around her petite biceps as he forcefully yanked her tiny frame back down to his. "Come *back*."

"I'm not going anywhere, love." Kennedy profusely giggled, flattening her lax frame along his as their lips met in a rushed kiss—hot, nicotine flavored breaths dancing along their tongues as Andrew tightly laced his fingers in her hair, tugging her skull forward as their noses arduously flattened against one another's cheeks.

"We're really gonna do this," Kennedy murmured, the words elegantly slipping into Andrew's parted lips as he simply grunted in reply, lanky legs tangling with hers as his left palm claimed the center of her lower back, assertively applying a vast amount of pressure as he forced her hips downward against his.

"Mmm," Andrew hummed, claiming Kennedy's bottom lip between his teeth as he cautiously chewed. "I'm gonna be a daddy."

Kennedy widely grinned, the pad of her thumb intently tracing the smooth features of his face as she swiped her touch along his swollen bottom lip. "You're going to be an amazing father, Drew."

Andrew's eyelids fluttered open, blurred gaze focusing on Kennedy's conflicted features as he softly caressed the extended bone of her cheek. "I love you, Ken. We're really doing it this time."

Her forehead collided with his, dry lips placing a soft kiss to the tip of his nose as she inhaled his glorious, musky scent—a lovely mixture of cologne, nicotine, and cigarette smoke.

"Yeah, we are. I love you too, grumpy butt." She giggled, placing an array of firm kisses along his neck as he impatiently squirmed beneath her torturous touch. His skull jutted backwards, lips parted in tranquility as staggered pants slipped sloppily through, the simplistic sonance prompting patches of goosebumps to arise on Kennedy's exposed flesh as she tore open the button on his slacks.

"Forever and a day."

XVI

Adelaide insistently picked at the frayed concrete of the severed wall, her outgrown fingernails yanking at the material as she picked at the sloppily constructed hole.

Her lazy, hazel gaze momentarily flickered in the direction of the vacant bed in the neighboring cell, the unpigmented sheets precisely folded at the foot of the measly mattress. The air was still and musky, an insistent sonance of evenly-spaced water droplets emerging from the sink faucet as Adelaide eventually tore her frail frame from the distressed wall.

Three harrowing days had passed since Switch's banishment to maximum security. For a moment, the dainty woman had quite honestly forgotten what it was like to live in complete isolation. For a solid seventy-two days, Switch had kept her company, his exaggerated speech patterns and enthusiastic hand gestures had managed to occupy the typically stale and lonely nighttime hours.

Quite frankly, the past 794 days had passed by remarkably quick. It felt like just yesterday when the wretched Alice Lynch had abandoned a sorrowful Adelaide in the lobby of Stillwater Sanitarium; her distressed frame held tightly within Briar Cunningway's reassuring grasp as the artificially blond woman had solely vowed to protect the younger girl at any cost.

Although Adelaide was entirely alone within the dingy, concrete walls of her cell, she couldn't help but dream of an absolute abditory—a place where she could squeeze her petite frame into and be completely concealed— completely invisible.

Just as the woman had managed to settle upon her rickety mattress once more, the hefty steel door of her cell abruptly opened, revealing an exhausted Nurse Briar—her features partially illuminated by the dull blue lights as she slunk into the confined space. A weak, tight-lipped grin enveloped her features at the sight of a fully-alert Adelaide, precisely drawn winged eyeliner smudged and smeared as the door clipped closed on her heel.

"They've got me working late," she dryly explained, her tone hoarse and thick as she lowered herself into a sitting position at the foot of Adelaide's exceedingly small bed. A soft, paper cup was held tightly in her manicured clutch, artificially lengthened fingernails stained a vibrant orange as she thrust the pills into Adelaide's wary grasp.

The shy woman uneasily retrieved the object, dirt-riddled fingers elegantly lacing around the flimsy paper as she tore it from Briar's clutch, widened gaze fixated on the woman's conflicted expression as she tossed the pills into the depths of her mouth.

"How is he?" Adelaide inquired, chewing on the severed skin of her lower lip as Briar claimed the empty cup from her grasp. A sigh escaped the woman's lips, avoiding Adelaide's desperate stare as she shifted her weight upon the paper-thin mattress.

"Greenwald's giving him a hard time," Nurse Briar defeatedly revealed, the pads of her oily fingers insistently tearing at the bleak paper of the cup as Adelaide's prying gaze burned blatant holes straight through her skull. She couldn't bear to look at her—the guilt was eating her alive. After all, if she hadn't fibbed to Dr. Blake about Switch's apparent negligence, he'd be pacing about in the neighboring cell—constantly muttering incoherently beneath his breath as the tip of his tongue intently traced the scarred tissue on the inside of his cheek.

"He's got a black eye," she croaked, pulse quickening beneath her ribcage as she thoroughly recollected the horrific scene from only hours prior. Greenwald thought it would be wildly entertaining to stick the criminal into a straight jacket—obviously, the greasy-haired man did not willingly comply. "Refuses to even speak to me. He seems—different. Distressed, even. Keeps talking to himself and yelling and—"

"Stop." Adelaide sternly scolded, eyelids squeezing agonizingly shut as she clearly envisioned a vexed Switch, mangled curls concealing his vision as he anxiously tugged at the innards of his jacket, an extreme sense of claustrophobia setting in as he desperately attempted to rid his limbs of the constricting material.

Adelaide's palms met her sullen complexion, cracked fingernails digging deeply into the flesh of her forehead as her knobby knees met her chest, heart erratically thumping against the protruding skin as Nurse Briar's cobalt gaze refocused on the worrisome woman.

"Ad," Briar cooed, shy digits meeting the thick fabric of Adelaide's clothed kneecap, which had managed to instinctively jerk out of the woman's unexpected touch. A sharp inhale filled the stiff void, Adelaide's trembling fingers threading through her tangled locks as she cautiously eyed a frowning Briar opposite her.

"I know I'm your caretaker, and this entire—*friendship*—is greatly discouraged and ultimately forbidden, but I want you to know that you can always be honest with me. I care about you so much. I think of you like the little sister I never had, and I promise to always protect you. No matter what you say or do, I'll never put you in harms way." Nurse Briar confidently rambled, the words spilling off of her tainted tongue with ease as she revealed her innermost feelings for the woman beside her, thick tears prickling at her vision as she hastily blinked them away.

"I like him," Adelaide admitted, quivering fingertips meeting the silky flesh of Briar's moisturized knuckles as she daintily traced the soft skin. "A lot. I haven't felt this way about someone since—" the woman instantaneously fell silent, Emmett DuPré's handsome features riddling her mind as she forcefully swallowed a mouthful of bile. "–since *him*."

"Him?" Nurse Briar unintentionally pried, lacing her fingers with Adelaide's as she clearly recalled the gorgeous diamond ring that had once claimed Addy's ring finger—the very same ring they'd forcibly removed from her hand as she'd lewdly sobbed. Unfortunately, the woman had landed herself in maximum security on her very first day, courtesy of her overgrown fingernails and the obscene gashes she'd left upon the guard's face who had removed her ring.

"Since Emmett," Adelaide breathed, a single tear slipping down the slope of her prominent cheekbone as she audibly sniffled. "W-We were engaged. He died in a car accident a few years ago."

Nurse Briar's face fell at Adelaide's brave proclamation, hazel-hued orbs masked by a thick layer of blinding tears as the elder woman rubbed reassuring circles against Adelaide's fingers.

"I'm so sorry, Addy." She cooed. "Thank you for opening up to me. It means so much."

Adelaide simply nodded, patting Briar atop her palm as she contemplated spilling the details of hers and Switch's recent—*affair*. However, after much contemplation, she decided to keep her mouth sealed tightly shut.

"Try and get some sleep, Addy. I have a late show tomorrow, so I'll be in around supper time." Nurse Briar awkwardly explained, crumbling the petite paper cup between her rigid fingers as she bid Adelaide a final goodnight before slipping from the cold, concrete cell.

The hefty steel door sealed shut, Briar's left palm flattening against the frigid surface as she attempted to steady herself. Suddenly, her legs had turned to utter goo, knees violently wobbling as she choked back ghastly cries. She had the opportunity to tell her—to be completely open with Adelaide and admit to the horrific thing she'd done. Adelaide had been entirely and unreservedly open with her, audibly admitting her feelings for the madman, and Briar had *betrayed her.*

Briar clamped a clammy palm over her gaping mouth, eyelids squeezing tightly shut as she attempted to conceal the hefty cries that threatened to emerge. Cora's obnoxious snores filled the otherwise stale air present within the cell block, her legs wobbling frenziedly. She stumbled into the direction of the exit, silent tears claiming her flushed cheeks whilst her chest achingly throbbed.

Slowly, the woman defeatedly ascended up the evenly spaced cement steps, lazy lids fixated on her feet as she climbed towards maximum security. She was required to tend to Switch once more before the ending of her shift, and following hers and Adelaide's surprisingly sentimental bonding session, the very last person she wanted to see was *him.*

Maximum security was exceptionally barbaric. Unlike the routine cement walls, this particular cell block was lined with transparent glass—several inches thick and completely soundproof. The cubicles were eight feet by eight, complimented with a paper-thin mattress that resembled a pile of newspapers laid upon the dusty concrete floor, sheets and a pillow entirely absent as a profusion of miscellaneous stains littered the surface of the material. Per usual, the back wall was accented with a single metal toilet and neighboring sink, the left tap permanently screwed slightly open as insistent water droplets littered the bowl every three and a half seconds.

Unfortunately, the absolutely odious presence of Elliot Greenwald remained, his bottom solely glued to the uneven surface of an aging metal chair as his gaze lay transfixed on Switch's unmoving form beyond the thick glass.

Nurse Briar stumbled through the hefty steel double doors of the cell block, a slight skip in her step as her lazy gaze refocused on a rigid Greenwald, his fingers laced together in a tight fist upon his lap as his exhausted gaze met hers.

"How is he?" She ushered, the door clipping her heel as it swung abruptly shut, a slight wince overcoming her sullen features as she rapidly approached the very last cell on the left. Only four glass cells occupied this particular block, and currently, only one was occupied.

"Hasn't said a word," Greenwald grunt. "Tried to get something outta him, but he's not giving in. Seems on edge, keeps muttering to himself. It's almost like he's going through drug withdrawals or something, he's acting funny physically."

Briar raised a considerable brow. "Drug withdrawals?"

"Just my observation," he grunts. "He's puked three times. Keeps clawing at his face and shit, so Farley and I put him in a jacket a few hours ago."

Nurse Briar's wary stare collided with a restrained Switch on the opposite side of the glass, her thin lips curling into a tight frown as she observed the distressed man within the cell.

His torso was clad with the unpigmented fabric of a straightjacket, arms tightly concealed by the claustrophobic material as he sat cross-legged upon the measly mattress. Blank, soulless eyes concentrated deeply upon a large speck of dust upon the floor, greasy, unkempt curls cloaking his line of sight as several moistened ringlets clung to the deep lacerations upon the half of his face. The soles of his bare feet were drastically filthy; cloaked with an assortment of dirt and grime, courtesy of the poor conditions of the cell floor.

"Go ahead and take your break, Greenwald." Briar firmly stated, dainty fingers curling around the thin plastic of her ID as she tore it from the depths of her shirt pocket.

"Briar–" the man firmly pressed, brows knitting together in vexation as his palms met the prominent skin of his knees, allowing the man to swiftly stand from his position on the old, rickety chair.

"I'll be fine, Greenwald." Nurse Briar reassuringly countered. "I've been alone with him plenty of times. I'll be okay, I promise. Go take your break so I can go home afterwards."

Greenwald tossed his palms into the air in surrender, the sleeves of his uniform dowdily rolled as an essence of colorful tattoos littered every inch of his flesh. "As you wish. I just wish Stillwater would install cameras in this damn place, so we don't have to sit and watch him. He's boring."

Nurse Briar weakly smiled, nodding curtly in Greenwald's direction as she inserted her identification card into the slot, the translucent glass door unlatching with an audible *click* as she laced her fingers around the cool, circular handle.

Greenwald wordlessly excused himself from the premises, running a large palm through his disheveled crimson locks as Briar slunk into the depths of Switch's cell. The madman, however, hadn't even glanced upwards to view her sudden intrusion.

"Switch?" She whispered, the door obnoxiously sealing behind her timid frame as she meticulously dragged the soles of her matted shoes along the floor, prompting the dirt to audibly shift beneath her weight. He, however, failed to respond. Instead, his unmoving form simply claimed the center of the mattress, which hugged the very left wall of the cubicle.

The sleeves of his black and white striped jumpsuit were sloppily rolled several inches above his ankle, displaying his bony ankles as well as a profusion of brunette leg hair. Per usual, his shoulders lay hunched, broadening his already wide frame further as his jaw intently twitched, determined tongue insistently poking at the uneven flesh within his mouth as Briar fell to her knees beside him.

"Hey," she whispered, a confident palm meeting the destroyed skin of his cheek as she carefully cupped the surface.

Switch blatantly flinched beneath her sudden touch, jaw obscenely clenching as his beady, black gaze met hers. With a disgruntled tone, the man murmured a simplistic, *"Ken?"*

Briar blandly blinked, features contorting into that of immense confusion as Switch's eyes widened, lips parting in angst as he rigorously shook his head from side to side, an unattainable series of phrases tumbling off his tongue as he eventually settled back into the warmth of her palm. Briar intently eyed the now silent madman, the uneven crevices of his scars tickling the inner flesh of her palm as a weak smile yanked at her chapping lips.

"I'm sorry," she added, the pad of her thumb curiously tracing the rugged flesh beneath his eye as she inched upward toward the gaudy bruise that claimed the supple skin directly above. Several scarlet-tinted raised marks littered his forehead and cheeks, courtesy of his aggressive scratching. It appeared as if he'd actually attempted to claw his complexion right off . . .

"Blake has you on some heavy-duty meds. Are they not sitting right with you?" Nurse Briar politely inquired, tearing her greedy palm away from his features as his gaze refocused on the ground before him.

Silence.

The woman awkwardly cleared her throat, shifting her weight against the heels of her shoes as she settled into a more comfortable position upon the floor. Switch's features continuously twitched, his jaw jerking slightly sideways as the tip of his pink tongue toyed with the corners of his lips.

"Can you tell me about Ken?" She breathed, instantly regretting her intrusive query as Switch's hardened gaze flickered in her direction, jaw arduously tightening as his chin jutted outward.

"No more *needles*." He croaked, his tone hoarse and uneven as his lazy stare bored deeply into hers. "I'll take 'em. The *pills*."

"O-Okay," Briar breathed, anxiously tugging her bottom lip between her teeth as she scanned Switch's conflicting complexion. "No more needles. I'll tell Blake, I promise."

Switch nodded, audibly smacking his lips as he shifted his position against the sorry excuse for a mattress.

"Switch?" Briar cooed, dainty fingertips toying with the stray strand present on the rolled sleeve of his trousers as he intently observed her every move.

"Hm?" He murmured, tugging his leg away from her greedy touch as she frowned.

Were you a junkie? She thought, lips forming to create the words as staggered breaths hastily emerged in their place. For some reason, she couldn't quite spit the statement out.

"Cat got your tongue, toots?" Switch lowly muttered, his tone lazy and uneven as he irritably eyed the nearby toilet before grumbling a choppy, *"fuck."*

Briar silently observed as he tore himself from the mattress, wobbling legs inching over towards the shiny metal bowl as he violently emptied the remaining contents of his stomach into the u-bend, limbs contorted at a wildly awkward angle as the jacket seemed to suction to his rigid frame.

The blond woman immediately darted upwards, falling to the madman's aide as her fingers curled around the greasy strands of curls that cloaked his irate features, hastily tugging them backwards as he continued to obnoxiously hurl into the toilet bowl.

"Get off me!" Switch deeply exclaimed, his tone magnified by the thick metal of the toilet bowl as Briar hastily pulled away, gaze significantly widening as violent trembles consumed his spine beneath the hefty fabric of the jacket.

"S-Switch–" she stammered, but he hadn't allowed her to finish.

"Get *out!*" He irritably exclaimed, forehead arduously colliding with the ridge of the bowl as he painfully heaved, struggling to catch his breath as the woman blinked away several hot tears.

"It's okay, I'm here to help you!" She proclaimed, fingers contorting into clenched fists at her sides. "Greenwald isn't here to fuck with you–"

"Are you *deaf?*" Switch spat, tearing his forehead away from the cool metal as his furious gaze collided with hers. "Get the *fuck* out. I don't *want* you in here."

"Don't say that–" she pressed, voice uneven and wary as Switch released a considerably sarcastic chuckle, which eventually eased into a heightened laugh as he tossed his head back in glee.

"Oh–*God*," Switch drawled, tongue caressing the destroyed flesh of his lower lip as he sat in an exasperated heap upon the grimy ground. "You're truly an idiot, aren't you, baby Briar? So gullible and *weak*–shit, all I gotta do is *look* at'cha and you're already falling to your *kneeees*."

"I am *not!*" Briar exclaimed, cheeks flushing a drastic scarlet hue as she eyed Switch's thoroughly amused expression.

"You're no-*t what?*" He taunted, insistent giggles slipping off his parted lips as he shifted his position against the floor. "A little *whore?*"

Briar's lips sealed, pulse drastically quickening beneath her ribcage as her stomach violently churned. She hated how right he was–all he had to do was *look* at her and she'd willingly fall to her knees before him and give him anything he pleased . . .

"C'mon, Bri-Bri. *Ob-vious-ly* you're-*uh*, nice'n *comfortable* with me, considering you felt the need to touch the *scars* on my face," Switch sternly spat, pausing momentarily to gauge her reaction. "It's a *great* story, actually."

"We're finished here." Briar countered, thickly swallowing as she shot

Switch a rigid stare.

"Oh–*c'mon*, toots," Switch purred, batting his eyelashes seductively in her direction. "I may be all doped *up*, but my *pee-pee* still works. Why don't you put that *big mouth* to use."

"Piss off." Briar murmured, twisting sharply on her heel as she abandoned the cell, fingers fumbling with the thin plastic of her ID as Switch's haunting cackle filled the claustrophobic void. In that moment, Briar Cunningway felt worse about herself than she ever had before.

XVII

"There's a room where the light won't find you
Holding hands while the walls come tumbling down
When they do, I'll be right behind you"
–Tears for Fears,
"Everybody Wants to Rule the World"

Day 805.

Eight-hundred grueling days—Adelaide Rhea Lynch had been isolated within the bland, colorless walls of Stillwater Sanitarium for over eight-hundred *fucking* days. Despite her unalloyed hatred for her mother Alice and the dreadfully forlorn life she lived before her days of extreme isolation— Adelaide was considerably exultant within this imprisonment. Besides, the undeniably charming features of the notorious criminal—more commonly known as Switch—made Adelaide happier than she's been in years.

A plethora of dirt and grime currently raided the overgrown nails upon Adelaide's lengthy digits, moderately ulterior eyebrows knit together in uncertainty as she attempted to rid the nail of the abundance of dirt.

Whispers currently consumed the rec room, several pairs of wild-eyes settling upon the incredibly lax form of the previously mute woman as she shot them perplexed glares. She timidly shifted her weight against the dolorous concrete wall, the bones creaking beneath her flushed flesh as the broad double doors of the large room dramatically opened.

The dainty woman's pulse accelerated, features brightening at the sight of a disheveled Vern and a cocky Greenwald, their fingers tightly laced around the biceps of a rigid man with greasy brown hair as they strut into the room.

The whispers immediately ceased, curious heads tilting in the direction of the sudden intrusion as Adelaide tugged her knees to her busty chest. Infrequent mounds of dirt slipped through the bothersome hole present along the ridge of her toes, prompting a scoff to overcome her features as she irritably wiggled her petite toes to rid the flesh of the sticky sand.

Switch's hardened glare met hers, a profusion of dreadfully oily ringlets dangling within his line of vision as a pair of dark, callous eyes met hers. Goosebumps instantly littered the exposed flesh of her slender forearms, breaths incredibly thinning as the soles of his unlaced boots dragged along the dusty floor. Per usual, the scarlet-riddled flesh of his wrists were bound by a set of remarkably shiny metal cuffs, fingers heartily discolored as he trudged in the direction of Adelaide's rigid frame.

He looked absolutely dreadful–the skin surrounding his left eye flushed a mute yellow hue. The ghastly, healed scar was swollen and also somewhat bruised—ugly and bulging and downright *painful* to look at. The typically untouched flesh of his right cheek was currently coated with a profusion of raised scratches, light crimson in color and slightly faded in intensity.

It actually appeared as if the man had attempted to claw his complexion completely off.

Adelaide thickly swallowed, tears welling up in her eyes as she rose to her feet, knees wobbling as Greenwald and a significantly healed Vern abandoned a silent Switch in the center of the room. The moment their hold had faltered on his arms, however, the man appeared to halt in place—shoulders hunched as his jaw profusely tightened.

An uneasy Adelaide scurried in his direction, trembling fingertips colliding with the uneven folds of his face as he impulsively flinched beneath her abrupt touch.

"Shh," she cooed, the pads of her incredibly smooth skin gently massaging his flesh as his jaw tightly clenched beneath her fingertips. "It's okay. I'm here now."

Switch's nostrils obnoxiously flared as he released a considerable exhale, lazy gaze drooping downwards to meet Adelaide's socked feet as she daintily moved him in the direction of their distinct corner. Several sets of stares remained transfixed on the peculiar couple, mouths agape in awe as they observed the scenario. It appeared that the intemperate and dauntless persona of the notorious Switch had temporarily dissipated, leaving behind a cold, empty shell in his place.

Both Adelaide and Switch lowered themselves onto the ground, the man's slender digits curling into distressed fists as his bottom arduously collided with the uncomfortable concrete. Adelaide's reassuring touch never once left his cloaked flesh, uneasy fingers curling around the dowdily rolled sleeve of his jumpsuit as her fingers elegantly traced the permanent ink imbedded upon his left wrist.

"What'd they do to you?" She mutely murmured, index finger looping beneath the cool metal of his left cuff as Switch's glare remained glued to the ground before him, features twitching as his left foot expeditiously bounced.

Her inquiry remained unanswered, prompting the woman to boldly frown as her right knee met his left, prominent chin meeting the bony skin of Switch's hunched shoulder. The man stiffened beneath her soothing hold, fingers insistently rubbing together in an invariable fashion. Suddenly, Kennedy Carter raided his mind once more, his bottom lip aggressively tugging between his teeth as he heavily blinked.

You're weak, she thickly spat, her bothersome tone echoing deeply within his skull as violent trembles enveloped his spine. *I knew you wouldn't be able to do it. You can't even handle one single needle without spiraling back into the pits of addiction.*

Switch's nose wrinkled in disgust, stomach turbulently turning as the blood curdled beneath his veins. Fingers curled into fists once again, lengthy nails digging deeply into the flesh of his palm as the warm, comforting feel of crimson blood met his fingertips. Once again, Kennedy's stern tone reappeared.

I know how bad you want it, she taunted, a sarcastic giggle slipping off her lips as the blood oozed between his fingers. *Admit it. You can't live without it.*

Adelaide's eyes widened at the sight of the harsh liquid seeping between his fingers, her lips parting in angst as her quivering fingers met his, determinedly tugging his razor-edge nails from his palms as she attempted to cease the bleeding.

"Oh my God, Switch!" The woman muttered, her digits becoming slick with the liquid form of his life as her pulse drastically quickened. "I'll go get Nurse Briar—"

You're nothing, Kennedy's voice loudly reappeared. *You're no one. You're nowhere.*

"Get *out*." He darkly murmured, head insistently twitching as his eyelids squeezed agonizingly shut. Several beads of blood dribbled onto the concrete, seeping between the harsh surface as Adelaide's brows perplexedly raised.

"What?" She whispered, tongue darting outward to wet her dry lips as she craned her neck to view his distressed expression.

"Out of my *head*," he clarified, breaths staggered and shallow as the speed of his tapping foot rapidly increased. "Get her out *get her out*–"

"W-Who?" Adelaide defeatedly muttered. "Get who out, baby? Tell me so I can help you–"

"Get her out!" Switch exclaimed, wild-eyes flying open as his dilated pupils met Adelaide's timid form. "Fuck off, Ken! *Fuck off fuck off*–"

Adelaide rose to her feet, heart thumping thickly in her throat as she darted in the direction of the sealed double doors, Switch's blood coating her fingers as she laced them around the circular handles of the doors, smearing bold streaks of crimson along the surface as she harshly yanked them open.

Nurse Briar met Adelaide in the middle of the doorway, her heart momentarily jumpstarting at the unexpected sight of the distressed woman as her gaze instantly diverted to meet her bloody fingers.

"*Addy?*" Briar gawked, lids significantly widening as her palms met Adelaide's. "What happened? Is this your blood?"

Adelaide shook her head, salty tears slipping down the slopes of her cheeks. She glanced over her shoulder to view a defeated Switch laid slump against the wall, scarlet-riddled fingers tugging at his distressed features as Briar gasped. Tracks of crimson littered his marred complexion, courtesy of his prying fingers.

"Crap–*Switch*!" She gasped, brushing past a frozen Adelaide as she darted directly towards the man in the back-left corner, beady pairs of eyes instantaneously focusing on the interesting scenario as Adelaide's rigid gaze met a chirpy Nayeli.

"Guess max really broke your little boy toy." The olive-toned woman blatantly mocked, earning a profuse set of giggles from a shy Cora beside her.

"Screw off." Adelaide boldly dismissed, prompting the giggling woman to openly gawk at her reaction.

"Holy hell," Nayeli gasped, meeting Cora's equally bewildered expression. "The mute actually *speaks*! What changed, princess peach? Did he stick his pecker in you or something and now you magically talk?"

Adelaide's jaw tightly clenched, her worrisome gaze meeting Briar and Switch as the woman desperately attempted to calm the man down. Apparently, he wasn't in his right mind, and it was undeniably *mortifying.*

"Addy," Nurse Briar announced, assisting Switch to his feet as he insistently murmured a profusion of incoherent terms beneath his breath, expression consistently twitching as he dragged his boot-clad feet along the floor. "Westlynn's here to see you."

Adelaide's breaths immediately thinned, her heart plummeting as Westlynn's abhorrent expression raided her mind. Swiftly, she shook her head from side to side, an abundance of obscenities escaping her partially parted lips as Nurse Briar shot her a puzzled glare.

"It's just your sister, Addy. Maybe you can talk to her this time?" The woman gently offered. "Vern'll escort you there. He's waiting outside. I'm going to take Switch to his cell."

Adelaide rubbed the pads of her moist fingers together at an alarming rate, her straggly ashen hair irritably sticking to the slick skin of her neck as she avoided Westlynn's glare. A soft, reddish-tint consumed the dainty flesh of her fingers, courtesy of Switch's harsh blood as her sister curiously eyed the peculiar hue.

"Ad," her identical twin sister murmured, arms outstretching along the remarkably cold metal table as they eventually met Adelaide's. Impulsively, the timid woman tugged out of Westlynn's embrace, wild-eyes reconnecting with an identical pair of hazel orbs as she thickly swallowed.

"Mum left," Westlynn dryly explained, her tone hoarse and uneven as she claimed a stray strand of brunette hair from her eyes, eyelids briskly blinking as several miniscule chunks of mascara flaked off, coating her flushed cheeks. "She's back with the roos. Haven't heard from her much, not that it really matters—she's a bit of a bitch."

Dr. Blake boldly cleared her throat from the far-right corner, brows knitting together in vexation as Westlynn shot the woman a scolding glance. It was unfair that she had to invade on hers and Adelaide's privacy. All Westlynn wanted was a moment alone with her sister—her other half.

"Talk to me, Laide." Westlynn pressed, blinking away blinding tears as Adelaide's fingers met the thick sleeves of her jumper, elegantly twisting around the fabric as she rolled the sleeves up the length of her arms. Compared to Westlynn's moderately healthy physique, Adelaide was drastically skinny and looked considerably unwell, strutting forearms so thin that they could truly pass as a pair of toothpicks.

Adelaide's jaw slackened, an exasperated exhale escaping her lips as she shifted her weight upon the rickety metal chair.

"Why are you here?" She croaked, the statement earning a heightened gasp from the woman opposite her as her palms met her gaping mouth.

"Oh–*Ad*!" Westlynn cheered, choking back hefty sobs as she obnoxiously sniffled. "You're back! You have no idea how happy I am to hear your voice–"

"Save it, Westie." Adelaide gruffly clipped. "Just tell me what you want so we can get this over with. I'm not feeling well." She partially lied—truth be told, she desperately wanted to return to her cell, to return to *him.*

"I put some money in your commissary fund," Westlynn bluntly explained, periwinkle pink painted lip tucked between rows of artificially whitened teeth. "Consider it an early Thanksgiving gift, I suppose."

"How're you and Jasper?" Adelaide awkwardly murmured, left foot tapping expeditiously against the multi-hued tile floor as a broad smirk danced along Westlynn's lips, pearly white teeth on display as she glanced downward at the elegant ring laid upon her finger. *"Mrs. Harris."*

Westlynn obscenely blushed at the mention of her married name, petite giggles slipping off her lips as her heart immediately swelled. *Finally*–she had her sister back.

"He's great," she mused. "Really, really great. Marriage is lovely, Ad. I wish you'n Emmett could've experienced it."

Adelaide's face fell, her chest clenching as the haunting features of Emmett DuPré's handsome mug littered her mind. Words could never properly portray how much she missed that man.

He was everything to her.

"Sorry," Westlynn added, avoiding Adelaide's weakened stare. "I didn't mean to bring him up. How've you been? Are the voices gone? You seem better–"

"Westie," Adelaide croaked, a single tear slipping through the confinement of her lid as she hastily wiped it away with her palm. "I miss it. I miss being free."

Westlynn frowned, bottom lip tucked between her teeth once more as she simply nodded in reply. "I wish you could be free, Ad. Don't worry, you will one day. By the way–"

Oh God, here we go . . .

"–do you know him?" She whispered, inching closer to Adelaide as she glanced warily over her shoulder at a nosy Dr. Blake. The woman jabbed her index finger at the center of her thick-rimmed spectacles, slipping the glasses up the slope of her oily noise as she glared in their direction.

"Who?" Adelaide feigned uncertainty, head cocking sideways as she uneasily glanced in Blake's direction.

"Switch, o'course." Westlynn pressed. "What's he like? Tell me 'bout him. I wonder if he's anything like they made him out to be on the news."

Switch's complex features raided her mind—the unruly mop of brunette locks atop his skull, which were partially curly, especially around his pierced ears. She could clearly visualize the selcouth scars that lined his otherwise flawless features, severing the left side of his cheek and partially splitting his bottom lip—as well as claiming the underneath of his eye and nearly the entirety of the very side of his face. For a moment, the woman was almost certain that she could actually feel the comforting touch of the ragged pockmarks, the uneven bumps and crevices slipping between her needy fingers as she effortlessly explored his tainted complexion . . .

"Addy?" Westlynn pressed, thrusting the woman from her momentary trance as she inexplicably cleared her throat.

"Uh–" Adelaide stammered, daintily tearing at the excess skin around her fingers as Dr. Blake audibly shifted her weight in the chair behind her. "I-I don't know him."

"Oh," Westlynn defeatedly muttered. "You've never crossed paths?"

"I mean, I've *seen* him," Adelaide lied, glancing once more over her shoulder to view a perplexed Dr. Blake in the back. "But we've never spoken. He keeps to himself. As do I."

Westlynn left a solid twelve minutes later, lanky arms lacing tightly around Adelaide's neck as she held the identical woman close. Although Adelaide was still rather pissed about her sister failing to visit her for so long, something deep within her had boldly instructed her to not push the desperate woman away. Besides, outside of these thick, musky walls—Westlynn Harris was the only living person she had.

184 // ALYSSA DICARLO

Dr. Blake escorted a timid Adelaide back to the rec room, her petite, inch-tall heels colliding with the thick cement floors in a series of irritable clacks as Adelaide's hands lay buried deeply within her jumpsuit pockets.

"So," Dr. Blake confidently began, clipboard held tightly to her busty chest. "Why'd you lie to your sister?"

Adelaide's heart sank, her throat running impossibly dry as she shot Dr. Blake a puzzled glance. "What d'you mean?"

"About the Switch," the elder woman confirmed. "You told your sister that you've never spoken to him. We both know that's a fat lie."

"It's none of her business," Adelaide dismissed, avoiding eye contact with the woman beside her as they awkwardly trudged down the dingy hallway. *It's none of yours, either.*

"You better watch yourself, 4210." Dr. Blake firmly pressed, glasses slipping down the ridge of her nose as she irately shoved them back up to her face. "Don't get too—comfortable—with the man. He's bad news. Besides, this is a sanitarium, not a brothel. Don't even *think* about becoming physically intimate."

"Deadset," Adelaide lazily murmured, earning a confused glare from the American woman as she directed her into the obscenely noisy rec room.

"Try and have a good day, 4210." Dr. Blake weakly grinned, strutting a faux smile as Adelaide swallowed a mouthful of bile.

"G'day, doc."

Nurse Briar clutched her identification card between several quivering fingers, breaths emerging in staggered pants as the softened paper cup nearly crumbled within her moist grasp. Hastily, she ran the card through the provided slot upon the keypad, the door instantly springing to life as the steel unlatched with an audible *click.*

The mahogany door creaked open, insistent patches of goosebumps immediately littering the exposed flesh of Briar's forearms as she anxiously strutted into the depths of Switch's occupied cell. It was nearly nine-thirty—the low, blue hue of the nighttime lights illuminating the bleak cell block as the door clipped closed on her heel.

The defeated man lay in a heap upon the mattress, torso cloaked with a straight jacket as several strands of oily curls lay draped over his lazy eyes.

The beady, black orbs collided with the woman, the scarred side of his mouth instinctively twitching as his lacerated bottom lip jutted outwards, timidly blowing away the strands of hair from his eyes at the best of his ability. After all, his hands were good as dead underneath the confinement of that damn jacket.

"Hey," Briar breathed, bleakly observing the sullen man laid upon the aging mattress.

There was no reply.

The blond woman hastily cleared her throat, glancing downward at the vibrant paper cup held within her grasp as a profusion of pills littered the basin.

With one final burst of bravery, the woman took several considerably large strides sideways, legs colliding with the rim of the metallic toilet bowl as she quickly rotated the cup. Five circular pills sank deeply to the pit of the toilet, the stale water rippling from the sudden intrusion as Briar's fingers met the handle.

Switch rose to a sitting position upon the mattress, brows knit together in wonder as the soles of his bare feet met the floor. His jaw fell agape in curiosity, the tip of his tongue tracing the severed corner of his lips as Briar flushed the pills down the drain.

"What're *you*–" he grunted, his tone low and husky as Briar crumbled the paper cup into a miniscule ball within her palm, brightened gaze meeting his once more as she boldly smiled.

"This'll be our little secret," she spoke, a single index finger meeting her lips as she cheekily smiled. "These are the devil's pills. You don't need them. If Blake asks, I'm still giving them to you. Alrighty?"

Switch weakly nodded, eyes scanning Briar's confident frame as he yanked at the innards of the jacket. Briar seemed to get the memo, the bile rising to her throat as she cautiously approached his bed.

"If I take this off, do you promise not to claw your eyes out?" Nurse Briar whispered, rapidly approaching his rigid limbs as her fingers met the constricting bonds of the jacket.

Switch mutely nodded, arduously chewing upon his bottom lip as the dainty woman unlatched the drastically tight straight jacket, ultimately freeing the man from his bonds as he released a considerable sigh, shoulders elegantly rolling as he stretched out his aching arms.

"Uh," he lowly spoke, avoiding Briar's gleeful expression. "Thanks."

"You're welcome," Briar smiled, clutching the jacket to her chest. "Goodnight, Switch."

XVIII

*"Sometimes you're better off dead
There's a gun in your hand
it's pointing at your head"
–Pet Shop Boys, "West End Girls"*

Adelaide awoke from a dreamless slumber to the persistent shaking of her scrawny shoulders, heavy eyelids flickering open in bewilderment as stunning arrays of hazel hues focused on a profusion of curly blond locks.

Nurse Briar's fingers detached from Adelaide's sullen skin, a measly, tight-lipped grin enveloping her exhausted features as she inaudibly urged the mute woman to rise from the rickety mattress. After all, it was nearly seven-thirty, and a tasteless, routine breakfast currently awaited the prisoner on the first floor.

"They've made pancakes today," Briar dryly explained, her winged eyeliner habitually smudged in the corners as she crossed the petite, concrete cubicle, slender digits curling around the heap of black and white striped fabric discarded upon the floor. Her gaze lay level with the obscene hole present between Adelaide and Switch's cells, her curious stare focusing on a grinning Switch beyond the opposite side of the wall.

Her heart nearly burst right out of her chest at the sight of him—exposed elbows claiming his knees as his thumb intently traced the skin of his lower lip. A stygian stare glared deeply into hers, menacing grin slapped upon his lively features as the woman shivered at the sight of him.

Determinedly, the blond woman shook her head from side to side, claiming the discarded fabric from the ground as she thrust Adelaide's jumpsuit into her open arms. Gleeful bursts of butterflies currently raided her belly, insistent thoughts of a dashingly handsome Switch beyond the severed wall riddling her mind as her conscious thoroughly argued with her doting thoughts—*knock it off! He nearly killed you!*

"Morning, Briar." Adelaide throatily spoke, a weak grin plastered along her cheeks as she tugged the heavy material over her head, several unbrushed strands of straggly, ashen-brown hair thrown awry as her eyelids furiously blinked, attempting to rid her eyeballs of the sudden obtrusions.

"Good morning, Ad." Briar croaked, ushering Adelaide from the cell as the hefty steel door audibly latched behind them. The young, Australian woman's hair was a dreadful mess, scarlet-tinted cheeks severely sunken as a harsh charcoal hue raided the underneath of her eyes, physical evidence of her lack of proper sleep as Nurse Briar visibly frowned at the sight.

"Having trouble sleeping?" She inquired, approaching the Switch's sealed cell door as she aligned the thin plastic identification card within the tight grooves of the keypad. A bold, miniscule green light illuminated in approval, granting the woman access to the cold, stiff cell as Adelaide shifted her weight from either foot.

"Medication gives me insomnia, I think." Adelaide awkwardly explained, gaze solely fixated on her boot-clad toes as she wiggled them beneath the claustrophobic leather.

"Hm," Briar simply grunted, fingers encircling Adelaide's dainty bicep as she practically yanked the woman into the depths of Switch's humble abode. "They should be doing the exact opposite."

Adelaide's palms claimed her slender arms, eyes significantly widening at the sight of a disheveled set of brown curls as several particularly wavy loops elegantly pranced along the lacerated flesh of his face. Admittedly, the woman loved the greasy curls.

Switch's dark gaze instantaneously illuminated at the sight of the women as they strut into his confined cell, a hearty smirk tugging at his lips as he inexplicably rose from the sorry excuse for a mattress.

"Morning," he lowly greeted, left eyelid flickering momentarily closed as he delivered a sultry wink in Adelaide's direction. An immediate crimson tint overcame her features, curled fingers meeting her mouth as she weakly attempted to conceal her raging grin. God—she oh-so-absolutely *adored* the apparent psychopath with every fiber of her being. She wanted nothing more than to thrust herself forwards—to toss her dainty figure into the warm, comforting embrace of his tainted arms and nuzzle her nose into the crook of his neck. To feel the erratic, uneven thumping of his heightened pulse as she held him close, deeply inhaling his natural scent— glorious mixture of man and musk, a peculiar but nevertheless riveting smell. She needed to feel his marred lips against hers once more, or she'd surely succumb to the pits of insanity—mirroring the time where to her, the Switch was nothing more than a name.

"Feeling better, Switch?" Nurse Briar queried, chest heaving as she glanced warily in the direction of a blushing Adelaide beside her.

"Much," Switch gleamed, lanky digits precisely curling around the sleeve of his matted jumpsuit as he intently rolled the fabric up the slopes of his arms. An abundance of permanent ink rapidly appeared, littered miscellaneously along the flesh of his forearms as his determined tongue poked and prodded at the innermost corners of his lips.

"I'm glad to hear that," Briar forcibly smiled, retracting a shiny pair of metal cuffs from the pocket of her scrubs. "You look significantly better as well."

Switch's gaze met Adelaide's once more, a generous heat promptly invading her chest as she shied away from his piercing, inky glare. It was as if he'd managed to strip her bare using only his eyes; shedding her lithe frame of the miasmic striped jumpsuit to reveal the flushed flesh that lay buried beneath. She wondered how he'd look at her—how he'd actually admire (or, possibly disapprove) of her nude form. Surely, her drastically thin physique was horrifically insalubrious, but maybe—just *maybe*—he wouldn't even mind. Besides, she was almost entirely certain that he could fit both palms around the entirety of her miniscule waist, the tips of his thumbs and middle fingers would surely touch. And yet—still, after all of this time, he stayed true to his word—keeping his eyelids tightly sealed whilst she undressed during bath time every night.

Paroxysms of lust coursed thickly through her veins, lucid images of a panting Switch before her thoroughly raiding her mind as her body virtually cried out for more—*more more more* . . . she'd gotten a little taste of him, a little *feel*, and she couldn't help but simply crave the sensation of raw, pure intimacy once more with him. Being imprisoned within these bland, concrete walls for over two years truly took a considerable toll on her every limb . . .

Nurse Briar latched the chains around Switch's wrists, earning a sigh from the madman as he merely rolled his eyes at the sight of his bound wrists.

"You're still high risk," she instantly explained, clearly understanding his audible sound of detest as she led both him and Adelaide from the cold, lonely walls of the old cell.

The trio strut through the dingy halls in an unnerving silence, the emphatic sonance of their weighty boots colliding with the unkempt concrete clearly ricocheting off the drastically thick walls with ease. Adelaide stole several considerably lengthy glances in Switch's direction, her heart skipping a blatant beat when his gaze locked on hers as a miniscule squeak emerged from her ajar lips.

"It's Wednesday," Nurse Briar began, turning sharply to lead them into the dining hall. "So, the commissary is open. Switch, you know how the deal works–you're provided with five dollars weekly. Addy, I believe Westlynn put some money in your account, so you may have a bit more."

Adelaide managed to tune out Briar's insistent babbling, her attention diverting to a rather cheery Switch as a smile pranced upon his maimed mouth. Based off of the morbid tales individuals told within the rec room prior to the infamous Switch's initial arrival—their little escapade was nothing less than grotesquely sordid. The young woman was entirely certain that if her miserable mother had ever come to learn about her inconspicuous affair with the iniquitous Switch that she'd possibly drop dead. Either that, or she'd simply put Adelaide out of her misery.

An aging, plump lunch lady with a headful of salt-and-pepper hair and drooping jade eyes tossed a trio of silver dollar pancakes onto Adelaide's multi-hued plastic tray, muttering a rigid *good morning* before meeting Switch's stern stare. It was common knowledge that nearly the entire staff either resented—*or somewhat feared*—his presence, and as the stubby woman slapped four petite pancakes onto his tray, Adelaide was nearly one-hundred-percent sure that she had nearly shit herself at the sight of his mangled face.

The weary woman drew her bottom lip between rows of yellowing teeth, failing to stifle a cheerful giggle as both her and the hunched-shouldered man inched toward their nearly secluded table. Per usual, four chairs remained vacant beside the murderer, allowing both him and Adelaide substantial privacy as their bottoms collided with the circular disc shaped chairs.

"Not fair," Adelaide grumbled, irritably eyeing Switch's extra pancake as she claimed a maple syrup packet in her grasp. "What do I have to do to get an extra pancake?"

Switch's lips strung into an amused grin, tongue darting out from the depths of his mouth as he intently caressed the flesh of his cheek, audibly smacking his lips before replying with a husky phrase: "Implement *fear.*"

"What've you done that's so bad?" Adelaide innocently wondered, coating her stiff pancakes with a profusion of sticky syrup. "Why's everyone so afraid of you?"

Switch had failed to answer her inquiry. Instead, his slender fingers curled neatly around a single dry pancake, thumb and pointer finger determinedly pinching the stiff surface as he tore the pancake in half before tossing a large chunk into his mouth. Adelaide openly grimaced at the sight, sticky fingers scooping a chunk of mutilated pancake onto her plastic spoon as she spat out a vexed, "no syrup?"

"So many *questions,*" Switch purred, darkened gaze colliding with a stunned set of orbs. She slowly chewed her food, jaw parting in angst as she helplessly wished he'd just answer her goddamn question.

An unusually silent Vern had escorted Adelaide to the commissary immediately following the completion of breakfast. The young chap looked utterly exhausted—strutting deep, inky bags beneath his dull, watery eyes as the skin upon his typically smooth lips lay cracked and broken. His fingers were laced weakly around Adelaide's scrawny bicep, gaze fixated on the dingy ground as the duo navigated the hellish halls.

"Feeling okay, Vern?" Adelaide chirped, her tone shy and uneven as they turned a sharp corner, nearly colliding with an unnamed nurse and a giddy Nayeli, who had managed to spit several obscenities in the stringy-haired girls' direction.

"Not necessarily," the man grumbled. "My mother is dying."

"Oh." Adelaide murmured, regretting her wildly obtrusive inquiry as they rapidly approached a vacant wide window.

The commissary was located in the back corner of the first floor, somewhere between the exceedingly large rec room and the compact dining hall. A single woman worked behind the foggy glass window, standing less than five-feet tall and strutting a shade of deep, olive skin. Her head was routinely buzzed, which added a good decade onto her already aging self. Constellations of charcoal freckles raided her cheeks, dipping between the creases of her hooked nose as her beady eyes collided with an extremely rigid Adelaide.

"Hello," the middle-aged woman croaked, her tone masked by a thick, Spanish accent as her murky glare lay glued upon the four numbers present on Adelaide's jumpsuit. With an audible smack of her lips, the corpulent woman's fingers collided with the faded keys of the desktop keyboard, swiftly entering Adelaide's patient number as information regarding both approved and disapproved items filled her vision.

"List?" The woman monotonically wondered, clearly recalling Adelaide's peculiar condition as Vern stepped aside, unlatching his frigid fingers from the younger woman's arm as he allowed her minimal privacy.

"I can just tell you," Adelaide bluntly explained. "How much is in my account, though? My sister said she put in money."

The woman beyond the glass openly gawked at the foreign sound of Adelaide's accent, crooked teeth on display as she struggled to search for the dollar amount present in the woman's account.

"Uh," she stammered, gaze steadily flickering over the screen as she momentarily forgot the location of the amount. "You have thirty-two dollars, it seems."

Adelaide's jaw fell, a forced burst of air emerging from her nostrils as she inaudibly thanked her identical twin sister for the extra cash.

"Oh, wow," she heartily mused, glare peering around the middle-aged woman's abundantly short frame as she scanned the shelves for particular items. "I'll take a roll of toilet paper, please, and some deodorant, for starters."

The woman merely nodded, falling to her knees behind the jade-hued counter as she retrieved a single wrapped roll of one-ply toilet paper from a hefty box. She dismissively tossed it onto the counter, a heightened grunt slipping through her parted lips as her limbs obscenely cracked with every miniscule movement. Her gaze collided once more with the computer screen, the vibrantly-colored surface illuminating her otherwise dull orbs as nearly non-existent eyebrows knit tightly together.

"You're not approved yet for deodorant. Your personal nurse must've forgot to submit the paperwork." She spat, claiming a nearby scanner as a fluorescent crimson LED light read the barcode along the sealed toilet tissue. "Anything else?"

"*What?*" Adelaide exasperatedly shrieked, palms meeting the curled edge of the metallic window as she shot the commissary clerk a wild expression. "Since when is deodorant restricted?"

"Since 1167 decided to start eating it," the woman simply replied. *Fucking Lloyd.* "Anything else? Toilet paper is fifty cents."

"Er–" Adelaide stammered, observing the stacked shelves as her gaze settled upon several neatly wrapped individual packs of Newport cigarettes, which were clearly untouched as they lay in heaps within a faded plastic bin. "How much are the durries?"

"The what?" The commissary clerk thickly countered, a single brow considerably raising at Adelaide's confusing request.

"Sorry," the woman muttered, irritably shaking her head from side-to-side. "The cigarettes."

"Eleven dollars," commissary clerk revealed. "Matches are three. So, total, you're looking at fourteen dollars. And," she slightly paused, fingers grazing over the noisy keys as she read Adelaide's online file. "Lucky you, you're approved to get them."

So she can buy cigarettes but not deodorant?

"I'll take a pack, please. And some matches as well."

Adelaide lay in an exhausted heap upon the grimy rec room floor, considerable chunks of hair claimed between trembling fingers as she day-dreamt of the taunting pack of untouched cigarettes within her sealed cell. She couldn't *wait* to poison her lungs once more with the toxic substances.

The withered copy of *Sense and Sensibility* lay abandoned at her feet, her sock-clad toes persistently grazing along the softened cover as Switch adeptly shuffled a deck of cards between his confined grasp. The sight was rather mesmerizing—the simplistic way he managed to ease each individual card between skillful fingers as a series of incoherent terms slipped off his slightly ajar lips.

Suddenly, the silent woman became exceedingly aware of the forgotten playing card buried deeply within her trouser pocket. Swiftly, she shoved a free hand into the depths of the thick fabric, the hidden card slipping between her grasp as her pulse instantly quickened.

"You're unusually *quiet*," Switch observed, his gaze solely glued upon the rapid rotation of cards between his large palms as Adelaide shifted her position, her head confidently meeting his vacant lap. His boot-clad ankles were neatly crossed, disheveled leather scraping together as he irritably readjusted his stance.

"Tired." Adelaide shyly spoke, eyelids flickering tightly closed as she drifted into a temporary euphoria. Her greasy hair lay sprawled out in divergent directions, coating the madman's lap entirely as he raised a curious brow at the sight of her lax form.

"You *know*," he mutely purred, discarding the neatly stacked cards beside his hip as steady fingers met the silken skin of her neck. She naturally nuzzled into his lower stomach, her slender digits curling around the bulky fabric of his top as she deeply inhaled his glorious scent. Switch's fingertips elegantly traced the lining of her jaw, easing downward to meet the supple skin of her pale neck as her pulse steadily drummed against his fingers. The curly-haired man's neck immediately lulled backwards, skull arduously colliding with the uneven concrete wall as he applied ample pressure to her neck, her rapid heartbeat persistently thumping against his calloused fingers as involuntary shivers immediately enveloped his spine.

It'd be so easy for me to kill you right now . . .

"Goodnight, Adelaide." Nurse Briar collectively dismissed, a tight-lipped grin plastered on her droopy features as she vacated the musky cell. Adelaide's pulse instantaneously accelerated, her fidgety fingers detaching from the paper-thin sheet as she shuffled from the stained mattress.

The soles of her bare feet met the frigid floor, disarrays of prominent goosebumps briskly littering her exposed flesh. Her breaths thinned as she approached the nearby wooden dresser. With shaking palms, the woman pried open the middle drawer of the tri-shelved furniture, her quivering digits shuffling through heaps of unfolded, fetid clothing as the fabrics slipped between her weakened grasp. Eventually, she located the fresh pack of cigarettes hidden beneath.

Adelaide stifled an amused giggle, retrieving the pack of matches from beneath a particularly old crème-hued tank top as she nudged the drawer closed with a bony hip. Giddily, she fell to the cement floor, her shoulders uncomfortably resting against the solid metal frame of her tiny bed as she crossed her legs Indian-style.

Determinedly, Adelaide anchored an exceedingly long fingernail beneath the flap of the paper pack, nudging the container open as she elegantly shuffled a single cigarette out. Tiny pink tongue darted out from the depths of her mouth, playfully toying with the innermost corners of her chapped lips as she retrieved a single match. With a deep breath, the woman slid the match against the rigid floor, igniting a vibrant flame as her breaths ran jagged.

Adelaide shakily wedged the unlit cigarette between her lips, teeth softly clamping down on the stick as she held it firmly in place. Uneasily, the timid woman rose the lit match to meet the end of the cigarette, speedily lighting the object as the comforting taste of nicotine immediately invaded her taste buds.

An exaggerated sigh of relief slipped through the woman's partially parted mouth, eyelids fluttering closed as a beautiful warmth flooded her lungs. The woman ran a free hand through her disheveled locks, her once quivering limbs instantly laying lax as the thick smoke invaded her senses.

"Well well well," Switch throatily mused, his lacerated features partially illuminated by the low glow of the nighttime lights as he peered through the gaping hole. "Where'd you get *those?*"

"Commissary," Adelaide mumbled, taking a long drag off of her cigarette as her eyelids fluttered open. Her temporarily blurred vision eventually focused on a dashingly handsome Switch, a cheeky smirk yanking at his lips as he glared at the consistent strand of smoke that emerged from her lit cigarette. "Expensive as shit. Cost me fourteen bucks."

"*Yeeesh,*" Switch slurred, swaying from side to side as he audibly smacked his lips. "You care to *share*, princess?"

Adelaide tore the burning stick from her lips, uneven chuckles resonating through her busty chest as she side-eyed the madman beyond the severed wall.

"What'll I get in return?" She dryly teased, voice muffled beyond the hefty obstruction as she inhaled deeply once more, warm nicotine expanding her lungs as she drifted into a blissful euphoria.

"*Mmm,*" Switch mused, eyes dramatically rolling sideways in his skull as he clicked his tongue. "Whaddaya *want*, toots?"

Adelaide's brows seductively raised, her legs untangling as she drew her knees upwards, pressing them beneath the thin fabric of her aging spaghetti-strap tank top as she slightly raised her voluptuous set of breasts.

"You?" She sang, obscenely battering her eyelashes in his direction as she twirled the cancer stick between two fingers.

"Why don't-cha *slither* on through this little hole, *hm*? That way you can gimme that cigarette, and I can give *you* whatever your heart desires, pumpkin." Switch purred, tongue lapping out to taste his words as his husky gaze lay transfixed on the now squirming woman upon the floor.

"I'm not *that* skinny," she lightly argued, gaze drooping as she shuffled into a standing position, inching closer to the hole as she eventually fell to her knees before the portal. "But I wish I was. I could use another one of those washroom dates."

"*Speaking* of," Switch interjected, keenly eyeing the nearby cigarette as he thoroughly wet his dry lips. "When are they gonna do another one'a those?"

Adelaide audibly sighed, heels colliding with her numb bum as she slipped the lit object between the choppy-edged hole. Switch's lips generously parted, allowing the woman to gracefully slip the cigarette into his mouth as she mindlessly chewed on the torn skin of her bottom lip.

"I don't know," she admitted. "It's not a thing they do often. But I wish it was . . ."

Switch's lips sealed around the burning object, the smooth skin just barely grazing Adelaide's fingertips as violent bolts of electricity promptly consumed her spine at the extraordinary feel. Adelaide's already staggered breaths drastically thinned, her chest inordinately heaving as she admired the uneven folds of his face and how they twitched in relief. The man took a considerably long drag, deeply inhaling the warm nicotine as Adelaide bluntly smiled, the pads of her fingers prancing along the severed wall as she awaited her turn.

"Smoking kills, y'know." She playfully stated, abruptly snatching the cigarette from his mouth as she yanked her arm back onto her designated side of the concrete wall.

Switch intently wet his lips once more, slowly blinking as he released a throaty, "then why do *you* do it?"

His inquiry remained unanswered momentarily, the cancer stick lodged between Adelaide's yellowing teeth once again as she took another long drag. With an exasperated exhale, the woman tore the object from her lips once more, balancing the dwindling material atop her fingers as her gaze bore deeply into his.

"Because," she confidently began, her voice laced with amusement. "I'm not afraid to die."

Switch's heart froze within his chest at her revelation. The phrase repeated several times over within his jumbled mind, replaying like a broken record as virtually every single breath escaped his withering lungs.

I'm not afraid to die.

Suddenly—as if on cue—the morbid fantasies arose once more. Vivid visuals of a dainty Adelaide beneath his hips, his desperate fingers latched agonizingly tight around the supple skin of her glorious throat as he physically stole her every last breath. However, this particular fantasy was entirely different—in this fantasy, she *allowed* the monstrosity to occur. There wasn't any obsessive clawing—any begging or pleading or sobbing. No—the lovely woman wholeheartedly *enabled* the horrific gesture. In fact, the incomparable glare had ultimately reassured him that this entire scenario was—in fact—*okay*.

Switch thickly swallowed, blinking several times as he plummeted back down to Earth. Adelaide seemed to be in her own little world, willowy frame balanced against the dense wall as his stomach twisted into excruciating knots.

Allow me to do the honor, princess.

XIX

"You play tricks on my mind
You're everywhere but you're so hard to find
You're not warm or sentimental
You're so extreme, you can be so temperamental"
–Foreigner, "Urgent"

There was something relatively exuberant about Thanksgiving Day at Stillwater.

A majority of the inmates—*or patients, as they prefer to be labeled*—expressed their keen sense of excitement for the particular holiday in a variety of ways. One individual, in particular, was entirely convinced that Thanksgiving was the dawn of the Christmas season. His name is Charlie—a thirty-one-year-old chap with a head full of greasy, jet black curls and wide, beady eyes that resembled the color of a grotty, swamp-like lake. The sleeves of his mandatory jumpsuit were extremely frayed, courtesy of his excessive chewing upon the thick material whilst he attempted to sleep at night. Word on the street was that Charlie relied heavily on narcotics before his Stillwater days.

Nevertheless, the typically antisocial bloke had managed to resurface from his sequestered shell on the morning of Thanksgiving, his eyes wild with elation as he skipped around the rec room. The lithe man nearly tripped over his sloppily-laced boots several times, slightly stumbling as his quivering palms grasped onto a nearby object to stable himself.

"Santa's coming!" Charlie exclaimed, a toothy grin plastered on his features as he approached each and every individual seated silently within the room, his fingers sometimes lacing within the shy fabric of their identical jumpsuits as he repeated the phrase several times over in pure joy.

Switch readjusted his weight upon the grimy ground, shifting slightly to the left as various stray curls tickled the flesh of Adelaide's extended cheek.

"Somebody *has* to tell'em," the theatrical man muttered, fingering the cool metal of his routinely latched cuffs as Adelaide shot him a perplexed glare.

"We *can't*," she boldly countered, side-eyeing an elated Charlie as he hovered over the withered sofa several yards away, exclaiming an exuberant: "*Santa's coming!*" as he claimed a fist full of Nayeli's shirt.

"C'mon," Switch thickly pressed, his speech temporarily interrupted by the tedious flick of his tongue. "The dude's *clearly* older than myself. And I'm *old*. The sooner he learns, the better."

Thus, the buoyant bloke rapidly approached the seated duo, a hearty grin strung across his lips as his gaze flickered merrily between a timid Adelaide and a clearly amused Switch seated hip-to-hip.

"Guess what," Charlie breathed, his tone rigid and throaty as he struggled to regain his breath. His slender shoulders heaved, gaze consistently bouncing between the two individuals as he hastily awaited a plausible response.

"What?" Adelaide playfully countered, a broad grin claiming her lips as Switch—surprisingly—remained deathly silent beside her.

"Santa's coming!" Charlie cheered, clapping his eczema-riddled palms together in glee as he sharply twisted on his heel and abandoned the glowing couple at once.

Switch immediately released a strangled chuckle, which emerged as a half-snort as the sonance caught in his nostrils in the form of a forced exhale. Curious fingers fiddled with the bunched fabric at the knee of Adelaide's trousers, her neck slightly craning to properly view the amused man as batches of butterflies brewed in her belly.

"Speaking of," she confidently began, re-adjusting her position on the ground so that she could fully face the madman. His fingertips promptly detached from her clothed flesh, brows inexplicably raising as he awaited the continuation of her statement. "How old are you? I don't think you've ever mentioned it."

"*Hmm*," Switch purred, brows knitting together in mock concentration as his bound palms met his chin, index finger playfully tapping at the protruding flesh. "Guess."

Adelaide thickly swallowed, several numbers bombarding her jumbled mind as she struggled to spit any of them out. Truth be told, she was—quite frankly—afraid to guess incorrectly. After all, she didn't want to insult the man.

"Twenty-four." She shyly guessed, knowing damn well that he wasn't any less than twenty-five. *Oh well, it was worth a shot.*

"No-*pe*." Switch grinned, enthusiastically smacking his lips as a yellowed grin overcame his lively features. Scattered strands of oily ringlets framed his freckled face, one particular strand swaying irritably in front of his lacerated left eye as he brushed it away with the swipe of his conjoined palms.

"Ugh," Adelaide grumbled, fingers anxiously yanking at the ankles of her trousers. "Twenty—*three?*"

"*Colder.*" Switch mused, clearly enjoying their playful, childlike banter as the woman avoided his piercing gaze, her cheeks growing hot as the flesh flushed a bright scarlet hue.

"Twenty—*six?*" She guessed again, earning an exasperated sigh from the man beside her as he murmured a vexed: "*Warmer.*"

"Er–" Adelaide paused, collecting her thoughts as she wiggled her partially exposed toes beneath the aging fabric of her disheveled socks. "Twenty-seven?"

"*Warmeeer…*" Switch dryly teased, tugging his left leg upwards as his knobby knee met the broad surface of his chest. The bones beneath his skin irately creaked with every precise movement, earning a nettlesome scoff from the man as he stretched his lanky limbs.

"Twenty-eight?" She guessed, quite defeatedly. Her heart sank lower and lower as she feared the inevitable: *this man may be an entire decade older than myself!*

"Keep *goin',* dollface." Switch amusingly teased, tongue explicitly lapping outwards as it caressed the severed skin of his lip.

"Thirty?" Adelaide chirped, her breaths thinning as Switch released an exaggerated sound, something along the lines of a buzzer as the woman instinctively flinched.

"*Colder.*" He teased, pupils severely dilated as Adelaide swallowed a mouthful of bile. *Phew.*

"Twenty-nine, I reckon?"

"*Bingo.*" Switch gleamed, arms extending outward as two dainty fingers met the base of Adelaide's chin. He delicately swiped along the surface, the momentum prompting the woman's chin to vaguely raise as she brightly blushed before him.

"Wow," she muttered. "When do you turn thirty?"

"Nuh-uh," Switch teased, rapidly shaking his head from side to side as several ringlets tumbled into his line of sight. *"Your* turn."

"I'm twenty-four," Adelaide simply revealed. "Turning twenty-five near the end of January."

"Aw," Switch pressed, giggling wildly as he inched closer to the frozen woman. "Such a wittle *baby."*

"What the hell?" Adelaide spat, brows knit together in irritation as Switch continued to chuckle opposite her. "I'm only five years younger than you. I'm hardly a baby. You were my age once, too. Anyways, I have another question."

"Ugh." Switch grunted, tossing his hands up in angst as he collapsed in a heap against the drastically uncomfortable wall. "Always asking so many damn *questions."*

"Come on, Switch. Just one more." Adelaide urged. "Please?"

"Fiiiine." Switch mewled, meticulously rolling his eyes in their sockets as his right palm met the scuffed skin of his chin, petite patches of beard hair tickling his fingertips as he intently scratched the surface.

"Okay," Adelaide huffed, eyelids flickering closed as she took a deep breath. "Tell me."

"Tell you *what?"* Switch urged, eyes excessively darkening as he intently licked his lips in anticipation.

"Your name," Adelaide urged. "You know mine. Please tell me yours so I don't have to keep calling you by the name of Switch."

"Oh? And-*uh*, why should I tell you *that*, hmm?"

"I mean, you don't *have* to–"

"Bob." Switch keenly interrupted, bottom lip tucked between rows of teeth as he stifled a giggle.

Adelaide flatly frowned, a deep sigh emerging from her chest as she observed his giddy form as she spat out an irate, "liar."

"–Rob?" He teased, his tone slightly muffled by the obstruction of his bottom lip as he intently bit down, mindlessly chewing upon the skin.

"Switch–"

"Patrick." He firmly stated, wiggling his eyebrows seductively in Adelaide's direction as the woman's jaw significantly dropped.

"Like—Patrick Star?" Adelaide thickly teased, earning a simplistic eye roll from the broad-shouldered man as he cocked an eyebrow.

"Okay—*okay*," he exclaimed, tossing his hands into the air in mock surrender. "It's *Norman*."

"You're a damn liar," Adelaide scoffed. "I know about Norman Bates from *Psycho*, asshole."

"*Oooo*," Switch purred, claiming Adelaide's timid fingers in his warm palms as he gently cradled them. "Someone's *feisty*."

Adelaide begrudgingly yanked out of his reassuring hold, trembling fingers lacing around her nearby discarded boots as she ushered them back onto her cold, socked feet.

"I get it," she dismissed, blatantly avoiding Switch's quizzical glare as she slipped her petite feet into the leather shoes. "If you don't want to tell me, it's fine."

With that, the woman claimed the withered copy of *Sense and Sensibility* in her clutch, shooting Switch an additional irritated glance as she removed herself from their designated corner and approached the nice guard named Vern near the exit doors.

"Hello, Adelaide." The apprehensive man greeted—thick, charcoal bags consuming the flesh beneath his blank, soulless eyes as the woman's lips contorted into a soft frown.

"Hey, Vern. How's your mum?" The woman politely inquired, clutching the book tightly to her chest as the man released a strangled sigh.

"Dead." He revealed. "Do you want me to take you back to your cell?"

"Yes, please." Adelaide politely requested, allowing the man to claim her upper bicep with faulty fingers as they exited the premises. "I'm sorry about your mum."

Per usual, the dining hall served a hardly edible version of Thanksgiving dinner that night at six-thirty sharp. The meal consisted of an exceedingly dry slab of turkey, chunky mashed potatoes, and—of course—*peas*. Occasionally, the inmates were surprised with a small sliver of key lime or pumpkin pie as well, but it looked like the tasty desserts were nonexistent this year.

Adelaide swirled a chunk of mushy peas around her lilac-tinted tray, top teeth intently kneading upon her lower lip as Switch nibbled on a dry slice of turkey.

They hadn't spoken a single word to one another since their reunion in the supper line fifteen minutes prior. It was evident that Adelaide had smoked a cigarette back in her cell—the man could practically taste the smoke that radiated off of her skin. The scent was so glorious that it made him salivate in line. For some peculiar reason, the madman couldn't quit envisioning Adelaide's tiny hips below his, their tongues frolicking about as he physically tasted that damn cigarette that she so selfishly enjoyed while he spent the remainder of his recreational time staring at a blank, concrete wall. He wanted to taste her again—he *needed* to. He wanted to take her bottom lip between his teeth and feverishly clamp down—to sever the skin and devour the magnificent metallic flavor of her blood as it seeps into his gaping mouth . . .

"Switch!" Adelaide pressed, calling out his name for the third consecutive time as she fiddled with the plastic spoon in her grasp.

The distracted man crashed fleetingly back down to Earth, eyes ablaze as he rigidly shook his head to rid his brain of the torturous thoughts. Besides, the mere thought of Adelaide's sweet blood on his tongue was enough to make his head spin.

"How's the turkey?" The woman wondered, her stare reconnecting with the scattered peas upon her plate as she nudged at a particularly lumpy portion of potatoes.

"Belongs in the *trash*." Switch dismissed, dropping the half-eaten slice onto the bulky plastic of the tray.

The duo sat in a stale silence for several agonizing moments, exchanging curious glances as the man eminently poked and prodded at his untouched potatoes. This meal was definitely the worst Thanksgiving dinner he'd ever consumed—which was a slight shock considering he had eaten nothing but processed turkey and cheese Lunchables the previous year. Even those salty packs of artificial food tasted better than whatever the hell this shit was.

"Ad," Switch huskily pressed, leaning forward on the circular seat as his abdomen collided with the edge of the table. Adelaide's hazel gaze flickered upwards, meeting a set of dilated pupils. Her stomach impulsively churned.

"Yes?" She whispered, wedging a single nail between her teeth as she aimlessly chewed. Quite frankly, that single, dirty nail tasted better than the entire meal she'd managed to choke down, (all besides the revolting pile of peas, of course).

"I-*uh*," Switch murmured, glancing warily over his shoulder as his stern gaze met hers once more after a considerable pause. "*Need* you. There's gotta be somewhere we can go—a supply closet, another *bathroom*–"

Adelaide's cheeks flushed, her pulse drastically accelerating as she shifted her weight upon the stool, heart thickly hammering in her throat as vivid visuals of a blissful Switch raided her mind once more. If anything, she needed him more than he'd ever need her—and in more ways than strictly physical.

"Don't worry," she assured him, tearing the nail from the depths of her mouth as her palm met his. He physically tensed beneath her sudden hold, a staggered breath hitching in his throat as the supple, moistened skin of her index finger traced miscellaneous shapes along the top of his palm. "We'll figure something out."

"Ade-*laide*," Switch impatiently grumbled, gritting his teeth as he forcefully attempted to ward off the extremely venereal thoughts that currently consumed his skull.

"Patience, Switch." Adelaide countered. "I promise. I'll figure something out for us. I want you, too. So bad. We'll make this work."

"The voices are still at bay?" Nurse Briar politely wondered, thrusting a vibrantly-colored paper cup into Adelaide's unwilling grasp as a grimace overtook her features.

"Yeah," the woman softly agreed, tossing the multitude of pills into her mouth as she filled the empty cup up to the brim with tap water before chasing down the pills with the liquid. "For now, at least."

"I'm glad to hear that, Addy." Briar heartily grinned, retrieving the empty cup from Adelaide's grasp as she turned it over in her palm. Her stare heavily avoided Addy's, instead it lay firmly fixated on her toes as the artificially blond woman struggled to collect her scattered thoughts.

"Happy Thanksgiving, Adelaide." She simply stated, several additional statements threatening to spill from her sloppily painted lips as she hastily choked them back down. *Not today, Briar.*

Adelaide merely nodded, a weak, tight-lipped grin plastered up on her sullen complexion as she bid the nurse an inaudible goodbye, watching carefully as the slender woman slunk toward the door. The low hue of the nighttime lights pranced along the split ends of Briar's hair, which was pulled into a messy bun atop her skull as she rummaged around the pockets of her scrubs before releasing a heightened grunt.

"Shit," Nurse Briar mumbled, glancing uneasily over her shoulder to view a curious Adelaide as she'd realized the inevitable: She'd forgotten her ID in her locker.

"Everything okay, Nurse Briar?" Adelaide nosily squeaked, brows raised in immense curiosity as she carefully observed Briar's timid frame.

"Just forgot my ID," the woman simply dismissed, manicured fingers colliding with the provided key pad upon the plastic box as she entered a four-digit code. A tiny, fluorescent green light suddenly appeared, granting Briar access to the cell block as Adelaide's broad, steel mahogany door swung widely open. "Goodnight, Ad."

With that, the door sealed shut on Briar's heel, leaving behind an immensely sweaty Adelaide as she thickly swallowed.

Briar's password was Adelaide's inmate number.

Adelaide's fingers met the bulky fabric of her jumpsuit, fingertips grazing along the raised material of the sewn-on patch as her digits intently traced the numbers etched upon the surface.

4210.

Anxious trembles currently consumed the woman's spine, her fingers intently tearing at the dilapidated fabric of her top as she aggressively yanked it from her torso, revealing a patchy, crème-hued spaghetti strap tank top with a particularly large stain on the bottom left corner. A massive ball of bile had managed to find refuge in her throat, uneasy fingertips prancing along the aging wood of her dresser as she rapidly tore the center drawer open to reveal a half-full pack of Newport cigarettes and several unused matches.

Suddenly, the lithe, once-mute woman had all the power in the world. She currently held the key to unlock every single door in all of Stillwater Sanitarium—and this entire time, the ball was *already in her court*. For two years, Adelaide's inmate number has been used to unlock numerous doors within this hell hole.

Briar truly was an idiot.

Impatiently, the rigid woman stepped out of her leather boots, holey, socked feet meeting the frigid cement floor as an immediate shiver consumed her spine. She'd managed to wedge the flimsy pack of cigarettes into her trouser pocket, along with several fresh matches as the items lay buried within the fabric, nuzzling nicely between the previously forgotten playing card and a fuzzy ball of lint.

The woman's eyelids fluttered elegantly shut, hasty breaths emerging from partially parted lips as she mustered up the strength to inch forward–the strength to press her quivering fingertips against the keypad and enter in the almighty code.

With one final burst of bravery, the petite woman lunged forward, right palm colliding with the sleek black keypad as the raised buttons slipped between her curious digits. Steadily, her index finger hovered over the number four, sweat consuming the fine hairs of her upper brow as she finally applied a bit of pressure to the button, which audibly clicked beneath her firm touch.

An instantaneous gasp slipped off her tongue at the foreign sensation, heart beating rapidly beneath her ribcage as her finger migrated toward the number two, chest inordinately raising as she firmly pressed the button inward. Once again, the object audibly complied, sinking inwards from the pressure of her finger before popping back into place.

Swallowing thickly, the woman ushered the pad of her finger in the direction of the number one, a steady strand of sweat oozing down the slope of her prominent cheekbone as she pressed the button firmly. For a third time, the keypad responded with an audible click, which prompted the woman's stomach to heavily churn.

One more number.

Confidently, Adelaide's finger hovered over the number zero, pulse beating so rapidly against her chest that she feared she may actually succumb to cardiac arrest at any waking moment. She knew the code . . . she'd seen Briar enter it only moments prior.

It was Thanksgiving. On holidays, only one guard stood duty, and they typically remained in maximum security or on the first floor overnight. Besides, nobody cared enough to do the proper rounds in the middle of the night, (besides Greenwald, who only did them so he could get a proper nut off).

With a final, deep inhale—the woman pressed the final button, the breath immediately eluding her lungs as her knees locked firmly into place.

A tiny, vibrant viridescent light instantly appeared, granting the woman access to the cell block as the heavy steel door unlatched with a noisy *click*.

Adelaide stood frozen in the doorway, eyes wide with wonder as she glanced around the deathly silent cell block, her heart heavily hammering within her throat as the weight of the cigarette pack tugged fleetingly on her trousers.

Holy shit holy shit holy shit holy shit holy—

Quickly, the woman scurried from the confinement of her assigned space, yanking the large door closed behind her as she struggled to contain her screeches of delight. *Free at fucking last!*

Determinedly, the woman hooked slightly to the left, rapidly approaching Switch's sealed cell door as she efficiently entered the code onto the key pad. Once again, the light beamed a bright, confident green hue, which jump started her heart as the hefty door swung widely open.

Quivering fingers laced around the obscene circular handle as she roughly tugged the door closed on her heel, blurred vision struggling to adjust to the unfamiliar surroundings as the low glow of the blue nighttime lights softly illuminated Switch's sleeping form. He laid sprawled out on his back, left arm dangling off the side of the measly mattress as several sleepy fingers unconsciously twitched.

Surprisingly, the criminal had managed to slip into a dreamless slumber, marred lips heartily parted as soft snores emerged from deep within his chest. A shirt was absent, displaying arrays of scattered chest hair and a profusion of entirely random and oddly intriguing tattoos. The white and black striped jumpsuit trousers still claimed his bony hips, hanging low upon the skin as a distinct patch of pubes peeked out from the waist of the pants. Sealed eyelids were hidden by a mess of brunette curls, chest evenly rising and falling with every deep breath as Adelaide's stomach violently churned.

He was beautiful.

Adelaide's socked feet inched closer to the snoring heap of man, her heart inexplicably racing as her palms began to profusely sweat. A tiny sliver of pale midriff appeared beneath the shy fabric of her tank top and above the waistline of her trousers, which clung to her petite hips by hardly a thread as she cautiously approached the bed.

The lacerated skin of Switch's cheek unconsciously twitched, exasperated snores emerging from his drying lips as he audibly smacked them in a weak attempt to moisten the cracked flesh. Adelaide's stomach churned at the innocent action, her arm outstretching as slender digits uneasily parted, fingertips just barely grazing his tattooed wrist as her warm flesh met his.

Before Adelaide could even process a single thought—she'd found herself pinned to the frigid concrete, the base of her skull arduously colliding with the harsh surface as arrays of blinding stars littered her vision. A sturdy palm clamped down tightly onto her pulsating neck, fingers laced agonizingly tight around the supple skin as she struggled to intake air. Her hips were painfully pinned, fresh tears escaping the corners of her choppy vision as Switch released a puzzled statement: "Addy?"

Thus, the blinding stars ceased—the unbearably strong hold on her throat instantaneously vanishing as Adelaide obscenely gasped for air, dainty fingers grazing the sore skin of her throbbing skull as she met a wild-eyed Switch, who currently sat snug upon her hips.

The sleepy man blinked several times, his temporarily weakened vision struggling to adjust to the shy lighting of the cell as he eventually clambered off of the tiny woman, who lay in a gasping heap upon the concrete.

"G-God—" Adelaide croaked, climbing to her knees as she eagerly massaged the tender skin of her throat. She swore she could already feel vibrant purple bruises in the shape of fingertips forming along the flesh. "You could've *killed* me—"

"In my *defense*," Switch huskily pressed, his voice laced with sleep as he settled back onto the rickety mattress. "You snuck up on *me*. By the way, how the hell did you get in here?"

"Briar's an idiot and forgot her ID," Adelaide throatily explained, knees violently wobbling as she stood to her feet. "I saw her code. It's my inmate number."

A strangled snort emerged from Switch's nostrils, a weak, cheeky grin tugging at his lacerated lips as dainty fingertips pranced along Adelaide's wrist, gingerly tugging her toward the mattress. "What an *idiot*."

"Yeah," Adelaide breathed, collapsing onto Switch's lax form as he maneuvered his broad frame fully onto the surface, desperate fingers digging into the silky flesh of her wrist as he positioned her petite self directly on top of his hips in one fluid motion.

"*Yeaaaah*," Switch murmured, fingers knotting into taunt fists at the back of her skull as he suddenly yanked her rigid frame forward, noses dolorously colliding upon impact as the woman audibly moaned against his flesh.

Magnificent arrays of vibrant colors instantaneously raided Adelaide's sealed eyelids—her heart skipping several blatant beats as she grew lax within his arms, bony hips meeting his as her clothed breasts flattened against his pale, bare chest. Desperate fingers kneaded an assortment of pictures against her scalp, several unkempt strands of straggly brown hair slipping between untamed fingernails as wet tongues messily collided. Lecherous fingertips tore at the marred flesh of Switch's complexion, slipping elegantly between the uneven folds as the duo openly groaned into one another's mouth—whilst swallowing the glorious sounds with absolute glee.

"I've missed this," Adelaide moaned against his pockmarked skin, fingers threading through a particularly curly loop of brunette hair as Switch's palm flattened against her throbbing skull, forcing her lips to his once more as he tasted every bit of her luscious mouth.

Adelaide released a throaty sigh as she tore her swollen lips from Switch's determined mouth, enthusiastic giggles escaping her as she heavily blushed. At the sudden absence of her prying mouth, the madman decided to travel south—peppering sporadic, open-mouthed kisses along the prominent skin of her jaw as he dipped down to meet the bruised flesh of her neck. His hand abandoned the unbrushed strands of her hair, slipping *down-down-down* to meet her rounded bottom as his palms flattened against the heavily clothed surface, applying the faintest amount of pressure, forcing her hips downward to meet him.

"Switch—" Adelaide gasped, toes curling within the wilting fabric of her holey socks as her eyes rotated to the back of her skull, breaths emerging in staggered pants as his hips bucked upwards to meet hers. All the while, his lips remained firmly planted along the supple skin of her neck, severed skin painting invisible portraits along her discolored flesh as she stirred within his hold.

Adelaide abruptly tore out of his needy embrace, wide, cocoa-hued eyes staring fleetingly back at her figure as she tore the bothersome material of her tank top from her clammy skin. The fabric elegantly fluttered to the floor in a discarded heap, Switch's widened gaze fixated on her bare chest as she felt her cheeks grow hot. Her nipples seemed to have realized the drastic temperature shift, as they promptly hardened—accompanied by raised patches of goosebumps along Adelaide's chest as several bumpy spots dipped down onto her navel.

"S-Sorry," she murmured, arms curling inward in a shy attempt to conceal her busty chest. Switch's hands immediately claimed hers, tugging her uneasy touch away as he reveled in the sight of her bountiful breasts, as well as the prominent goosebumps that littered her pale skin.

"Hey, *heeey*," he lazily cooed, inching upwards (with some difficulty) on the mattress, his hips slightly shifting beneath her agile form. "You're *beautiful*."

Adelaide heavily blushed at his declaration, a toothy grin stretching along her cheeks as the man leaned forward, hot breaths fanning along her scaled skin as he peppered dainty, open-mouthed kisses along her prominent collarbones.

The woman's head lulled back on her shoulders, hushed groans slipping through significantly cracked lips as rigid fingers buried into the tangled mess of hair atop his skull. She claimed several ringlets between her fingers, insistently tugging the strands away from his scalp as deep moans resonated throughout his chest, the audible sonance tickling the flesh of her chest as his tongue wrote poems against her skin.

There was something truly surreal in regards to the rugged flesh of his destroyed cheek—the way the jarred skin helplessly caressed hers, how the uneven edges of the shaped scar on his lower lip sent violent shivers down the length of her spine as he efficiently marked every inch of her flesh.

Switch hungrily nipped at her throat, the flat of his tongue teasingly toying with the supple skin as his free palm claimed her jaw, the pad of his calloused thumb intently tracing the raised surface of her goose bump riddled skin as Adelaide practically crumbled within his embrace.

"Switch—" the woman merely purred, yanking a considerably large chunk of his curls away from his scalp as he released a heightened grunt—swollen lips ultimately detaching from her abused throat as dark, callous eyes met hers.

Their lips reunited in a rushed peck, teeth fervently latching onto one another's skin as Switch's fingers hooked into the waistline of her trousers. Her palms blindly met his whilst exchanging hearty, wet kisses—petite fingers interlacing with long, slender digits as she assisted the man in removing the article of clothing. Their mouths parted momentarily; a disgruntled murmur emerging from her swollen flesh as she struggled to rid her lanky legs of the bothersome material.

Her hands were trembling immensely–staggered breaths escaping through red-rimmed lips as she eventually discarded the material onto the dingy floor. Switch noticed how badly she was shaking–which, in turn, made his pulse drastically quicken beneath the pale skin of his chest. Truth be told–he absolutely *loved* how uncomfortable and anxious people got around him. It was–to say the least–quite arousing to observe how jittery they got– and *all because of him!*

The curly-haired man's arms extended backwards, palms flattening against the rugged surface of the lumpy mattress as slender fingers unvaryingly spread. His head hung limp on his shoulders, husky gaze observing an anxious Adelaide as she remained only in her unappealing pair of faded white panties, hair a massive mess as she eased back onto the warmth of his lap.

An involuntary moan emerged from the madman at the simplistic feel of their tepid groins colliding–enthusiastic bolts of electricity consuming his spine as his Adams apple bobbed gleefully about beneath the flesh of his throat.

Adelaide curiously leaned forward, delicate lips capturing the raised skin as she placed gentle, even kisses along the flesh. Raspy groans emerged from the antsy man beneath her hips, his head leaning further back as more surface area of his throat immediately opened up to her. The Adams apple promptly shifted beneath her prying lips–*quite possibly due to his excessive whimpering*–and the woman found herself slightly grinding down on his lap, desperate fingers toying with the waist of his jumpsuit as she inaudibly begged for him to remove the material. Eventually, every article of clothing had been promptly removed; leaving the two entirely naked before one another.

Although they bathed naked next to one another every single night, something about this time was entirely dissimilar. The charged energy between the pair was unmistakable; as if an invisible rope bound the two together, aggressively yanking them closer and closer until they ultimately merged into one. One body, one soul—one rapidly beating heart and arrays of goosebumps.

For a moment, the two of them simply admired the sight. Switch's fingers danced along her blushing skin, calloused fingertips etching along the clearly visible set of ribs beneath her strikingly small form as Adelaide's lips met his collarbone, sucking diligently upon the skin as Switch writhed beneath her sturdy frame.

"Switch–" she breathed, admiring his curious glare as her stare met his cocoa-hued gaze. His thumb met her throbbing lower lip, gently grazing over the angry flesh as he intently wet his lips in preparation to speak.

"It's *Andrew*."

XX

One considerably flawed trait of the human mind is that of true adoration and admiration. Like most, Briar Cunningway falls victim to this very flaw—especially in regards to the impeccably shy Adelaide Lynch.

The thirty-four-year-old woman's hair was tugged back into a sloppy, loose blond bun, several stray strands dangling within her line of sight as unpolished fingernails dug deeply within the shy fabric of her shirt pocket. The tip of her forefinger dipped along the side of a smooth plastic card hidden deeply within, a forced, tight-lipped frown enveloping her lips as she feigned frustration.

Adelaide glared skeptically in her direction, nearly nonexistent brows raised in curiosity as Briar's greedy hold retracted from the thick material of her scrubs. An exasperated *shit* slipped off of her lips as she glanced in Adelaide's direction, bottom lip tucked between rows of artificially whitened teeth as she shifted her weight upon the ground.

"Everything okay, Briar?" Adelaide wondered.

"Just forgot my ID." Briar said, noisily exhaling as her quivering fingers met the keypad. *This was it.*

Boldly, the woman entered the four-digit code—the very same combination that lay sewn into the fabric upon Adelaide's breast—when she was promptly greeted with a tiny, vibrant green light. Her chest clenched at the sight, the broad, steel door audibly unlatching as the Nurse bid a timid

Adelaide goodbye before slipping from the cold, concrete cell.

Once outside, Nurse Briar flattened her back against the frigid frame, heart inexplicably hammering beneath her ribcage as she fished her aging ID from the confinement of her pocket. Uneasily, she turned the object over in her palm, wide eyes admiring the dainty plastic as a faux grin stared upwards at her beneath the weak blue lighting of the nighttime lights. She damn well knew what she'd done, and the persistent thumping of her heart ensured the woman that she hadn't made any mistake at all.

Besides, Adelaide deserved this. She always would.

Confidently, Nurse Briar's painted lips curled into a gleeful smirk, her fingers effectively slipping the ID back into the depths of her breast pocket as she trudged down the bleak hallway and abandoned the cell block.

"It's *Andrew.*" Switch assuredly revealed, the pad of his calloused thumb digging deeply into the dainty flesh of Adelaide's sullen complexion as her gaze instantly widened.

"W-*what–*" she thickly stammered, maneuvering her petite frame off of Switch's heaving figure as she rotated onto the mattress beside him, her skin slick with sweat as her slender fingertips claimed his jaw.

"That's it. My *name.*" He firmly stated, glare significantly darkening as he wet his lips in wanton abandon. "Ugly, *innit?*"

"Unexpected," Adelaide breathed, tracing the tumescent skin of his lacerated lower lip with her nail. "But not even remotely ugly. I really, really like it."

A forced burst of air emerged from Switch's flared nostrils, a simplistic grin overcoming his blushing features as a yellow, toothy smile invaded Adelaide's vision. She heartily giggled at the sight of him, heart inexplicably racing as she leaned forward to press a firm kiss to his mouth.

Switch heartily obliged to the confident display of affection; his jaw falling slack as swollen lips instantly parted. Adelaide released a pleasant sigh at the glorious feeling—her thin lips curling into a cheeky grin as she peppered feather-like kisses against his open mouth, tongue occasionally lapping out to caress the silky skin as the woman drifted into euphoria once more.

The severed, choppy flesh of his mangled face elegantly pranced along the swollen skin of her lips, eliciting blatant goosebumps along every square inch of her glistening, exposed flesh. The miniscule hairs upon the back of her neck promptly stood at the magnificent feel of the pockmarked skin, curious mouth exploring every inch of the artificial deformities as Switch willingly allowed the wildly intimate gesture.

Curled fingertips roughly kneaded the reddened flesh of Adelaide's dainty hips, eyelids fluttering tightly shut as the comforting pair of cocoa-hued orbs immediately disappeared from sight; replaced only by persistently squeezing lids and tightly-knit brows. Voluntarily, the criminal drifted heavily into submission, heart heavily hammering beneath Adelaide's firm chest as she continued her gentle assault upon his scarred flesh.

Eventually, the dainty woman yanked away from Switch's lax form, a hearty grin displayed upon her joyful expression as she rotated her nude form toward the edge of the measly mattress. Switch's brows raised in curiosity, tiny pink tongue darting outwards from the depths of his mouth as he intently poked and prodded at the lacerated flesh of his cheek.

"What'cha *doin'*, toots?" He throatily mused through half-lidded eyes, fingertips dancing along her flushed flesh as she retrieved the softened paper pack of Newport cigarettes from her jumpsuit pocket. The woman readjusted her position, plopping down beside the madman on the exceedingly tiny bed as his gaze significantly widened.

"Oh, *baby*," he purred, desperate digits lacing around the pack of cigarettes as he positioned the nail of his thumb beneath the flap. Adelaide's breaths thinned as he inordinately opened the container, revealing several fresh cancer sticks as needy fingers rotated upwards to retrieve one of the cigs.

An instant, scarlet-tinted blush captured her sunken cheeks as she snatched an unlit match from the bottom of the pack, breaths momentarily thinning as she ran the edge of the wood against the harsh, concrete wall—emitting a bright, fluorescent flame.

"Thanks, *pumpkin*." Switch mused, a lengthy grin yanking at his mouth as he positioned the cigarette between lacerated lips, greasy, unkempt curls fanned outward against the drastically thin pillow as Adelaide intently observed his every move. Once more, his eyelids fluttered tightly closed, concealing the perfect shade of orbs beneath as Adelaide's stomach violently churned.

There was something morbidly handsome about the way Switch smoked cigarettes—in fact, there was something morbidly handsome about the way Switch did anything at all, really. It was as if he did everything with absolute confidence—with grace and precision and overall authenticity. Sometimes, Adelaide somewhat doubted that the nude man beside her was even real at all—could it be possible that he was merely a figment of her very own imagination? A result of a wildly imaginative reverie—a complete phantasmal individual that was strategically constructed by her maniacal mind?

"I really like you," Adelaide confidently spilled, free fingertips brushing along the defined lining of his jaw as her opposite hand claimed a lit cigarette, mindlessly twisting the cancer stick between two slender digits.

Switch's eyelids crept open, widened gaze refocusing on the woman beside him as she anxiously brought her bottom lip between rows of yellowing teeth. Although the stirring sense of discomfort present in her belly reminded her of how utterly idiotic she was to even admit her feelings aloud; she couldn't quite bring herself to regret letting the statement slip.

She knew virtually nothing of the Switch's true identity beyond these four secluded concrete walls—*and yet*—the insistent thumping of her erratically racing heart heavily reminded her of the sheer fact that once again, she *didn't even care.* In this moment, the amount of lives Switch had stolen beyond the walls of Stillwater simply did not matter. Whether he was a mass-murdering psychopath or simply a crappy criminal who enjoyed dressing theatrically and murdering children—it simply *did not matter.*

Because within these four lonesome walls, the Switch she knew was nothing of that at all.

Black Friday—otherwise known as day 813.

Adelaide Lynch lay accompanied in the furthermost corner of the rec room, eyes solely glued to the written word of her routine novel as dirt-riddled fingertips caressed the aging pages.

Switch lay slung over her petite legs, greasy ringlets sprawled out over her clothed skin as his chin met the exposed flesh of his neck, fingers threaded between a dilapidating deck of cards as he efficiently shuffled the stack. Determined glare flickered momentarily in Adelaide's direction, chocolate-colored gaze brightening at the sight of her concentrated glare as a vibrant cartoon King pranced along his fingertips.

"D'you-*uh*," Switch slurred, wedging the corner of the flimsy card beneath an outgrown nail. "Still *have* it?"

Adelaide lowered the novel from her sullen complexion, a hearty grin overcoming her features as she daintily folded the corner of the yellowed page into a miniscule triangle before discarding Jane Austen's written masterpiece onto the dusty floor.

"Have *what?*" She dryly teased, becoming completely aware of the playing card wedged between the thick fabric of her jumpsuit pocket. Her straggly, ashen-brown hair was gently parted slightly to the left side, creating a volumetric illusion as several strands efficiently framed her heart-shaped face. Her big hazel eyes were bright and cheerful, a genuine smile stretched across her plump lips as she struggled to stifle a giggle. For once, Adelaide actually looked considerably pretty.

Switch merely rolled his eyes, tearing his ringlet-riddled skull from the confinement of her lap as confined wrists irritably brushed away several bothersome strands from his eyes.

"Oh *God*," Switch spat, flattening his back against the drastically uncomfortable cement wall as he fingered the bothersome set of metal cuffs. "*Look* at us. Like an old *married* couple or some shit. It's *disgusting*."

Adelaide's playful expression immediately slackened, lively features instantly contorting into that of immense hurt as she awkwardly shifted her weight against the wall.

"Lemme guess," she lowly murmured, avoiding Switch's expressionless gaze as she intently eyed Emmett's gifted copy of *Sense and Sensibility* laid beside her right leg. "You're against marriage or something? Think it's nothing but legal documents binding two individuals together or some rubbish?"

Switch flatly frowned, cards inelegantly slipping between parted fingers as he mindlessly toyed with the loose lace of his boot.

"Whose *E?*" He thickly inquired, clearly recollecting the blatant message imprinted upon the front cover of Adelaide's paperback novel.

The woman shyly swallowed, blinking back several blinding tears as Emmett DuPré's strikingly handsome figure bombarded her fragile mind. A wide, toothy grin—an essence of chopped, chestnut curls which outlined his perfectly sculpted face like magic, as if he was produced in a factory. *The perfect boy*; he would've been called. Created to make even the most miserable woman considerably happy for all of eternity.

"Since you seem to be so against marriage, I assume your stance on children is wildly similar?" Adelaide snapped, shooting Switch a vexed glare as a forced burst of air emerged from his flared nostrils, several curls tickling the lining of his jaw as he profusely shook his head.

"Y'*know*," he thickly began, obnoxiously smacking his lips as vivid visuals of his past raided his mind. "You've got some pretty *big balls*, love bug. In-*uh*, the *outside* world, nobody would *dare* to speak to me the way *you do.*"

"Well, in the *outside world*," Adelaide irritably mocked his exaggerated tone. "You'd probably pull a knife on anyone that would. But in here, you're all talk—nothing but."

A heightened, sarcastic giggle emerged from the criminal sat directly beside her, pupils immensely dilated as he struggled to stifle the obnoxious sound. Several curious heads immediately turned at the sudden intrusion; eyes wild with fear as several patients actually shifted their weight further away from the laughing man in the back-left corner.

Adelaide's blood curdled within her veins, fingers curled into agonizingly tight fists as she glanced warily in Switch's giggling direction. She *hated* that laugh—the way it so clearly *mocked* her, like some sort of uneducated child.

"Why do you *ask*?" Switch drawled, choking back the final round of giggles as the pad of his thumb swiped against his bottom lip. "D'you have a *bun* in the *oven*? If so, it's certainly not *my* bun—"

"*No*," Adelaide sneered, her voice slightly wavering as she clearly remembered her pregnancy scare with Emmett only six months after they began dating. "I always wanted my own set of ankle-biters, and I even thought that I was carrying one at one point. Turns out it was just some kind of phantom pregnancy, or something. I didn't even know that was a thing."

Switch fell silent, bottom lip jutting outwards as he thickly swallowed.

"Did you ever want kids at one point in your life?" Adelaide gently wondered, fingers desperately itching to creep over to Switch's lap, to curl around his slender digits and torturously squeeze.

The curly-haired man's eyebrows slightly raised, an inordinate sound emerging through partially parted lips as he inefficiently cleared his throat.

"You-*uh*," Switch began, briefly pausing to collect his thoughts as he picked at the frayed skin surrounding his fingernails. "Ever seen a *baby coffin?"*

Adelaide's jaw fell ajar, her heart instantly stilling beneath her ribcage as she avoided Switch's sullen complexion. Although the statement was entirely simplistic and extremely vague—she felt as if he'd just revealed his entire life story to her in just one single sentence. She wanted to ask him about it, to convince him to spill every single aspect of the baby he'd lost.

Switch's inquiry went painfully unanswered—Adelaide's breaths emerging in short, staggered pants as she swallowed back hefty sobs. Within such a short time span, she'd learned so much about the madman sat beside her, all from one teeny-tiny statement, one exceedingly small factor of his life; the fact that he, too, has endured the horrors and hells of loss—of losing someone that meant the absolute world to him.

Suddenly, Adelaide felt closer to the Switch than she ever had before.

Supper that night went surprisingly well. Unlike the usual abundance of tasteless food that tended to litter their multi-hued plastic trays—the cafeteria had decided to go an alternative route, one that involved perfectly mashed potatoes and absolutely tasty green beans, accompanied by a juicy slice of ham.

Nurse Briar hadn't shown her face all day, and Adelaide was beginning to grow antsy. Sure, the artificially blond woman had gotten sick over the past two years and taken several days off, but something about Briar's absence today seemed abnormally strange. It was as if she was avoiding something—possibly even running *away* from something . . .

"Why aren't-*cha* eating your *potatoes?*" Switch muttered, dipping a forefinger into the mushy pile of potatoes as he scooped a spoonful into his gaping mouth.

Adelaide shook her head, ridding her mind of the conflicting thoughts of Briar's absence as she retrieved the unpigmented plastic spoon from the surface of the oblong table.

"Lots on my mind. Got distracted." She simply dismissed, twirling the potatoes around on her tray as she avoided Switch's curious stare. After several moments of utter silence, the woman eventually spoke once more.

"Switch?" She whispered, dropping the plastic spoon once again as it messily collided with the scoop of potatoes.

Switch's jaw clenched mid-chew, brows raised in wonder as his gaze trailed over Adelaide's worrisome expression. Following pursuit—he, too, mockingly dropped his spoon, dainty fingers curling around the angry flesh of his cuffed wrist as he quizzically stared.

"*Yeees?*"

Adelaide dramatically exhaled, shifting her weight upon the circular stool as she avoided his unblinking stare. "Have you noticed Nurse Briar's absence?"

Just as Switch's jaw parted in preparation to speak—a shy Nurse Jackie approached the isolated side of the table, hands inordinately trembling as she consistently smoothed down the bunched material of her scrubs.

Both Adelaide and Switch's stares immediately collided with the rigid woman, brows raised in bewilderment as she struggled to spit out a simplistic greeting.

"H-Hello," the woman stammered, bottom lip slightly extending outward to blow away a stray strand of irritable brown hair from her eyes. "Briar's out sick, so I'm her replacement until she returns. I'll be bathing the both of you tonight. Switch, you'll remained cuffed during bathing time."

"*Cuffed?*" Switch spat, brows knitting together in vexation as he glanced downward at the routine set of handcuffs around his tainted wrists. "That's *bullshit–*"

"What I say goes, Switch. If you have an issue with it, you can take it up with Dr. Evers." Nurse Jackie confidently pressed, shifting her weight from either foot as she glanced in Adelaide's direction. "How're you feeling, Adelaide?"

"Fine." Adelaide dismissively spat, wedging her thumb nail beneath the opposite one as she inexplicably attempted to lift the nail from its bed. "Imagine how uncomfortable it would be to bathe while handcuffed, Jackie."

"Gosh," Nurse Jackie unprofessionally hissed beneath her breath, before continuing with an irate, "forget it. Neither of you are getting baths tonight. You can wait until Briar returns tomorrow."

"*What?*" Switch sneered, accompanied by an exasperated exclamation from a furious Adelaide opposite him.

"You're joking!" The woman yelped, immediately standing to her feet as the table shifted beneath her abrupt shift in weight. "You can't do that–"

"I can do anything I want, Lynch. I'm your temporary Nurse and if I don't feel comfortable with bathing an uncuffed Switch and you can't seem to keep your mouth shut about the circumstance, then you both can wait until tomorrow. Not another word." Nurse Jackie sharply snipped, turning on her heel to abandon the duo as Adelaide furiously shook.

"But—"

"Enough!" Nurse Jackie exploded, prompting the entire cafeteria to fall exceedingly silent. "If you say one more word, I'll send you straight to Evers' office. *No exceptions*." Nurse Jackie's threat made the twenty-four-year-old woman feel as if she was in high school once again. Jackie took the place of some measly teacher who everyone hated, and vice-versa; and here she was, threatening to send Adelaide to the Principal's office over a dumb dispute over something totally immoral. The Switch was human, and it was apparent that Adelaide was the only one to see him as such. Everyone else within this prison treated him as if he were some type of wild animal.

Adelaide angrily bit her tongue, a sudden metallic taste filling her senses as her digits curled into painful fists at her sides. She glanced curiously over her shoulder to view Switch's expression, a broad grin plastered on his taunting features as her stomach promptly churned. He delivered a sultry wink in her direction, tongue routinely caressing the skin of his lip as Adelaide's mouth curled into a vicious grin.

"Hey Nurse Jackie," she announced, inching forward toward the taller woman as her glare met a confident Adelaide several feet away.

"Lynch, what did I just say?" Nurse Jackie countered, crossing her slender arms across her impeccably tiny chest as she cautiously avoided Switch's amused expression.

"Well, I think you said that you enjoy masturbating with a cucumber in the nurses' lounge. Or *maybe*—" Adelaide taunted, her wildly inappropriate comment earning a profusion of giggles from surrounding inmates. Nurse Jackie's jaw fell.

"You like to send nude photos to Elliot Greenwald in hopes that maybe— *just maybe*—you can get some action for the first time in a decade, because Lord only knows that the little valley between your legs hasn't even been thought of by anyone for as long as you can coherently *remember*—"

"*Enough!*" Nurse Jackie exploded, thick tears cloaking her scarlet-tinted cheeks as she struggled to contain her obscene cries. "Evers' office—*now!*"

A nearby guard quickly captured Adelaide's miniscule biceps, roughly yanking the tiny woman forward as she released a series of enthusiastic giggles. Confidently, she cocked her head in Switch's direction, delivering a playful wink in his direction as he returned the flirty gesture.

"Knock'em *dead*, kiddo."

XXI

"So sweet to see you
Writhe and crawl and scream for life
But I can't listen now
I'm too busy with the knife"
–Motörhead, "Sweet Revenge"

Tick.

Adelaide persistently laced and unlaced her clammy fingers, glancing warily around at the unfamiliar surroundings as a thick bead of sweat consumed her nearly invisible brow. An obscenely noisy clock lay plastered up on the opposite wall, persistent sounds irritably interrupting her worrisome thoughts as time ticked idly by.

Tock.

The cramped space was particularly warm—which, in turn, had prompted the lithe woman to claim the bunched sleeves of her jumpsuit. Determined fingertips curled beneath the thick fabric, rotating swiftly as she inordinately rolled the material up the length of her tiny arms before hooking the rolled sleeves behind her pointy elbows.

Tick.

The office was extraordinarily unkempt and cluttered—filled nearly to the brim with an abundance of antediluvian furniture, obscene splotches of paint absent in various spots as Adelaide insistently picked at a considerably large speck of chipping wood. Her chair was old and unstable; accessorized with a moldy mahogany cushion. The furniture obnoxiously creaked with every miniscule movement—so Adelaide found herself absolutely rigid, resembling a statue; the perfect addition to Dr. Evers' offices' aesthetic.

Tock.

After several agonizing minutes, the air seemed to drastically thin—creating an overwhelmingly dull atmosphere as Adelaide repugnantly gasped; her lungs neglecting to intake air as the latch on the door audibly clicked.

Tick.

A slender individual with slicked, jet black hair and exceedingly long eyelashes cockily strut into the petite premises; a confident, tight-lipped grin displayed upon his insipid features as he offered Adelaide a dull greeting.

Tock.

"Good evening, 4210." He said, a half-empty glass of enigmatic liquid sloshing about within a murky cup. An abundance of miscellaneous golden rings littered his slender, bony fingers—resembling that of brass knuckles as the thin man slunk into the room.

Adelaide failed to respond, her very last breath eluding her lungs as she viewed an overwhelmingly confident Dr. Evers, who'd managed to collapse into the depths of his inky black swivel chair on the opposite half of the ginormous oak desk.

The foggy glass promptly met the dusty surface of the desk, several drops of the malign liquid inordinately spilling over the sides as several beads met the wood. Adelaide intently observed as the thick liquid soaked the surface, slipping between the indifferent cracks as she drifted into a slight trance.

"Miss Lynch?" Dr. Evers pressed, brows knit together in uncertainty as the frail woman's beady eyes suddenly met his, a particularly bothersome strand of unruly hair clinging to the severed skin of her bottom lip as he awkwardly cleared his throat. Still, the woman failed to muster up the strength to reply. Even after 800 grueling days, she'd never found herself in this office, and the suffocating atmosphere made her realize just exactly why she'd chosen to remain inconspicuous up until recently . . .

"So," the man thickly began, cautiously avoiding Adelaide's unblinking glare as the tips of his rounded fingers persistently toyed with the base of his glass. "Miss Kleever tells me that you've been—*intolerable* tonight. What are your thoughts on this matter, 4210?"

Adelaide shifted her weight upon the rickety chair, thickly swallowing a mouthful of bile as she brought her bottom lip between her teeth, a stray strand of unbrushed hair slipping into the depths of her mouth along with it.

Dr. Evers released a strangled sigh at the entirely unsatisfactory situation, bright eyes intently studying Adelaide's sullen complexion as her features gradually paled.

"M-Mister Evers, sir," she inordinately stammered, her voice emerging in a half-whisper as she desperately avoided his piercing stare. "I'm not typically intolerable—"

"No," Dr. Evers clipped, lounging sideways in his leather swivel chair as Adelaide instantly bit her tongue. "Usually, you're practically invisible—aren't you, 4210? Tell me, what's changed?"

Switch's marred appearance suddenly bombarded her mind, a cheeky, yellow grin prancing along her thoughts as a multitude of giggles filled her ears. An impulsive grin immediately invaded her features, her palm clamping down over her lips to conceal the hearty expression as Dr. Evers frowned.

I'm sucking the infamous Switch's dick, that's what changed.

"Dr. Blake's inhumane practices must've cured me, sir." Adelaide boldly announced, clearly recollecting the horrific meetings and the countless rounds of electrotherapy . . .

"What exactly did you say to Miss Kleever in the dining hall, 4210? Just so I can get a proper picture formed in my head of the scenario." Dr. Evers blandly inquired, pausing momentarily to take a generous sip from his unwashed glass.

Adelaide's closed-lipped grin rapidly transformed into a toothy smirk, Nurse Jackie's horrified expression promptly raiding her thoughts as she spat out an amused: "I told everyone that she enjoys casually fucking herself with a cucumber in the staff lounge."

Dr. Evers' brows inquisitively raised, a forced frown tugging at his remarkably thin lips as he ineptly cleared his throat once again before speaking.

"Was that everything that was said, 4210?"

"No," Adelaide profusely giggled, twiddling her thumbs atop her lap as Elliot Greenwald's ugly mug replaced Nurse Jackie's mortified expression. "I also teased her for sending graphic nudes to Greenfuck."

"Greenfuck?" Dr. Evers queried, gnawing harshly on his bottom lip as a hefty snort wormed its way through Adelaide's nostrils.

"That's what I call Elliot Greenwald," she forwardly explained. "Besides, he earned the nickname when he decided to start sticking his little pecker in nearly every female patient—"

"That's enough, 4210." Dr. Evers monotonically scolded, immediately rising from his chair as he avoided the woman's incredibly confident physique. Oddly, she seemed like an entirely different person, as if the Adelaide Lynch persona had disappeared—perhaps one of her voices had taken over . . .

"Dr. Blake tells me the voices have disappeared," Dr. Evers taunted, irritably pacing the tiny space behind his desk as Adelaide's cocky expression slightly faded.

After a considerably lengthy pause, the man approached the aging desk, his palms flattening upon the surface as his bony back slightly arched. "Tell me, 4210. Who am I currently speaking with?"

Adelaide's brows cocked slightly upwards, an expression of pure disgust plastered upon her features as she released a vexed statement: "With all due respect—*sir*—I don't have Dissociative Identity Disorder."

"Ah," Dr. Evers mused, removing his hands from the table as he stood tall once more. "Textbook name and everything. I take it you're a fan of psychology?"

"I was always curious of what really went on in my head," Adelaide fumed, furious trembles enveloping her spine as her session with Dr. Evers took an incredibly sharp turn. "I might suffer from an acute form of Schizophrenia, but I don't have multiple personalities—"

"You're dismissed." Dr. Evers clipped, clearly avoiding Adelaide's bewildered glare as he retrieved the glass from the table. The wide-eyed woman watched as he tossed his head back, draining the dark liquid from the glass with one giant swig as he discarded the cup onto the desk.

"Pardon me?" Adelaide croaked, claiming a fist full of her jumpsuit between clammy fingers as Dr. Evers crossed the floor in three giant strides, fingers encircling the brass handle of the door as he aggressively yanked it open.

"Marvin," Dr. Evers exclaimed, signaling a nearby guard as Adelaide hesitantly rose from her chair. "Take 4210 back to her cell."

"Was it something I said, Doctor?" Adelaide dryly teased, her voice inordinately cracking during nearly every syllable as a raven-haired guard rapidly approached her quivering frame.

Her question remained unanswered—a tight-lipped frown plastered on his bleak features as the woman was efficiently escorted from the office.

"He doesn't even *care*!" Adelaide shrieked, tempestuously pacing the grimy ground of her cell as several flakes of dirt invaded the holed fabric of her socks.

"Like, I literally told him about Greenwald and how he assaults nearly everyone and he didn't even bat an eye! I told him point-blank and he was *expressionless!*"

"Are you really that *surprised*, bug?" Switch lazily drawled, his upper half lounging against the frayed wall as his fingertips toyed with the severed concrete wall. "I mean, it *is* the owner of *Stillwater Sanitarium* we're discussing."

"He's j-just—" Adelaide stammered, tossing her arms into the air in defeat as she struggled to spit the words out. "He's *foul*. Utterly foul!"

"You're *cute* when you're all angry." Switch hungrily pressed, amused chuckles resonating throughout his chest as Adelaide briefly paused, rigid glare meeting the smiling eyes of Switch—of *Andrew*.

"We need to get the hell out of here, Andrew." She whispered, collapsing in an exasperated heap upon her measly mattress as Switch released a lengthy sigh.

"In due *time*, princess."

Adelaide managed to slip into a pleasant slumber a solid seventy-three minutes later, her greasy locks fanned outward in diverse directions upon her unwashed pillowcase as Switch irritably tossed and turned.

The mattress felt unusually firm, and the madman just couldn't seem to get comfortable. Plus, the idea of slithering into Adelaide's impossibly tiny bed was a much better idea than attempting to sleep upon this old, lonely bed.

The soles of Switch's feet collided softly with the frigid floor, array of goosebumps instantly littering the exposed flesh of his permanently inked arms as he hastily retrieved his discarded striped jumpsuit several feet away.

"I can't believe you forgot to give the Switch his pills! He'll probably kill himself for something if he already hasn't!" A foreign, chirpy voice emerged beyond the sealed cell door. Switch froze, brows raised in immense curiosity as he settled back down onto his lumpy mattress.

"I know, I know," Nurse Jackie hurriedly dismissed. "Stop reminding me of how much of an idiot I am. I'm not used to dealing with the extreme psychopaths."

"Yeah," the second voice amusingly cheered. "You only deal with the moderately psycho ones."

"Exactly." Nurse Jackie's muffled voice agreed, the broad steel door suddenly unlatching as Switch's stomach violently churned.

Instead of fully entering the cell like Nurse Briar normally did, the woman simply set the vibrant paper cup upon the dusty ground, completely avoiding Switch's stern glare before tugging the door closed once more and disappearing from view.

"Any plans tonight?" The unnamed woman wondered. Switch rose from his bed once again, heart imprudently racing beneath his ribcage as he approached the sealed door. Hesitantly, he peered out the gaping hole present near the top of the door, awkwardly hiding behind the thick bars as the two women stood directly outside his confined space, their backs facing him as the low glow of the nighttime lights partially illuminated their scrawny frames.

"Actually, I have to take a bath here tonight." Nurse Jackie defeatedly spoke. "Forgot to pay last month's rent so my bitchy landlady shut off my hot water until I get her the money. I'm going on three days without a shower so I desperately need one."

"That really sucks, boo." The other woman said, rigidly patting Jackie on the shoulder. "Maybe clean the tub before you use it, the weirdos in this place are so gross."

"Tell me about it," Nurse Jackie lowly giggled. "Especially *him*. I wish I knew which bath he always uses so I don't accidentally use the same one. Gross."

Switch openly scoffed at Nurse Jackie's insensitive remarks, his palms pressed firmly against the cool metal of the door as the women eventually disappeared from the cell block.

Here it is, S. Here's your one chance.

Take it.

Switch thickly swallowed, palms profusely sweating as his heart erratically raced. Adrenaline coursed through his veins, trembling fingertips meeting the vacant keypad as he confidently entered the code—the very same arrangement of numbers that lay sewed upon Adelaide's left breast.

His forefinger sharply collided with the buttons, breaths sharply hitching as a vibrant viridescent hue invaded his vision.

The man struggled to stifle a hearty giggle at the sight, the cell door audibly unlatching as his fingers curled around the thick surface. Slender fingers heartily buzzed, toes practically curling beneath the leather of his boots as he silently slunk from the confinement of his cold, cement cell.

The cell block was eerily quiet, Cora's routine snoring temporarily absent as the Switch's cell door clicked tightly shut, signaling for him to quickly depart before Greenwald decided to show his ugly mug.

Switch rapidly approached the end of the block, unblinking eyes colliding with an additional silent keypad as his fingers persistently buzzed. It's been too long since he's felt this free . . . way too long . . .

Unsurprisingly, the stealthy man had managed to navigate the vacant, dark halls of Stillwater Sanitarium, cautiously avoiding a pacing Vern somewhere down on Level 2. Deep bags cloaked the sunken skin below his black, beady eyes—evidence of his lack of rest and extreme exhaustion. In all honesty, if Vern had noticed Switch's presence in the hall, he probably wouldn't have bat an eye . . .

Evidence of Nurse Jackie's presence was available to Switch directly outside of the wash room; an old, withering periwinkle pink leather purse lay abandoned outside the ajar door, a set of vibrantly colored keys taunting the man's vision as his brows perplexedly raised.

Curiously, Switch fell to his knees before the discarded purse, fingers delicately brushing against the profusion of miscellaneously shaped keys upon a bulging key ring, outgrown nail hooking beneath a particularly sharp key as his breaths promptly thinned. Suddenly, a strikingly beautiful thought bombarded his mind—a thought that made his toes curl and chest painfully ache.

With that, the man claimed the keys in his hold before slipping into the humid room once and for all.

It was as if there was an actual God looking out for Switch on this very night—an all-power who was literally handing him everything he needed at this very time. Lucky for him, Nurse Jackie's eyes were sealed exceedingly tight, fingers lightly laced around the circular edges of the porcelain tub as her drenched locks lay over the edge. Consistent drips of lukewarm water slipped off her soaked hair, coating the concrete floor with ease as a substantial puddle began to gradually form.

Jackie's obnoxious set of keys lay buried within his calloused palm, several slightly sharp edges leaving behind considerable imprints upon the shy skin as he rapidly approached the tub.

Nurse Jackie's drastically tiny tits lay concealed beneath the bubbly water, a strong scent of lavender invading Switch's senses as his nose crinkled in disgust. The woman was in pleasurable trance, indistinguishable phrases slipping off her tongue as she muttered the lyrics to an unfamiliar tune.

Switch slowly fell to his knees behind the tub, keys still held firmly in his grasp as the left sleeve of his rolled jumpsuit threatened to slip down the slope of his arm. Irritably, he yanked the material back over the protruding flesh of his elbow, dainty fingertips just barely grazing Jackie's skull as she jolted awake.

Her sudden shriek was effectively concealed by the flesh of Switch's palm, his thumb and index finger easily constricting her airflow as she painfully gasped. An abundance of water sloshed over the sides of the tub, soaking the toes of Switch's boots as she violently thrashed beneath his firm hold. Hot tears soaked his greedy palm, manicured fingernails desperately clawing at the angry flesh as his scarred lips met the cold lobe of her ear.

"*Shh*," he cooed, lips curling into a firm grin as he peppered hot, open-mouthed kisses along the raised skin. "S'only *me*."

His gaze traveled downwards, eyes significantly widening at the sight of her breasts as petite giggles slipped off his marred mouth.

"*Oh*, look what we have *here*." He mused, clamped palm curling around the woman's quivering frame as he reached for her exposed skin. In return, the woman aggressively yelped beneath his hold, desperately attempting to tear out of his uncomfortable embrace as she continued to heavily sob.

"*Mmm*," the man purred, the knuckle of his thumb just barely grazing her skin as she defiantly thrashed. "Don't *worry*, buttercup. That's *not* what I *came* for."

Nurse Jackie suddenly stilled—big, bright eyes wild with pure fear as she glared upwards at the giggling mess of man. Slowly, Switch tore his sweaty palm from her swollen lips, revealing an utterly stunned woman as she intently held her breath.

"Y'know *what*, princess?" Switch murmured, gently caressing her quivering jaw with the tips of his fingers. After a moment of silence, the man continued. "You *really* should've given me that *bath*."

Nurse Jackie's lips parted in angst, a mortified expression overcoming her flushed features as Switch's palms met her bony shoulders. Without a moment to spare, the criminal managed to slip the woman beneath the warm water, muffled cries of protest emerging from beneath the rippling waves as she squirmed against his hold.

The sloppily rolled sleeves of Switch's black and white striped suit were undeniably soaked—exaggerated cackles slipping off of his tainted lips as Nurse Jackie continued to obscenely scream beneath the bubbling bath water, surely ingesting an unfathomable amount of liquid as he cautiously avoided digging the keys into her skin. He had big plans for those surprisingly sharp metal keys, but imprinting her shoulder with them was definitely *not* the plan.

After several agonizing moments beneath the water, a giddy Switch eventually released his grip on the woman, allowing her to quickly resurface. Jackie openly sobbed, spitting up mouthfuls of warm water as her chest furiously burned. *Was this what it felt like to die?*

"P-Please—" she throatily begged, voice ultimately destroyed by her muffled shouts beneath the bath as Switch rotated himself to the left side of the bath. The madman tightened his hold on a particularly sharp key, slender digits encircling her left wrist as he assertively tugged her arm outward and toward his electrified frame.

Nurse Jackie outwardly cried at the sudden sensation, features immensely flushed as Switch held her trembling wrist tightly in his grasp, so tightly that the tips of his fingers managed to flush a ghastly white, as if he'd dipped them into a can of unpigmented paint. Before the distressed woman could protest, he managed to dig the razor-edge tip of the key into the supple flesh of her wrist, his free hand clamping down on her mouth once more in order to effectively muffle her obscene cries.

Once the deed was done and Jackie's cries had faded into nothingness, the madman strategically placed the keys onto the ground beside the tub and directly beneath her frozen fingers. A profusion of dark crimson steadily oozed into the still water, rapidly intermixing with the minimal amount of remaining bubbles as he slipped through the partially cracked door and abandoned the silent room once and for all.

XXII

"I swear we need to find some comfort in this run-down place
To bridge the gap of this conscious state"
–Underoath, "Writing on The Walls"

Briar was a solid eleven minutes late to work the following morning.

Her overgrown platinum blond hair was a dreadful mess, tugged into a half-ponytail as the remainder lay draped over her shoulders. Deep, chestnut roots began to peek through, courtesy of her extreme negligence with keeping up with dying her hair. The Scooby-Doo printed scrubs were wrinkled and slightly damp, due to the woman oversleeping and not having enough time to fully dry her uniform.

She trudged into the nurses' lounge, nearly tripping over her own two feet as the slight stumble prompted her fingernails to dig into the thinning plastic of her nearly empty water bottle. The material obnoxiously cracked beneath the abrupt pressure, causing the jumpy woman to somewhat flinch as she shuffled towards the nearly vacant lockers.

"Briar!" Nurse Lora exasperatedly exclaimed, thick tracks of dark mascara coating her prominent cheekbones as she rapidly approached the exhausted woman. Nurse Briar rotated on her heel, eyes widening at the sight of nine nurses seated around the room. Each of their eyes were rimmed with a deep scarlet hue, most likely due to their persistent sobbing.

"What the hell?" Briar spluttered, her aging purse slipping from the comfort of her shoulder as it sunk into the pit of her elbow. "What's going on?"

"It's J-Jackie Kleever," Nurse Lora stuttered, shaking palm claiming her agape mouth as she choked back several ugly sobs. "She slit her wrists in the tub last night."

"I should've seen the signs. She practically handed them to me last night," a dark-skinned Nurse Everly stated, her voice slightly muffled by the shredded nail between her teeth as a redheaded Nurse Angelica tossed her arms around the distressed woman. "She told me that her landlady had shut off her hot water, and that's why she needed to take a bath here. I should've known something was up. I should've checked up on her before I left for the evening."

"Stop it, Everly." Angelica pressed, swollen lips curling into a sympathetic grin as she tightened her hold around the measly woman's shoulders. "There's no way you could've known. It was entirely unexpected."

"Where?" Nurse Briar simply stammered, heart inexplicably racing as she dismissively tossed her purse into the open metal locker on her direct left.

"The wash room, of course. She did it in the bath." Nurse Lora blandly explained, eyes widening as Briar quickly turned on her heel and abandoned the room full of crying women.

The hallways were eerily quiet, even more so that someone had died. And not just any someone—a staff member, a coworker, an acquaintance. Sure, Jackie Kleever annoyed the living shit out of Briar ninety-nine percent of the time and was unbearably nosy; but the woman had a kind heart. Besides, the naturally pretty woman was only aged twenty-six years at her time of death—she'd just barely scraped the surface of a long, fulfilling life . . .

Briar stumbled around the corner of the partially cracked single door, quivering fingertips arduously curling around the frigid frame as her heart leapt into her throat at the undeniably morbid sight.

The body had been removed, but the evidence still remained. A tainted set of keys lay forgotten upon the grimy ground, the bright silver accented with a bold crimson hue as Briar's heart cleanly stopped. Stagnant, bloody water lay abandoned within the basin, the lavender bubbles had dissipated entirely over time as Dr. Evers paced the premises.

A heavily-tattooed and pale faced Elliot Greenwald stood frozen opposite him, palms folded into a taunt fist behind his back as he glanced warily in Briar's direction. Their glares conflictingly met; prompting arrays of painful goosebumps to arise on the exposed flesh of Briar's forearm as she trudged into the generously sized room.

"When did they take her?" Briar lowly croaked, uneasily approaching a persistently pacing Dr. Evers as Greenwald thickly swallowed a mouthful of bile.

"Nearly thirty minutes ago," Greenwald flatly explained, glancing painfully in the direction of the pool of dark blood as he clearly reminisced on Jackie's lifeless form, which had occupied the basin only less than an hour prior . . .

"No cops," Dr. Evers rigidly spat, halting in place before the haunting tub as he skeptically viewed the horrifying sight. "No investigations, no nothing. The media will find a way to misconstrued this story, and I am not going to have Stillwater be the headlining news. Absolutely *not.*"

Briar and Greenwald keenly nodded, lips partially parted in identical states of angst as the woman attempted to imagine a dead Jackie in the tub before her. Suddenly, this morning's breakfast began to resurface, and the woman found herself stumbling over sideways and toward a vacant tin trash bin, where she proceeded to empty the contents of her stomach.

Both Greenwald and Evers openly grimaced at the sight, Dr. Evers' slender digits anxiously tearing through his disheveled locks as he occasionally glanced in the soiled tubs direction.

"We need to get rid of it," he simply stated. "The tub."

Greenwald wordlessly nodded, blinking back blinding tears as he imagined a distressed Jackie within this room just last night, her trembling fingers laced around the hefty set of keys as she dug the sharpest of the bunch into the supple skin of her wrist. They'd only been on one simple date, but no matter the circumstance, Elliot couldn't help but mourn the loss of the young and gorgeous Jackie Kleever, who fed into her own personal demons and took the ultimate plunge.

"How selfish," Dr. Evers seethed, a raging scarlet hue overcoming his pointy cheekbones as his fingers curled into exasperated fists. "How selfish of her to take her own life within this establishment. Within these walls! I'm disgusted—even more so that I even hired someone as—as *weak* as she—"

"Nothing about what Jackie did was selfish, nor weak." Briar gurgled, palms flattening against the surface of the can as she irritably tore her shaking frame away from the object. "Suicide is *not* selfish. She was obviously struggling—"

"It was selfish of her to do it here, Cunningway. You'll never understand, at least from my perspective." Evers argued, reverently kicking the side of the tub with the toe of his shoe as he audibly cursed.

"I understand that you're being a heartless asshole," Briar countered, heart inexplicably racing beneath her ribcage as Evers' brows slightly raised.

"Cunningway—" he thickly warned as Greenwald stumbled forward, eyes wild with wanton abandon as he thrust a single index finger into the air, insistent phrases slipping off of his lips as he inaudibly begged the woman to stop speaking. Briar, however, wasn't quite having it.

"It's sickening that you'd even pair the word selfish in regards to a suicide, especially since you run a Sanitarium, doctor." Briar thickly spat, cobalt eyes contorting into thin slits as Greenwald's expression fell slack.

"Think of Lynch, Briar. Whose hands would she end up in if you got fired?" The guard lowly murmured, careful not to allow Dr. Evers to overhear as Briar shot in a bewildered glance.

"What do *you* care about Adelaide Lynch, Elliot?" She countered, shifting her weight from either foot as Greenwald's mouth lay agape. *She knew*—he wasn't quite sure how she'd found out, but she definitely *knew*.

Greenwald's prominent cheekbones flushed a deep scarlet hue, pure humiliation overcoming his every limb as he sidestepped and allowed Briar to seal her own fate.

"I'm not going to continue this conversation," the woman continued, glancing curiously in Greenwald's direction as his glare remained glued upon the grimy ground. "Mainly because I value my patients and appreciate my job. With all due respect, Mr. Evers, you should really watch what you say in regards to mental illness."

"Duly noted, Miss Cunningway." Dr. Evers irritably growled, slender digits lacing around his crooked tie as he hastily readjusted the theatrical fabric. "Like I said—no cops. No investigations. Let the rest of the staff know that Jackie's death was officially ruled a suicide and the case is officially closed. Anyone who attempts to bring outside investigators into the situation will immediately be terminated."

With that, the lanky man wordlessly excused himself from the room, glancing one last time in the direction of the bloody porcelain tub as the liquid form of Jackie's life tortured his mind.

Growing up, Adelaide always told herself that she'd become an artist one day. The idea in itself was entirely ironic, considering the woman could hardly write a decent essay, nor could she draw anything more complex than a choppy stick figure. In fact, even at the age of twenty-four, Adelaide could hardly keep the colors inside of the lines in a coloring book.

She wasn't entirely certain what had generated that extremely far-fetched aspiration; perhaps it revolved around her childhood friend Taylore, who was quite good at painting and used an assortment of vibrant colors to portray her inner thoughts. At twelve, Taylore took a liking to constructing masterpieces out of oil paintings, and her mother spent a whopping three grand on art supplies for her daughter within the time span of one single year.

Taylore Remmings was a bright, cheerful girl with a mediocre set of auburn eyes and bland brown hair. Her lips were incredibly thin and nearly nonexistent, mirroring the presence (or lack of), of her eyebrows, which were more blond than brown and didn't even remotely match the natural hue of her hair. Although her parents made a considerable amount of money annually, the young girl chose to wear boring outfits on the regular—outfits that lacked vibrancy and were nearly always coated with miscellaneous splotches of vivid paint.

Being the polite person that she was, Taylore always encouraged Adelaide to chase after her goals—even though the woman didn't even have a lick of artistic talent in her. By the time the girls turned fifteen, Taylore had shyly suggested that Adelaide construct a new (and perhaps more reasonable) set of goals; particularly ones that didn't include any type of artistic talent (which she very painfully lacked).

Thus, Adelaide was absolutely stumped. If she couldn't be an artist when she grew up, what could she possibly be?

Long story short, Adelaide Lynch never quite managed to figure out what she wanted to do in life. Lucky for her, she no longer needed to decide, as it was entirely apparent that she had a lifelong sentence to the macabre Stillwater Sanitarium.

However, ever since Switch's unannounced and unintentional appearance in Adelaide's life, she felt as if she'd truly achieved that goal. For once, the woman was an artist—because she was with him. Switch himself was nothing less than an extravagant piece of incomparable art, just waiting to be admired. From the fraternal bunch of gruesome scars that claimed his handsome left cheek, to the oily, dark-hued hair that claimed his skull—Switch, nevertheless, was an absolute *masterpiece.*

He sat in an exhausted heap upon the ground, oily nose buried in the aging pages of a dreadfully old copy of *The Great Gatsby* as Adelaide fingered the prodigious hole present on her left sock.

The audible reading of Emmett's gifted copy of *Sense and Sensibility* had been temporarily discounted—mainly due to the fact that only thirteen pages remained, and Adelaide couldn't quite bring herself to finish the story—to say goodbye to *him*. Her Earth—her wind and fire and entire soul—her *Emmett*.

Adelaide would've never pegged the Switch to be interested in reading; however, being secluded within these thick, lifeless walls could turn even the most wretched individual into something entirely divergent. She hadn't had a clue what the mysterious man was like before his admittance, but even since his arrival, he's changed. Maybe—just *maybe*—he was actually *healing*.

The rec room was considerably quiet for a Saturday.

The irritable voices of Nayeli and Cora were entirely absent. Word on the street was that the duo was arguing over a Czechoslovakian patient named Novak Holecek; who was six-foot-two and had a head full of natural blond hair. He was nearly thirty and partially blind, but the pair couldn't care nonetheless. Besides, he was fresh meat, and Nayeli and Cora always preyed on the new arrivals.

His skin was pasty and dry, freckled bottom lip awfully chapped and slightly peeling as he glared quizzically in both Adelaide and Switch's direction. He knew quite a bit about the notorious criminal, and although his biological mother had nearly died during one of Switch's violent episodes over the summer—he wanted to know more about the scarred-face man. After all, the murderer was—by far—the most feared man in all of Chicago. *But why?*

Adelaide's gaze flickered upwards, momentarily colliding with a pair of striking chocolate orbs as Novak diverted his stare, quivering fingers reclaiming his fallen deck of cards as the lithe woman directed her gaze towards Switch.

"Andrew," Adelaide croaked, glancing warily in Switch's exceedingly silent direction as he cocked an eyebrow.

"*Who?*" He grumbled, slowly lowering the wilting book from his mangled expression as the woman hastily gulped.

"Sorry," she murmured, pulse instantly quickening beneath her ribcage as she repugnantly gasped. "I meant Switch. It just slipped out."

"*Mhmm*," Switch drawled, eyes rolling dramatically in their sockets as he raised the book once more, refocusing on the professionally printed text. "What's up, butter*cup?*"

Adelaide's cheeks glowed a bright, stunning scarlet—bottom lip tucked between yellowed teeth as she insistently picked at her uneven nails.

"Nothing," she dismissively whispered, shifting her weight against the intolerable wall. "Just thinking about stuff." Switch raised a curious brow, tongue lapping out to caress his lacerated lips as he released an exasperated: "ex-*pand?*"

"Thinking of how my life would be if certain things wouldn't have happened." She said, avoiding his piercing gaze as the aging pages glided closed on Switch's calloused knuckles. The madman inched closer to the wary woman, cuffed wrists tossing the deteriorating book aside as deep cocoa eyes met a profusion of hazel.

"Hey," he cooed, conjoined wrists inching upwards to meet her sullen expression. Adelaide flinched at the sudden feel of his thumb against her flushed cheek, wild eyes clearly avoiding his as he sighed.

"Adelaide," Switch muttered, dropping his unwanted hold from her complexion as she thickly swallowed. *"C'mon,* I thought we were-*uh, closer* than this. You can tell me *anything.*"

Adelaide's free fingers laced around her empty ring finger, an excessive amount of bile rising in her throat as she insistently tapped her foot. She could still vividly picture the gorgeous diamond that once claimed this very finger—the physical evidence of Emmett DuPré's love for her. A beautiful promise that he'd made—to care for her, to love her and adore her for all of eternity.

"Ad?" Switch pressed, confident digits claiming her trembling ones as she released a hefty exhale.

"I would be married right now." She revealed, tongue lapping out to caress her cracking lips. "With kids, probably. We wanted several ankle-biters, remember when I told you that?"

Switch's brows inexplicably raised, jaw falling agape as he tugged his grasp from hers.

"Oh," he simply said, jaw tightening as he fidgeted upon the dusty floor. "That makes *two* of us."

Adelaide's neck snapped sideways, widened glare meeting Switch's surprisingly soft stance as she reclaimed his fingers in hers.

"You were engaged? Or married?" The woman wondered, her inquiry remaining unanswered when a sudden blistering headache invaded her skull. Adelaide harshly retaliated, clammy palms colliding with her flushed features as the pain intensified; a persistent throbbing present in the left side of her skull as a magnitude of blurred tones filled her ringing ears.

"Babe?" Switch purred, brows knit together in confusion as his palms met her knobby knees. Several straggly strands of ashen brown hair dipped into her line of sight, eyelids screwed agonizingly shut as the woman uttered a profusion of illiterate phrases beneath her breath, palms flattening against her reddened ears.

"Addy–" the man muttered, cuffed hands meeting her flattened palms as he attempted to pry them from her head. However, his actions only seemed to make matters drastically worse.

The woman violently thrashed beneath his comforting hold, irate sobs escaping through parted lips as her knees achingly met her chest. Clammy toes curled within the thin material of her discolored socks, thick tracks of salty tears coating her sunken cheeks as Switch attempted to quickly wipe them away.

"Sweet *heart*," Switch thickly cooed, attempting to yank the trembling woman into his open embrace as she thrashed beneath his rough hold. *"Breathe."*

"They're back," she warily gasped, an additional bolt of electricity overcoming her spine as her frail frame collapsed upon the concrete. Her dreadfully skinny form violently met the surface, emitting a ghastly crack as Switch's eyes immediately widened, broad-shouldered frame rotating forward to meet her convulsing self.

He doesn't care about you.

He never will.

They were louder than ever before—literally *screaming* at her; trying to convince her that the raging maniac that hovered above her didn't give a rat's ass about her.

You're wrong, she spat, blinking back hot tears as Switch lay suspended over her wriggling frame, locked wrists attempted to claim Adelaide's thrashing arms as she sobbed profusely beneath him. *He does. He cares.*

You're pathetic, Adelaide Rhea. The first voice teased, hiccupping immediately after her statement. Thus, the second chimed in.

You'd be better off dead. You're worthless.

Worthless bitch.

No, Adelaide pointedly argued, a sharp breath hitching in her throat as

Switch shouted a plethora of statements—none of which reached Adelaide's ears. *I'm not! I'm not!*

"Adelaide!" Switch shrieked, right palm meeting her blushing cheek as he roughly slapped the surface. His hand eventually claimed her distressed features, four fingers digging into the flushed flesh as his thumb flattened against her bottom lip. "Don't listen to them! *Control* them! I *know* you can do it—because *I* can do it—"

Adelaide brushed away his reassuring touch, arched back rising off of the uneven ground as exaggerated screeches slipped off her lips. The voices had managed to blend together—intermixing to create a deafening buzz as her ears throbbed. Quivering fingertips met her earlobes, the pads of her digits becoming slick with oozing, crimson blood as she obscenely cried.

"M-My ears!" She exclaimed, suspending her bloody palm above her face as Switch blinked away several stray strands of curls within his eyes.

"What?" The criminal interjected, claiming her floating palm in his as he thoroughly inspected the dainty flesh.

"They're bleeding! My ears!" The woman beneath his hips sobbed, choking on her cries as the madman inspected her bloodless hand.

"They're *not*," he pointedly pressed. "Look, Ad. They're *not bleeding.*"

Once more, her eyes flickered shut, masking the stressed hazel hue once more as she released a series of extended shouts. Switch lay awestruck above her, at a complete loss for words as he simply watched the woman violently crumble beneath his lanky form.

Suddenly, the broad double doors of the rec room burst open, the obscene brass handles colliding with the cement walls as several onlookers blatantly flinched at the noise.

Novak Holecek glanced fleetingly in their direction, blurred vision attempting to focus on the situation at hand. Through his sketchy vision, he was able to somewhat form a collective photo—one of a greasy, curly-haired Switch suspended over a distressed younger woman, her split-ended hair fanned outward in divergent directions upon the floor. From the looks of it, Switch was attempting to calm the woman down, but to no avail.

"4210!" Lyra Blake exploded, eyes widening in awe as her pointer finger collectively collided with the center of her glasses. The thick-rimmed spectacles slipped back up the slope of her oily nose, pointed stilettos continuously clicking against the ground as she rapidly approached the pair. "*Switch*—Get off of her! This is a Sanitarium, not a brothel!"

"Jesus, *Blake*," Switch irritably spat, rotating his stiff frame off of Adelaide's convulsing torso as he boldly eyed the psychiatrist. "It's not like *that*. I'm trying to *help* her."

"Lynch," Dr. Blake pressed, falling to her knees beside the trembling woman. A pair of hazel-hued, bloodshot eyes immediately widened at the sight of Blake's unwelcome stance, a worrisome expression instantaneously enveloping Adelaide's complexion as she attempted to wiggle out of Blake's grasp and crawl back toward her Switch. His expression slackened at the sight, fingers prancing along the exposed flesh of Adelaide's wrist as he reassured the woman of his presence.

"What is it?" The middle-aged woman queried, claiming Adelaide's thrashing wrists between several bony fingers.

Get rid of her!
Kill her!
Kill her!
Kill her!

"NO!" Adelaide shrieked, left leg extending upwards to meet Dr. Blake's busty chest. A muffled grunt tumbled from Blake's partially parted lips at the abrupt action, brows knit together in vexation as she shoved Adelaide's knees aside.

"Get up, Lynch." Blake ordered, latching her frigid fingers around the significantly younger woman's thin wrist. She attempted to yank her upwards, tossing the distressed girl around like a limp doll as several beady-eyed guards came to her aid.

"Leave her *alone*." Switch brashly ordered, immediately rising to his feet as he attempted to tear Adelaide from the guards. They, however, retaliated immediately—a broad palm flattening against the criminal's chest as they shoved him to the ground. Switch's bottom collided with the harsh cement, a distressed hiss tumbling off his ajar lips as his fingers irritably brushed several stray curls from his eyes.

"You'll regret *that*." Switch spat, dismissively spitting on the unnamed guard's boot.

"Take her to my office," Dr. Blake slyly ordered, blatantly ignoring Adelaide's manic episode as she cleared her throat. "Emergency session. After

244 // ALYSSA DICARLO

that, she'll spend the rest of the night in her cell. No supper. No bath."

"That's not *fair!*" Switch exclaimed, tugging at metal restraints around his scarlet-riddled wrists. His chest inordinately heaved, furious shakes overcoming his spine as Adelaide attempted to crawl her way out of their hold.

"That's not up for you to decide, now is it, 4428?" Dr. Blake countered, earning a spiteful glare from the madman beneath her.

"She needs *help*, can't you see?" Switch pressed, expression slackening as he met Adelaide's mortified gaze. Dr. Blake released a sarcastic cackle, lanky arms crossing across her chest as she wet her perfectly painted purple lips.

"*Oh,*" she giggled, shifting her weight from either foot. "And I suppose that you think that you can help her more than I can? Need I remind you, I'm the licensed professional here, buddy."

With that, the woman turned sharply on her heel, inaudibly instructing the two men to escort Adelaide from the premises as she glanced confidently over her shoulder to view a surprisingly silent Switch behind her.

"Hope you ate a hefty lunch, pal. One night without supper won't hurt, will it?" She said, ignoring Switch's appalled expression as she followed the pair of guards from the rec room—a silent and shaking Adelaide held in their grasp.

Switch intently stared as the group disappeared from sight, the hefty doors sealing once more on their heels as his jaw promptly tightened.

She's going to wish she was never even born.

XXIII

Tremendously oily digits ran along the smooth fabric of a considerably dark and slightly short black dress. It was an incredibly weak attempt to dry the slick flesh—one that had left her clammy fingers slightly damp and full of lint. The shrunken material tended to ride up the length of Briar's legs, which, in turn, prompted the woman to irritably tug the article of clothing downwards to cover the exposed flesh of her thighs.

A profusion of prickly goosebumps persistently coated the pale skin of the woman's arms, manicured fingernails toying with the hem of her dress as she glanced anxiously over her shoulder. A series of unfamiliar faces blended together into a bland blur, hushed voices and intermixed conversations raiding her jewelry-riddled ears as a pair of striking cobalt eyes met an abundance of beady black orbs.

Vern shuffled through the frozen crowd, hands buried deeply within the pockets of his sleek dress pants as a tight-lipped smirk enveloped his features. The toe of his left dress shoe sloppily collided with the heel of his right; prompting the elephantine man to stumble forward as an elderly woman glanced warily in his direction.

Briar stifled a giggle as she awkwardly observed from a distance, left leg expeditiously bouncing as she positioned her lanky legs upon the frigid wooden pew. She watched as Vern proceeded to tear a clammy palm from the pits of his trousers, waving politely in the white-haired woman's direction as he offered a nonverbal apology for nearly trampling over her.

"Hey," Vern exclaimed, slightly out of breath as he rapidly approached the pew where Briar currently sat. It was the second row from the stage, the entirety of the section nearly vacant as the woman scoot sideways, allowing an open spot for Vern to sit.

"Hey, Vern." She breathed, adjusting her dress as it irritably hiked up the length of her thighs once more. "Recognize any of these people?"

"A majority of the Stillwater staff are outside," Vern pointedly explained, collapsing onto the pew as he released a strangled sigh. "The infamous Evers himself is not here, though. Not much of a surprise."

"He's an asshole." Briar murmured, avoiding Vern's amused glare as she picked at a stray strand of skin along her thumb. "He had the nerve to call Jackie selfish for what she'd done to herself."

"Huh," Vern said, running a broad hand through his disheveled locks. "Ironic, isn't it? He runs a mental hospital but mocks a woman for taking her own life."

"It's more disgusting than ironic," Briar countered, slipping an auburn-tinted nail into the pits of her mouth as she dismissively chewed. "Maybe *he's* the selfish one."

The duo shuffled into a stagnant silence—her bright, cheerful blue eyes gazing around at the surroundings as Briar admired the particularly large portrait of Jackie sat perched up on the stage. She looked a tad bit younger, naturally dark hair parted directly down the center as a thick line of inky liquid eyeliner claimed her upper lids. She looked impeccably happy—a broad, artificially whitened, toothy grin sat slapped upon her features as a pair of rosy red cheeks lit up the entire room.

A unique and elegant font displayed her birth name directly above the professional headshot—*Jacqueline Ray Kleever.* It was a fancy and sophisticated name, totally and completely chic and totally and completely *her.*

She was twenty-six. Young—*so* young and full of life and ambition. As Briar squirmed in her seat, tedious fingertips irritably tugging at the hem of her insanely small dress—she couldn't help but wonder what could've been done if she'd actually befriended Jackie. It wasn't that Jackie was a bad person—no, not even *remotely*—Briar was just simply a recluse. She hardly had many friends, none at all, actually. Sadly, the only person that Briar Cunningway could actually consider her friend was her patient Adelaide

Lynch.

How pathetic.

"Excuse me, *sorry–*" A deep, muffled voice grunted from several pews back, feet inordinately shuffling against the dilapidating carpeting as Briar craned her neck.

Elliot Greenwald strut a head full of severely unkempt crimson locks, which paired rather nicely with his auburn tie and wrinkled black dress shirt. The sleeves of the shy fabric were messily rolled at his wrists, a considerably sloppy attempt to conceal the assortment of tattoos that littered the flesh. Curious eyes instantly collided with Briar's stern glare, an instant, lippy grin enveloping his features as he struts in both Briar and Vern's direction.

"Jesus," Briar muttered, swallowing a lump of bile. "Look who showed."

Vern curiously glanced over his shoulder, bushy brows knitting tightly together in irritation as he loudly cleared his throat. Greenwald, however, didn't seem to mind the duo's dismissive glares.

"Hey guys," Greenwald throatily greeted, thrusting a quivering hand outward in the direction of Vern's stern expression. Vern slightly hesitated, a single brow raising as he glanced curiously in Briar's direction. After much consideration, he eventually took Greenwald's stiff hand in his, shaking it firmly before letting it drop nearly as quickly as he'd claimed it.

"People seem to be trickling in," Greenwald observed, taking a seat on Briar's opposite side as she shot him a perplexed and uninviting glare. Once more, the red-haired man didn't seem to take notice to her peculiar behavior.

"Jacqueline Ray," he spoke, voice slightly wavering as he ran his palms along the length of his legs. "Pretty name."

Briar and Vern remained deathly silent beside a chatty Elliot, stares securely locked on Jackie's closed casket as a profusion of guests flocked into the room. Although it was an easy seventy-two degrees, Briar Cunningway couldn't help but sweat. The thick fabric beneath the pits of her arms were beginning to moisten, and her bare toes became slippery within her silky shoes.

Several of Stillwater's personal nurses eased into the premises, most of them wearing a flat frown as they searched for places to sit. Nurse Everly, in particular, strut a head full of frizzy hair and red-rimmed eyes, the back of her palm constantly swiping against her nostrils in a weak attempt to rid them of the abundance of runny snot.

Briar diverted her attention, avoiding Everly's defeated complexion as she refocused her gaze on Jackie's pristine portrait, a haunting smile brightening the room as Vern's palm met her naked knee. Impulsively, the rigid woman jerked sideways, yanking her knobby knee from the confinement of Vern's considerably warm and cozy palm as he shot her a perplexed glare.

"Sorry," she said, her voice a hushed whisper. "I'm just really anxious."

"It's okay," he kindly replied, a sincere, closed-lip grin overcoming his features. "I think we all kind of are. It's a sad day."

Once the guests were all seated and quiet, an aging woman with a profusion of white curls and beady brown eyes took the stage. She was exceedingly fit, slender legs easily climbing the several mahogany-carpeted steps toward the podium as she inexplicably cleared her throat. Elegant, dangly earrings claimed her saggy earlobes, occasionally brushing against her wrinkled expression as she offered the crowd a generous smile.

Her makeup was pink and perky, short torso cloaked with a flowy black blouse as her index finger met the microphone, emitting a shrill buzz. Several members of the audience visibly flinched at the sudden sonance, prompting the woman to innocently giggle.

"So sorry," she spoke, confident voice ricocheting off the walls as she shifted her weight from either foot.

"I think I speak for all of us when I say that Jacqueline's demise came as quite a surprise," the woman boldly began, shy gaze studying the timid group of exceedingly silent individuals.

"However, we must not dwell upon this tragedy—instead, we must celebrate the life Jacqueline lived, whether or not it may qualify as a long and fulfilling life to all."

Briar blinked back hefty tears, slender legs insistently crossing and uncrossing as she struggled to situate herself upon the drastically uncomfortable bench. Greenwald glanced curiously in her direction, brows heavily furrowed as she blatantly ignored his nonverbal inquiry.

"I found out that I was pregnant with Jacqueline when I was forty-six—and don't any of you dare do the math!" The woman exclaimed, a series of giggles immediately following her statement as several members of the audience hesitantly laughed.

"I was vacationing in Aruba for the summer. It was a way for me to celebrate the finalization of my five-year-long divorce. At forty-six, I was absolutely shocked to read a set of bold, blue lines on a pregnancy test. It couldn't be possible, not for an old hag like myself! I already had two children; sons, respectively. Charlie and Nathan. Charlie was born when I was nineteen—don't judge, I married young—hence the very, very ugly divorce—and Nathan arrived three days prior to my twenty-third birthday. The boys, being in their twenties—*Charlie almost thirty*—were not very pleased to hear that their old woman was knocked up." Jackie's mother momentarily paused, gaze diverting to meet the unoccupied podium as she took a second to collect her thoughts.

"Jacqueline was a little blessing in disguise. Quite frankly, I was worried that she'd come asking about her father one day, and I, of course, was terrified to tell her the truth." She said. "But, when she finally did ask about her dad, the last thing she wanted to call me was a whore. In fact, she was rather amused to know that she could be the love child of five different men!"

A brief pause—muffled laughter.

"Anyways," the elderly woman trailed off, wrinkled fingers fiddling with the circular edge of the podium. "Jacqueline was truly a blessing in everyone's lives. Although she was persistent and undoubtedly nosy—she had a kind heart. No interest in marriage—*or at least that's what she'd told me*—no interest in children or settling down. She loved her job and loved her family."

Vern's grasp crept over towards Briar's pointy knee, frigid digits curling around the discolored flesh as he lightly squeezed. A million thoughts instantly raided the blonde woman's mind at the simplistic gesture, a generous lump of bile taking refuge in her throat as she struggled to listen to Jackie's mother's speech.

"Our dear Jacqueline dealt with demons. All I can say is," the woman paused, sucking in a generous breath. "I'm happy if she's happy. I miss you, Jacqueline. Mommy loves you."

"I'll take a Strawberry Martini," Briar politely requested, handing the laminated menu into the waitresses' hands.

"Just a Bud Light for me." Vern spoke, collapsing against the squishy cushion of the booth as the leggy waitress excused herself from their table. The pair sat in a comfortable silence for several moments, Vern's fingers messily laced together atop the sticky table as Briar twiddled her thumbs.

"Thanks for asking me out for a drink," Briar whispered, wedging her left thumb nail beneath the right. "I wish I could eat something, but I just can't seem to stomach it."

"Yeah, me neither." Vern agreed, yanking his clamped palms from the surface of the table as he uneasily readjusted his posture. "That whole speech from her mom really stung."

"I wish my mom cared about me that much." Briar spoke, her tone faltering at the thought of her mother. Unfortunately, she hadn't seen her birth giver in nearly eight years. In fact, she didn't even know where she lived anymore.

Vern's gaze grew glossy, bottom lip tucked between rows of teeth as Briar's breath hitched in her throat. She'd heard of Vern's mothers' death, and right now, she wished she could slap herself in the face for what she'd said.

"I'm so sorry–"

"Don't apologize, Bri." Vern interjected, arm extending outward to claim Briar's fidgeting fingers. The moment their hands met, an unexplained spark immediately ignited within Briar's bones, causing her to deeply gasp. Vern raised a questionable brow, fingers tearing away from hers as pink, plump lips parted in awe.

"Hey," he murmured, pausing suddenly when the waitress returned with their drinks.

"Sorry," Briar chirped, picking at the hem of her dress. "I'm really jumpy today. It's nothing personal. Plus, I can't even remember the last time someone tried to hold my hand–"

"*Awww*," Vern taunted, lips curling into an amused smirk as he took a swig of his foamy beer.

"What?" Briar playfully spat, the pad of her pointer finger toying with the ring of thick sugar around her glass.

"You sound like a cute little teenage girl whose never been on a date, or something." The man taunted, placing his half-drank beer back onto the table as Briar's drink remained untouched.

Her jaw fell ajar, a mocking cackle slipping off her lips as she fiddled with the base of her glass. "Am *not*," she countered, finally taking a miniscule sip from her drink. "Totally not a virgin or anything–"

"Nobody said anything about virginities," Vern teased, a cheeky grin enveloping his lively features as his foot accidentally brushed against hers. "Plus, aren't you like, thirty-three?"

"Thirty-four," Briar kindly corrected. "I swear I still feel fifteen sometimes, though. How despicable is it, that I'm halfway through thirty and working some dead-end job at the most controversial insane asylum in town–"

"Don't talk like that, Briar." Vern darkly scolded, setting his empty glass aside as a stream of foam dribbled down the length of the glass. "Stillwater's given you many things. It's given you Addy. Plus, I'm thirty-one and working there, too."

"Yeah, *yeah*." Briar dismissed, avoiding Vern's complicated glare as she hastily swallowed. "I should be thankful. Adelaide's my best friend. I adore her."

"She's a really great girl," he said. "She's come a long way. A very long way. You should be proud of her. You're a very admirable person, Bri. Especially taking on Switch, too. He's a complicated individual–"

"*Ohoho*," Briar sarcastically giggled, tone slightly muffled by the martini glass between her smudged lips. "You have *no* idea..."

"Enlighten me, princess." Vern gleamed, requesting an additional beer from the waitress as she simply nodded. Briar audibly gulped at his request, Switch's complex features raiding her mind. The mere thought of him writhing in pleasure beneath her greedy mouth made her head fleetingly swim . . .

"He's just–" she began, pausing briefly to collect her thoughts, and push away the ones of a ecstasy-ridden Switch. "–something else. Extremely manipulative. Always gets what he wants, or so he assumes."

"He's got a mean right hook," Vern chuckled, the pads of his fingers meeting the healed flesh of his eye. "I swear that bruise took weeks to heal."

"Is Vern your first name?" Briar suddenly switched the topic, brows knit together in uncertainty as the man opposite her merely laughed.

"Wow," he spoke. "That was random."

"Sorry," she defeatedly whispered, taking another sip from her glass before continuing with, "I just randomly thought of it. Maybe because I don't even know Switch's real name."

"I have a feeling that Adelaide does." Vern suggested, beady gaze focusing on an uneasy Briar. She looked absolutely exhausted—her eyeliner heavily smudged and lipstick nearly nonexistent. However, to him, she looked beautiful nonetheless. "I also have a feeling that Lynch knows what Switch's dick tastes like."

Briar nearly spat out her drink, the liquid burning down the slope of her throat as she obscenely choked. Vern gawked in her direction, jaw parted in angst as he struggled to comprehend her reaction.

"What?" He wondered. "What's wrong?"

"*Jesus*–" Briar coughed, claiming a nearby paper napkin as she rid her chin of the excess liquid. "Why do you say that?"

"Oh, c'mon, Briar." Vern pressed, eyes rolling within their sockets as he took another generous sip of his second beer. "They practically eye-fuck each other on the daily. They're totally and completely infatuated with one another. It's obvious."

"Yeah, *but*–"

"Don't worry," Vern reassured the woman, palm clamping down over her cool fingers. "I'm not going to rat them out. God, the dude's gotta be horny as shit being locked up in that place. Good for him to get out there and get some."

"Y-Yeah," Briar choked. "Totally. Good—uh—good for both of them, I guess."

Once more, a stale silence littered the air, the persistent, low grumble of mixed chatter filling their ears as Vern requested a third drink from the pretty waitress. Finally, after and amplitude of silence, Vern spoke up once more.

"Ulysses." Vern announced, sucking diligently on his bottom lip. Briar blinked several times, at a complete loss for words as she struggled to comprehend his sudden outburst.

"What do you mean?" She wondered, shaking her head from side to side. "Ulysses? I'm confused."

Vern let out an exaggerated sigh, scooting forward on the leather booth as the material crunched beneath his weight. "That's my name," he said, shaking his head. "No middle name. Just Ulysses Vern."

Briar's jaw fell, an amused twinkle present in her sparkling eyes as she brought the sugar-rimmed martini glasses to her lips. Vern released a generous snort, one that vibrated its way through his flared nostrils as he downed the third glass of alcohol.

"It's weird," Briar said, her voice a slight gurgle from the massive amount of liquid present between her lips. "But I like it."

"I like you." He confidently countered, left eye delivering a sultry wink in her direction.

Briar wiggled her clammy fingers between Vern's slick digits, emitting a joyful giggle from the nude man beside her as she toyed with his fingers.

"So, *Ulysses*," she teased, pressing a feather-like kiss to his collarbone as the man blatantly stirred beneath her mouth. "Do you sleep with all of Stillwater's nursing staff?"

Vern simply chuckled, pointy chin meeting the base of his throat as several additional chins magically appeared. His usually dull and lifeless eyes were bright and cheerful, a hearty grin plastered on his swollen mouth as his hand met her hair.

"You'd be the first," he coolly replied, threading his oily digits through her mangled locks. "Maybe you can tell all of the girls just how charming I am, eh?"

Briar delivered a light-handed smack to his heaving chest, sporadic giggles slipping off his lips as their mouths connected in a blissful kiss for the umpteenth time that night.

"I don't think I'd be particularly fond of having to share you with all of my coworkers." She said, placing a soft kiss to the corner of his mouth as she irritably brushed a stray strand of blond from her eyes.

Half of her face met his chest once more, his racing heartbeat consistently thumping against her skull as the pads of her fingers traced miscellaneous shapes along his exposed peck.

"Vern?" She softly whispered, digging her nose into his flesh as he let out a choppy: *"yeah?"*

"Can I tell you a secret?"

"Jeez, Bri." Vern deeply teased, pressing his lips against her hair. "It's like we're already married. Or something."

Or something.

"You have to promise not to tell anyone," she breathed, pointed chin meeting the center of his chest as a worrisome gaze met her conflicting complexion. "I'm serious, U. I could get fired. Or probably admitted to Stillwater myself."

"Jeez, Bri." Vern murmured, cradling her flushed face in his palms as he intently licked his lips. "What is it? What's wrong? I promise I won't tell a soul."

Briar momentarily paused, vivid visuals of a satisfied Switch taunting her thoughts as she blinked back regretful tears.

"It happened back in October," the woman uneasily began, a bitter taste on her tongue. "I didn't mean for it to happen, I don't know what got into me. He's manipulative and bossy and I guess he really managed to get inside my head–"

"*Switch?*" Vern interrupted, bushy brows raising.

"Yes," she breathed. "I sucked his dick, Vern. I got on my knees and blew him during his first physical."

The man remained deathly silent beneath Briar's trembling figure, features expressionless as he struggled to visualize the scene.

"Wow," he said, fingers tangling in her greasy locks once more. "I'm definitely surprised."

"I'm such a whore." Briar outwardly cried, choking back strangled sobs as Vern immediately locked his arms around her slim torso.

"Love," he pressed, thumbs gently caressing her cheeks as a single tear slipped down the slope of her face. "You're *not* a whore. You're human."

"But–"

"I'm serious, Bri." Vern pressed. "Stop being so hard on yourself. You've been through a lot. You weren't thinking straight. You even said it yourself, he's the master of manipulation. Hell, if he wanted to, he could probably get me down on my knees. It's not like he's an ugly guy or anything. Now, if you would've told me that you'd sucked *Greenwald's* cock, I probably would've already been out the door."

The duo burst into fits of cheerful laughter, complimented with greedy fingers and playful, open-mouthed kisses.

"Where've you been all my life?" Briar murmured against his mouth, the tip of her nose brushing against his as his thumb met her chin.

"Under the very same roof." He said.

XXIV

"She runs through the streets
With eyes painted red
Under a black belly of cloud in the rain"
–U2, "Running to Stand Still"

Switch didn't have a clue what went down during Adelaide's emergency session with the vindictive Doctor Blake.

Quite frankly, the criminal couldn't stand the sight of the wretched woman, who wore a face full of exaggerated makeup and foundation two shades too dark. Her plump purple lips were nearly always formed into a habitual faux grin, magnified eyes silently judging every single ill individual within these claustrophobic walls as her obnoxious stilettos clicked against the uneven ground.

As promised, Adelaide wasn't at supper that night. The news of Jackie's apparent suicide spread like wildfire, courtesy of the loose-lipped women in bland sets of striped jumpsuits. Just the mere speculation of her horrific demise during dinner was enough to paint a hearty grin upon the madman's mangled features, calloused fingers dismissively twirling the limp spaghetti noodles around his tray as Greenwald eyed him from a distance.

Surprisingly, the soulless ginger hadn't dared to cross the Switch all day. In fact, Elliot managed to keep to himself, mostly. His auburn locks were a disheveled mess; oily and uneven, most likely due to his clammy hands. Jackie's lifeless form consistently raided his thoughts, occasional beads of sweat consuming his upper brow as he attempted to shove the troublesome memories from his skull.

According to Nurse Lora, Jackie's funeral had been scheduled for the following afternoon. Closed casket, thankfully. It was a quick and exceedingly short decision on her family's part. Apparently, many were a bit too keen on closing Jackie's book of life for good.

Nurse Briar had gone home early, complaining of a raging migraine and sporadic spurts of extreme nausea. Unfortunately, the woman's early departure occurred mere moments before Adelaide's exaggerated episode. Surely, if the artificial blond would've been there, Addy wouldn't have fallen directly into Blake's arms.

A frizzy haired woman with extremely bloodshot eyes offered to give Switch his evening bath. According to her patient—*whose name Switch did not know*—her name was Nurse Penelope. She was a shy, timid woman; clearly over forty and physically and emotionally drained. Unlike Jackie's adamant request, Penelope did not require Switch to remain cuffed during the ordeal. Shockingly, Switch remained extremely silent during his bath, which, unfortunately, was rudely interrupted by the irritable presence of an utterly obnoxious Nayeli.

The persistent buzzing of the cerulean nighttime lights invaded Switch's vision the moment Nurse Penelope escorted his cuffed self into the depths of the nearly silent cell block that night. Cora's routine snores filled the premises; the deep sonance ricocheting off of the incredibly thick concrete walls as the tired and lanky woman directed the shockingly obedient man into the confinement of his cold, cement cell.

"Does Nurse Briar give you your medication like she's supposed to?" Nurse Penelope politely inquired, her tone low and husky as she avoided Switch's piercing gaze. A pair of frigid, slender digits encircled his scarlet wrists, effectively yanking the harsh metal from his flesh as he fell free once more.

"*Yeees,*" Switch swiftly lied, beady black gaze momentarily colliding with Penelope's bland glare as calloused fingers locked around his bony wrists, insistently massaging the swollen surface. "Why *wouldn't* she?"

"Just wondering," Penelope quickly defended, inching further out of the broad steel door as her ring-clad fingers fiddled with the mahogany surface. "I'm not quite sure what protocols she follows—"

"She's grea-*t*," Switch keenly defended, his tone dark and sinister as he distinctly wet his lips. "*Really*. She's-*uh*, really, *really* good at her job. *Truly*."

Nurse Penelope paused, artificial brows raised in curiosity as she shifted her weight from either foot.

"Oh," she said, diverting her stare. "Good to hear that. I'll be back with your medication."

"I don't need an *audience*," pressed, shuffling out of his hefty leather boots as he proceeded to tear the discolored socks from his feet. "In regards to the *pills*, o'course."

"Right," the aging woman stammered, tugging the door closed on her heel. "I'll be back."

Switch dismissively spat a profusion of obscenities in Penelope's direction, the majority of the phrases effectively concealed by the thickness of the door as he paced the petite premises. The distinct hole present upon the grimy old wall was impossibly dark and eerie, leaving behind zero evidence of life on the opposite side. In fact, he wasn't even quite sure if Adelaide was actually *alive* over there . . .

"Ad?" Switch croaked, inching toward the sloppily built hole. The unwashed material of his jumpsuit trousers lay bunched at the ankles, a multitude of bones irritably cracking beneath the flesh of his knobby knees as he fell to the ground before the glassless window.

A single sniffle filled the otherwise bland and buzzing void—indicating that the woman was, in fact, actually alive in there. An automatic, sealed-lip grin enveloped his features at the mere sound, dainty fingertips toying with the frayed flesh of the wall as he shifted his weight from either foot.

"Baby *giiirl*," he huskily cooed, nails curling around a considerably large chunk of cement. "S'*okay*. *Talk* to me."

Adelaide stirred beneath the impossibly thin fabric of her off-white sheet, violent shivers consuming her scaly spine as she attempted to stifle her sobs.

The mere sonance of Switch's soothing voice was enough to send a peculiar warmth throughout her core—but also managed to cue an additional round of hot, salty tears to spew from her squeezed eyelids. The top of her striped jumpsuit loosely clung to her incredibly thin form, chest inordinately heaving beneath the unkempt fabric as she profusely cried.

They were back.

The woman's lanky legs curled inward, pointed knees jabbing into the tender flesh of her breasts as she tugged herself into fetal position upon the mattress. She could still clearly feel Switch's piercing gaze upon her curled back, but she purposely chose not to acknowledge it. Besides, there wasn't much that he could do for her beyond that wall . . .

Worthless.

Pitiful.

Unwanted.

Nurse Penelope returned several moments later, a vibrant paper cup held tightly in her clutch as the moisture on her fingertips promptly softened the material. Three substantially sized pills lay snug at the bottom, circular in shape and coated with a shiny, silky coat invented for easy swallowing.

"4428?" The woman croaked, her voice barely above a whisper as she dragged her slightly chipped ID through the slot. A vibrant viridescent light appeared on the keypad, accompanied by a harsh click as the broad door swung widely open.

Switch immediately stood to his feet, the frigid concrete sending involuntary shivers down the length of his spine as his bare soles swayed against the flat floor. The wide-eyed nurse inexplicably raised her drawn-on brows, chapped bottom lip tucked between rows of crooked teeth as she awkwardly placed the paper cup onto the grimy ground.

"Should I stay?" She unprofessionally inquired, unsure of how to act around the notorious criminal. Switch's gaze momentarily flickered in the direction of the abandoned cup upon the floor, left brow raising in amusement as a cheeky grin yanked at his marred lips.

"For *what*?" He dryly teased, burying his palms into the pits of his pockets. "You *want* something?"

"I don't know what you—" Penelope stammered, fingers encircling the bold handle as she began to yank the cell door closed at an impeccably slow speed.

"*Cool* it, *Pe-nel-oh-pee*," the criminal drawled, twisting a particularly curly loop of hair around his forefinger. "I already *know* that I'm nearly every girls *wet dream* in this-er, *establishment*."

Nurse Penelope immediately gawked at Switch's highly suggestive statement, long nose crinkled in disgust as she slammed the door closed.

"Goodnight, 4428!" The woman dismissively spat, swallowing a mouthful of bile as she struggled to push the morbid images of a very naked Switch from her mind. *Gross.*

A jocular expression raided The Switch's appearance, a yellowed, toothy grin plastered up on his marred features as he kicked the softened paper cup aside. A profusion of pills littered the surface of the floor, entertainingly rolling along the concrete as the man intently studied the silent keypad beside the door.

Adelaide's inmate number raided his jumbled mind—a quartet of unique numbers which hovered her left breast, numbers that otherwise defined her identity within these suffocating walls.

Four simple digits—that's all that separated him and her.

Four fucking numbers.

With a simplistic sigh, the pad of Switch's forefinger collided with the faded plastic, swiftly entering Briar's passcode onto the keypad as a vibrant green light insinuated his apparent approval.

Freedom.

Confidently, the madman curled his broad frame around the partially parted mahogany door, calloused fingers twisting around the circular handle as he abruptly yanked the door closed. Cora's repetitive snores consumed the otherwise stale space, the deep, throaty sound slightly vibrating along the walls as Switch rapidly approached Adelaide's sealed cell.

"Bay-*beee*," the man purred, confidently entering the pin onto the pad as he was promptly granted access to the petite premises. "I'm *boooome*."

Adelaide silently stirred upon the measly mattress, beady black eyes rapidly colliding with the broad frame present in her doorway. A mess of unkempt curls littered his oily forehead, comforting cocoa eyes glistening beneath the artificial lighting of the cell block as the door clipped closed on his heel.

See, she irritably spat, countering the particularly harsh second voice as her fingers curled into exasperated fists up near her skull. *I told you. He cares.*

Yeah right, they harshly countered, a slight snicker in their tone. *He's just here to get his nut off.*

"Go away," Adelaide defeatedly rasped, her tone low and choppy as she buried her flushed features into the confinement of her unwashed pillowcase. "I can handle them myself."

Switch slunk into the depths of her cramped room, carefully falling to his knees beside the creaky bed as his curious fingertips met her goose bump-riddled arms.

"What're they *saying, hm?*" He thickly inquired, intently studying the features of her distressed complexion. Adelaide's hooked nose buried deeper into the pillow, disappearing from sight as his thumb met her pointed cheekbone.

"Bad things," she murmured, her tone hushed, courtesy of the drastically thin fabric of her pillow. "Very bad things."

God, you're so damn dramatic.

Yeah, the second voice chirped, inexplicably clearing their throat. *We're only telling you the truth.*

No, Adelaide shyly countered, breaths rapidly thinning beneath the soothing touch of Switch's fingers upon her cheek. *You're just making me feel worse about myself than I already do.*

"Don't *listen* to them, sweetheart." Switch clipped, tucking a considerably lengthy and greasy strand of hair behind her elf-like ear. "It isn't *true*. What they're sayin'n *all*."

"How do you know?" Adelaide wondered, weakened glare meeting his as she lifted her clammy skull from the unpigmented pillowcase. "How do you know that they're wrong?"

"*Because*," Switch impatiently spat, eyes dramatically rolling in their sockets as he briefly paused to wet his lips.

"The ones up *here*–" another pause, only this time, the man managed to tear his grasp away from her flushed face, pointed index finger colliding several times with his temple. "–try'n tell me the *same*. You've just gotta master the-*uh, art* of blocking them out, sugar plum."

Adelaide's brows furrowed, mouth falling dramatically agape as she lifted her head from the pillow entirely, several stray strands of frizzy hair partially concealing her appalled expression as Switch released a sarcastic snort.

"I know what you're *thinking*," the madman toyed, readjusting his kneeling form upon the ground as the soles of his feet went momentarily numb. Greasy strands of brunette drifted into his darkened eyesight, pupils dilated as the woman stirred upon the bed directly beside him. "What a *freak*."

"Am *not*." Adelaide immediately interjected, thrusting her lithe frame into a sitting position as a heightened frown claimed her lips. "Because if you are, that means I am, too."

"Now *now*," the curly-haired man scolded, rough hold claiming her jaw as he gingerly squeezed. "Don't *talk* like that, bug. You think so *lowly* of yourself. You don't give yourself enough *credit*."

Adelaide flatly frowned, nose nuzzling into the warmth of Switch's broad palm as she dramatically inhaled his natural, musky scent.

"Lay with me." She commanded, eyelids fluttering gently closed as she scooted sideways on the bed, allowing substantial room for Switch to lay down next to her.

"Yes *ma'am*." He enthusiastically replied, lacerated lips curling into an equally enthusiastic smirk as he nudged his way onto the surface of the paper-thin mattress. The material dramatically dipped beneath the drastic shift in weight, cold, bare feet sinking below the reassuring warmth of the sorry excuse for a blanket as Adelaide immediately settled into his side.

The moist surface of Adelaide's forehead keenly collided with the edge of Switch's jaw, an involuntary grin overcoming her softening features as the pair released a series of equal unison exhales through flared nostrils. The woman drifted into a considerably tranquil high—eyelids comfortably slipping closed as she deeply inhaled the madman's glorious, manly scent. How absolutely *wild* was it—here she was, laying completely vulnerable and exposed within his strong, sturdy arms—arms that could wrap around her impossibly tiny frame in the mere fraction of a second and easily squeeze.

She'd be dead before she could even realize that he'd actually moved.

"Have they stopped?" Switch innocently wondered, uncharacteristically threading his slender digits through her matted hair. His inquiry remained painfully unanswered, which, in turn, prompted the man to spit out a vexed clarification: "the *voices*."

"For now." She said, voice emerging as a pained whisper as the melodramatic voices briefly ceased.

"Hey," Switch uneasily began, eyesight focused mainly on the ceiling of the cell as his fingers continued to mindlessly flow through her locks.

"Yeah?"

"You know," he objectively stuttered, placing a lengthy pause between his scattered thoughts as the tip of his tongue intently traced the innards of his destroyed face. "It's *you* that keep 'em at bay. For the *most* part, at least. I'm pretty *good* at controlling 'em, but sometimes it gets a *little–*"

Per usual, the criminal momentarily paused, palms tearing from the confinement of her extremely tangled locks as he lifted the pair of them into the air, fingers theatrically wiggling as he managed to insinuate a pair of invisible air quotes before finishing with: "–*overwhelming*."

Adelaide lifted her skull from the comfort of his shoulder, brows perplexedly raised as a puzzled expression raided her features. Her lips parted in wonder, words ultimately failing her as a pair of equally uneasy eyes met hers.

"What're yours like?" Adelaide innocently wondered, stare curiously fixated on his wrinkled forehead as he mirrored her expression.

After several moments of agonizing silence, he eventually released a single syllable, lips theatrically smacking together in preparation to speak as he ushered a distressed: "*hell*."

Adelaide didn't dare pry after that. Interestingly enough, the pair managed to slip into a surprisingly comfortable silence, sporadic, deep breaths filling the otherwise stale and still void as Switch's fingers casually traced miscellaneous shapes onto the clothed surface of her arched back.

Truthfully, Andrew couldn't quite remember the last time he'd willingly cuddled with another human being in such an innocent fashion.

This shit had to stop.

XXV

"Father of mine
Tell me how do you sleep
With the children you abandoned
And the wife I saw you beat"
–Everclear, "Father of Mine"

An amplitude of moisture coated the shriveled flesh of Briar's thumb, dipping deeply between the innermost creases of her defined fingerprint as the condensation from her glass enveloped her skin.

"You're quiet today," Vern observed through hooded eyes, left hand intently circled around his half-full glass of lukewarm Natural Light. "What's on your mind?"

Briar's wary gaze met a rigid Vern opposite her, the once vibrant hue of her crimson colored lipstick immensely faded as she mindlessly ground her teeth.

Jackie had been dead for seven days. Following the funeral, many of Stillwater's finest had failed to mention the cheery woman with bright eyes and a constant grin. In fact, it was as if Jackie Kleever hadn't even existed at all. Nurse Lora happened to mention something about making some type of memorial rock or brick or something of the sorts to put on display outside of the building, but Blake almost immediately shunned the idea and had firmly stated that: *any and all personal items may only be displayed outside of the sealed gates.*

Yup, she was totally sleeping with Dr. Evers.

"Thinking about Jackie," Briar foolishly admitted, tearing her condensation-riddled thumb from the surface of her untouched glass of dark soda. "Thinking about how nobody even mentions her anymore. She might be dead, but why does that mean she has to just disappear? Just because people die doesn't mean they need to be forgotten."

A tight-knit frown lay plastered upon Vern's exhausted features, lips parting in angst as he simply shook his head.

"I dunno, Bri." He coolly replied, reassuring gaze boring deeply into hers.

"I think everyone's just been preoccupied. Besides, I heard Lynch has another electrotherapy session tomorrow, per Blake's request. You haven't even mentioned that, which is shocking—"

"I guess I've been trying to forget about it," Briar defeatedly gushed, blinking back hot, salty tears as she loudly cleared her throat. An aging woman at a table several yards away awkwardly glanced in the distressed women's direction, nearly nonexistent brows raised in wonder as Briar shot her a scolding glare.

"They've come back," the woman groaned, eyelids flickering shut as Adelaide's irritable frame bombarded her mind. "Her voices—they've returned. Blake immediately relabeled her as a catatonic. She's back on electrotherapy and lorazepam."

Vern released a heightened sigh, exasperated limbs collapsing against the squishy surface of the aging leather booth as his fingertips tempestuously tapped against the top of the wicker table.

"I don't think I'll ever understand why that bitch is in charge," he harshly spat, dismissively nudging his nearly vacant glass with a single knuckle. "She must be sleeping with Evers, or something. She's god awful, there's no way he's okay with the things she does—"

"Jesus, Vern. Just look at Greenwald!" Briar solemnly exclaimed, thrusting a single hand into the air as a passerby glanced curiously in their direction on her way to the toilets. "Evers *knows* of the things he's done, and he still roams the halls as if nothing's ever happened! F-fuck, he could be in Jasmine or Cora's or Nayeli's or even Addy's pants this very minute, since he's on the night shift…"

"Bri," Vern scolded, eyes contorting into thick slits as the woman shifted uncomfortably in her seat. "Let's not talk about that bitch anymore, or the wretched Elliot. Let's just enjoy our dinner and not let work put a damper on our personal lives."

"But work *is* my personal life," Nurse Briar argued, brushing a stray strand of blond from her cobalt eyes. "It's all I think about. My life literally revolves around Addy and Switch now. I've assumed responsibility of them both."

"It's like you're their mother," Vern cooed, a boyish smirk enveloping his features as his slender, warm digits met Briar's trembling frigid fingers. The shaking woman stilled beneath his reassuring touch, quivering bottom lip held firmly between rows of artificially whitened teeth as she released a heightened sigh.

"That's not a bad thing, Bri." He cautiously added, dark eyes sparkling. "You've assumed the guardian role for the both of them. They're troubled and seeking love and comfort, you provide both."

"I'm pretty sure that mothers aren't supposed to play with their sons manly parts," Briar rigidly spat, avoiding Vern's somewhat sympathetic glare as she tore her palm from his. Switch's complexion immediately raided her thoughts—yellow, crooked teeth bared in a highly suggestive smirk, pitch-black orbs piercing deeply into her soul as he simply studied her.

The man could read her like a bloody book.

"Fair enough," Vern amusingly countered, his back collapsing against the aging leather booth as the material shifted beneath his weight, as well as releasing an audible puff of air. "More of a babysitter, then? Or something?"

Or something.

"No," she murmured, irritably fingering the condensation present on her glass with the tip of her forefinger. "I don't know. I guess I'm just more of a distant friend or something to them. At least they respect me."

The duo sat in a snug silence for several prolonged minutes, Vern's fingers laced tightly around a nearly empty glass of tepid beer as Briar's drink remained untouched. The churning sensation present in her belly was enough to make her want to projectile vomit from one simple sip.

Six minutes later, a group of four unrecognizable faces rapidly approached the table, smug smiles etched across their mouths as foggy glasses of beer lay in their grasps. Vern's expression immediately brightened at the sight of the middle-aged men, a toothy grin enveloping his exhausted features as he removed his broad frame from the leather booth.

"Verny, boy!" The blond boy near the front cheered, claiming Vern's outstretched palm in his as he meticulously squeezed. "Fancy seeing you here!"

"Just having a drink with my girl," Vern giddily explained, maneuvering his slender digits into the depths of his pant pockets. "Guys, this is Briar. Briar, this is Archie, Zachary, Leonard, and Georgie."

A faux grin encaptured Briar's lips, wobbling knees rising from the surface of the sticky booth as her clammy legs agonizingly peeled away from the material. Her trembling palm met each of theirs, hushed greetings slipping through partially parted lips as she took her seat nearly as quickly as she'd stood.

"Listen, Verny," the one man apparently named Georgie began, a thick, black mustache claiming his incredibly thin upper lip as he occasionally eyed a rigid Briar. "It's been ages since we've seen you, mate. Listen, would it be fair if we stole your man from you for a few hours, missus?"

Briar shifted uncomfortably upon the booth, a single fingernail tucked between rows of sharp teeth as she awkwardly nodded before replying with, "yeah. That's fine. No problem."

Vern shot Briar a perplexed glare, brows raised as he shifted his weight from either foot. He could clearly tell that the woman was slightly hurt, and the very last thing he wanted was to let Briar down tonight. Sympathetically, his warm palm met the prickly flesh of her exposed shoulder, clammy fingers applying a fair amount of pressure as he reassuringly squeezed.

"I don't need to stay out tonight, Bri." He assured her, taking a seat on the edge of the plush booth beside her as she avoided his soft stare. "Besides, I drove."

"I can get a cab," she shyly protested, nudging his palm off of her shoulder as she weakly grinned. "Really. It's fine. My apartment really isn't too far, just a few streets over. I'll manage. Even if I walk, it's not a big deal."

"See, Verny!" Georgie cheered, moist tongue lapping out to meet his exceedingly chapped lips. "You've got a strong, independent woman, there! I'll go get you a drink so we can start this night off, yeah? Good evening, missus. Pleasure meeting you."

Briar dumbfoundedly glared at Georgie's outstretched palm, impossibly dry fingers spread in an unattractive fashion as he inaudibly requested for her to slip her hand into his.

Not a chance.

Instead, the quiet woman simply smiled, nodding curtly in both Georgie and the remaining men's directions before planting a firm kiss to Vern's partially parted lips.

"Keep your phone in your hand," Vern lowly spoke, cradling her sullen features in his warm hold as she nodded. "Call me if you need *anything*. I'll pick you up from anywhere."

"Ulysses," Briar nasally drawled, batting her mascara-riddled eyelashes as she placed a feather-like kiss to the tip of his pointed nose. "I'll be fine."

Ingleside is only three streets south, babe. You worry too much."

"I worry because I care. Besides, this isn't the best neck-of-the-woods, especially with how close we are to Stillwater." He boldly argued, the pad of his thumb colliding with her chin as he gently massaged the skin. "I just want you safe, darling. Maybe you should consider getting out of that worn-down apartment complex and finding a place somewhere up in Elmwood or around there."

The woman raised a curious, thickly painted brow, sucking diligently up on her bottom lip as Vern inconsistently cleared his throat.

"Elmwood is all the way Uptown," she rigidly spoke, claiming her impossibly dry left elbow with her right palm as she hastily cupped the lizard-like skin. "It would take me nearly an hour to get to work when traffic is bad."

"Oh, c'mon, Bri. You're just fishing for complaints. I do the commute daily, it doesn't bother me at all." He countered, awkwardly eyeing his idle friends nearby.

"Look," Briar began, avoiding their impatient glares. "I have my pepper spray and keys if I need them. I'll jog, even. Probably won't take me more than fifteen minutes to get home, and I'll ring you the moment I walk through the door. Okay?"

Vern momentarily paused, a rigid expression plastered upon his conflicted complexion as Briar weakly smiled.

"Okay," he finally breathed, fingers darting outward to caress her elbow. "Please keep in touch. It's late and dark and—"

"—stop *worrying*, U." Briar embarrassingly pressed, objectively eyeing his strange friends as they awkwardly observed the situation at hand. "I'll be all right. Goodnight, guys. Nice meeting you."

The strangers simply nodded, thrusting wide palms into the air as they dismissively waved goodbye to the pretty blond with striking cobalt eyes. Finally, Briar excused herself from the over-crowded bar—sniffling slightly from the drastic shift in temperature as she vacated the premises. A profusion of melting ice crunched beneath the soles of her boots, a soft sigh slipping through discolored lips as she shivered violently from the cold. It was officially December, and Chicago was getting its first (of many) waves of freezing weather.

Frigid fingers took refuge in the drastically shallow space of her jean jacket pockets, bottom lip sat snug between rows of chattering teeth as she quickly rounded the corner of the lively bar, the abundance of brightly hued lights instantly slipping from view as the nearby surroundings faded to black.

Woodlawn was poorly lit and smelt of sewage and sloppy condom sex. Old, decrepit businesses lined the eerily empty road, the broad, cracked shop windows displaying differing signs, all of which read the very same statement: *Out of Business*. Occasional whimpers escaped the woman's partially parted mouth as she speedily scaled the frozen sidewalk, gaze glued to her surroundings as she anxiously awaited the presence of another human being. However, Woodlawn seemed to lack any source of life at all at this particular time of night, especially on this long strip of empty road.

Crunch crunch crunch.

Rigidly, the woman glanced cautiously over her pointed shoulder, eyes wild with curiosity as she continued down the path towards her extremely outdated apartment, the settled snow crunching beneath her soles as she increased her pace. The outside temperature seemed to continuously plummet, painting her severely dry lips a harsh blue hue as her feet fell numb from the cold. Apparently, she'd chosen the thinnest pair of socks that she owned to go along with her exceedingly comfy leather boots.

"Hey!" A dark, ominous voice suddenly barked, heavily startling the timid woman as she nearly jumped from her skin in fright.

Briar stumbled sideways, her left foot curling at an obscenely ugly angle as she slipped from the comfort of the slippery sidewalk and collapsed flat onto her ass, shaking palms extending backward in a shy attempt to soothe her fall. Unfortunately for her, the choppy ice beneath her feet had managed to slice open the surface of her palms.

The defeated woman released a vociferous cry—hot, salty tears tickling the corners of her eyes as her precisely applied eyeliner began to slightly smudge. The unfamiliar voice promptly returned the moment she managed to view her bleeding hands, discolored bottom lip quivering with a mixture of conflicting emotions as she held back violent sobs.

"Oh, man," the raspy voice sighed, a sense of mockery present in its tone as a man (easily into his mid-fifties) lowered himself to the ground, extremely thick eyebrows raised in wonder as he observed the fluorescent liquid.

"You took quite the tumble," he said, stunning cocoa-eyes locking onto her sullen features. A sudden, eerie smile pranced along his thin lips, partially wrinkled features curling upwards in a blatant array of smile lines as he continued with, "Sorry if I startled you, I mistook you for someone else. Why don't we get you cleaned up a bit?"

"I'm fine." Briar shakily spat, shoving past the handsome stranger as she immediately climbed to her feet. A profusion of ice littered the surface of her jeans, soaking the material through and through as an abundance of goosebumps littered her freezing flesh.

"You're bleeding," he argued, warm fingers interlocking around her bony wrists as he quizzically stared at her fresh wounds. "I'm the cause of it, too. The least that I can do is clean you up. I promise you can go on your merry way once you've stopped oozing."

The woman hesitantly froze in place, heart heavily hammering beneath her heaving chest as she glanced worriedly over either shoulder. The entirety of the road was painfully vacant, prompting the woman's stomach to violently churn as the strange man objectively eyed her. A series of street lamps littered the road, all of which were completely burnt out, creating an extremely uninviting atmosphere as blackness consumed the area.

This was it. This was where she would die. Two streets away from her own home.

"Hey," the newcomer thickly pressed, his breath laced with smoke and beef jerky as Briar disgustingly flinched. His greedy palms fondled her elbows, assertively yanking her frail frame forward as she outwardly cried within his hold.

"You're such a wiggle worm," he murmured, his once soft, warm eyes instantly vanishing as a menacing dark hue enveloped the surface. "Stop fighting. All I want to do is clean you up a bit."

"C-Can I just c-call my boyfriend to let him know–" Briar uneasily stammered, thick tears clouding her vision as the aging man released a sarcastic cackle, tossing his head back with glee as several dark strands of jet black hair littered his vision.

"*Oh*," the man giggled, aggressively yanking her rigid form towards a nearby building as she outwardly sobbed into the thin air. "*Boyfriend*, eh? What's he like? Tell me 'bout him, don't be shy."

"P-Please," she shrieked, attempting to climb out of his surprisingly hard hold as he dragged her towards an improperly sealed steel door—originally silver in hue but littered with an abundance of dark crimson rust. "Let me go! I can clean the blood up myself–"

"God, will you just shut up?" The older man irritably clipped, ungloved fingers lacing around the circular handle of the door as he abruptly tore it widely open. "Go."

"You c-can't do this," Briar defeatedly exclaimed, heart thumping thickly in her throat as she dug her fingernails into the exposed flesh of his pulsating neck. "I know the Switch! He'll—he'll *kill* you if you lay a single finger on me—"

The man immediately halted his actions, eyes widening considerably as his jaw hung low. The pair still stood between the ajar doorway, occasional gusts of warm, comforting heat intermittently slapping her flushed cheeks as he snarled.

"The Switch, huh?" He mused, dark, callous gaze slightly twinkling as he exchanged his weight from either frozen foot. "Last I heard, the fucker landed himself in Stillwater from all the ruckus he caused last summer. How does a pretty girl like yourself know ickle Andy?"

His name was Andy?

"I'm his personal Nurse," she shamefully revealed, audibly gulping as the man's smirk grew. "And a friend of his."

"*Friend,* hm? What kind of friend? Because the Switch I know—this *new Andy*—doesn't have any friends, and a gorgeous girl like yourself is probably more of a girlyfriend than anything..."

"We're just friends. I swear if you lay a single finger on me he'll surely skin you alive when he gets out of Stillwater—" Briar exclaimed, heartbeat accelerating as her breaths emerged in short, staggered pants.

"*When?*" The stranger mocked, an additional chuckle slipping off of his lips. "Are you helping a notorious criminal escape from captivity? That, my dear, would surely land you a spot in his place."

"Please, just let me go," she dryly begged, attempting to tear away from his extremely tight grasp. "Please. You have no use for me."

The strange man slightly paused, the tip of his tongue curiously fondling the innards of his smooth complexion as he contemplated his next series of actions. Briar was young, blond, and abundantly pretty; complimented with silky coat of hair and precisely applied makeup, a series of colors that perfectly accented the gorgeous set of eyes that claimed her flawless features.

"Oh, but I do," the man said, admiring her striking features. "Just look at yourself, dolly. Do you even realize how much I could make off of you? Hell, I bet someone would pay thousands for a face like that…"

An immediate, horrified expression enveloped Briar's face, realization setting in as she attempted once more to tear out of his arms, but to no avail. It was evident now that this strange man in his easy fifties had planned on selling her into sex trafficking—*and for what?*

"But," he interjected, swaying sideways as he contemplated on what to do with the stunning woman before him, whose eyes were the size of the moon and cheeks flushed a ghastly white. "Since you know little Switchy, I have an even better idea. One you may actually prefer, in fact. One that doesn't involve pawning you off to some foreign creep with too much money and a pitiful pencil penis."

"Just let me go and I promise I won't say a word. Besides, I don't even know your name or anything. It'll be like none of this ever happened." Briar spat, her words blending into a jumbled mess as she choked back vociferous sobs. The unnamed stranger sympathetically smiled, the left back heel of his boot resting against the hefty steel door as it lay propped open.

"They call me King Cici." He confidently revealed, a slight snicker in his tone as the tips of his fingers agonizingly tickled the clothed flesh of her forearm. Instinctively, Briar jerked away from his inappropriate touch, a slight scoff overcoming her flushed complexion as she silently begged for release.

"Mister Cici, please just—" she slyly began, attempting to wriggle away from the doorway as his brows mockingly raised.

"—Jesus," he throatily mocked, harshly claiming her elbow is his palm as she openly winced. "Just knock it off, all right? Since you seem to be on such good terms with Switch, that changes *everything* about this little scenario."

"What d'you—"

"Just tell me one thing, gorgeous." King Cici began, disgustingly sharp nails digging into the fabric of her sweater as she swallowed a mouthful of bile. "Are you afraid of needles?"

"Not particularly, but—" she stammered, only to be interrupted by a sarcastic cackle as he confidently laced his arms around her torso.

"Perfect," he mused, clammy palm flattening against her ajar lips as he dragged her into the building. "Oh, and uh, one more thing…"

Before she could protest, he'd managed to lift her entire weight from the dusty concrete floor, a series of horrified shouts slipping through trembling lips as he carried the broken woman into the impenetrable abyss of the foreign building. His lips tickled the flesh of her earlobe, a horrifyingly dark voice emerging as he whispered a distinct phrase: "Tell him that Papa says hello."

An old, withering tennis ball claimed the warm flesh of Switch's greedy palm, the fluorescent green material faintly frayed in several sections as he twisted the round ball around in his grasp. A dark-haired Vern had gifted Switch the peculiar object only a day prior, explaining to the madman that it was an old chew toy from Vern's dog, apparently named Tootles. Vern's reasoning for providing the notorious criminal with such a random doodad was, quite frankly, unknown. It was as if the particularly friendly guard had actually grown to like and admire the curly-haired bloke with extremely violent tendencies and a vastly scarred appearance.

The aging ball slipped sharply from Switch's grasp, rippling precisely through the still, stale air as the rounded surface just barely grazed the concrete ceiling before speedily stooping downward and slipping comfortably back into his confident grasp. This particular action repeated on a continuous loop for a solid thirty-seven minutes that morning—all the while: the persistent, deep breaths of a somewhat pretty(*ish*) Adelaide in deep slumber occasionally squeezed through the glassless window as Switch lay wide awake nearly the entire night.

Immediately following Adelaide's recent visit with the horrid Dr. Blake, the scrawny woman managed to sleep an astounding eleven hours nightly, and occasionally took sporadic, hour-long naps midday. Just yesterday, the straggly-haired woman managed to slip into a nearly comatose state within the rec room, her nose buried deeply within the fabric of Switch's dilapidating jumpsuit trousers as she curled up into a petite ball upon his lap. Routinely, Switch had passed the time by fiddling with a shabby deck of cards, slender digits persistently shuffling the thick paper as Adelaide silently observed. Eventually, her heavy-lidded eyes had slipped closed, shielding the madman from her twinkling orbs as she drifted into a silent slumber, chest lightly falling with every staggered breath as he astonishingly allowed the wildly intimate gesture.

Alas, the soft, snug scenario was cut excruciatingly short by an unfamiliar face wearing a Stillwater uniform. She called herself Wren, and was a shockingly short woman with a profusion of freckles and fiery red hair. Her eyes were a deep shade of unmatched black, creating an illusion of invisible irises as they were nearly identical in hue to her pupils. Luckily, she'd let the duo off with a soft warning, but dismissed a sleepy Adelaide to her cell where she would succumb to an even deeper and extremely lonely slumber.

Unceasing bolts of electricity continually consumed Switch's spine as he tossed the tennis ball into the air, frequent recollections of last night's events continuously bombarding his mangled mind as his stomach physically churned. He almost swore that he could still feel the intoxicating sensation of Adelaide's lips up on his collarbones—an extremely sensitive spot of his—where blatant blemishes had consumed the surface: clear, distinct evidence of her lovely, prying mouth. His dark gaze reconnected momentarily with the specific spot, the base of his chin flattening against the exposed flesh of his neck as he viewed the destroyed skin with a sneer smile.

Sure enough—two tiny, purple bruises claimed the center of his protuberant right collarbone, courtesy of the shy woman who lay fast asleep on the opposite side of the wall. A cheeky grin immediately consumed his features, free fingers claiming the spot where Adelaide's lips laid only hours prior as he intently studied the flat flesh with his fingertips. It was utterly bizarre—really—how some random woman with sunken eyes and bulbous cheekbones and incredibly dry skin managed to drive the infamous Switch somewhat wild, but also managed to vaguely tame him. But for what price?

He knew damn well that this little honeymoon phase wouldn't last long. Things this good never did seem to last, especially for a guy like him.

A guy like him . . .

And yet—the overwhelming desire to snatch Adelaide Lynch's every last breath continued to intensify day by day. Just hours prior, he'd gotten a torturous tease of how absolutely glorious her skin tasted—how it felt beneath his needy, gruesome grasp. Her breathless sighs were addictingly intoxicating—heart thickly thumping beneath his confident hold as his fingers had encircled her throat. She'd wanted it, she'd *asked* for it—*oh daddy, will you just choke me already?*—and, being the dutiful man, he was—he did it. Hell, he could've sworn that his heart might've actually, literally, *physically* burst out of his heaving chest the moment she'd uttered those very words—*oh princess, you know* exactly *what daddy likes*—and as his fingers twisted around her supple skin, he could've sworn that he'd nearly burst just from the simplistic feel of her erratic pulse beneath his fingertips.

An involuntary groan emerged from significantly scarred lips, eyelids fluttering closed as Switch stirred upon his measly mattress. God, Adelaide was just so effortlessly *sexy* with everything she did—and she didn't even have to try! Perhaps the sexiest, most intricate part of her very being was the very fact that she—admittedly—was not even remotely fearful of death.

Please, baby girl—Let me take all of your pain away . . .

Just as Switch's greedy palm met the growing bulge beneath his matted trousers, the distinct click of his broad cell door thrust him from his dazed trance, eyes wild with wanton abandon as a tired Vern strut into the petite premises.

"Morning." The guard lowly greeted, completely oblivious to Switch's aroused state as the madman hastily adjusted his growing length beneath the waistband of his pants. Awkwardly, the killer rose from his position, withering tennis ball concealed within his palm as the soles of his bare feet met the cool concrete.

"S'abit *early,* innit?" Switch murmured, snapping his head from side to side as he audibly cracked the stiff bones within his neck. "You caught me with my morning *stiffy.*"

"Yeah," Vern grumbled, running a hand through his messy locks. "It's six-forty, so a little earlier than usual. Nurse Briar's asking for you, it's the beginning of December and time for your physical. She wants it done before breakfast so you don't miss out on any food."

Dismissively, Switch placed the ball onto the mattress, empty palms flattening against the discolored sheet as he applied ample pressure to the surface before rising to his feet. The aging, striped jumpsuit clung lowly to his hips, persistent patches of untamed pubes peeking out from the waist of his trousers as Vern claimed the discarded top piece of his suit from the ground and tossed it in his direction.

"Er, thanks." Switch uncharacteristically said, heavily-lidded eyes keenly observing a silent Vern as he tugged the material over his head, sending several unkempt curls awry as a multitude of ringlets concealed his vision. The hair was shoulder-length, a messy mop of unclean curls claiming his scalp as slender fingers intently pried the stray strands away from his eyes.

"Jeez, bud," Vern chuckled, shifting his weight from either foot as he tore a set of shiny, new handcuffs from his utility belt. "You could use a haircut."

Switch flat-out ignored Vern's friendly comment, calloused fingers unconsciously picking at his mangled flesh as the madman approached the guard, palms eventually outstretching in preparation to be cuffed, per usual.

"I hate how you still have to be cuffed," Vern said, latching the cool, silver material loosely around Switch's bony wrists. "I personally think you've made a lot of progress since you've been here. If it were up to me, I wouldn't even label you as high risk anymore."

Switch curiously observed the chatty man, brows amusingly raised as the duo clambered from the cold, dingy cell and entered the vacant hallway of the cell block.

"Yeah, well it isn't *up* to you, now is it?" Switch dryly teased, gaze strictly focused upon his unlaced boots as they quickly navigated the building, dull lights constantly flickering as several of them eventually burnt out. It was clear that Dr. Evers didn't give a rat's ass about the upkeep in this establishment—Nor about the overall wellbeing of his admitted patients.

Most of the souls within these walls were left for dead, anyways.

The hospital wing was dark and dingy—courtesy of the absence of lights and warmth, for that matter. Truth be told, it was freezing in this enormous room, and even Vern found himself quivering within his boots from the dramatic dip in temperature.

"Hopefully the little physical rooms are warmer, otherwise I'll feel awful bad about you having to strip down." He lightly explained, a slight chuckle present in his tone as he directed Switch in the general area of the sealed rooms. The madman curiously eyed the overly-friendly guard, a series of queries bombarding his mind as he wondered the inevitable—why was Vern treating him like an old friend instead of a widely-despised criminal?

"Totally," the curly-haired man began, marred mouth etching into a cheeky smirk. "Wouldn't want any *shrinkage*."

Vern audibly gulped at his wildly inappropriate remark, lazy glare refocusing on the nearby surroundings as they rapidly approached the sealed room where Briar patiently waited. His freezing fingers weakly gripped onto the thick fabric of the elbow of Switch's suit, vivid visuals of his girl doing certain—*things*—to the murderous psychopath instantaneously raiding his mind.

Eventually, they approached a tightly sealed door, Vern's free fingers curling into a limp fist as he politely knocked upon the unpigmented wood. Nearly three seconds following, the door swung widely open, revealing an exhausted Briar with severely smudged eyeliner and chapped lips.

"Morning." She throatily greeted, waving the pair into the comfortable, warm room as she inaudibly sniffled, greasy blond locks tugged away from her eyes as the hair lay held back with an old rubber band.

"If you need anything at all–" Vern began, directing Switch towards the examination table, complimented with a thin sheet of wrinkled paper.

"–press the red button. Got it." Briar sleepily dismissed, her back facing the two men as she shuffled through Switch's medical files.

Vern's expression tightened, an immediate sense of worry overcoming his complexion as he excused himself from the room without another word. Switch playfully smirked at the current scenario, teeth bared in a cheeky fashion as the tip of his tongue intently traced the top row of yellowed teeth.

"Ge-*zuuuuus*," he throatily drawled, taking his spot up on the table as the paper audibly shifted beneath his weight. "Even I could feel all of that *sexual tension–*"

The manila folder inelegantly slipped from Briar's weakened grasp, noisily tumbling to the surface of the nearby counter as several pieces of ink-littered paper spilled from inside. Swiftly, the woman rotated on her heel—azure-hued eyes bloodshot as she choked back hefty sobs. Switch's jaw inordinately fell, confusion riddling his features as her shaking fingers claimed the thin fabric of her scrubs, digits curling beneath the surface as she anxiously yanked upwards to reveal her midriff.

Before Switch could release some type of sarcastic remark, his eyes immediately widened—every single last breath instantly eluding his lungs as he viewed the angry flesh that was once concealed by her white and pink polka-dot shirt.

A very distinct mark claimed her skin—four inches by four—permanently embedded into the flesh by dark, black ink. A cartoon-ish outline of a pointed crown—one that maybe a King would wear—hovered the flesh directly above her pant line, accented with a very distinct set of initials directly in the center of the drawing—two C's, respectively. The first forward facing, whereas the second lay backwards, the opening of the second letter directly facing the opening of the first.

As if on cue, the madman climbed from the safety of the table, eyes unblinking as he worriedly approached the silently sobbing woman, shirt still clutched between quivering fingers as the lining of her strawberry red bra lay on display. His attention, however, wasn't on that particular spot—*no no no*—his attention was primarily glued to the absolutely *horrific* branding that marked her flesh, directly above her privates and stamped permanently into the skin—*his marking,* King Cici's marking.

Switch fell to his knees before the violated woman, cuffed wrists raising to meet her ruined flesh as the very tips of his fingers met the raised skin, intently tracing the surface as his breaths drastically thinned. Unintentionally, an abundance of unwelcome memories instantly raided his mind, sending the man flat onto his bottom as an audible gasp slipped through lacerated lips.

"This is all your fault, y'know. Only you could've prevented this!" King Cici exclaimed, a slight chuckle present in his condescending tone as he wrestled the petite woman down onto the rickety old table. "It'll teach you not to steal from me–"

"Don't fucking touch her!" Andrew cried, salty tears coating his flushed features as thrashed within the hold of two exceedingly tall men, who currently held tightly onto the raw flesh of his arms. Several brown curls stuck to the dampened skin of his cheeks, bottom lip quivering as Kennedy released a vociferous cry beneath Cici's weight. A single stream of dark, crimson blood slowly oozed from his right nostril, the thick liquid occasionally dipping into his agape mouth as a harsh, metallic taste filled his senses.

"Get the hell off of me!" She shrieked, palms flattening against King Cici's chest in a weakened attempt to shove him off. "I have nothing to do with this! We're separated, pending a divorce! I refuse to settle whatever debt he has with you–"

Kennedy immediately swallowed her words the moment King Cici's palm met her cheek, emitting a horrific sonance as it ricocheted off the paper-thin walls. Once more, Andrew audibly protested, attempting to yank out of the strong men's holds as one of them clamped downward on his unruly locks, aggressively yanking the man backwards as he released a heightened cry— immediately followed by a sarcastic sneer.

That felt good.

"Stop wiggling." King Cici scolded, assertively tugging Kennedy's

jean shorts down the length of her legs as she outwardly sobbed, blurry gaze meeting a horrified Andrew only yards away as she silently begged for help. He, however, was utterly helpless—occasionally releasing a series of heightened cries and harsh obscenities as the man openly violated his girl— right before his very eyes.

"Get your hands off of her, you freak!" Andrew cried, receiving an immediate punch to the jaw as painful tears slipped from the corners of his bloodshot eyes. He slightly stumbled sideways, slipping out of their hold only momentarily as the older man yanked down his zipper.

"He's a pretty boy, isn't he, Kennedy?" King Cici teased, wiggling out of his slacks as he held Kennedy's wrists taunt against the table top. "Spitting image of his Momma, he is. Would've been a lot handsomer if he'd gotten his good looks from myself, though."

Andrew froze, eyes instantly widening as realization suddenly set in: This couldn't be real . . . this couldn't be happening . . .

"Switch?" Briar pried, dropping her shirt to conceal the horrid marking as she fell to her knees before him, a genuine look of concern etched upon her features as her hands met his distressed complexion. His hands were in his hair, aggressively yanking and tugging at the messy curls atop his skull as heavy eyelids remained glued shut, vivid visuals of a horrific memory tainting his vision as Kennedy's cries echoed throughout the petite premises.

"Drew! Help me, please!" Kennedy had cried, releasing another sob as the older man continued to explicitly violate her. Andrew defeatedly watched, a profusion of bile rising into his throat as he noticed something quite bizarre—something precisely and permanently placed right above Kennedy's pant line.

A marking. A specific symbol that signified that he'd officially claimed her all for himself.

Violated her.

Tortured her.

Unfortunately for her, the two henchmen had yanked a screaming Andrew from the room, sharpened blades held tightly in their clutch as they held his squirming frame flat against the dusty floor, the tips of the serrated knife inching closer and closer to his distressed features . . .

"Switch!" Briar exclaimed, palm meeting his face as her thumb claimed the top of his cheek, whereas her forefinger collided with his brow—fingers quickly spreading as she aggressively yanked open his eyelid.

Wild, inky eyes met a stunned sea of blue—airy gasps escaping through mangled lips as he yanked out of her reassuring hold.

Switch scrambled backwards, the back of his skull arduously colliding with the leg of the examination table as he released a throaty exhale, fingers anxiously tearing at the restraints upon his wrists as Briar desperately attempted to calm him down.

"Hey, hey!" She cooed, retrieving the key for the cuffs from the table top as she unlatched the metal restraints from his scarlet-riddled wrists. "What is it? Who is he?"

"What did he do to you?" Switch darkly inquired, eagerly massaging the angry flesh up on his wrists with his fingers. Once more, that haunting look on Kennedy's face struck his mind, prompting his left eye to irritably twitch as Briar's glare promptly hardened.

"Don't make me say it," she whispered, swallowing thickly as fresh tears arose. "I bled everywhere. He had absolutely no remorse—and the tattoo—"

"He's my dad." Switch revealed, point-blank. The words tasted bitter on his tongue, King Cici's ugly mug raiding his vision as he aggressively chomped down on the muscle, drawing blood.

The pair sat in an uneasy silence for several agonizing moments, Briar's stomach painfully churning as she admired Switch's blank expression.

His father.

"She has it, too." He nonchalantly added, picking at the excess skin around his nails as he avoided Briar's firm glare. "The *tattoo*."

"Who, Switch?" She shyly wondered, collapsing onto her bottom as she sat crossed-legged on the floor, pulse inexplicably racing beneath her ribcage as she blinked back blinding tears. She *hated* King Cici for what he'd done to her, and apparently—she wasn't the first.

Switch simply swallowed, mouth ajar in mortification as Kennedy Carter's beautiful face invaded his thoughts.

"My *wife*."

XXVI

"Holy shit, Vern! I just—I just don't think I can even *begin* to comprehend any of this! The infamous, psychopathic Switch has a *wife*!" Briar elatedly exclaimed, hands thrust boldly into the air as she paced in vigorous circles around the vacant staff lounge. The toe of her dilapidating Chuck Taylor side-swiped one of the metal chairs, prompting the legs to obscenely scratch against the tile surface as she blatantly flinched.

The vending machines on the far wall groaned with dissatisfaction, the refrigeration sporadically kicking in to cool down the highly carbonated canned sodas as Briar paced the premises. Her lover, Ulysses Vern, currently strut highly distressed expression; eyes widened and slightly watering as he struggled to comprehend the information that his darling beau had just effortlessly spilled–*as if it was no big deal!*

"You were *raped?*" He croaked, clammy palms meeting the disheveled locks atop his skull as he arduously tugged. "See, Briar—*see!* This was *exactly* the reason I told you not to walk home. *Shit*—you were raped! Oh my God, we need t-to get you to a hospital! Get you plan B! G-Get you–"

"Vern, that's not the focus right now." Briar irritably clipped, anxiously twirling several greasy strands of blond between pinched fingers as the man's eyes promptly widened and his jaw fell agape. Several spurts of ice-cold air suddenly spluttered from the air vent directly above his frigid frame, causing an involuntary shiver to arise as he violently shook.

"Not the focus? Geez, Bri—do you even *realize* how serious this is? You could've been kidnapped—or killed—oh God, what if you're *pregnant*—" Vern vented, bottom lip quivering with angst as an abundance of bile instantly crept up his throat.

"—I'm *not*." She immediately interjected, accidentally yanking several individual strands of hair from her scalp. "I'm definitely not. I ran to CVS and took a Plan B. I'm not pregnant with Switch's father's child—"

"*Switch's father?*" Vern exploded, his tone harsh and thick as Briar slightly flinched. The raw flesh below her bellybutton irritably twinges, the physical evidence of King Cici's assault imprinted up on her body as a fresh set of tears littered her bloodshot orbs.

"A-Apparently so—" Briar stuttered, arms crossed as she turbulently twitched. Her statement, however, had unfortunately been interrupted by the irritable presence of an additional human being, one who'd abruptly entered the staff lounge.

An abundance of fiery red locks strut into the area—dark, callous eyes wild with wanton abandon as she froze in place within the parted doorway. Awkwardly, the baby-faced woman thrust her freckled arms into the air, a slight snicker overcoming her blushing complexion as the metal cuffs attached to her utility belt clinked together.

"Bad time?" She giddily inquired, immediately lowering her tiny palms as she released a sarcastic cackle. Her eyes promptly scanned the stunned duo, nearly invisible brows raising in curiosity as she flicked her tongue.

"Wren Tribeca." The ginger woman introduced, extending her arm out towards a frozen Briar as she inaudibly requested the presence of her palm. She walked with a slight skip in her step, rounded eyes sparkling beneath the artificial lighting of the luminous staff room.

"Uh," Briar uneasily stammered, objectively claiming Wren's palm in hers as she weakly squeezed. "Briar Cunningway."

Wren simply nodded, gaze detaching from a rigid Briar as she met Vern's equally awkward physique, one hand buried deeply in his uneven locks as the opposite met Wren's confident grasp. "Vern."

Wren nodded curtly, a thin-lipped grin etched upon her freckled features as she navigated the petite premises, heading directly towards the soda machines as she fished a wrinkled dollar bill from her breast pocket.

"Hope I haven't interrupted anything important," she loudly began, placing the softened bill upon her busty chest as she attempted to smooth out the paper with clammy fingers. "You two seemed a bit distressed."

"What kind of accent is that?" Vern wondered, blatantly ignoring Wren's straight forward inquiry as the woman shot a puzzled glare at the duo over her pointed shoulder, ring-clad fingers lacing around the straightened paper bill as she messily shoved it into the machine.

"I'm from South Dakota." Wren simply said, watching closely as the machine swallowed up her money with glee before spluttering to life and dispensing her can of Coca-Cola.

"What brings you to dreary ole Southern Chicago?" Briar pried, side-eyeing an equally uncomfortable Vern as the tips of her fingers agonizingly brushed against his lonely hand.

"A girl," Wren snickered, claiming the dispensed soda can between desperate fingers as she twisted on her heel. A pair of electric eyes immediately collided with objectifying orbs; ginger brows raised in wonder as the new security guard tore open her drink. "My wife, actually—Julianna. She came to work for the CPD about a month ago as a detective. She's working on the infamous Switch's case, actually. She's absolutely obsessed with the guy—everything about his case and crimes fascinates her. If she wasn't a raging lesbian, I could've sworn she was in love with him."

Briar and Vern exchanged glances, the persistent buzzing of the overhead lights filling the otherwise gruesome void as Wren obnoxiously cleared her throat.

"You're his personal nurse, ain't cha, Missus Briar?" Wren wondered, bringing the cold can to her lips as she took a generous swig.

"I am," Briar said, transferring her weight to the opposite foot. "I'm also Adelaide's. She's patient 4210."

"Yeah, we've met." Wren chuckled, lively gaze colliding with the dusty floor as Briar raised a questionable brow. "She's a tired little thing, isn't she? Fell asleep in the rec room yesterday on Switch's lap—the *Switch*! Can you believe it? I wasn't even aware that a monster like himself could even be able to feel affection towards someone—"

"They're friends," Briar interjected, her tone wary and choppy as Vern audibly cleared his throat. "Good friends. Addy's on some heavy-duty medication for her schizophrenia, which explains the drowsiness. I appreciate your concern over her, but I can handle things from here."

With that, Wren tossed her palms into the air, a heavy can of soda laced between parted, slender digits as she headed towards the door.

"I guess I'll see you two around." She said, voice slightly muffled by the can pressed fleetingly to her lips as she wordlessly excused herself from the staff room, isolating both Briar and Vern once more.

Vern released a staggered sigh, a severe sense of discomfort consuming his chest as his watery glare met a timid Nurse Briar opposite him.

"Show me it again." He requested, clearly referring to the permanent ink that littered her abused flesh. "Please."

Briar gulped, trembling fingers curling around the hem of her scrubs as she shakily lifted the material from her midriff. A profusion of dark, scaly ink immediately appeared—the mark of a monster. He'd claimed her, in every way somebody physically could. It *sickened* her.

Vern fell to his knees before her, eyes profusely watering as his quivering fingertips met the raw flesh of her lower belly. Cautiously, he traced the precise shape of the crown, the raised, angry flesh tickling his digits as he choked back vociferous sobs. He could've prevented this . . . it was all his fault . . .

"Stop internally blaming yourself," Briar suddenly spoke, immediately dropping her shirt as the tattoo disappeared from plain view. "This isn't your fault. At all."

"I'll fucking kill him," Vern pressed, rising to his feet once more as he vigorously paced the area, heavy footsteps ricocheting off the paper-thin walls as Briar audibly gulped. "I'll do it. I swear."

"Vern—"

"He'll wish he was never *born*—"

"Ulysses—"

"I'll do it. With ease, actually. I have the greatest weapon of them all." He slyly said, a snicker enveloping his raging features as his girlfriend's brows quizzically raised.

"What is it?" She thickly inquired, clammy palm claiming her exposed elbow. Vern's glare grew dark, lips curving into an enthusiastic grin.

"I have his son."

The aging engine of Lyra Blake's 1995 manual Hyundai Accent spluttered back to life after a momentary stall—a dissatisfied grunt emerging through purple painted lips as her fingers curled around the cool silver of her keys.

She was a whopping eighty-two minutes late to work that morning, and she could practically hear Dr. Evers' gravelly, condescending tone already—*God Lyra, you need to be more punctual!*—as the little blue car roared back to life momentarily, old rubber wheel vibrating beneath her calloused fingertips as she thrust the vehicle into first gear.

Nearly seven minutes following, the woman arrived upon the sealed, rusted gates of Stillwater Sanitarium; her fender nearly colliding with the crooked keypad as her foot suddenly slammed on the brake a bit too quickly for her liking. Her broad-shouldered frame inordinately thrust forward, a petite whine escaping through an irately parted mouth as her fingertips met the dilapidating buttons.

Timidly, the middle-aged woman entered the unique code used for the front gate, magnified glare keenly focused on the crooked text etched upon the tippy-top of the inky black gates.

Home sweet home.

Creakily, the metal gates began their ascent, slipping backwards with momentary difficulty as the gates groaned outward in annoyance. Just as Lyra Blake's fingers met the gear shift, her irritated stare met the sight of a foreign object to the left of the nearly open gates. Curious brows quizzically raised, lips momentarily parted as the woman dropped the clutch and voluntarily allowed the vehicle to stall once more. As if in a trance, the woman slipped from the confinement of her seatbelt, needy fingers curling around the discolored plastic of the door handle as she kicked it open.

"What the—" she murmured, cautiously approaching the elegant stone placed neatly on the surface of the dirt, a series of sparkling, silver letters claiming the face of the fancy rock as Blake blatantly scoffed.

Jacqueline Ray Kleever
In loving memory of
a truly beautiful human

The disgruntled woman fell to her knees before the precious stone, lightly freckled features contorting into a look of immense disgust as she lifted the object from the ground with difficulty. Oddly enough, the rock was a lot heavier than she'd anticipated, and as she'd attempted to stand back to her feet, her knees defiantly locked beneath her, followed by a distressed cry as it slipped through tainted lips.

Ineptly, the woman tossed Jackie's pleasant memorial several yards aside as she stifled a sigh. The oblong object bounced several times before eventually colliding with an adjacent rock, which, in turn, caused the small memorial to split directly into two choppy pieces. The exceedingly kind tribute to Jackie Kleever lay forgotten off to the side as Lyra Blake clambered back into her vehicle, whitened teeth insistently chewing on her lipstick-riddled mouth as an additional vehicle pulled in behind her.

Begrudgingly, Blake slipped her car through the partially parted gates, manicured nails constantly picking at the moderately torn skin as the color began to flake off in tiny chunks. Her assigned parking space lay vacant, the chalky white paint displaying her surname was beginning to fade as her tires came to a screeching halt within the perfectly painted lines.

Her frigid digits met the cracked leather of her purse, obscenely lengthy thumbnail unintentionally digging into the elderly material as the object tumbled sideways, spilling its contents all over the passenger floor.

"Fuck!" She exasperatedly exclaimed, dipping downward to meet the surface of the floor as she quickly claimed the assorted items, dismissively shoving them into the depths of her purse. Frequent gusts of freezing wind collided with her fogged windows, goose bump-riddled limbs persistently shivering as she yanked the strap over her shoulder and finally vacated the vehicle once and for all.

"Freaking freezing," she lowly groaned, the toe of her boot kicking aside several vibrantly hued pebbles as an abundance of squishy footsteps raided her mind. Nosily, the woman glanced over her shoulder to view the intruder, which was an extremely cheery woman with rosy-red cheeks and curly brunette locks.

"Excuse me, Missus!" The stranger chirped, a toothy grin etched across frozen features as she skipped towards a vindictive Dr. Blake. The older woman glanced dismissively in her direction, muttering a profusion of unattainable phrases as they mounted the steps towards the broad front doors.

"My name is Julianna Tribeca, I'm a detective for the Chicago Police Department and I–" Julianna exclaimed in one long breath, hands theatrically waving as she took the stairs two at a time to keep up with Blake's ridiculously large strides.

"Yes—yes, detective—I get it. Who is it you need to see?" Dr. Blake spat, tearing open the hefty oak door as Julianna followed closely on her heel.

"I'm supposed to be meeting with perhaps one of your most nefarious inmates, Missus–"

Dr. Blake abruptly halted in place, brows disapprovingly raised as the strap of her purse slipped from the comfort of her pointed shoulder, easing into the crook of her elbow as Julianna's glare widened.

"You want to see the Switch, don't you?" Blake thickly queried, vexingly tugging the purse back up the length of her heavily clothed arm as Julianna loudly cleared her throat.

"Y-Yes, ma'am. I've been assigned to his case–" Julianna ranted, avoiding Blake's deprecatory stare as the pair of them spilled into the building.

"Switch actually has a *case?*" Dr. Blake mocked, a slight snicker present in her tone as she routinely navigated the premises. The receptionist glanced fleetingly in their direction, concerned gaze following Julianna's every move as Dr. Blake nodded curtly in her direction, instructing for her to stand down and allow the strangers presence.

"There's honestly nothing to look into with that man. He's a lost cause. A freak." Blake amusingly added, snickering at her own words as Julianna's jaw fell agape.

"With all due respect, Missus–"

"Doctor Blake to you." Blake hurriedly interrupted, thrusting her left hand outward to instruct Julianna to turn left. The soles of their boots obnoxiously scraped against the dusty old floors, lights constantly flickering as Julianna struggled to admire her surroundings.

"Sorry—Doctor Blake—I just do not believe that the–the Switch is necessarily a freak—maybe misunderstood–"

The rubber soles of Dr. Blake's boots agonizingly squealed against the uneven concrete floor as she froze in place, a stern expression plastered across her features as she waved a slender digit in front of Julianna's face.

"Let's get one thing perfectly clear," she boorishly began, the tip of her bubblegum pink fingernail uncomfortably jabbing the woman's' nose as Julianna went cross eyed. "Switch is not some kind of charity case. He can't be cured and he's not misunderstood. He's a monster. Plain and simple."

"Everyone has a reason for the things they do. A motive. Something." Julianna brashly argued, little fingers curling around Blake's single digit as she aggressively tore it from her face.

"Not everyone, Miss Tribeca." Dr. Blake sneered, lips pursed as she brushed past Julianna's shoulder and abandoned her in the hallway directly beside the vacant meeting room.

"It's Mrs. Tribeca, you ignorant bitch." Julianna spat, easing into the chilly room as she took her spot at the tiny metal desk in the center.

The area was eerily quiet and smelled of bleach and metal, prompting Julianna's skin to agonizingly crawl as she spilled the contents of her messy briefcase onto the table top. A heaping mess of assorted pencils and multi-hued pens scattered in diverse directions, several of them rolling off the rounded sides of the surface as they found refuge on the checkered tile floor. A thick, manila folder claimed the very center, several loose-leaf pages sticking out from every end as she inordinately stuffed them back into the depths of the file . . . of *his* file.

She'd been waiting for this day since the first time she'd seen those greasy brown curls on the nightly news. Widespread terror had consumed all of Chicago; a magnitude of frightened individuals begging for answers—answers that she'd hoped to find. His partially lacerated complexion had stuck to her mind like super glue—always watching, always lurking. Cold, lifeless eyes had seemingly observed her every move—haunted her every thought, every dream and every visual. She was utterly and unremorsefully obsessed.

Her wife of two years—Wren—had known about this disturbing obsession from the get-go. In fact, the natural ginger could vividly recall the exact memory of Julianna's first encounter with the man strutting a haunting complexion, the left portion of his features brutally mutilated as if he'd narrowly escaped some sort of brutal knife attack—*A switchblade attack.* They'd binged an amplitude of episodes of *Grey's Anatomy* that night—a starless, cloudy evening full of laughter, kisses, and buttery popcorn. Thus, his features soiled the utterly romantic night half-past seven; a clear image of his giddy physique laid plastered upon the television in high-definition, along with an alleged story about some type of robbery/hostage situation, or so they said. It was peculiar, really, for a small town like Sturgis, South Dakota to receive news about a crime hundreds of miles away—but she immediately knew of the consequences. She knew by the way Julianna had literally and quite confidently tugged out of her locked embrace, eyes wide with wonder as she army crawled towards the television, as if she were viewing a photograph of her long-lost lover. Then came the day Wren's darling beau had requested that the couple pack up, sell their home, and move up to some dingy, rat infested apartment complex in the center of Chicago City.

Anything for you, Julie Bear.

Julianna quickly retrieved her fallen items, sloppily stuffing them back into the confinement of her gifted briefcase as she clearly recollected the time that Wren had given it to her.

For your first day at the CPD, she'd said, freckled features flushed. *You'll do great. You always do.*

An immediate smirk overcame Julianna's features, Wren's doting expression prompting a series of butterflies to erupt in the hollow of her belly as she tore open the flap of the folder to reveal Switch's mugshot. Disorderly clothes and a triumphant sneer had overcome his permanently scarred face, as if he'd wanted to be caught, as if he'd *planned* it.

A trio of knocks on the hefty steel door disrupted Julianna's daze, sending a series of shivers down the length of her spine as she released an exasperated, "yes! Come in!"

"Knock, knock." Wren Tribeca gleamed, balancing her weight between the ajar door as her wife's expression brightened.

"Baby!" Julianna cheered, clapping her hands together enthusiastically as she jumped up from her spot. "What's up?"

"I've got a surprise for you," Wren slyly spoke, glancing anxiously over her shoulder as Julianna's brows immediately raised. Nosily, she attempted to peer through the crack in the door, but to no avail. "Just wait, give me a damn second. So impatient."

The door slammed abruptly closed on Wren's heel, causing Julianna to violently flinch as she took several nervous steps backwards, involuntary shivers consuming every inch of her exposed flesh as a profusion of goosebumps arose along with them. *He was here.*

Moments later, (although it seemed like an eternity to a drastically impatient Julianna), the sleek silver door reopened, revealing a smiling Wren, along with a brunette, curly-haired man bound by a set of shiny metal cuffs. Julianna was almost entirely certain that her heart had stopped clean in her chest.

His wrists were flushed a nasty scarlet hue beneath the bothersome handcuffs, calloused fingers steadily gliding against one another as a pair of beady black orbs instantly collided with hers.

Julianna openly gawked at the notorious criminal, nearly losing her composure as her mouth went dry and her stomach did several flips. Wren, however, didn't seem to notice this—nor did Switch. In fact, the murderer seemed to not even notice Julianna's presence, besides their three-and-a-half second long eye-lock moments prior.

The detective silently observed as her wife, Wren, instructed Switch to take a seat at the file-ridden table, her dainty, boyish fingers claiming the chains atop the table as she quickly and efficiently tied him down before removing her personal set of cuffs from his tainted wrists. Several particularly loopy curls dangled fleetingly within his line of sight, bottom lip jutted outward in a disorderly fashion as the heel of his boot rapidly rapped against the tiled floor.

"He's all yours," Wren spoke, smiling gingerly in Julianna's direction before delivering a hasty pack to the square of her back. "I'll be right outside if you need anything."

Before Julianna could adequately respond, Wren had physically excused herself from the room, completely isolating the shy woman with Chicago's most feared criminal. They sat in a still, stale silence for several moments too long, yellowing teeth aimlessly chewing upon his lower lip as he intently studied the surface of his fingertips.

"H-Hello," Julianna croaked, her voice ultimately defeating her as she diligently paced the room, arms folded anxiously across her unfortunately flat chest as Switch avoided her entirely. "My name is Detective Tribeca, and I'm here to have a little chat with you today, Switch."

Once again, the criminal remained deathly silent. Puzzled, Julianna continued with her carefully rehearsed speech.

"If you will," she defeatedly began, taking a shaky seat upon the freezing metal chair as she openly flinched at the drastic drop in temperature beneath her exposed thighs. "I'll need you to state your first name, last name, and date of birth before we can officially begin."

Switch's glare momentarily flickered upwards, partially concealed by a mess of frizzy, brown locks as he irritably clicked his tongue. With a heavy sigh and an obscene squeak of his chair, the man readjusted his posture; lanky legs inelegantly spreading outward as the toe of his unlaced boot just barely grazed the very tip of Julianna's shoe—chained wrists collapsing atop his lap as he blew away the bothersome strands from his eyes. For the first time, he truly looked at her.

"First name *'The'*," he mockingly began, his tone deep and entirely serious as his tongue audibly clicked against the roof of his mouth.

"Last name *'Switch'*," he giggled this time, stare straying away from Julianna's hardening features as he consistently toyed with the deepest crevices of his scar between every intentional pause.

"Date of *birth*," the man mused, conjoined palms raising upward to meet his mauled flesh as the side of his thumb dismissively itched a particular part of his freshly shaven chin.

"December twenty-fifth—*uh*—*oh, oh, oh, oh*, I suppose." Switch meticulously growled, intentionally brushing his boot against Julianna's once more as she vastly flinched.

"So," she steadily began, rifling through several miscellaneous pages within his file as he intently studied her. She was *so* nervous, he could practically taste it on his tongue. "We're playing games, huh?"

Switch heartily grinned, bottom lip slipping between yellowed teeth as it noisily popped back into place.

"Only if you *want* to." He pursed, snapping his neck from side to side as the bones audibly cracked. "I know a lot of games, princess. Just tell me which one you wanna *play*."

"How about we play the game where you tell me what I need to know so I can go on my merry way?" Julianna unprofessionally pleaded, immediately disgusted with her choice of dialect as Switch released a joyous cackle; one so menacing and dark and horrifying that it made the little blond hairs on the back of her neck stand sky-high.

"*Because,*" the madman drawled, a distracting flick of his tongue momentarily interrupting his dialogue as Julianna's skin crawled. "That's just no *fun*, dollface."

Julianna thickly swallowed, manicured fingers mindlessly rummaging through a series of unnecessary paperwork as Switch positioned himself once more; broad, square shoulders raising as his back arched at an awkward, ugly angle. He leaned dangerously forward, several obscenely long curls dipping into his line of sight once again as his palms met the top of the table.

"So," he tauntingly began, arching a brow as he playfully cocked his head to the side. "You like *girlies*, don't-cha?"

Julianna's pulse instantly quickened, Wren's beautiful features immediately raiding her mind as her jaw parted in angst—*how. . ?*

"No sense try'na *hide* anything from me, buttercup. You're like an *open book*. Just gimme some time to study yah a little." He pressed, staring deeply into her awestruck eyes as she slowly shook her head.

"We're not here to discuss me," she said, a random bout of nausea consuming her belly. "I just want to know why you did it."

"Did *what?*" Switch slickly countered, thick eyebrows knit together in genuine uncertainty as he looked Julianna up and down. "Do you ever think about what it'd be like, *hm*? To feel the warm *touch* of a man . . ."

"No." She lied, picking at the excess skin surrounding her nails. "What you did this summer. Causing uproar in Chicago. Tell me why you did it."

"*Hmmm,*" Switch purred, a cheeky, toothy grin enveloping his lips. "Bossy, bossy. I *like* bossy. Tell me-*uh, De-tec-tive*—are you the dominant one in bed? Or the submissive?"

"T-This is not—"

"I'm typically a major-*er, dom,* myself—buuut, *Lordy*, girly—I really, *really* think I'd let'cha dominate *meee*." He teased, right hand brushing against his lacerated lips as two particular fingers generously parted, insinuating an extremely inappropriate activity.

"Stop avoiding the subject." She snidely snipped, a whirlwind of butterflies consuming her empty stomach as it audibly cried outward for food.

At the surprisingly booming sound, Switch merely smiled, a giggle overcoming his tone as he spilled an extremely amused: "Hungry, baby?"

"No." She lied once more, avoiding his cheerful expression. "Was it for revenge? Or something entirely divergent?"

"Lemme fill you in on a little *secret,* sugar. Y'see, I do things because I fucking *want to*. No catch, *kind of* a gimmick . . . Listen, sugar. When all goes to hell, it's everyone for *themselves*. Always."

Julianna stared blankly back at the criminal, eyes wide with shock as she truly, wholly attempted to soak up everything he was willingly feeding her. To be entirely frank, she wasn't quite sure how this session would go down, and this entire confession was entirely—*unexpected*. But maybe that's exactly what he'd planned all along . . .

"I'm always several steps *forward*, bug. Just when yah think you've *got* me, I'm already *gone*."

"Lloyd," Elliot Greenwald clipped, the toe of his boot colliding several times with the torn fabric of the sofa as the jumpy man merely flinched. "Time for your appointment with Doctor Blake."

Per usual, Greenwald directed an exceptionally silent Lloyd down the skinny halls of Stillwater, unused handcuffs persistently slapping against the meat of his outer thigh as they rapidly approached the sealed room on the right-hand side. Dr. Blake stood rigidly outside the door, a clipboard held tightly in her clutch as her beady, magnified gaze slowly came in contact with the approaching duo.

"Afternoon, Elliot." She politely greeted, nodding her head curtly as the tattooed man returned the kind gesture, his cheeks flushing an amorous scarlet.

"Afternoon, Lyra." He blatantly blushed, fingers curling around the bunched material of Lloyd's jumpsuit as he yanked the frail man forward. The sudden sonance of the hefty steel door opening had sent a series of shivers down Lloyd's crooked spine, brows raised in immense curiosity as an unfamiliar red-haired guard directed a broad-shouldered man with greasy, curly locks from the room.

Switch's gaze immediately locked onto Lloyd's; an instant smirk plastered across his mangled features as Wren impatiently tugged his cuffed frame forward. Nearly the very second their eyes met, Lloyd felt himself instantly stiffen—every single last breath vanishing from his withering lungs as his vision went white. Panic immediately sunk in as his blinded frame stumbled forward, colliding messily with Elliot's defined chest as the guard shoved Lloyd off of him. What he failed to notice, however, was the mere fact that the inmate's eyes had—quite literally—rotated to the back of his skull, leaving behind an eerie, chalky white hue in their wake.

"Let's get this over with." Dr. Blake muttered, leading the way into the uncomfortably cold room as Lloyd dipped back into reality; eyes wild with pure fear as his pulse violently accelerated.

Routinely, the fifty-year-old man took a seat opposite an unquestionably inattentive Dr. Blake, who persistently jabbed her pink-rimmed spectacles back up the slope of her oily nose as she rummaged through a mess of loose-leaf papers. Lloyd's palm met the scaly skin of his clothed chest, heartbeat thickly drumming against his warm flesh as he feared he may go into cardiac arrest at any given moment.

"How's your day been, 1167?" The uninterested woman confidently began, wedging a pen between ring-clad fingers as Lloyd shifted uncomfortably upon his chair. Thus, the man was suddenly thrust back into his momentary trance, limbs stiffening as a series of vivid visuals plagued his mind.

"Algort. Blake. Greenwald. Jackson. McGregory. Schmitt. Tribeca." He monotonically stated, stare remaining unblinking as Dr. Blake's brows quizzically raised. The pen slipped from her weakened grasp, dismissively colliding with the metal table as she inched forward in her chair.

"What?" She queried, tucking a bothersome strand of hair behind her ear as Lloyd's lips parted in preparation to speak.

"It will happen on the Eve of Christ's birth." He specifically added, fingers vigorously rubbing together as the woman opposite him grew rather curious.

"What will happen, 1167?" Blake softly urged, reclaiming the pen in her manicured grasp as she swiftly etched several sloppy notes into his files.

"On the Eve of Christ's birth, Satan will demand the release of his only son." Lloyd vaguely explained, stare remaining unblinking as Blake quickly wrote down the peculiar information.

"Who's Satan's—"

"Lightning will strike," Lloyd blandly interrupted, fidgeting slightly. "Thunder will clap. Chaos will consume the crowd."

"I don't underst—" Dr. Blake began, only to be cut short once more by the extremely strange inmate.

"Powerless. Powerless."

Dr. Blake lowered her pen once more, a general feeling of unease raiding her belly as sloppy chicken scratch raided his files; a mess of several phrases that made absolutely no sense to the middle-aged woman, even in the slightest.

"Algort. Blake. Greenwald. Jackson. McGregory. Schmitt. Tribeca." Lloyd repeated, glare suddenly connecting with an uneasy Dr. Blake as she thickly swallowed.

"What do those names mean, 1167?" She anxiously pressed, shoving the loose pages back into his file as she collected her things.

"Those who impede will fall."

Another lengthy pause.

"It's coming," Lloyd mutely whispered, his threatening statement caused Blake's skin to warily crawl. "It's coming."

Alas, Dr. Blake stood from her chair, messily stumbling towards the door as she anxiously tore it open to reveal a puzzled Elliot Greenwald on the opposite side.

"Algort. Blake. Greenwald. Jackson. McGregory. Schmitt. Tribeca."

"Can you come get him? Please?" Dr. Blake defeatedly begged, her tone choppy and gravelly as the guard immediately entered the premises.

"Danger," Lloyd snipped, glare steadily focused on the empty chair before him. "It's coming. It's coming."

"1167," Greenwald objectively began, left hand cautiously placed over his set of cuffs. "Come with me, please. This session is finished."

Lloyd's head meticulously craned, hollow gaze boring deeply onto Greenwald's confused stare as an eerie, toothy grin overcame the elder man's features.

"He's gonna *get'cha!*" The inmate exclaimed, giggling profusely as Greenwald determinedly lifted him from the chair. "He's gonna *get'cha!*"

"Take him to max for the day," Dr. Blake instructed, stepping aside to allow Greenwald substantial space as he yanked Lloyd from his chair. "Sedate him, if you can. He's having some kind of manic episode."

"Danger!" Lloyd screeched, eyes rolling to the back of his skull as Greenwald's sturdy arms laced tightly around his incredibly thin torso. The deranged man, however, immediately rejected the guard's reassuring hold—his limbs inelegantly thrashing about as he desperately attempted to tear away from him.

"Danger! Danger! DANGER!"

Greenwald and Blake unnervingly ignored the man's cries, eyes quickly locking in a unison state of worry as the heavily tattooed guard exited the premises, along with an estranged Lloyd and the repetitive phrase consistently slipping off of his dry, cracked lips.

Once the voice had faded into nothingness, Lyra Blake collapsed into an exhausted heap up on the frigid metal chair, an exasperated sigh slipping through quivering lips as she ran a shaky hand through her hair. Lloyd's proclamation persistently ran circles around her mind, clear visuals of a scarred-face Switch bombarding her thoughts as she wondered what in the actual hell this inmate meant by his words.

The fact of the matter was; No one could prepare themselves for what was to come.

Because just as Lloyd had said, it was coming. Whether they wanted it to or not.

It was coming.

XXVII

*"My mind is in total decay,
I'm coming to take you away
There's nothing more that I can do, this maniac's in love with you"
–Alice Cooper,
"This Maniac's in Love With You"*

"Does that *hurt?*" Switch lightly purred, his warm breath fanning over Adelaide's left ear as patches of goosebumps instantly arose upon the flesh. The rough, ragged surface of his calloused fingertips dug deeply into the tissue of her back, daintily kneading against her tense muscles as Adelaide released a throaty sigh.

"No," she reassured him, craning her neck to plant a generous kiss to his parted lips as she gingerly rocked back onto him, earning a satisfied grunt from the madman above her as she continued with: "It's perfect. This is perfect."

"*Mmm,*" Switch lowly mused, the tip of his nose agonizingly trailing downward against the scaly skin of her bare back as a multitude of lukewarm water splashed upwards from their wriggling selves, dipping over the curled edges of the porcelain as it coated the concrete floor. "It's *exhilarating*, ain't it? Let's hope we don't get *caaaaught.*"

Sporadic, sloppy kisses were placed along Adelaide's flushed skin as a pair of scarred lips replaced his needy fingertips, her eyelids fluttering closed as low, pleasurable moans escaped through her ajar mouth. The palms of her hands were beginning to wrinkle from the exposure to the water, prompting her frail form to slightly slip as Switch weakly attempted to hold her in place within the tub. Her knees were beginning to grow weak, legs violently quivering as she inched dangerously close to her high.

Whore. A voice suddenly spat, prompting Adelaide's mouth to curl into a dissatisfied frown.

Leave me alone, she pressed, her jumbled thoughts momentarily interrupting her pleasant trance as the feeling of her thriving peak instantaneously vanished. *Will you let me enjoy something for just once?*

Suddenly, Switch's actions ceased; a pair of warm, reassuring palms softly cradling her belly beneath the water as his lips tickled her jaw, lips pressing soft, feather-like smooches to her flesh.

"Whassa *matter?*" He murmured, playful fingers tracing miscellaneous shapes along the fair flesh of her belly.

"They won't leave me alone." She said, neck twisting sideways to meet his bewildered expression. Their noses briefly met in a whimsical fashion, toothy grins enveloping their amused features as the woman inaudibly urged him to recommence.

Nimbly, Switch's parted mouth met Adelaide's temple; eyelids fluttering tightly shut as he murmured a series of phrases against her skull, ones that made the shy girl giggle with glee as a rather peculiar phrase escaped his lips: "Listen here, you little *shits*. You better leave my girl alone, or we're gonna have some *serious* issues."

"Ew," Adelaide mused, adjusting her legs as her knees fell numb. "Look at you being all sappy. Who the hell are you right now?"

"Mmm," Switch hissed, taking her exposed earlobe between sharp teeth as he unexpectedly bit down, nearly severing the skin. Adelaide released a painful yelp, which was shortly masked by a series of exaggerated moans as the madman resumed his erratic movements only moments later. Suddenly, his digits curled around her matted locks, aggressively tearing her head backwards as a hearty mixture of pain and pleasure coursed through her throbbing core.

"I'm your worst *nightmare,* baby." Switch characteristically spat, nails achingly digging into her bony hip as he somehow managed to increase his already wild pace.

An abundance of water littered the floor, exiting the basin on every single side as Adelaide struggled to stabilize herself. Her legs were shaking immensely; knees falling notably numb as her scalp painfully throbbed. His hold on her hair seemed to intensify with every waking moment, deep, throaty whimpers filling the stale void as patches of prickly goosebumps raided Adelaide's flesh. That familiar feeling of immense warmth had already consumed Switch's spine; eyelids fluttering securely shut as his hand abandoned Adelaide's hair, causing her head to slip suddenly forwards as a profusion of water coated her features. She, however, was so caught up in the conflicting feel that she couldn't find the energy or time to actually care.

His now free hand, (the other still claimed Adelaide's prominent hip, keeping her squirming self in place against his waist), had snapped sideways, calloused fingers intensely curling around the edge of the exceedingly small tub as his knuckles flushed a ghastly white.

"Andrew," Adelaide whined, right arm extending backwards as several droplets leapt upwards to soak Switch's wild curls. He simply groaned in reply; a throaty sigh colliding with the skin of her back as several more exhausted kisses claimed the in-between of her prominent shoulders. "N-Not yet. Please."

Switch grunted as her pruned palm claimed his thigh; cold, wet curls tickling the flesh of her goose bump-riddled skin as the top of her skull arduously collided with the inside of the tub. With a slight wince, the woman stirred within Switch's tight grasp, exceedingly lengthy locks soaked beneath the surface of the water.

Three little words teased Adelaide's mind—three words that her lips physically begged to say, to scream it from the rooftops and bask in the phrase for all of eternity—to make it *known*.

Instead, Adelaide simply swallowed the pitiful proclamation, her thoughts masked by an additional series of soft, girlish groans as her mind drifted into euphoria once more.

The hours bled into days, which slipped into blissful nights. An abundance of kisses, touches—laughter, adoration and admiration blossomed between the strange duo; thrusting Adelaide down a haunting path as she succumbed deeper into the pits of the nefarious Switch. However, amidst their seemingly romantic relationship, things were beginning to spiral out of control.

Or, more specifically—*he* was spiraling out of control.

The amount of times he'd "accidentally" hurt Adelaide during their steamy moments seemed to drastically multiply, as if this dark, ominous cloud managed to clog his thoughts and he'd lost all sense of reality. Sometimes, it was merely the fact that his fingers laced just a bit too tight around the supple skin of her neck, or he'd grip onto her hips agonizingly tight, leaving behind violent, violet bruises in his wake. These nights, Adelaide seemed to spend an extensive amount of time simply admiring these specific markings; markings that ensured that she belonged to him.

Somehow, she was okay with it.

Soon, the fourteenth of December had rolled around, and the cheery, holiday season at Stillwater was in full swing. Multi-hued lights littered the rec room, strung along the peeling concrete walls by sloppily stamped tacks, some of which had managed to tear from the shallow holes and disappear for good. Word on the street was that Lloyd managed to nick most of these tacks—for what reason, nobody quite knew.

It was as if he was preparing for something drastic—something violent and dangerous and flat-out *bad.*

Three days prior, Nurse Briar had gotten the all-clear to finally remove the tempestuous set of handcuffs from Switch's scarlet-tinted wrists. According to Dr. Blake, the madman was no longer "high risk", and was officially granted substantial freedom around noon within the rec room. For as long as Adelaide would live; she'd never forget the doting expression that had raided his features—the smirk was almost sinister, haunting and threatening and flat-out creepy. She wanted to know the things that went on in that meticulous mind of his, but she knew quite well that she could never comprehend the sheer magnitude of his thoughts.

Per tradition, the cleared inmates within these smothering walls were granted the opportunity to participate in crafting, a weak attempt to brighten their spirits and bring a bit more joy to their dark and dingy cells during the holiday season. Christmas trees littered the premises, artificial and wildly crooked as a plethora of old, deteriorating ornaments weakly clung to the bent branches.

Stillwater's craft room was buried in the back-left corner of the lower level and reeked of mildew. For most of the year, the surprisingly small room laid abandoned, the door improperly sealed as an abundance of thick cobwebs consumed the quarters. A profusion of thick, sticky webs covered the old wicker tables, which were vandalized with an abundance of carvings; assorted letters, numbers, and even an occasional profanity or two. The wilting wooden stools were nearly attached to the tables by thick webs, accented by defensive and territorial spiders as the inmates irately attempted to rid the seats of the bothersome bugs.

Adelaide openly grimaced at the sight of a particularly large one, with an ass so fat that she swore it contained a million babies. Hesitantly, she scanned the exceedingly small area for an additional stool, but to no avail. It appeared that all of the extra stools were already claimed by extremely antisocial inmates.

"What's *wrong*, bug?" Switch dryly teased, dismissively swatting an inactive cobweb away from the three-legged chair as he popped a squat upon the dilapidating wood. The rickety legs boorishly scraped against the multi-hued tile floor, emitting a ghastly shriek as several curious necks craned in his direction. Nurse Briar nosily glanced over her shoulder from the opposite side of the room, her fingers curling around a stack of various colors of cardboard paper as her wild blue eyes viewed the source of the abrasive sound.

"Big bug." Adelaide simply said, shaking index finger jutted outwards as she pointed directly at the terrifying spider that currently occupied her seat. The incredibly tiny room was poorly ventilated and absolutely reeked, prompting Addy's lungs to neglect fresh oxygen as she audibly choked.

A sincere smirk skipped along Switch's partially mangled lips at the mere sight of the generously sized spider, fingers unvaryingly spread as his palm quickly met the surface of the stool. Adelaide impulsively flinched at the action, pulse erratically thumping beneath her prominent ribs as the madman slowly lifted his flattened palm from the dusty surface of the chair, a tight-knit grin displayed upon utterly handsome features as he flashed his hand in her direction.

A very smushed and somewhat twitchy spider lay glued to the stiff surface, eight extremely lengthy legs occasionally flinching as the beady-eyed bug lay lifeless in his palm.

"See," Switch heartily teased, his free hand swiftly swiping against the insect-riddled palm as the deceased specimen fluttered to the floor. "Easy as *cake*."

"Well *yeah*," Adelaide muttered, trembling fingers claiming her elbows as she awkwardly took a seat beside him. "Killing a big ass bug might be easy for a someone who kills for sport. I hardly like killing flies."

Switch's face fell, eyes meticulously rotating within their sockets as the toe of his habitually unlaced boot met the thick wooden leg of the table.

"It ain't for *sport*, sugar plum." He defensively murmured, mindlessly picking at the excess skin surrounding his untrimmed nails as Adelaide uncomfortably stirred up on her seat. "They-*uh*, all had it *coming*."

He briefly paused, tongue routinely darting outwards to wet his drying lips as his palms dramatically rose into the air to further enunciate his speech. "Every single one'a them."

Adelaide rigidly observed as the theatrical bloke tossed his curled hands into thin air right before speaking each individual syllable; curly-haired scalp inching sideways as he cocked a considerably raised eyebrow in her direction. Reclusively, the woman failed to reply, saddened gaze meeting her empty lap as she patiently awaited the return of Nurse Briar with an armful of art supplies.

Briar scurried over moments later, an abundance of wildly colored sheets of thick, cardboard paper held within her clutch as various markers, pens, and crayons lay snug between curled fingertips. The items began to slip from her hold, eventually toppling to the table as several plastic objects slipped off of the oblong sides. Both Adelaide and Switch's brows raised, curious fingertips poking and prodding at the Crayola brand markers as Briar released an exasperated sigh.

"I tried to grab as many vibrant colors as I could," she breathlessly exclaimed, falling to her knees to claim the fallen objects as she irritably tossed them back onto the dusty tabletop.

"Most of the markers didn't have any lids and were drier than a bone. Hopefully these work. I also grabbed two pairs of child scissors for you two, but I have to watch you guys carefully when you use them—especially *you*," she murmured, index finger extended outwards to meet Switch's faux, innocent grin as he claimed a sleek sheet of black paper. "Little troublemaker."

"Oh, *stop*," Switch mockingly giggled, calloused digits curling around the tiny, baby blue scissors as he began to trim the corners from the inky paper. "You're makin' me *blush*."

Adelaide perplexedly eyed the madman, an old, orange crayon held snug in her grasp as she began to trace a sloppy Christmas tree upon a pale-white sheet of paper. The lines were rough and severely uneven; as if a three-year-old had attempted to draw their very first Christmas tree.

"Hey *doll*," Switch amusingly began, marred mouth curling into a gleeful smirk as he continued to cut the paper with the weak pair of scissors. "With all due respect, I think that Christmas trees are typically *green*."

Pitifully, the woman's fingers curled into frustrated fists, balling the thick paper between embarrassed palms as she tossed it to the side and decided to start her sketch from scratch. Switch stiffly diverted his glare, shards of unwanted paper fluttering to his feet as he effectively cut an octet of legs and a broad, circular body out of the rectangular page—without the use of a stencil.

"A spider?" Adelaide thickly inquired, brows quizzically raised as she began to cut out her sloppy stencil of a vibrant viridescent Christmas tree. Briar stood opposite the duo, shifting her weight from either foot as her distracted stare eventually collided with a sleek black spider within Switch's greedy grasp.

"*Correct,*" Switch nasally pressed, placing the picture-perfect spider off to the side as he reached out to claim an additional sheet of thick, dark paper. "She's nice'n *purdy*, isn't she?"

"What does a spider have to do with Christmas, though?" Adelaide innocently wondered, placing her cut-out of the handmade Christmas tree off to the side as she mindlessly twisted the green crayon within her slender fingers.

Her inquiry, however, remained unanswered. Instead, the low grumble of mindless chatter filled the musky void, occasionally riddled with Nayeli's irritable laughter as her and Cora sat several tables back—gleeful grins stretched across their mouths as they created vibrant one-dimensional ornaments out of paper. Adelaide warily glanced over her shoulder at the ear-splitting sonance of Nayeli's voice, bottom lip draped between razor-sharp teeth as the olive-skinned woman's gaze suddenly met hers.

"What the hell are you looking at, freak?" Nayeli clipped, her voice ricocheting off the walls as rage consumed Adelaide's spine.

Get up, the first voice commanded, their tone hoarse and thick as Adelaide's hazel stare reconnected with the half-colored Christmas tree before her.

C'mon, Addy. You know you want to do it. An additional voice interjected, prompting arrays of goosebumps to consume her exposed flesh. Adelaide fiercely shivered at the sound of the particularly bothersome voice.

Wring her fucking neck.

"Addy-bear?" Switch politely purred, placing an additional, evenly cut spider within his finished pile as the dark, mysterious creatures continued to stack up before him. "What're they *saying?*"

Adelaide's jaw achingly clenched, her fingers curling into furious fists as Switch placed his pair of scissors onto the table, uncuffed hands meeting the woman's timid frame as she violently shook within his grasp. Briar's brows inquisitively raised at the sight, her pulse dramatically accelerating as she rounded the rectangular table and plopped onto her knees on Addy's opposite side.

"Sweetie, what is it?" She nervously questioned, warm palm claiming Adelaide's elbow as the opposite met her jumpsuit-clad thigh, fingers reassuringly squeezing as Switch's hands claimed her scrunched features.

"Baby," Switch nearly whispered, hand cupping her chin as his nails unintentionally dug into the frail flesh, urging her head sideways to meet his worrisome glare as she shook within his embrace. "Tell us."

"I-I need to leave," Adelaide admitted, vicious, violent thoughts consuming her skull as the voices intensified tenfold—vivid visuals of Nayeli's dead body riddling her mind as the urge to claw her eyes out grew by the minute.

"It's okay, Addy. Just ignore them and keep making your decorations." Briar said, softly placing a pat atop the tiny woman's thigh as she slowly stood to her feet.

"No." Adelaide uncomfortably countered, eyelids fluttering shut as her ears deafeningly rang—palms instantly flattening against her earlobes as she desperately attempted to cease the obnoxious sound. However, the bothersome voices seemed to blend back together, repeating a clear phrase over and over and over and over . . .

"P-Please, Briar." Adelaide defeatedly begged, sobbing profusely within Switch's affectionate hold as he brought her tiny torso close to his. "Take me back to my cell. Now."

Nayeli and Cora nosily peered over the surrounding heads, desperately attempting to view Adelaide's apparent manic episode.

"What's wrong with her?" Cora nasally wondered, consistently sniffling as inconsistent trails of snot constantly consumed her upper lip.

"I dunno," Nayeli shrugged, brushing several thick curls from her dark eyes as Adelaide's wild glare met hers once more. "She's a freak, that's what. Just like the weirdo next to her. They're perfect for one another."

"Oh, stop." Cora pressed, coloring in her second oval ornament as she avoided her extremely intense urge to stare at the dynamic duo. "You're just jealous that someone like her managed to find a boyfriend within these walls."

"I don't need a *boyfriend,*" Nayeli slurred, insistently picking at the dead skin present on her bottom lip. "Besides, I have you. I don't need anyone else, especially not someone like him."

Cora's cheeks flushed an amorous scarlet, quivering fingers tautly tucking a stray strand of greasy blond behind her pierced ear as she avoided Nayeli's suggestive gaze.

"Yeah," Cora said, smiling weakly in her direction as she shifted her weight upon the rickety stool. "You'll always have me, Yeli."

Adelaide angrily rose from her chair, aggressively tearing out of Switch's weak hold as she turned to face the blushing mess that was Nayeli Schmitt. She hated that curly-haired bitch with every fiber of her being, and she wanted nothing more than to wrap her little fingers around her neck and squeeze the life right out of her.

Look at you, the primary voice returned, a slight snicker in their tone. *Such a hardass, aren't cha? All talk but no balls. You're just trying to be like him—to impress* **him**.

Am not, Adelaide clipped, shoving Briar's needy touch off of her as she took an additional step in Nayeli's direction. *He likes me the way I am. Big baby and all.*

Although, the woman could clearly picture the statement that would slip from the selcouth bunch of scars—*Oh, princess! Look at you go!*—he'd probably rejoice in her actions: celebrate her triumphs and even go as far as smear Nayeli's warm, crimson blood all over the floor, where he'd pin Adelaide's frail frame to the ground and remind her of just how much he truly adored her. Oh—how *riveting* it would be to roll around in the thick, liquid form of that bitches' life—they'd be so loud, *hell,* she'd let the entire building know just how glorious he'd made her feel—all while fornicating in Nayeli's fluorescent blood . . .

Stop, Adelaide weakly commanded, shaking palms meeting her extremely dry elbows as she began to shake. *Stop putting these morbid thoughts into my head. This isn't who I am.*

You have no idea what your full potential is, sweetheart. One of them spoke, urging Adelaide's legs forward as she approached Nayeli and Cora's table. Briar's pleading tone descended into a buzzing blur; desperate fingertips constantly tugging at the loose arms of Adelaide's top as her stringy hair draped her heart-shaped face in full, thick sheets.

Let us guide you towards it. The second said, providing additional visuals of Switch assisting Adelaide in murdering Nayeli. *Let us help.*

NO! Adelaide sharply shrieked, her knees buckling beneath her as she collapsed into an exhausted heap up on the grimy ground—heightened cries escaping her gaping mouth as she curled into a defeated ball.

"Addy!" Briar cried, calling out to a nearby guard for assistance as Nayeli openly snickered at the sight. A white, toothy grin lay slapped upon her clear complexion, a single curl twisted around her pointer finger as Adelaide's vision promptly blurred.

"Stay back, Switch! Sit down!" Briar barked, beckoning an unnamed guard forward as they roughly claimed Adelaide's thrashing body within their arms.

"Let me *help*–" Switch pressed, shoving past several surrounding guards as Adelaide's fists delivered several weak punches to the burly man's chest.

"No, Switch." Briar scolded, pressing her palm flatly to his chest as her eyes contorted into thin slits. "Don't make them cuff you again. Stand down."

"Jesus, mute," Nayeli giggled, nudging Cora in the side as the pair of them erupted into vibrant chuckles. "You've really gone off the deep end, haven't you? Is it because you're carrying the devil's baby within your belly? Is it eating away at your brains and making you *crazy*?"

"Nayeli!" Nurse Lora exploded, perfectly manicured digits nestling into the dark-skinned woman's hair as she forcefully yanked her skull backwards. "Quit it!"

"There's consequences for sleeping with the Switch, y'know! It's a sin to screw a serial killer!" Nayeli shrieked, her wrists tugged backwards by her irate personal nurse as a set of shiny, silver cuffs claimed the surface. "Don't act all innocent, sweet pea. *Everyone* knows—it's written all over your face! He probably sticks his dick through that hole between your cells and–"

"ENOUGH!" Nurse Lora screeched, delivering a harsh slap to Nayeli's cheek as the woman burst into sarcastic laughter.

"Watch your back, *bitch*." Switch seethed, taking a seat up on his old, aging stool as he continued to cut out a series of perfectly sculpted spiders. "I can't wait to feel how warm and *silky* your blood is."

"Switch–" Briar heatedly warned, assisting the guard in removing a squirming Adelaide from the room as he tossed his hands into the air in mock defense.

Thick, salty tear tracks coated Adelaide's flushed cheeks, fingernails persistently digging into the raw flesh of her exposed forearms as she uncontrollably sobbed. Briar followed closely on the guard's heels, worried glare fixated on Adelaide's swaying legs as they navigated the dingy hallways. Lights constantly flickered—some occasionally burning out for an eternity as the sound of the guard's boots echoed within the nearly vacant halls.

"S-Spiders," Adelaide gasped, her nails rubbing her skin raw as several scratches cracked and bled. "Spiders. Biting me."

"Addy," Briar breathed, taking several large steps forward as she struggled to keep up with the guard's impeccable speed. Intently, she studied the flesh of Addy's arms, only to find them free of spiders or any type of bites, for that matter. "There's no spiders. No bites. You're hurting yourself, sweetie."

"S-So many spiders." Adelaide sobbed, eyes sealed shut as she persistently picked at the frayed flesh. "N-Need Andrew. Need Andrew to k-kill the spiders."

Briar openly gawked at Adelaide's confession, heart inexplicably racing beneath her chest as the trio entered the eerily quiet cell block where Adelaide currently lived.

Andrew. Andrew. Andrew. Andrew. Andrew.

"Should we sedate her? Throw her in max?" The guard wondered as Briar quickly opened Adelaide's chilly cell, instructing the man to place the shaking woman onto the bed as she simply shook her head.

"I'll stay with her for now," Briar explained, taking a seat at the foot of Adelaide's bed as she waved the guard from the room. "Keep an eye on Switch. Let him finish his art project and then you can bring him back, too."

"Can I cuff him?" The guard weakly wondered, chubby fingers mindlessly toying with the cuffs attached to his utility belt as Briar shook her head from side to side.

"Only if he's a threat."

The guard nodded, exiting the cell as Briar added an additional statement to her already strict instruction, "and Devlyn?"

"Yeah?" The guard—apparently named Devlyn—questioned, peeking through a substantial crack in the door as he audibly cleared his throat.

"Him looking at you isn't considered a threat, okay?" Briar thickly pressed, cold fingers laced around Adelaide's bony ankle as she removed the unlaced boots from her feet.

Devlyn stiffly nodded, the steel door sealing shut on his heels as his footsteps disappeared into oblivion, officially isolating Briar and Adelaide within the stale, sticky-aired cell block.

"Oh God," Adelaide whined, abruptly sitting up on the paper-thin mattress as her head fell defeatedly into her clammy, bloody palms. Tracks of crimson smeared along her moist complexion, violent trembles wracking through her every limb as her vision went white.

"What is it, Ad?" Briar cooed, gently stroking the younger woman's back as she physically attempted to calm the distressed girl down.

"I'm gonna hurl." Adelaide confessed, tearing her sweaty frame from the bed as she catapulted her weak form towards the metallic toilet bowl. Her knobby knees painfully collided with the drastically uncomfortable ground, several strands of oily locks dipping into her line of sight as she retched into the basin.

"Oh, sweetheart," Briar throatily mused, her oily nose crinkling in disgust as Adelaide collapsed onto her bottom, trembling palm brushing the irritable chunks of hair away from her clammy complexion. Briar fell to the floor beside her, the ankles of her scrubs bunching up as she pressed shy smooches to Adelaide's temple. "Breathe, Ad. It's going to be okay. I'm going to talk to Blake and get you on some new medication—medication that'll make those damn voices go away."

"T-The spiders," Adelaide hoarsely cried, glaring suspiciously at her arms as an abundance of blistering red dots coated the surface. "They bit me all over my arms. It looks like hives, Briar. I might be allergic!"

Briar carefully cradled Adelaide's left arm, gently wiping away the dry, cracked blood from her arm as she openly frowned at the sight of angry, blistering scratches up on the surface. However, what she didn't manage to see was a single insect bite on the skin.

Hallucinations.

Weakly, the woman smiled with sealed lips, forehead colliding with Adelaide's thick skull as she gingerly massaged the angry flesh of her arm.

"You're not allergic, sweet pea. I'll get you some ointment for those bites, okay? Can you stay here while I go and get those?"

Adelaide silently nodded, blinking back blinding tears as she choked back an additional spurt of bile. Briar placed a shy pat upon Adelaide's shoulder before climbing to her feet once more and excusing herself from the sad, pitiful cell.

The moment the door sealed shut behind her, Adelaide managed to spew the contents of her stomach once more into the cold, metal basin—severe shivers overcoming her malnourished body as she prayed for the end to come.

I can't do this anymore, she boldly thought, wiping her lips with the back of her palm as the voices sarcastically snickered.

No one's stopping you from ending it, darling.

By the time Briar had returned less than fifteen minutes later, Adelaide Lynch had fallen into a deep, dreamless slumber, lanky frame collapsed into an uncomfortable heap beside the frigid toilet as the woman flatly frowned.

Rigidly, the thirty-four-year-old woman approached the sad heap of girl, a thin bottle of ointment held tightly in her clutch as she lifted Adelaide from the dusty floor with ease. The sickly girl did not stir, soft snores emerging through partially parted lips as Briar cautiously lifted her from the ground and placed her onto the aging mattress.

"Oh, Adelaide," Briar muttered, petting the greasy girl's hair as Adelaide silently slept. Her hands were stained a shy pink, raised cuts cloaking her exposed arms as the woman uncapped the ointment and squeezed a dime-sized amount onto her fingertip.

"You'll be free again one day," she said, massaging the thick ointment into Adelaide's flesh as the exhausted woman slightly stirred. "I promise it. I'll do everything in my power to let you live the life you've always dreamt of. Even if it costs me mine."

"Did she get *dinner?*" Switch irately inquired, stirring the watery mashed potatoes around his yellow hued plastic tray as Nurse Briar sat opposite him in the cafeteria.

"I brought her some food but she's been asleep for hours," Briar timidly explained, avoiding Switch's hardened gaze as she fingered the edge of his tray. "She's really sick, Switch. I'm worried about her."

"Sick *how?*" Switch pressed, a single brow raised as he discarded the unpigmented plastic spoon onto the top of the table.

"Her schizophrenia is getting worse, I think." Briar revealed, swallowing a mouthful of bile as she choked back hefty sobs. Truthfully, she feared for Adelaide's health—and most importantly, Adelaide's future. What kind of future would she have if she never got better? As long as Dr. Blake was in charge, Adelaide had zero chance of ever being dismissed from Stillwater.

Ever.

"She needs to learn how'tah *control* it." Switch grumbled, running a hand through his unruly curls as Briar shuffled the thirteen handmade stygian spiders within her clutch. "Like *me*."

"She's different than you, Switch." Briar countered, inspecting the identical spiders with awe as she wondered how in the hell he'd managed to create such beautiful creatures without the assistance of a stencil. "You're a lot stronger than she is."

"You under-*estimate* her." The scarred-face man spat, visualizing Adelaide's undeniably strong physique as he stirred in place upon the circular stool.

"She's a helluva strong girl, Bri-Bri. It's-*er*–" Switch briefly paused, glancing over each shoulder before thrusting his palms into the air and waving them about theatrically, before continuing with, "*inspiring.*"

"You're right." Briar whispered, eyeing his untouched tray before thickly swallowing.

"Always am." He cheekily grinned, winking suggestively in Briar's direction as he stood from his chair, calloused fingers encircling his uncuffed wrists as the woman blatantly stared at the permanent ink imbedded upon his left wrist.

"C'mon," Briar pressed, palm meeting Switch's shoulder as he assertively tore out of her reassuring hold. "Let's take you to your cell so we can hang up these—*spiders.*"

The pair trudged towards the cell block, fingers occasionally brushing against one another's as Briar's heart leapt into her throat. Her opposite hand claimed the odd number of arachnoids, the pad of her thumb intently tracing along the edge of the legs as they rapidly approached his vacant cell.

"I'm going to hang them up with sticky tack," Briar monotonically explained, swiping her ID through the keypad as a vibrant green light granted her entry to the enclosed area. "So please don't rip them down and eat the tack."

Switch snickered, fingernails scratching away at a particularly itchy spot beneath his unwashed curls as they strut into the cell. Briar removed the azure-tinted sticky tack from her pocket, carefully applying it to the direct center of the oblong body as she placed the spiders around the vicinity. Switch intently observed from his spot on the mattress as her oily fingers smoothed out the legs of his spiders, ensuring that the paper would stick to the concrete.

"So," she began, glancing curiously over her shoulder to view Switch's lax form as he kicked off his bothersome boots. "Why spiders? Are you some kind of obsessive Spiderman fan?"

Switch erupted into a fit of giggles, broad frame collapsing against his mattress as the metal frame audibly shifted beneath his shift in weight. His brunette curls lay sprawled out against the itchy pillowcase, chest inordinately heaving as the red and blue cartoon instantly invaded his thoughts.

"He's *amazing*," he playfully murmured, admiring the inky spiders that littered his walls as Briar hung the thirteenth one.

"God," she laughed, shaking her head. "You're obsessed with that character, aren't you?"

Try obsessed with Adelaide . . .

"Not as obsessed as I am with *yooou*." Switch purred, tugging his lip between yellowing teeth as Briar playfully rolled her eyes. *What a manipulative little shit.*

"Addy's afraid of spiders." Briar blandly informed, rolling the tiny mound of remaining sticky tack between oily fingers as a pair of dark eyes met hers.

"I *know*." He said.

"Goodnight, Switch." Briar whispered, stuffing the leftover sticky tack into her scrubs pocket before offering the man a sincere smile. "Sweet dreams of your little Spidey."

"Spiderman." Switch shrewdly interrupted, the tip of his tongue clicking against the roof of his mouth as Briar sarcastically shrugged.

"Whatever. Sweet dreams." With that, the woman left, leaving Switch to his scattered thoughts as Cora's habitual snores enveloped the area.

Once the exterior door of the cell block had tightly sealed, Switch's bare feet met the cool floor, palms flattening against the sinking mattress as he propelled his lanky frame from the bed. Darkness consumed the cell, the only light source being the persistent, buzzing nighttime lights as streaks of blue painted the walls. Thirteen lively spiders littered the corners, their legs eerily crawling along the surface as the madman lowered himself to his knees before the glassless window, a devilish smirk overcoming his wild features as he ushered a throaty: "Addy?"

No reply.

The man released an impatient *tsk*, lips irritably smacking as he rose to his feet once more. A tired hand raked through his curls, chest heaving as he hummed an unidentifiable tune beneath his breath. Just as he'd approached the old, sad bed—a soft, subtle voice slithered through that very hole.

"Andrew?" It croaked, sending a mess of shivers down Switch's spine as his birth name effortlessly slipped off Adelaide's lips.

"*Yeeees*, sweet pea?" Switch gruffly spoke, approaching the black hole as a pair of pink stained fingers slithered through the concrete, coaxing him forward as he impulsively fell to his knees to view her.

"I'm sorry." She shyly said, empty eyes avoiding his sympathetic gaze as his arm slithered through the choppy hole, rough fingertips tangling with her knotted locks as he elegantly stroked her cheek.

"For *what*, doll?" He cooed, just barely touching her flushed skin as she blushed a bright scarlet. Half of her face lay invisible beyond the low blue hue of the lights, masked by extreme darkness as the lack of light threatened to consume her pure soul.

"I wanted to kill her," she revealed, referencing the completely idiotic Nayeli Schmitt as her pulse drastically accelerated. "They were telling me to do it. They almost convinced me . . . *almost*."

"But they *didn't*," he snipped, the tip of his forefinger colliding with her greasy nose as she dramatically exhaled. "You're *so* strong, Ad. You don't give yourself enough *credit*. You've put up with a whole lotta shit—*hell*—you put up with *me*–"

"You're not even remotely difficult, Switch." Adelaide grumbled, brushing his hand away as she sucked on her lower lip. "If anyone's difficult in this relationship, it's me."

Switch raised a mocking set of brows, ushering a choppy: *"relationship?"*

"Sorry," Adelaide gulped, standing to her feet as she cleared her throat. "Y'know what I mean. Friends with benefits, I suppose. Acquaintances with benefits—"

"Shut it, lovebug." Switch scolded, mindlessly picking at the frayed flesh of the wall as Adelaide collapsed up on her dilapidating mattress. "You're my *girl.*"

Adelaide's elbows claimed her knees, left leg expeditiously bouncing as she released a staggered sigh. *My girl my girl my girl my girl my girl my girl my girl my girl my girl my—*

"I was engaged," Adelaide suddenly revealed, hesitantly swallowing as she pulled her straggly locks from her eyes. "He died."

"S'okay," Switch slurred, rubbing his eyes with a dirty set of fingers. "I'm *married.*"

Adelaide's stare immediately collided with his once more, slicked back locks glistening beneath the low lighting as her lips curled into a grin. The pair of them slipped into lively laughter, a beautiful blend of pure joy filling the void as Adelaide picked at her nails.

"I want to be free," Adelaide spoke, intently wetting her lips as Switch's face fell. "Mentally and physically."

"Don't *worry*, baby doll." Switch reassured the drastically skinny woman as she weakly smiled. "You will be soon. I'll make *sure* of it."

XXVIII

*"My baby is a freak like me
and she knows just what I like /
I swear by God you are an angel
Ironic how you help me raise hell"*
–NoMBe, *"Freak Like Me"*

Briar Cunningway awoke in a panic somewhere around three in the morning, the thick material of her yellow and green striped comforter tangled around her left ankle as several beads of salty sweat claimed her upper brow. Her palms sunk deeply into the surface of the mushy mattress, pinky finger accidentally clipping the corner of a snoozing Styx's tail as the kitten wailed in protest.

"Shit. Sorry, Styx." Briar breathed, sympathetically stroking the angry kitten as the little ball of black fur eased into a steady purr, glowing eyes fluttering closed once more as the animal slipped back into a peaceful slumber.

Shakily, the sweaty woman untangled her lanky limbs from the sheets, tugging trembling palms through her tangled hair as she slipped from the bedroom and entered the exceptionally small bathroom.

The sticky tile floor was cold against her bare feet, triggering a series of involuntary shivers to consume her spine as her fingers met the light switch. Aging, fluorescent bulbs spluttered to life, blinking several times before eventually easing into a low, steady glow.

Briar scoffed at the sight of her sulking expression, a profusion of old acne scars littering her features as her manicured fingers poked and prodded at several spots of active acne. Her upper half lay draped over the stained porcelain sink, greasy nose nearly colliding with the toothpaste splattered mirror as she intently picked at the blemishes around her mouth.

Vivid visuals of her tempestuous nightmare consistently littered her mind—visuals of a very real and very scarring event that made her skin crawl and her hair stand tall. His face—*the face of King Cici, as he called himself*— lay imprinted within her memory like a permanent stamp; features hardly faltering as painful recollections of that night clung to her mind like super glue.

Defeatedly, her fingers trailed downwards towards her concealed belly, fingertips dipping below the hem of her incredibly thin pajama top as her breaths grew short and erratic. Labored breaths immediately ceased the moment the healed ink appeared, chest heaving as her forefinger collided with the tip of the perfectly etched crown. *A pretty crown for a pretty Queen,* he'd said—as if what he'd just done to her didn't matter in the slightest.

Blinking heavily, uninvited recollections crossed her vision, and she could almost feel the warmth of her blood upon her fingertips as it oozed from her parted, quivering legs that night.

A mortified shriek emerged through trembling lips as Briar dropped her top, collapsing onto the frigid floor in an exasperated heap as the tears freely flowed. It was as if the walls were slowly caving in, threatening to suffocate her pitiful little self and everything she stood for.

Briar Cunningway would continue to profusely sob until dawn.

Simultaneously, several miles North—a distressed Adelaide Lynch woke up in a cold sweat; thick tears clouding her blurred vision as untrimmed fingernails tugged and tore at her flushed features. Almost instantly, the haunting moments of her nightmare returned—very real images of a dead Emmett DuPré at her side, gorgeous green eyes flushed a ghastly gray as they stared infinitely into nothingness, cracked lips slightly parted as flies persistently ate away at the rotting flesh.

In the dream, her darling boy had slowly begun to decompose in his hospital bed, digital monitor displaying a clear, flat line as Adelaide begged and pleaded for help. Her sweaty, slippery bare feet had slipped and slid around the corridors, blinding tears cloaking her hazel gaze as she attempted to search for any living sign of medical staff. However, the hospital had laid completely vacant; dead and empty, just like her Emmett upon his stiff, cardboard bed.

Oily locks lay within the woman's grasp, chest rising and falling in uneven gasps as her lungs physically cried out for air. She, however, couldn't quite seem to get ahold of herself, and feared that she very well may hyperventilate within the dark, dingy cell she called home.

"I'm sorry, Emmett." She defeatedly whispered, several hefty tears colliding with her unpigmented sheets as she brought her knees to her chest. "I'm sorry I failed you."

One cell over, Andrew Carter—*or, more commonly known as The Switch*—lunged forward, the nape of his stained off-white t-shirt irritatingly sticking to his drenched chest as he repugnantly gasped for air.

Profound, recurring memories persistently raided his mind that night—memories of the daughter he'd never had the chance to know. Gruesome recollections of a teeny, tiny baby; an innocent little girl with a head full of impossibly dark hair that stuck up naturally as if it were slicked upwards with gel. Deep purple lips—crusty, sealed eyelids that hid the most beautiful pair of stunning blue eyes, eyes she'd inherited from her mothers' mother. Eyes that would've had men falling to her feet and women lusting for such a gorgeous set of orbs.

Eyes that never even had the chance to see.

She's got your nose, Kennedy had said to a traumatized Andrew—choking back sobs as she admired the cold little bundle of joy in her arms, an insanely small human with perfectly sculpted arms and legs, curled inward to cradle her body as she lay wrapped within her own customized blanket. Kennedy's mother had knit that very blanket for that darling little girl—bubblegum pink in color, with the name Sydney Leigh imbedded into the thick material with striking red thread.

They'd never heard the end of her name—an endless stream of complications, of pitiful arguments that'd left Kennedy in tears and her mother a red-faced mess. *Sydney? Really? What kind of name is that?— Drew picked it out, Mother, and I happen to like it!*

Switch's clammy palms met the brown curly locks atop his skull, anxiously tugging at the unwashed hair as a series of incoherent murmurs escaped through ajar lips—the very same name slipping off of his tainted tongue as it painted the walls red. Red like the color of Kennedy's blood, which had spilled from the between of her thighs as she grievously delivered her fully-developed daughter dead. Red like the shade of Sydney's supple skin, flushed and irritated from passing through the birthing canal as a bitter silence consumed the room—a haunting silence that ensured the couple that their worst fears had come alive.

Sydney Leigh. Sydney Leigh. Sydney Leigh.

Thirty-nine weeks of pregnancy.

Thirty-nine weeks of sobriety. Of hardships and morning sickness and depression and pain. Thirty-nine weeks of preparation—of conflicting sobs and torturous nights. Thirty-nine weeks of looking the other direction when they'd passed by an old friend on the street; a ghost of their old selves. Thirty-nine weeks of bettering themselves in preparation of what was to come—of becoming better for her. For their Sydney Leigh.

For the first time in seven months—not even an hour following Sydney's official time of death—Andrew slunk towards a nearby bathroom, which reeked of sanitizer and bleach as he uneasily tore the used syringe from his exceedingly tight pant pocket. The silver of the needle was tinted a taunt crimson; courtesy of the abundance of rain and wear and tear from being discarded in the outside trash can. He'd found it one morning while getting the newspaper and simply kept it—*just in case just in case just in case*—and Kennedy hadn't had a damn clue, or so he assumed.

And as a grieving and absolutely doleful Andrew lay slumped against the precisely cleaned tiled wall—a horrendously filthy needle injected into his prominent vein as the venom freely flowed—Kennedy Carter lay abandoned in her hospital bed, flushed features buried in the depths of her clammy palms as she pitifully wept.

Not only for the loss of her daughter, but the loss of her husband, too.

Adelaide blushed as the madman placed sporadic kisses along her naked jaw, a hearty grin tugging at her lips as she squirmed beneath his lanky form.

"Stop," she throatily mused, arching her skull backwards as a large portion of her dainty neck was instantly exposed to the mans determined lips. "I'm ticklish."

Switch merely chuckled, the vibrations of the handsome sonance sending violent shivers down Adelaide's spine as blissful butterflies raided her belly. The deep, choppy folds of the left portion of his face effortlessly explored her neck, her hips bucking upwards with pleasure as he sunk his teeth into the surface, emitting a ghastly gasp to emerge from the woman beneath him.

"Hey," Adelaide murmured, glare settling upon a specific spot of permanent ink hovering his left hip as she flattened her palm against his chest, inaudibly urging him to climb off of her. "I've been meaning to ask you about this one."

An impatient snort slipped through Switch's flared nostrils, a hand running through his disheveled curls as he neatly tore them from his eyes. The measly mattress shifted as he adjusted his nude form, collapsing directly beside the equally naked woman with a lengthy sigh.

"Which *one*, dollface?" He teased, knowing quite well that she was referring to the woman's name that laid imprinted upon his flesh for an eternity.

The tip of Adelaide's forefinger jabbed the slick flesh of his hip, wide, hazel eyes intently studying the surprisingly neat penmanship as she read Kennedy's name aloud. At the mere mention of her name, the man instantly stiffened—labored breaths catching in his throat as he avoided Adelaide's innocent stare.

"She's your wife, isn't she?" She softly spoke, more of statement versus a question as the madman shuffled from the comfort of her bed, fierce trembles wracking through his limbs as he sloppily slid his legs into his unkempt jumpsuit trousers.

"Where're you going?" Adelaide abrasively clipped, inching upwards on the mattress as her greedy fingers claimed his elbow. A petite whine slipped off her quivering lips the moment he'd shoved her off, left leg missing the pant hole entirely as his heel met the floor with an exasperated *thump*.

"Please stay," the shy woman sappily begged, blinking back embarrassed tears as she tugged her somewhat stained, off-white tank top down over her head. "I'll tell you all about Emmett."

"I don't give a rats *ass* about *Emmett*." Switch coarsely clipped, prompting Adelaide's cheeks to flush a bright scarlet as she wiped a fallen tear from her cheek.

"Besides," Switch monotonically continued, eventually easing his leg into the pants as he concealed his softening erection. "There's nothing to say. It's in the *past*. It's a–" Switch briefly paused, eyelids contorting into a thick squint as he loudly cleared his throat before continuing.

"*–lost cause.*"

"Okay," Adelaide uneasily replied, bare feet meeting the frigid floor as she, too, shuffled back into the confinement of her jumpsuit. She intently observed as the man mindlessly toyed with the waistline of his trousers, a profusion of thick, brown curls erupting from the underneath of his bellybutton as the teasing trail dipped into the lining of his pants. "I just need to know that someone won't come searching for me or anything."

Switch raised a questioning brow, urging her to continue.

"I just—" Adelaide choppily sighed, her bottom meeting the mattress once more as the rickety metal frame whined in protest. "I just don't want to be— like a *homewrecker* or anything because I'm not that kind of girl and—"

"Okay, okay," Switch rigidly pressed, taking several steps towards her as he waved his hands in protest. "*Listen.* You're *not* a homewrecker because like I *said*—it's in the past. If she could have *her* way, we wouldn't be legally married anymore."

A stale silence plagued the duo, Adelaide's heart thickly thumping as the blood rushed to her ears, displaying a heated blush upon her skin. Switch cautiously avoided her curious stare.

"She can't divorce me, though. I guess that's her punishment for *everything*, I dunno."

"Why can't she?" Adelaide croaked, tucking a loose strand of hair behind her ear as Switch's menacing glare collided once more with hers—an array of shivers consuming her spine as goosebumps physically appeared all over her exposed flesh.

Switch's palms claimed his wide hips, bare feet mindlessly kicking around invisible objects as a sinister giggle filled her ears. Brunette, oily curls persistently slapped his cheeks as he vigorously shook his head, a ghastly, toothy grin plastered on his eerie features as Adelaide stirred upon her mattress.

"*Oh,*" he lightly mused, tossing his head back with glee. "Let's just say that— *uh,* ickle ole Andrew Carter doesn't *exist.*"

Adelaide raised a bushy brow, bottom lip yanked between chattering teeth as Switch habitually ran a hand through his hair—scarred cheek extended outward as his tongue toyed with the mutilated flesh on the inside of his mouth.

"What do you mean?" She softly inquired.

"I *mean,*" Switch aggressively spat, teeth barred as he rapidly approached the stiff woman a mere yard away. Impulsively, she flinched—eyelids screwing agonizingly shut as a series of amused cackles consumed her thoughts.

"*Mmm,*" Switch mockingly purred, falling to his knees before her trembling frame as his hips rest against the low-set bed frame, bare torso pressed flat against the oblong edge of the mattress as his prying hands met her face. "*Look* at me, pumpkin."

Adelaide violently shuddered—eyes slowly reopening as his slender, callous-ridden fingers vigorously tugged at the dainty flesh of her chin, thumb occasionally applying pressure to an irritable pimple upon the surface as she openly scoffed.

"Ow." She murmured, attempting to bat his hand away but failing miserably. Instead, her estranged actions seemed to fuel his already flaming fire—sparkling orbs immediately widening as a series of *tsks* slipped off his tainted lips.

"Hey hey *hey*," he taunted, digging his thumb nail into the angry mound of flesh as her eyes watered, petite whines slipping off of her lips as she attempted to back away from his aggressive hold. "Where yah goin', *hm*? I thought you wanted to *knooooow*."

"I don't need to know." She measly defended, blinking back pained tears as she mustered up the strength to officially tear his palm from her face, effectively squirming away from him as that haunting laugh filled the void once more.

"*Oooh*," Switch profusely giggled, tongue flattening against the bottom of his sliced lip as he choked back muffled giggles. "What do we have *here*? A little game of *cat* and *mouse*, hmm?"

"Andrew—" Adelaide anxiously pleaded, backing further away from his agile form as his back lay severely hunched, arms extended outward as his fingers lay unvaryingly spread. Almost immediately, his entire expression shifted—soft, comforting glare transforming into a dark, mocking hue as the woman's pulse rapidly quickened.

"Don't *fucking* call me that!" He exclaimed, brows knit tightly together in vexation as he took several steps forward; whereas Adelaide took several steps back.

"Be *quiet*!" She shrilly scolded, index finger meeting her lips as she peered through the evenly spaced bars upon her sealed cell door. "You'll get us caught!"

At that, Switch simply sneered—arms lowering as he cocked his head to the side. Adelaide flatly frowned, highly disapproving of the way he stared—as if she were a slab of meat.

"Stop looking at me like that." She whispered, clammy palms meeting her elbows as she shied away from Switch's cocky stance.

"Like *what?*" He teased, slowly approaching the frightened woman as he pinned her frail frame against the hefty steel door. An impulsive gasp emerged from the conflicted woman before him, greedy fingertips claiming her biceps as he yanked her arms upward to effectively pin them against the smooth surface.

"L-Like–" Adelaide stuttered, eyes fluttering closed. Her hips instinctively jut forward, colliding timidly with his as a pair of mangled, severed lips met the exposed flesh of her neck.

"Go *oooon.*" He darkly urged, fingernails digging deeply into the saggy skin of her biceps. She outwardly groaned, skull sinking further back as Switch claimed a particular patch of shy skin between his teeth.

"Like you want to hurt me." She said, chest heaving as Switch tore his amused complexion from her botched neck. Somehow, just by the simplistic look in his eye—she knew that she was right.

"Goodnight, Adelaide." Switch spoke, pressing a stiff, sealed-lip kiss to her mouth before approaching the vacant keypad.

"Wait!" She called, claiming his perfectly sculpted bicep between desperate fingers as she harshly squeezed. "Please don't leave. I didn't want things to end up this way tonight. Besides, it's almost Christmas and I just want to be happy for once in my life!"

Switch froze, fingers just barely grazing the worn buttons as he let several obscenities slip beneath his breath. His hands curled into taunt fists, forehead crinkled in frustration as he foolishly attempted to ward off the homicidal thoughts.

Don't strangle her don't strangle her don't strangle her don't strangle her don't—

"I just want to be happy." Adelaide sobbed, multi-colored irises invaded with a harsh crimson hue as she choked on her words.

"I don't know why, but it's you. It's you who makes me happy, Switch! I know what you've done and I know that w-what we have isn't anything but for just once, I wish I could pretend! I haven't felt this way since Emmett, and he died, Switch. He's *dead!* He's not coming back and I'm going to just disappear into nothingness one day and I just have to learn how to accept that, but for now can you at least pretend to enjoy my presence? Please? I don't know why my heart or my brain has picked you, but it did.

And it's too late to change anything now. I'm in too deep." The woman spilled, laying all of her feelings out on the line as salty, suffocating tears stained her flushed cheeks.

"Don't do this to me, Switch." She warily added, frantically tugging at her greasy locks as the man stood exceedingly silent opposite her. "Don't make me hate myself more than I already do. More than the voices convince me, at least. I don't expect anything out of this—Really, I don't. I don't dream of us escaping hand-in-hand and running off into the sunset and getting married or anything like that. I don't, I really don't."

The words spilled out of her like vomit, emerging at an impeccable speed and extremely jumbled. Some of her syllables even managed to blend together into a buzzing blur—thick tears slipping into her agape mouth as she audibly choked on her cries.

Switch heavily sighed, inching forward to cradle the sobbing heap of woman within his arms as she hideously wailed; lengthy nails tearing at the raw skin of her cheeks as it suddenly became difficult to breathe.

Suddenly, an abundance of undeviating voices clogged her mind, voices that yelled—that pleaded and shrieked and begged for her to tear every single strand of hair from her scalp—to litter the floor with extremely long strands of old, dead hair. Deceased like her heart, which had shriveled up and died the day her darling Emmett took his very last breath.

Adelaide's knees promptly gave out, lanky limbs collapsing into a jumbled mess within Switch's reassuring hold as she gasped for air, nearly hyperventilating as her chest achingly heaved.

You're nothing.

You'll never amount to anything.

You're as good as dead.

"I-I can't breathe." She confessed, crying loudly against Switch's chest as he awkwardly stroked her hair, fingers constantly tangling within her unbrushed locks as she concealed an exaggerated scream against his bare chest.

"Make it stop make it stop *make it stop!*" She pitifully begged, back arching at a drastically ugly angle as Switch ushered a series of phrases—phrases that merely fluttered directly over her head as she fell from his grasp and tumbled to the ground.

"Addy!" Switch exclaimed, hovering over her hips as his palm met her cheek, persistently slapping the skin in a weak attempt to knock her out of her horrifying trance, but to no avail. Fierce, violent trembles overcame her every limb, mimicking that of a seizure as she spilled several defeated phrases, phrases that she was entirely too strong to speak aloud. Phrases that the voices had managed to convince her were true.

"Stop it, Ad." Switch scolded, resting his body weight upon her wide-set hips as she shook beneath him. "You're *stronger* than this, babe. *Breathe.* Count backwards from *ten*. Clear your mind."

"I-I c-can't—"

"You *can*." He softly cooed, leaning down to press soft, subtle kisses to her sweaty scalp as his left hand constantly caressed her cheek, whereas his right lay plastered against the grimy ground, steadying his weight. Several grains of sand and dirt dug into the flesh of his palm—leaving behind minuscule marks as his lips met her forehead.

"Breathe." Switch purred, voice muffled by her skin as open-mouthed kisses littered her face, neck and chest—the brutal trembles gradually calming as she crumbled within his embrace.

"That'a *girl*." He wheezed, straying sideways to meet her mouth as their noses faintly collided.

Adelaide's pulse eventually returned to normal, slightly shaken palms gently brushing through Switch's curls as he continuously placed slow, warm pecks to her mouth, dry bottom lips occasionally sticking together as a mixture of salty tears and warm breaths invaded his senses.

Their glares collided once more, features partially illuminated by the soft shine of the tame nighttime lights as a genuine grin crawled across Adelaide's lips.

For the second time, a trio of tremendously significant words bombarded her disorganized mind—words that were undoubtedly consequential and held more meaning than any other phrase known to man. Her lips parted, breaths shallow and uneven as the words teasingly danced along her tongue, eyes sparkling as she stared deeply and longingly into his unblinking gaze— *this was it! Say it!*

"What?" He murmured, brushing a bothersome strand of brunette from her eyes as her eyelids briskly fluttered.

In the place of a verbal reply, her lips hurriedly met his once more, playful fingers knotting in his hair as she swallowed those damn accursed terms once and for all.

XXIX

"And a new day will dawn
For those who stand long
And the forests will echo with laughter"
–Led Zeppelin, "Stairway to Heaven"

Nurse Briar's clammy fingers met the creased collar of her lilac scrubs, persistently attempting to smooth down the wrinkled surface as she rapidly approached Dr. Blake's office. The woman was running on a solid thirty-two minutes of sleep, and even the heaviest coat of concealer hadn't managed to hide the inky black bags that claimed the underneath of her eyes.

Dr. Blake's office was located in the far-right wing of Level 2, a stuffy little room with too many bookshelves and an old, wilting wooden desk directly in the center. Hundreds of miscellaneous titles claimed the dusty surface of the bookshelves; books all about the human mind and everything in between. Books that hadn't been touched in years.

Briar's knuckles met the dilapidating door, taunt fist rapping several times against the sealed surface as a distinct sonance of shuffling papers emerged from within.

"Come in!" Dr. Blake's muffled voice exclaimed, the second syllable hiking up several octaves as her voice defeatedly cracked. Briar raised a suspicious brow, pulse anxiously accelerating as she twisted the circular brass door knob clockwise and entered the premises.

Dr. Blake's perky, magnified gaze dulled at the sight of her, an exasperated sigh slipping through bubblegum pink lips as she collapsed against the back of her leather chestnut-hued swivel chair, which had managed to obnoxiously shriek beneath her sudden shift in weight. Her coffin-shaped nails met her forehead, irritably picking at a particularly itchy portion of skin as she reclaimed the discarded file within her clutch.

"What is it, Briar?" Blake lazily requested, pinky finger flattening against the center of her thick-rimmed spectacles as the glasses slipped back up the slope of her crooked nose.

"I just wanted to discuss Adelaide Lynch's medication." Briar firmly stated, rapidly approaching the manila folder littered desk as she thickly swallowed.

The hefty folder met Blake's lap once more, lanky legs unraveling as she released an uninterested sigh, fingernails colliding once more with her forehead as her dull, colorless gaze cautiously avoided Briar's bloodshot orbs.

"What about it?" The elder woman inquired, several chunks of dead skin flaking away against her fingernails as Briar uncomfortably shifted her weight from either foot.

"With all due respect—Mrs. Blake—I just don't believe that Lorazepam is appropriate for Adelaide's particular diagnosis—"

Almost instantly, Dr. Blake thrust a pointed index finger upward, stingy glare meeting Briar's unkempt appearance as she physically scoffed.

"First off," Blake began, claiming the file from her lap as she dismissively tossed it onto the heaping pile of patient records. Briar stiffened as the woman rose to her feet, fingers lacing around a crumpled pack of cigarettes upon her desk as she tore a single cancer stick from within the pack.

"You look like shit." Blake pointedly explained, fishing a vibrant yellow lighter from depths of her cracked leather purse as she shoved the stick between perfectly painted lips. A brief, stale pause enveloped the room—a hot, fluorescent orange flame emerging from the handheld lighter as the aging woman lit the object between her lips.

"Have you been sleeping?" The doctor sarcastically snipped, considerably deep voice muffled by the intrusion. Briar shook her head.

"Not really, but I'm more concerned about Addy. We can discuss my insomnia at a later date—" Briar hurriedly discussed, only to be rudely interrupted by another spurt of completely irrelevant information.

"I'm a licensed psychiatrist, you know." Blake said, pointing out the obvious as she twirled the lit cigarette between perfectly manicured fingers. "I can prescribe you anything you need. Restoril. Lunesta. Ambien. Edluar—"

"I know what you're doing," Briar hissed, defiantly crossing her arms as her temples achingly throbbed, a second heartbeat consuming her skull as intermittent bursts of nausea overcame her belly. "You're avoiding the subject. Do you even care about the general well-being of your patients, Mrs. Blake? Or do you just care about that pretty little paycheck that you pick up every Friday afternoon?"

An exaggerated snort spilled from Blake's flared nostrils, cigarette sloppily shoved between curled lips once more as the woman began to mindlessly rummage through a profusion of disorganized files.

"Since you seem to know *oh-so-much* about patient 4210, why don't you go ahead and recommend a list of medications that would better suit her specific needs?" Dr. Blake queried, fishing Adelaide's skimpy file from the very bottom of the stack as she tore the folder open to reveal its contents. An undeviating stream of thick, murky smoke emerged from the shortened tip of her unpigmented cigarette, mimicking a consistent stream of misery as Briar audibly cleared her throat.

"I have a few suggestions." She confidently began, taking a seat in one of Blake's squishy, mahogany guest chairs as she made herself comfortable. At this, Blake merely frowned, lips tightly sealed around the oozing object as she studied Adelaide's current list of medications.

"Go on." Blake irritably urged, tearing the cigarette from her mouth, discarding the ash onto a nearby ashtray.

Briar lightly sighed, palm sinking into the innards of her scrubs pocket as she extracted a petite piece of paper, a profusion of hideous chicken scratch littering the surface as she effectively read the information aloud.

"Well, as you know," Briar cockily began, prompting Blake's brows to curiously raise. "Lorazepam is primarily used to treat anxiety. While Adelaide may express certain symptoms of anxiety, she primarily suffers from catatonic schizophrenia."

Briar briefly paused, bottom lip pulled between rows of teeth as her brows arched in curiosity. Inaudibly, the woman rose from her chair, the tip of her toe accidentally clipping the wooden leg of the chair as the object emitted a ghastly sound, one that made Blake physically flinch and nearly drop her half-smoked cigarette.

"What're you–" the doctor slurred, brows knit tightly together in annoyance as Briar rummaged through the dusty books upon the shelves, inaudible sounds slipping amusingly off of her lips as she released an enthusiastic *a-ha!* the moment she'd found a particular book.

Cockily, the blond woman tore the aging textbook from the third shelf of a particularly packed bookcase, pale lips curling into a blatant o-shape as she blew the thick layer of dust from the cover of the hardcover text.

"Here we go!" Briar cheered, approaching Blake's desk as she cradled the weighty book within her stick-like arms, tiny pink tongue claiming the corner of her unpainted lips as Blake distinguished her cigarette. Briar quickly thumbed through the thick pages of the exceedingly large textbook, bloodshot gaze effectively scanning the printed text as she settled upon a specific portion of information.

"I assume that you're familiar with the term *comorbid*, yes?" Briar mused, a hearty grin plastered across her features as Dr. Blake lowered herself onto the disheveled leather of her chair, an irritated series of sighs emerging through painted lips as Briar's inquiry went unanswered. "Comorbid is when an individual simultaneously suffers from more than one mental disorder, yes? Please tell me you know this, I mean, you *are* a licensed professional, and all. I'm just a dimwitted nurse, aren't I?"

"Watch your tongue, Cunningway. I'm technically your boss, and you're treading on very thin ice." Dr. Blake dryly threatened, but the bubbly blond didn't seem to hear her.

"When Adelaide first came to me two years ago, she was primarily diagnosed with catatonic schizophrenia. However, over time, she'd developed additional disorders, probably due to the shitty living conditions of this absolute joke of an institution—"

"Briar—" Blake warily warned, but Briar only continued her improvised rant with glee.

"Comorbidity typically tends to develop when the primary problem directly causes a secondary problem, which would most likely explain Adelaide's clear signs of generalized anxiety disorder, as well as bouts of trauma and stressor-related disorders, commonly known as PTSD—"

"I know what PTSD is—"

"*And!*" Briar squealed, thrusting a finger into the air to silence the nettlesome Lyra Blake as the gears in her brain briskly twirled. "The poor girl suffers from delusions and hallucinations—a series of imaginary sensations ranging from the bothersome voices in her head to the physical things she sees, things that lack true existence! By feeding Addy the incorrect type of medication, you are blindly and almost *deliberately* provoking a horrific episode, one in which the voices will take over and quite possibly convince her to do the unspeakable—"

"Jesus, Briar! What medication do you recommend, since you're *oh-so-passionate* about this doomed damsel in distress getting better! News flash, honey! She won't! Whether she dies in here or out in the real world, it's going to happen. She's psychotic and will never be able to function on her own. It's best that she lives out the rest of her days under our watch–"

"You're so damn ignorant!" Briar yelped, the hefty book tumbling from her trembling palms. It messily collided with the cement floor, pages splitting and tearing at an ugly, unfavorable fashion as Blake's features flushed a furious crimson.

"You don't give a rats ass about any of these patients, do you? Because if you actually, genuinely, *truly* cared, you would have reevaluated Adelaide's medication *months* ago. In fact, if your small-minded, teeny-tiny brain was able to properly process *basic fucking psychology,* you would've never prescribed Lorazepam in the first place! Nor the electroshock therapy, which is undeniably *barbaric*–"

Blake visibly shook with imminent rage, fingers curling inwards at her sides as she contorted her palms into furious fists.

"Have you failed to realize that following my treatments, 4210 emerged from her catatonic state and actually turned relatively *normal?*" Blake exclaimed, showering Briar with sporadic spurts of spit as her curled fist collided with her own chest several times as if to further prove her point. "I did that! *Me!* If it weren't for me, that little shit would still resemble some type of sad, sorry statue in the corner of the rec room, wearing that same pair of ungodly socks and reading the same stupid fucking book!"

"That book is *extremely* important to her–" Briar boldly defended, only to be rudely interrupted . . . *again.*

"That *book* should be *burned.* Maybe then she'll realize the significance of this place. The significance of *me.* The significance of healing! She can never heal if she holds onto whatever keeps gluing her down!"

A heightened, sarcastic cackle slipped off of Briar's lips, quivering digits claiming her greasy, unwashed locks as her eyes grew to the size of marbles.

"Do you even hear the bullshit that spews out of your mouth?" The nurse accused, shaking her head profusely as she fell to her knees to claim the fallen textbook. "Or do you just shit it out and turn your back, pretending that you hadn't heard a damn word of it?"

Dr. Blake instantly stilled, bottom lip jutted outward in angst as she tempestuously tapped her foot. She'd never liked Briar Cunningway—*always getting in her way in her way in her way*—and this had been the absolute final straw. It was *her* who was in charge, not this faux blond woman with sloppily painted nails and hideous scrubs and a big, fat mouth . . .

"Let's consider this your resignation, yes?" Dr. Blake coolly replied, dramatically exhaling as her sweaty palms met the wrinkled material of her pencil skirt. "You'll have until the first of the year. After then, I don't ever want to see your face in this building ever again. If you comply, I'll be sure to let Evers know that you'd chosen this route, and you won't have a negative strike on your work record–"

Briar blinked back horrified tears, bottom lip violently quivering as she continuously shook her head.

"N-No," she cried, pointer finger and thumb claiming her lower lip as she heartily yanked at the skin. "You can't do this, Blake! What about Addy? And Switch? Nobody could possibly replace me as their nurse, they wouldn't allow it!"

"They'll survive." Blake simply spat, avoiding Briar's defeated expression as she sealed Adelaide's file once more. "I will reevaluate 4210's medication, but she will still undergo electrotherapy as I see fit. She is under my care, and my care is the best there is ever going to be for her."

"Please don't do this, Lyra. I didn't intend for this to happen, I just wanted to get Adelaide on the right track–" Briar shakily sobbed, her words emerging in a choppy fashion as Blake mockingly rolled her eyes before lounging back in her chair, as if to imply that she didn't give a damn about Briar's feelings.

"You have until the first of January." Blake strictly stated, toying with the rounded edge of her nail as she playfully clicked her tongue against the roof of her mouth. "Y'know—Briar—If I wasn't mistaken, I could actually interpret your passion as *lust*, yes? Tell me, what exactly happens when you're alone with 4210? How about 4428?"

Briar paled, a thick ball of bile rising up the length of her throat as she tensely tore at her hair.

"You feel something for the both of them, don't you? Something naughty, something *forbidden*. In fact, I wouldn't be surprised if the three of you engage in sexual intercourse–"

"ENOUGH!" Briar exploded, blinking away blinding tears as she took several lengthy steps backwards. "I'd never! *Ever!* I'm—I'm *offended* that you'd even suggest–"

"Get the fuck out of my office, Cunningway." Blake monotonically ordered, repositioning her glasses as the spectacles began to habitually ease down the generous slope of her nose.

With that, the heaving heap of woman excused herself from the office, heart officially plummeting into the pits of her belly as realization of her consequences truly sunk in. The door clipped closed on her heel, abandoning an enraged Blake at her desk as she snatched Adelaide's file once more from the towering stack.

Vengefully, the middle-aged woman thrust open the thin cover of the manila folder, revealing the very first page of Adelaide's file: which included her monotonical mugshot, basic details, diagnosis, and in the very top right corner—her sentencing.

Blake snickered, snatching an additional cigarette from the flimsy pack as she sloppily stuffed the unlit object between parted lips, buzzing digits claiming a nearby pen as she observed the clearly printed *TBD* directly beneath the term *SENTENCE*.

"To-be-determined my ass." The doctor wildly giggled, voice muffled by the cigarette between her lips as she messily scratched out the trio of letters, etching several *x*'s over the print as her lips curled into a devious grin, teeth clamping down on the filter of the cancer stick to keep it in place.

After ensuring that the *TBD* was entirely scratched out—absolutely no trace of the letters remaining—she inched downwards, directly beneath the original sentencing, where she clearly wrote a very specific term before dropping her pen: *LIFE.*

Simultaneously, Nurse Briar had managed to shuffle towards a nearby toilet, where she found herself vomiting into the porcelain rim of a heavily used toilet bowl—a distinct, planetary ring of crimson rust coating the inside of the bowl as she defeatedly sobbed into the echoic basin.

"Bri-Bri looks like *ass* today, have you noticed that?" Switch mumbled between heaping helpings of lumpy mashed potatoes.

Adelaide intently observed his uncuffed wrists, an abundance of permanent ink littering his muscular arms as the sleeves of his striped jumpsuit—*white and black, respectively*—lay attentively rolled, efficiently hooked behind the protruding flesh of his elbows as she audibly gulped.

"Yeah," she said, voice barely above a whisper as she stirred the untouched potatoes around her tray with the circular edge of her spoon. "She looks sick. And tired."

"Like *shit*." Switch mused through a mouthful of food, left heel expeditiously tapping against the cracked butterscotch-hued tile beneath the sole of his foot as Adelaide's appetite promptly vanished.

Her worrisome gaze drifted downwards, colliding with the fair flesh of her remarkably skinny forearms as her jaw cleanly dropped at the sight of pustulating pimples—dozens of them, in every shape, form and size— effectively coating every square inch of her exposed flesh as an impulsive gasp slipped off her tongue.

Switch raised a curious brow, lazy tongue toying with the frayed flesh of his mouth as he silently observed the distressed woman opposite him, with eyes as big as marbles and jaw nearly scraping the floor. She cautiously observed the shy flesh of her arms, bottom lip violently quivering as she poked and prodded at a specific spot in the center.

"What'cha *doin*, pumpkin?" Switch huskily pried, twirling the plastic spoon within his grasp as Adelaide anxiously picked at her pale, blemish-free skin.

"Do you see those?" She gawked, voice faltering as she dug her untrimmed nail into the angry surface, nearly drawing blood. Instinctively, Switch's uncuffed hand extended outward, aggressively claiming her wrist between tight-knit fingers as she outwardly gasped.

"Hey," she whined, gently tearing out of his hold as she blinked back pitiful tears. "That hurt."

"Stop picking at your *skin*." He simply said, arm returning to his assigned side of the table as she carefully studied the scarlet-hued spot upon her arm. "You'll make yourself *bleed*, hon."

"I want them to go away," she revealed, resisting the urge to violently claw her skin off as Switch raised a suspicious brow. "The pimples. Or boils. I don't quite know what they are, but they're gross and I want them gone. See them, Switch? All over my arms?"

Switch flatly frowned, steadily studying the smooth, supple skin of her arms as he failed to find any evidence of the ghastly pimples that she'd described.

She's getting worse.

"Hey-*uh, toots*." He reassuringly spoke, audibly clearing his throat as several patients—including a typically antisocial Jasmine—glanced their way. "Just leave 'em. You're pretty as *ever*, marks'n all."

Adelaide's cheeks grew a gleeful scarlet, toothy grin plastered on her features as Switch shoveled an additional spoonful of improperly mashed potatoes into the pits of his mouth.

Suddenly, a harsh, blinding field of white consumed her vision, nearly turning her eyeballs inside-out as she momentarily disassociated from reality and was transported to an unknown universe—one where the air was light and feathery and undeniably fresh, filling her lungs with ease as she aggressively inhaled. A place where the grass felt like tiny little pillows beneath her bare feet—bushes accented with flavorful lollies as well as dripping, caramel apples—which clung to vivacious tree branches nearby.

And then there was *him*.

A little boy, no older than six years of age, with deep, chestnut curls that swirled around the lobes of his ears. Sparkling cocoa eyes—a distinct color that reminded Adelaide of those never-ending cases of freshly shredded cocoa powder from her father's old factory job. Pearly white teeth, agonizingly straight and almost too large for his little face, which was plastered with extremely faint constellations of freckles, nearly invisible but nevertheless present.

This little human was—without a doubt—Andrew Carter's carbon copy.

Directly behind him sat a beautiful broad staircase, the rails encrusted with diamonds and jewels of varying shapes and hues, leading hundreds of stories upwards and disappearing between the fluffy white clouds. The gorgeous set of translucent stairs actually reminded the woman of her favorite Led Zeppelin song, prompting a lively snort to emerge from flared nostrils as the boy removed his hands from the depths of his jean pockets, dark denim Chuck Taylors messily laced as he took several particularly large steps forward, inching closer to the puzzled woman.

"Who are you?" Adelaide asked, her voice emerging as a melodic whisper as the child broadly grinned, a scarlet blush overcoming his features as he tucked a lengthy curl behind his ear.

"Don't worry," he softly spoke, his voice laced with a hint of an Australian accent—Adelaide's native tongue—as he habitually wet his lips. "I'll be waiting for you on the fluffiest cloud in the sky. I picked it out all by myself."

Adelaide's brows drew together, a dumbfounded expression plastered across her features as she shook her head, words temporarily eluding her.

"Are you alone?" She croaked, falling to her knees before the undeniably stunning child as he shook his head.

"Don't worry, Mummy, for I have Emmett." He cheerfully revealed.

Mummy?

Adelaide's blood ran cold, eyes widening as she stood to her feet once more. Wide, hazel orbs immediately collided with fields of graceful green; conflicted tears welling up in her eyes as her palm met her mouth.

A very alive and undoubtedly happy Emmett DuPré claimed the boys' shoulder with his palm, toothy grin plastered along flawless features as the child glanced upwards to view him, broad smiles all around as Adelaide stood completely starstruck across from them.

"I've had Emmett, and he'll continue to raise and love me as his own until Daddy can join us, too."

Daddy?

"Go back, Mummy." The boy sternly spoke. "It isn't your time yet. Go back to Daddy, he isn't ready for you to leave him just yet."

"B-But–" Adelaide stammered, but the boy and her Emmett didn't seem to hear her. Instead, the duo spun around on their heels, climbing onto the glittering steps of the elegant staircase as the woman ushered a distressed: "Wait! What's your name?"

"Aiden!" The little boy—apparently named Aiden—exclaimed, smiling softly in her direction before beginning his ascent towards the clouds.

"Uh, *Ad?*" Switch croaked, several tempestuous curls dipping into his line of sight as the woman lay rigid in her chair.

"He's here." She throatily gasped, the whites of her eyes sparkling beneath the artificial lighting of the cafeteria as she stared into nothingness.

"Who?" Switch pointedly pried, sliding his unwanted tray of food to the side as he attempted to tear Adelaide out of her apparent trance. The peculiar actions, however, seemed to catch the attention of a group of idle guards in the far-left corner. "*Who*, Addy? Who's here?"

"He knows, and he's *okay* with it! H-How can he just be so—so *accepting*–" she exclaimed, prompting several nosy heads to turn as Nayeli's slender lips curled into an amused grin.

Wren, Greenwald and another guard (whose name Switch did not know) rapidly approached their end of the table, inky black boots creating a series of incredibly noisy footsteps as Switch reached across the table to claim Adelaide's distressed face in his hands.

"*Look* at me, baby." He uneasily pleaded, delivering a soft slap to her cheek with his palm as Adelaide's glare remained vacant—eyes unblinking and unseeing.

"My Emmett," she raspily revealed. "He knows of us. He's—*happy*. He's content. He's with our—"

"Adelaide! Look at me! Snap *out* of this trance, baby—snap *out!*" Switch seethed, greedy palms tearing at his broad shoulders as Greenwald assertively tore his frozen frame from the circular stool.

"Our boy! *Our boy our boy our boy our boy—*" Adelaide continuously shrieked, eyelids fluttering agonizingly shut as her palms flattened against her earlobes, forehead heavily creasing as the vivacious voices overcame her mind once more, and Emmett faded into oblivion, exactly where he belonged.

"She needs *Briar*." Switch spat, lanky limbs wriggling about within Greenwald's rough hold as his stare remained entirely fixated on Adelaide.

"For what?" The fiery-red guard blandly questioned, maneuvering the set of cuffs from her utility belt as she prepared to restrain an abundantly agitated Adelaide.

"Just *get her!*" Switch impatiently seethed, slipping out of Greenwald's hands as he approached the terrified woman. His palms reassuringly cradled her shoulders, soft coos invading her senses as the man effectively attempted to calm her down.

Greenwald watched in awe as a puzzled Wren ran off to fetch a sickly Nurse Briar, eyes wide with wonder as Adelaide's stare suddenly collided with his.

"Why're you just standing there?" The other guard seethed, taking a step forward towards a very free Switch as Greenwald's palm met his chest.

"Stop." The crimson-haired, heavily tattooed guard commanded, tongue lapping out to wet his lips as Adelaide eased into a pleasantry trance within Switch's warm embrace.

"See," Greenwald spoke, shifting his weight from either foot. "It worked. She calmed down."

"But why?" The other guard queried, bushy brows etched tightly together in bewilderment as Switch threaded his fingers through Adelaide's knotted hair. "He's not even acting like himself around her."

"Because he *isn't* himself around her." Greenwald said, mindlessly fingering the cold set of cuffs attached to his belt. "It's . . . *strange*."

Wren reappeared shortly, followed by an exhausted Briar with extremely frizzy and greasy hair as she consistently called Adelaide's name in an extremely worried manner.

Adelaide simply sobbed against Switch's chest, sudden spurts of extreme nausea and overwhelming cramps suddenly overcoming her teeny tiny form as she howled outward in pain. Her hand darted downwards to meet the source of her agony, blatantly cupping the in-between of her legs as Switch's gaze followed her actions, only to significantly widen at the sight of an extremely dark and ever-growing scarlet spot.

"Briar." Switch rasped, his hand confidently replacing Adelaide's as his fingers grew slick with blood. An involuntary shudder consumed his every limb at the undeniably glorious feel—eyes nearly rotating to the back of his skull as his breaths drastically thinned. He wanted more, he *needed* more—he needed to tear her chest open and bathe in that beautiful, warm substance . . .

"Shit," Briar rasped, pulse inexplicably racing as she glanced at a curious Wren over her shoulder. "We need to get her to the hospital wing. Now."

Switch nodded, slipping his arm beneath her shaking legs as he easily lifted her from the stool, cradling the petite woman in his arms as if she were his bride. Smears of bright, fluorescent red stained the torso of Adelaide's jumpsuit, courtesy of Switch's soaked fingers.

Nayeli glanced mockingly in their direction, a sarcastic cackle emerging from her side of the table as she released a vociferous statement, "Jesus, mute! Will you ever learn how to properly use a tampon?"

"Ignore that bitch." Briar lowly spoke, cradling Adelaide's suspended skull in her palms as she pressed a reassuring kiss to her forehead.

"Missus Briar," Wren hastily began as the trio headed for the double doors of the cafeteria. "Patient 4428 should really stay here—"

"He's coming with me." Briar pointedly spoke, shooing an exceedingly curious Wren off of her as she directed Switch towards the doors. "I need his help."

Adelaide had begun to bleed down the slopes of her thighs by the time they'd reached the hospital wing, where Briar directed Switch towards a nearby secluded room, the very same one where she'd fallen to her knees and taken him into her mouth (*like the little whore she was . . .*).

Briar closed and locked the door behind them, heart thickly thumping as Switch placed a profusely bleeding Adelaide upon the table, the fresh sheet of paper audibly scrunching beneath her rigid frame as she lay in a silently sobbing heap on the surface.

Switch fell to his knees beside her, stare fixated upon the sleek, red blood that lay sprawled across his fingertips. His breaths dramatically thinned, digits intently rubbing together as he basked in the absolutely glorious feel. To him, blood was like a fucking drug. In fact, he'd become so immersed in the feel of it, so much so that he'd failed to realize that Briar had slapped on a pair of latex gloves and torn down Adelaide's drawers, revealing a ghastly, rounded clump of black blood within her ruined panties.

"Addy," Briar croaked, swallowing thickly as Switch shook his head—*this wasn't possible, it couldn't be possible*—mouth growing dry as his pulse rapidly quickened. "When was your last period, sweetheart?"

"O-October." She throatily revealed, raising her head to take a peek at the clump of cells in her tarnished panties as she openly gawked. "I-Is that–?"

"Inevitable miscarriage." Switch mumbled, taking several large steps backwards as his heart leapt into his throat. Clammy palms claimed his disheveled ringlets, routinely yanking at the loopy hair as Briar immediately began to clean Adelaide up.

"It's okay, Ad." She cooed, claiming a handful of sanitary wipes from a nearby cabinet as she quickly cleaned between the woman's parted legs. "It's okay."

Switch persistently paced the premises, teeth achingly gnawing on his bottom lip as a series of queries littered his brain—*how was this possible how was this possible how was this possible! We were so careful! So careful!*

"Switch–" Briar pressed, discarding the soiled wipes into a nearby waste bin as the madman's eyes widened.

In the place of a verbal reply, the man simply did what he did best—for the man lacked reflexive empathy, so, he laughed.

Laughter that ricocheted off the walls. Laughter that made the little baby hairs on Briar's neck stand sky-high. Laughter that had the criminal completely doubled over, thick, blinding tears cloaking his stygian stare as he nearly collapsed onto the floor in a rolling heap of amusement. Laughter that generated prickly patches of goosebumps all along Adelaide's supple skin, dipping into the deepest crevices of her thighs as the nurse continued to clean her ruined drawers.

He laughed—and he laughed and laughed and laughed and *laughed*—he laughed until his face flushed purple. Until salty tears cloaked his cheeks. Until he was short of breath and nearly wheezing in the place of a proper belly-laugh. He laughed in the place of pain. As a substitute for loss and despair and grief.

He laughed in response to the brutal loss of his daughter—*his Sydney Leigh, his darling, beautiful Sydney Leigh*—and the loss of this other child, the one who never even stood a chance.

XXX

"They tortured every inch of me
Then expect me to forget it
They thought that they would finish me
But I pull through every time"
–Alice Cooper, "Vengeance Is Mine"

"You've got to eat, Addy." Briar stiffly spoke, nudging the untouched tray of hardly edible eats closer to the cross-armed girl as she simply shook her head.

"Not hungry." Adelaide muttered, glancing warily in the direction of a tremendously bubbly Nayeli who sat several seats down, olive-hued fingers knotted deeply within Cora's hair as she attempted to braid the greasy locks.

Meanwhile, Mister Switch practically scarfed down his meal, acting as if it were the very last time he would be given the opportunity to eat. Smears of fluorescent red claimed his lower lip, physical evidence of his love for ketchup on clear display as he tore open his third packet of the afternoon.

Briar released a lengthy sigh, impatiently fingering the grooves of the mustard yellow tray as she studied the untouched mound of limp french fries and the crusty bun of an extremely processed fried chicken sandwich.

Temperamental black bags still lingered beneath the whites of Briar's eyes, clear evidence of her lack of proper sleep as she claimed a soggy, mushy fry from Adelaide's tray, quizzically eyeing the sad excuse for food as she slipped it into the depths of her mouth.

"See," Briar mused, a forced grin enveloping her lips as she hastily chewed the revolting food. "Yummy. Your turn."

"You're a crappy liar." Adelaide spoke, glaring at Briar through severely hooded lids as lengthy fingernails persistently picked at the dry skin of her elbow. "Can I go back to my cell now? I'm awful tired."

"You need to stay active and awake." Briar sternly said, stealing an additional fry as she fed her growling belly. "Blake's starting you on some new meds tonight, isn't she?"

Adelaide shrugged, stealing an additional glance at Nayeli and Cora, who simultaneously seemed to be in their own little world—multi-hued plastic trays practically licked clean as they lay forgotten atop the table.

The introverted woman spent the remainder of the afternoon within the confinement of her lonely cell, per request. Switch, however, had been escorted back to the rec room immediately following the completion of lunch hour, where he'd occupy his and Adelaide's corner, uncuffed fingers curiously rummaging through a box of board games as Novak Holecek uneasily approached him.

"Hey." The newcomer lowly greeted, his shy voice laced with a thick, foreign accent as his blurred, dilapidating vision struggled to focus on the scarred-faced man. Switch merely nodded, glare fixated upon the grimy box of games as he fished out an aging copy of Monopoly.

Novak collapsed into an exasperated heap opposite the cross-legged criminal, a genuine, sealed-lip grin strung across his mouth as he exhaustedly blinked; a weak attempt to focus his failing vision.

"They had me under suicide watch, that's why I haven't been in the rec room recently." Novak blurted, swallowing thickly as Switch's attention remained glued to the game within his clutch.

"I have major depressive disorder. I admitted myself after my third attempt. Obviously, some higher power wants me here, otherwise I'd be six feet under already."

Stagnant silence.

Switch's calloused digits curled beneath the wilting flap of the broken box, tearing the cover off as an assortment of playing pieces and a floppy, faded game board slipped into view. An enthusiastic lip-lick—followed by an immediate tongue click emerged—prompting scaly goosebumps to coat Novak's exposed flesh as he rolled down the wrinkled sleeves of his jumpsuit to conceal the blatant blush.

"I can't see very well," the Czechoslovakian man confidently claimed, several grains of dirt slipping between his fingers as he mindlessly toyed with the coarse filth. "I'm partially blind, but I love board games. They help bring positive thoughts—"

"You speak very *fluent* English." Switch nonchalantly observed, tossing a cold metal game piece into Novak's clutch. The timid man impulsively flinched, filthy palms cupping together to catch the flying object as it sunk into the depths of his marred flesh.

"I was born in Czechoslovakia, but moved to New York at a young age.

Grew up around fluent English speakers, so I learned the language young."
Novak said, holding the game piece rather close to his face as he intently
studied the little silver dog. "I inherited the accent from my parents, though.
That didn't rub off, but I'm also bilingual."

Switch raised an amused brow, clammy palms attempting to flatten out the
bent board as he placed it onto the dusty concrete floor. The old, withering
box containing the remainder of the unused pieces lay forgotten off to the
side, creased Monopoly money fanned outward in a distressed mess atop the
criminal's lap.

"Tell me *somethin'*." Switch dryly requested, claiming the discarded
money within his exceedingly large hands as he quickly organized the
drastically thin paper. "In-*uh, Czech*."

Novak released a staggered breath, palms steadying his weight behind his
lanky frame as the tiny metallic dog claimed his knobby knee. Switch's
hardened glare remained concentrated on the sorry excuse for money within
his grasp, arrays of anxious butterflies littering Novak's belly as a series of
inquiries bombarded his jumbled mind.

"*Všichni se tě bojí.*"

Switch's fingers ceased their swift movements, blackened stare colliding
with Novak's frozen frame as his brows knit tightly together in bewilderment.
The pair sat in an uncomfortable silence for several moments, the foreign
man's pulse instantly quickening as he cautiously studied Switch's uncuffed
wrists, as if he were anticipating some kind of alleged attack . . .

"*Cool.*" Switch finally said, his tone low and gravelly as he separated the
vibrant slips of money into orderly stacks. "Let's play."

Novak adroitly nodded, heart thumping thickly beneath his ribcage as he
ran the pad of his thumb along the frigid metal playing piece. A profusion of
naturally curly locks concealed Switch's stiff stare, vivid recollections of his
mother's near-miss with death raiding his mind as discomfort boiled within
his veins.

The man sitting opposite him—mere *feet* away—was the reason that
Novak's mother was confined to a manual wheelchair. This *fucker*—this
mangled-faced, lip-licking, head twitching *weirdo* was the reason Marta
Holecek couldn't feel a damn thing below the curve of her knees. He was the
reason her fingers were nearly rubbed raw from the rubber wheels of her

cheaply made chair. He was the reason she needed the assistance of a young nurse—a newly-found pregnant woman with *entirely* more potential than assisting some crippled old woman who hardly spoke a lick of English—who had to bathe her every evening before bed.

And yet . . . as Novak sat opposite the deranged psychopath—a little lifeless dog laced between trembling fingers—he couldn't help but feel somewhat content. Content about the fact that he'd managed to earn a spot on Switch's "no-kill-list", (or so he assumed). Content about the fact that the psychopathic criminal remained uncuffed, virtually free to move about in any way, shape or form—*free to lunge forward and lace his fingers around Novak's neck and securely squeeze*—free to act as an actual human being in a place where he was viewed otherwise.

And for that, a genuine grin overcame Novak's mouth as he placed his little silver dog onto the playing board and voluntarily fed into Switch's masterful mannerisms of manipulation.

Nurse Briar hovered the partially parted door of Dr. Evers' office, clammy palms persistently rubbing together as she exchanged her weight from either foot.

Widened, black-bag riddled eyes peered through the substantial crack present in the aging door, quivering fingertips colliding with the uneven surface as she viewed Evers' vacant desk, an untouched glass of dark, fermented liquid laying undisturbed within the foggy, unwashed cup as she slowly eased into the musty room.

Almost immediately, an uninviting gust of stale cigarette smoke consumed her lungs, a staggered cough catching in her throat as she swiftly choked it back. Blinding, disgusted tears momentarily obstructed her vision, heart painfully hammering as she slunk towards a metal, olive-hued filing cabinet on the opposite wall. She'd been in Evers' office only several times before, but not once had she ever entered the unwelcoming premises without permission.

It's not like she could get fired a second time . . .

Sloppy, inky penmanship littered the filing cabinet doors—six of them, respectively—the large, bold print laid slapped upon discolored sheets of printer paper as they lay crookedly taped onto the surface, directly above the rectangular handles. The unnaturally blond woman quickly navigated the drawers, breaths gradually thinning as she settled upon a particular piece of paper, which clearly and distinctly read: *Patient Belongings.*

Quickly, Briar's fingers curled around the handle, gently easing the drawer widely open as an abundance of multi-colored files raided her vision, the left-hand corners displaying a tall flap with the numbers of each admitted patient. The woman efficiently shuffled through the files, eventually coming across a bright blue folder with the digits "4210" pasted across the edge in bold, black ink.

Just as she'd managed to stuff her greedy palm into the depths of the nearly vacant folder, a peculiar sonance thrust her from her uneasy trance—prompting her heart to nearly drop into the pits of her stomach.

Hesitantly, the woman froze, the tips of her fingers just barely grazing the sticky plastic of a sandwich bag as a muffled grunt emerged from the sealed bathroom door to her right.

Fuck fuck fuck fuck fuck fuck fuck fuck fuck–

Anxiously, Briar resumed her determined quest, severely shaken fingers claiming the bag as she tore it from the folder. A glimmer of something shiny and silver caught her eye almost instantly, a hearty grin enveloping her features as she ushered the drawer closed and admired the beautiful ring at the base of the bag.

"Shit." A familiar, muffled voice exclaimed from beyond the bathroom door. Briar's jaw fell open almost instantaneously—the bagged ring held tightly within her moist clutch as she inched towards the exit. *"Harder."*

"What a little *slut!*" Briar hissed, her tone low and uneven as she made a beeline towards the doorway and promptly exited, her speeding pulse leaping into her throat as joyful phrases slipped off her tongue. *She'd gotten it! She'd gotten the ring!*

Blake was sleeping with Evers Blake was sleeping with Evers sleeping with Evers with Evers with Evers–

Almost immediately, the nurse took the unevenly spaced steps two at a time, nearly leaping towards Adelaide's cell block as the plastic bag became slippery within her embrace. The too-long sleeves of her mahogany scrubs occasionally slipped beneath the heel of her worn-out navy Keds, prompting her to nearly tumble forward and crack her slender nose on the concrete as she rapidly approached the sealed cell block.

"Addy!" The ecstatic woman cheered, retrieving her ID (*with difficulty*) from her breast pocket as she eased the object between the clunky plastic grooves of the keypad. "Addy-*beeeear!*"

Adelaide lay in a distressed heap beneath her exceedingly thin duvet, bloodshot eyes glancing warily in the direction of an extremely bubbly Nurse Briar as the blond woman fell to her knees beside the mattress, stiff bones arduously cracking beneath her skin as she waved the plastic bag within Adelaide's line of sight.

"What's that?" The shy girl croaked, voice laced with sleep as she shuffled against the drastically thin pillow, eyelids fluttering as she struggled to focus on the object held extremely close to her face.

"Just look, sweetheart." Briar cooed, steadying the bag as her hands continued to obscenely shake. Flawless diamonds glittered beneath the artificial lighting of the cold, lonely cell—the beautiful, sparkling entity catching Adelaide's eye as she thrust upwards in her bed.

"Oh my *God*–" she gasped, the attenuated pillow fluttering to the floor as a thick layer of dust erupted from either angle of the object. "Is *that*–"

"Your ring." Briar gleamed, slipping the bag into Adelaide's prying grasp as the jaunty girl maneuvered her nails into the creases of the sealed bag, aggressively tearing it open as the comforting object slipped into her open palm. Nearly the moment the warm material met her flesh, her heart instantly stilled, breaths thinning as she turned the familiar object over in her hand.

"Emmett." She breathed, slipping the band onto her ring finger with ease as she choked back vociferous sobs. "My *Emmett*."

"It's a beautiful ring, Ad." Briar complimented, threading her manicured fingers through Adelaide's unkempt locks as the exhausted woman admired the simple shiny rock that claimed her slender finger. The ring hardly fit after all this time (*and all the weight she'd lost*), and she nearly cried at the fact that the last thing that bound her to herself—her *true* self—didn't even fit her anymore.

"It doesn't fit." Adelaide sadly spoke, wiggling the loose band off of her finger as she turned it over several times to admire the expensive item. "Nothing fits me anymore. I'm just a ghost of my old self, Briar. I figment of my past. I'm practically dead in every way but physical."

"Stop." Briar clipped, warm palm claiming the sunken, bony cheek of Adelaide's sullen complexion. "Don't talk like that, Adelaide. You're amazing and you're loved. You can always wear it on a different finger, lovebug. Or I can put it on a necklace–"

"If I put it on a different finger or a necklace it changes the meaning of it." Adelaide countered, handing the ring over to an objective Briar as the nurse violently shook her head. "The fourth finger on the left hand has a vein that leads directly to the heart. That's why you wear wedding bands on that specific finger."

"That's beside the point, Ad." Briar snipped, forcing the ring back into Adelaide's palm as she curled her stiff fingers into a fist, the ring laid snug inside. "I know that you're grieving. I know that you're in pain. But *don't* take it out on yourself. It's not your fault, nothing is."

The duo sat in a stiff silence for several moments too long, the diamonds glittering beneath the harsh lighting of the tiny room as Emmett's flawless features consumed her jumbled mind, occasionally overcome by Andrew's contradicting complexion.

"It was a boy." Adelaide apprehensively spoke, guiding the ring back onto her immensely tiny finger as it slipped back into place. Briar's brows knit together in confusion, lips forming into unspoken queries as Adelaide hastily continued.

"The baby I miscarried," Adelaide confirmed. "It was a boy. Named Aiden. Emmett's raising him for Andrew and I until we can join him *in the clouds*, he said."

Briar's mouth ran dry, thumb flattening against Adelaide's cheekbone as she mindlessly massaged the skin. She wasn't quite sure how to respond to Adelaide's latest hallucination, and for some peculiar reason, this one seemed entirely divergent. As if it wasn't even an illusion at all.

"Blake fired me." Briar boldly spilled, tearing her palm from Adelaide's face as the ill woman instantly stilled, eyes wild with wanton abandon as she struggled to formulate a proper reply.

"My last day is New Year's Eve," the nurse uneasily continued, standing to her feet as the tempestuous bones within her knees audibly cracked once again. "I don't know who'll replace me, but–"

"You can't leave!" Adelaide shrieked, socked feet colliding with the cool concrete as she impulsively shivered. "Y-You can't leave us, Briar—you *can't*–"

"Listen to me, Addy!" Nurse Briar exclaimed, palms claiming Adelaide's shaken shoulders. "I'm not going to let this monstrosity unfold, okay? I'm not going to let you fall into the hands of someone entirely incapable of caring for you, I *promise*."

Adelaide profusely shook her head, mouth agape in awe as she tore out of Briar's strict hold. "B-But how will you—"

"You're going to get out of here." Briar whispered, her voice hoarse and choppy as a dumbfounded expression consumed Adelaide's face.

"You're going to get out of his hell hole. You are." Briar confidently repeated, leaning forward to press an awkward kiss to the center of Adelaide's forehead as her patient stood absolutely appalled within her embrace. "You are. You're gonna get out."

"Briar isn't sitting in on this session?" Dr. Chadwick wondered, brushing several strands of brunette locks from his eyes as he readied the Succinylcholine, hands somewhat shaking as he struggled to steady the syringe.

"Nope." Lyra Blake spat, enthusiastically popping the "*p*" as she readied the electrodes. "I'm having Greenwald bring her in, too. Vern seems like he's too far up Briar's ass and I don't trust either of them anymore. They're both little sneaky snakes."

"With all due respect, Mrs. Blake," Chadwick uneasily began, readjusting the uncomfortable cerulean pillow where Adelaide's head would soon lay. "I have a strong feeling that your feelings towards the pair of them has nothing to do with their work ethic. Or anything to do with work at all, quite frankly."

Blake harshly bit her tongue, mindlessly toying with the idle electrodes as she impatiently awaited the arrival of the irritable Adelaide Lynch.

"I'm going to be in charge of the machine this time." She rigidly announced, wetting her precisely painted lips as Chadwick shot her a perplexed glare. "You can hold the electrodes on her temples. Okay?"

"I can handle the machine, Mrs. Blake." Chadwick said, a general feeling of unease overcoming his belly as the broad double doors of the hospital wing abruptly opened, revealing a smug Greenwald and an extremely exhausted Adelaide. "Really. I can."

"Chadwick." Dr. Blake seethed, eyes contorting into inky black slits as

Chadwick waved Greenwald over. *"I'm* in charge of the machine. End of story."

Chadwick frowned, bottom lip strung between chattering teeth as Greenwald ushered Adelaide towards the drastically uninviting metal bed.

"Hello, Miss Lynch." Chadwick politely greeted, extending his arms as he welcomed the shy woman into her worst nightmare. "Ready for tonight's session?"

"No." Adelaide flatly replied, her bottom objectively meeting the mattress as she swung her pencil-thin legs onto the abnormally sticky surface. Her skinny torso was covered with an old, unwashed hospital gown— unpigmented and covered with an abundance of baby blue polka dots. "Where's Nurse Briar?"

"Not here." Blake announced, index finger flicking against the switch as the machine spluttered several times before groaning to life. "Lay down so Chadwick can administer the anesthetic."

Adelaide tossed her arms into the air in mock defense, stomach violently churning as she eased herself fully onto the surface of the sorry excuse for a mattress, keenly avoiding Greenwald's curious stare as she thickly swallowed. Nearby, Chadwick readied an incredibly pointy needle, flicking his middle finger against the rounded surface several times before smiling gently in Adelaide's direction.

"You'll just feel a little pinch." He said, threading a tourniquet around Adelaide's exposed bicep as her electric blue veins instantaneously protruded.

"A little pinch followed by an unwelcomed seizure." Adelaide sarcastically snipped, wincing slightly as the needle entered her thin skin.

Within seconds, the woman slipped into an artificial abyss, eyesight overcome by complete darkness as her body went rigid, imitating that of a poorly constructed statue.

"Go ahead and administer the Succinylcholine," Blake began, dismissing a vastly curious Greenwald as he angrily sulked and excused himself from the room. "I just need to adjust something on the machine."

"Everything's already pre-set, Mrs. Blake." Chadwick countered, filling Adelaide's veins with the drug as the middle-aged woman fumbled with the dial. "There's nothing you need to adjust. It's already ready–"

"Piss off, Chadwick!" Dr. Blake screamed, cranking the power up to its maximum voltage as she profusely shook. *Stop it, Lyra! You could kill the girl!*

Chadwick openly gawked at the sight of her adjusting the voltage, the pads of his oily fingers cautiously flattening against a rainbow-hued bandage as it effectively concealed the holes on Adelaide's arm.

"Let's get this over with." Blake murmured, claiming the electrodes in her palms as she yanked them in Adelaide's direction.

Adelaide wasn't quite sure how she managed to wind up back in her cell that night, but when she'd stirred from her involuntary slumber a mere hour later, she was greeted by the unfamiliar scent of juniper berries. Puzzled, the groggy woman blinked the sleep from her eyes, curled fists vigorously rubbing away at her crusty eyelids as a mysterious hand clasped down on her naked calf.

The scanty hospital gown clung loosely to her tremendously tiny torso, sporadic bursts of ice-cold air tickling the exposed flesh of her goose bump-riddled thighs as the hand gradually inched upwards, smooth fingers tickling her reptilian flesh as she stirred beneath their soothing hold.

"*Mmm,*" Adelaide sleepily purred, vision still blurred as her temples throbbed, a second, steady heartbeat consuming her skull as the room violently spun. "Andrew?"

The hand had managed to find her clothed buttocks, greedy fingers applying a generous amount of pressure to the rounded tissue as the woman pleasurably stirred within their hold. Eyelids eased closed once more, a hearty grin enveloping her lips as frigid digits agonizingly trailed around to the front of her panties.

"My head hurts really bad, Andrew." Adelaide whined, timid fingers meeting her skull as she attempted to massage the tender skin. "Something's wrong, I think. I usually don't feel this bad after a session—"

"*Shhh,*" a soft, eerie voice cooed, urging arrays of fearful goosebumps to replace the pleasure-ridden tracks as Adelaide's hazel gaze promptly reappeared.

The woman thrust upwards in bed, the room spinning on an uneasy axis as persistent bursts of immense pain consumed her temples, nearly doubling the woman over in pain as Elliot Greenwald's fingers nudged their way between her hostile thighs.

"Go away," she limply begged, collapsing back onto the rickety mattress as the frame creaked beneath her weight. "Please. Go *away*."

"It's *okay*, Lynch." Greenwald hoarsely explained, lips meeting her ankle as she violently tore herself away from his revolting mouth. "Blake sent me to keep you some company. Just relax."

"You're disgusting!" Adelaide shrieked, blinking back blinding tears as she squirmed underneath his remarkably strong hold. "Get off of me!"

One cell over, Switch lunged forward on his incredibly thin and somewhat lumpy mattress, temples throbbing as calloused fingers met the surface. Brows knit together in bewilderment as a soft, muffled plea danced along the walls, his pulse instantly accelerating as he tore his half-nude self from the surface and slunk towards the uneven hole present between their temporary homes.

"Ad?" Switch thickly croaked, digits meeting the edge of the choppy concrete as his knobby knees collided with the wall, eyelids warped into enraged slits as Greenwald's grotesque complexion appeared beneath the nighttime lights.

"You've *got* to be *joking*." Switch droned, furious stare clearly fixated on Greenwald's wandering hand as the opposite palm claimed Adelaide's mouth, effectively concealing her dreadful pleas.

"Go away, freak. This isn't a peep show." Greenwald spat, fingers digging against Adelaide's inner thighs as the angry, swollen flesh burned a bright scarlet. "Besides, I have permission to be here. Blake sent me to make Lynch feel better after her latest electrotherapy session."

"That's sweet of you—*truly*—but that's *my* job, pal." Switch sarcastically snipped, side-stepping away from the glassless window as he retrieved the forgotten article of clothing in the center of the cell, the musky, striped jumpsuit slipping between his fingers as his curls went awry.

"Seriously, *pal*," Greenwald confidently called, sweaty palm flattening against Adelaide's quivering lips as she attempted to bite at his flesh, but to no avail. Slick, salty tears coated his baby-soft skin, stirring something deep within the pits of his fully fed belly as a completely clothed Switch fell to his knees before the man-made hole once again. "If you don't give us some privacy, I'll give you another one of those lovely black eyes. Okay?"

"Riiiight," Switch chuckled, running a hand through his deep, chestnut curls as he swayed his weight from either leg. "You two have some *fun*, m'kay? Just remember–"

The killer momentarily paused, tongue toying with the pockmarked skin of his cheek as Adelaide's eyes pleading stared at him from beneath the warm blue hue, as if to inaudibly beg for some kind of—of *rescue* . . . What did she honestly *expect?* Did she expect him to just waltz right out of his cell using Briar's personalized passcode and just *skip* on into hers? To rip Greenwald's grubby, electrified frame off Adelaide's limp body and beat him to a bloody pulp right on the floor? No—*no no no*—it just simply *couldn't* be done! Not *yet,* at least . . . *no* . . . their cover can't be blown *just* yet . . .

"You'll get what's *coming* to you, douchebag."

"Just forget about it, babe." Adelaide murmured, stirring her liquidy applesauce around the rectangular section of her tray as Switch's eyes remained heavily hooded. "I'm fine. It's happened before, and I'll live. I promise."

"No!" Switch hissed through gritted teeth, fingers curling into furious fists atop the table, an oblong, unpigmented plastic spoon sat snug between curled fingers as the rigid edges left behind imprints on the rough flesh.

"He's *not* going to get off this easily. Neither is that *bitch* Blake." The man seethed, angrily eyeing the violent, violet and yellow colored bruises that claimed Adelaide's temples, as if Blake had managed to physically fry the poor woman's brain during their most recent session—as if she were trying to thrust Adelaide into a severe seizure, one that would have long-lasting effects on the poor girl and ultimately ruin her life for good . . .

"Really," Adelaide whispered, claiming Switch's chalky white knuckles in her palm as she reassuringly squeezed. "Sweetie, it's okay. Greenwald's a piece of crap and so is Blake, and they have what's coming for them. In due time, baby, in due ti–"

Switch tore his curled fist from Adelaide's warm grip, plastic spoon plunging to the floor as he dismissively stomped on it with the sole of his boot. Several heads turned inquisitively, curious orbs focused on the vengeful criminal as he rapidly approached a bubbly Elliot Greenwald on the opposite side of the cafeteria, tattooed arms playfully crossed as he exchanged chuckles with a guard named Devlyn.

Adelaide's strangled pleas filled the stale void, lanky legs awkwardly unraveling from the circular stool as she tumbled towards an angry Switch several yards forward. "Switch! *Stop!*"

Greenwald's gaze met his, an amused, cheeky grin enveloping the crimson-haired guard's features as he untwisted his crossed arms, palms flattening against either hip.

"Go back to your seat, 4428." He dryly demanded, exchanging hearty chuckles between an equally enthused Devlyn as Switch froze in place a mere three feet before the piece of shit.

"I mean it, 4428." Greenwald pressed, arm extending outward to meet Switch's jumpsuit-clad chest as his forefinger confidently collided with the tough tissue. "*Back* to your *seat.*"

Mere moments following his incredibly bold statement—*and the tip of his finger meeting the in between of Switch's pecks*—a sudden cry slipped off of his lips, arm twisted at an achingly awkward angle as Switch's fingers tightened around Greenwald's wrist. Devlyn's face fell, jaw parted in angst as he uneasily observed the scene unfold, a blubbering Adelaide swiftly approaching the duo as she assertively tugged at the nape of Switch's neck. The madman, however, didn't seem to even notice her existence, and as the neck of his striped uniform uncomfortably crushed his windpipe—he'd managed to punch Greenwald square in the nose, the tough cartilage audibly shattering beneath Switch's fist as a profusion of oozing, crimson blood spurted out from either nostril.

The whole scene seemed to unfold before Adelaide's eyes in slow motion—Switch's fingers quickly releasing Greenwald's irritated wrist as he claimed his profusely bleeding nose. The shocked woman needily grabbed at Switch's shirt sleeves, aggressively yanking his giggling form backwards as she buried her head into his heaving chest, salty tears consuming her vision as absolute chaos erupted within the decently sized cafeteria.

"Don't take him—*DON'T TAKE HIM!*" Adelaide shrieked, attempting to claim Switch's hands in hers, only to watch them slip cleanly through—a mangled, joyous expression disappearing from view as Nurse Briar held a screaming Adelaide back. The faux blond woman laced her arms around Adelaide's busty chest, holding her in place as several angry guards escorted a chuckling Switch from the premises, wild, curly locks vanishing from view as Adelaide's world fell completely apart beneath her feet.

XXXI

The twenty-fourth of December, 2008.

Adelaide Rhea Lynch lay in an exhausted heap upon her paper-thin mattress, grungy fingers tangled within her unruly locks as she floated in and out of consciousness. The tiny space she called home was colder than normal, prompting involuntary shivers to claim her spine as she struggled to slip into a deep slumber.

An hour prior, Briar came bearing gifts: simplistic, homemade decorations, considering Adelaide never quite had the chance to finish her individual crafts within the spider-infested craft room. Arrays of pointed, viridescent Christmas trees littered the walls, loosely clinging to the concrete by sticky tack as a pair of wide, hazel eyes admired the precisely drawn pieces. An occasional snowman lay plastered between the abundance of cheerful trees, crooked smiles slapped across their mouths as an orange carrot claimed the immediate centers of the oblong skulls.

In addition to the lively decorations, Briar had also managed to drop a bit of a bombshell—she and Vern were romantically involved, and she was packing up her things to move in with him somewhere Uptown (she'd said where, but Adelaide couldn't quite recall the exact location). Briar also attempted to spill something else, but the statement seemed to wedge within her throat, failing to emerge before she excused herself from the cell, murmuring a dismissive *Merry Christmas* in Adelaide's direction before disappearing for good.

Just as darkness managed to consume her vision once more—eyelids sealing tightly shut as insipid orbs attempted to roll to the back of her skull—a pair of lovely, lacerated lips met her forehead, delicately placing feather-like kisses upon the flesh as she outwardly gasped.

Blurred, multi-hued gaze met a plethora of cocoa—heavily scarred mouth curling upwards into a cheeky grin as the very tip of Switch's nose met hers. Almost instantly, the woman melted within his soothing embrace, pulse erratically thumping beneath the heaving flesh of her chest as their lips met in a rushed, sloppy snog. Desperate fingers kneaded against his scalp, loopy curls twisting around her fingers as she attempted to yank him closer—to swallow him up whole and hold him within her soul for all of eternity.

"Andrew," she breathed, marred mouth meeting her exposed neck as her hips abruptly met his, nails digging into his skull as he audibly groaned. "H-How did you get out of max?"

Her inquiry went unanswered, teeth gently nipping at the bruised skin of her neck as she molded into Switch's embrace, legs tangled together in a blissful heap as his palms flattened against her tiny hips, drawing her even closer, (if that were even remotely possible at this point).

"Hey," she pressed, palm flattening against his jumpsuit-clad chest as she lightly tapped the surface. "What's going on? How are you here? Talk to me."

Oh, darling, the first voice chirped, stifling a giggle as Switch murmured sweet nothings against her goose bump-riddled skin. *How gullible are you?*

What? Adelaide countered, dipping downward to meet his lips once more as teeth sorely clattered together. Lips parted in awe, tongues easing into either one's open mouths as the pair thoroughly tasted every single bit of each other's skin.

Tell me what you mean. Adelaide rigidly spat, struggling to focus on the situation at hand as Switch continued to mindlessly kiss her, tongue gently massaging hers as a multitude of voices giggled heartily in reply.

They were all here.

We'll let you figure this one out on your own, princess. The second said, earning an irate grunt from the woman as she attempted to ward off the irritating figments of her imagination.

"Andrew." Adelaide impatiently whined, voice severely muffled by the presence of his tongue as he blatantly ignored her pleas. Her eyelids flickered widely open, hazy vision struggling to focus on his features as a magnitude of precisely placed freckles appeared. Her heart nearly swelled twice its size at the glorious sight of his complexion—his eyelids lightly fluttering with every brisk flick of his tongue as the very tip of the gaudy scar curled to mirror the shape of his mouth, itching upwards towards his sealed eye as Adelaide abruptly tore away.

A puzzled set of menacing, black eyes suddenly met hers, the blood immediately running cold within her veins as the brisk ice threatened to tear through her thin skin at any given moment. It was as if the irises had disappeared entirely; replaced by an overly-large pupil as a weighty frown lay etched across his lips.

"Babe?" She murmured, brows knit together in bewilderment as his mouth remained tightly sealed, forehead creasing in vexation as his hold tightened on her hips. "I-I was just going to tell you that I think that I lo—"

NOOOOOOOOOOOOO!

Adelaide's palms met her ears, eyes screwed shut in angst as the voices blended together into an undeviating blur—a shrill, high-pitched ringing invading her skull as the room expeditiously spun beneath sealed lids. Suddenly, this evenings supper resurfaced, prompting the lithe woman to stumble from her mattress and hurl herself towards the open bowl of the toilet.

"Fuck!" She throatily exclaimed, thick, blinding tears clouding her vision as she craned her neck to view a surely puzzled Andrew abandoned on the bed. However, once she'd managed to blink away the hot, salty tears—she found the bed unoccupied. Cold. Lifeless. Vacant.

"What the--" Adelaide panted, wiping her mouth dry with the back of her palm as the floor suddenly steadied beneath her soles, violent shivers claiming her limbs as she shakily climbed to her feet.

"Andrew?" She called, gaze raking the dark cell as the low blue hue of the cell block lights partially illuminated the premises, painting dull, blue streaks along the concrete floor.

He was never here, Addy. Come on. You know this.

Defeatedly, Adelaide shook her head, trembling palms claiming her pointy elbows as she slunk towards the sink to rid her hands of the remaining bodily fluids, pure disgust etched across her pale complexion as she choked back a hefty sob.

"I want him here." Adelaide spoke aloud, splashing her flushed face with beads of lukewarm water as the voices remained silent.

Just as the woman started towards her bed once more, the sight of her nearby dresser offered a generous suggestion, one that she never knew she needed. The voices egged her on, easing her towards the ajar top drawer as she latched her fingers around the handles and tore it open.

The inside of the wooden box smelled musty and stale, courtesy of her additional, unwashed jumpsuit (laundry was on Tuesday nights) and several pairs of ugly underwear. Buried snug beneath several pairs of panties lay the crumpled box of Newport cigarettes and a single match, one last cigarette crushed between the softened cardboard as Emmett's gifted copy of *Sense and Sensibility* claimed the very bottom of the drawer.

Shakily, Adelaide reached into the depths of the compartment, fingers curling around the discarded pack of cigarettes and the aging novel as she tore the duo from the bottom of the dusty surface, elbow colliding with the drawer as she dismissively closed it once and for all.

And as the sun eventually dipped beneath the ground directly outside of the secluded Stillwater walls, day officially bleeding into night as black, ominous storm clouds consumed the sky, thunder rolling violently over the hills—the woman curled up beneath the shy fabric of her stained sheet, lit cigarette strung between chapped lips as she positioned the book perfectly beneath the shy blue-hued lighting.

For the first time since Emmett took his very last breath, Adelaide finally finished reading their book.

Julianna Tribeca sat upon the torn cloth seat of her idle car, oily fingers persistently massaging the thick rubber of her steering wheel as occasional beads of sweat consumed her upper brow.

The engine of the six-year-old vehicle groaned in dissatisfaction, suffocating bursts of warm air constantly claiming her brushed locks as she openly gawked at the enormous black building that was formally known as Stillwater Sanitarium. The twin front tires of her Toyota were frozen at seventy-two-degree angles, barely placed within the chalky white lines of the designated guest parking space as she eventually extinguished the engine.

Quite unlike her last visit to the sanitarium, the woman remained empty handed, vibrantly colored key ring looped around her index finger as patches of ice crunched beneath the soles of her worn sneakers. Her hooked nose almost instantly flushed a flaming scarlet at the dramatic dip in temperature, freezing fingers worming their way into the pockets of her parka as Julianna took the cracked concrete steps two at a time.

The sun had just begun its descent beneath the ground, eerily dark clouds cloaking the starry, dusk sky as frigid gusts of wind wailed and howled around the nearby trees.

Just as the woman claimed the circular handle of the broad double doors, a pentad of numbers invaded her vision. Inquisitively, the woman side-stepped, a profusion of piled-up ice outwardly groaning beneath her flat soles as the tips of her fingers met the dilapidating metal.

The final number, the number eight, was dreadfully crooked—barely clinging to the uneven brick wall by the assistance of a single screw, whereas the remainder of the numbers strut two sturdy screws. One at the top, and one at the bottom. Instead of limply dangling, the cold metal had managed to nuzzle itself into a protruding piece of grout mid-way, creating the illusion of something Julianna recognized as an infinity sign.

"Huh," the woman murmured, attempting to reposition the number back into its original spot, only to watch it dip back into its comfortable home within the grout.

With an exasperated shake of her head and a lengthy, sarcastic sigh, the woman strut into the premises, arms tightly knit across her chest as a preppy woman in her mid-twenties greeted her from a nearby desk, directly below an elegant chandelier.

"Oh, hello!" She exclaimed, tearing her petite frame from the comfort of her mahogany swivel chair as a staccato of clicks raided Julianna's ears, courtesy of the black-haired girls stiletto heels. "What can I help you with today? Here to see a patient? Visiting hours are nearly over, it's almost seven."

"Oh," Wren's wife squeaked, tucking a particularly bothersome strand of stick-straight hair behind her ear as she anxiously glanced around at her surroundings. "No, actually. I'm here to see a guard."

The receptionist raised a precisely sculpted brow, hands clapped together in curiosity as Julianna continued to awkwardly stammer before her.

"My wife." She uneasily spilled, avoiding the pretty girls stern glare. "Wren Tribeca. She's a guard here at Stillwater and—"

The woman opposite her tossed her hands into the air in surrender, a bright blue grin stretching across her mouth as she ushered an abrasive, "okay! Stop rambling, *yeesh*. I'll get you a guest pass."

With that, the high-heeled woman struts back into the direction of her desk, whereas Julianna audibly released a breath that she hadn't realized she was holding in. The air within the sanitarium lobby felt cold and utterly stale, sporadic bursts of nausea consuming her belly as her anxiety kicked into full-swing. Palms slick with severely uninvited sweat. Prickly goosebumps coating the exposed flesh of her neck and foundation-riddled cheeks, giving her the appearance of some kind of mutant reptilian human, like the kinds in those X-Men movies.

Frustratedly, she picked at her bumpy flesh, keenly avoiding the receptionist's bent-over frame as she scrawled the name *Mrs. Tribeca* onto a white and blue *"Hi, My Name Is!"* sticker. The high-heeled woman's skirt had managed to inch upwards on her thighs, displaying the vibrant yellow panties beneath as Julianna hastily diverted her wandering stare.

"Here." The unnamed woman said, easing the sticker into Julianna's frozen fingers as the brunette girl blatantly flinched. She hadn't even noticed that the heavy-footed woman had approached her.

"Wren's assigned to Switch tonight. They're up in Maximum Security," she dryly explained, clicking her heels together as her glare met her manicured fingers. "Max is up on Level 5. You're welcome to take the elevator, but just a forewarning: it's slow as all hell. The stairs'll be off to your left when facing the back wall. They're super choppy and uneven, so try not to lose your footing because you'll end up with a broken nose and it'll just add onto the copious amount of blood stains on those slabs of concrete."

Julianna raised a skeptical brow, occasionally meeting the woman's stern stare as a growing sense of discomfort appeared in the very pits of her churning belly.

"You'll need a code to enter solitary. For now, just use mine. It's 5050. Eventually, if you decide to make these visits more *frequent*,"

Generous pause. Sense of discomfort multiplies tenfold.

"Well then that'll be the day that we arrange for you to get your own personalized passcode. Any questions?"

Julianna shook her head, ungloved fingers toying with her pointed elbow as the receptionist excused herself and disappeared behind her desk once more, the persistent clicks of her heels reverberating down the length of the brunette's spine as she ushered further into the premises.

Just as the receptionist promised, the elevator was agonizingly slow, automatic doors clipping closed as the woman nearly suffocated to death within the unventilated cubicle. Suspicious stains claimed the old, shabby carpeting, varying in both size and shape as the woman eased into the back-right corner, clammy palms riddled tightly together as the elevator roared to life.

Gradually, the broiling box began its ascent, creeping up to the fifth floor with difficulty as the cables shrieked in mild discomfort, prompting anxious butterflies to raid Julianna's already twisted tummy. *She should've taken the damn stairs.*

Eventually—after what seemed like an absolute eternity—the cramped compartment arrived at the fifth and final story, a vivacious ding erupting within the elevator as Julianna blatantly flinched at the sudden sonance.

"Jesus, Julie." She lowly hissed, stepping through the partially parted doors as she inhaled deeply. "Relax. It's just your wife and Switch in there."

The Switch the Switch the Switch the Switch the–

Julianna cleared her throat, trembling fingers meeting the fingerprint-riddled keypad as she quickly entered the receptionist's code. The hefty steel door unlatched with an audible *click*, revealing a slender, open hallway with rows of nearly blinding scintillating lights. The long, circular tubes of light gave off an undeviating buzz, gently reminding a shy Julianna of the years she'd spent in the hospital, a place where the lights also audibly buzzed for hours on end.

A grimace overcame her features as she slunk into the unfamiliar area, a pair of dark, lively eyes immediately colliding with hers as Wren abruptly stood from her chair.

"Julie!" The red-haired woman exclaimed, freckled cheeks flushing an bright crimson as she jogged in Julianna's direction. The couple embraced in a wholesome hug, accompanied by an abundance of sealed-lip kisses as a look of pure puzzlement overcame Wren's boyish features.

"What're you doing here, Julie Bear?"

Julianna shrugged, fishing her badge from the depths of her jean pocket as she playfully flashed it in her wife's direction. "Just here on official duty, lovebug."

Wren's face fell, bottom lip extended outward as she tediously toyed with the inner flesh of her mouth. Julianna's badge glimmered beneath the harsh, fluorescent lighting of the room, catching Wren's eye as she intently studied the well-earned object.

"Oh," she said, fingernails mindlessly toying with the nape of her neck. "I'm actually glad that you're here, Julie Bear. I've been calling for a bathroom break for nearly an hour but I guess we're short staffed and nobody can or wants to cover for me. I don't blame them, it's dinner time on Christmas Eve, after all. Could you just watch him for a second while I go?"

Julianna gulped, widened gaze colliding with the occupied cell off to her immediate right as a mess of curly brunette locks concealed a haunting, partially marred complexion. Horrifyingly, the man was staring directly at her—his inky, stygian stare looking directly into her soul as she audibly gasped. He was seated on the floor in the direct center of the glass cell, legs crossed Indian-style as his unlaced leather boots lay discarded in the furthermost corner of the space. The ankles of his black-and-white striped trousers were crookedly rolled, displaying a profusion of curly brown leg hair as Julianna's glare met a pair of drastically filthy feet.

"A-Are you s-sure that's—"

"Sweetie," Wren impatiently clipped, warm palms claiming the shy flesh of Julianna's biceps as the significantly taller woman flinched beneath her abrupt hold. "He's locked in there nice and tight, okay? I won't be longer than ten minutes at the most. I might take a Tylenol while I'm down there too, my head's pounding."

Before Julianna could properly protest, Wren had disappeared, her tiny frame slipping between the sturdy steel doors as the brunette woman gawked in Switch's direction. Her lips were significantly parted, breaths shallow and uneven as her lungs neglected to intake air. The room seemed to expeditiously spin—the ground violently shaking beneath her feet as she inched closer and closer to the multi-layered glass.

"Hi." She shyly spoke, not even realizing that the thick glass was undoubtedly soundproof.

Switch remained frozen in place, head cocked slightly to the side as several loopy curls dangled within his vision. The choppy, bulging scar beneath his left eyeball looked angry and red, as if he'd poked and prodded at it only moments prior to her arrival.

Her sweaty palm met the glass, slick skin suctioning to the surface as she unintentionally batted her eyelids in his direction. At her peculiar action, the man merely grinned—a haunting, yellow, toothy grin, accompanied by a hand, which had suddenly met his smiling mouth. Curiously, Julianna raised a brow, palm still firmly pressed against the glass as the surface flushed a foggy hue beneath her skin.

"What are you doing?" She lowly murmured, eyes unblinking as she cautiously studied the madman on the opposite side of the glass, blackened fingers colliding with his lips as he flattened both his index and middle finger against the surface.

Before Julianna could react, he'd generously parted the two, insinuating a wildly erotic activity as the woman openly gasped, cheeks glowing a striking scarlet.

Moments later, the cell block door swung widely open, revealing a relieved Wren as she smoothed the palms of her damp hands along her clothed thighs, gaze aimlessly wandering as Julianna tore her palm from the glass. Wren froze in place, left brow immediately raising as she observed the hand print plastered upon the glass and an extremely flustered Julianna.

"Julie Bear?" She awkwardly pried, inching closer. "Everything all right?"

Julianna wordlessly nodded, redirecting her gaze to the translucent cell once more as a heightened shriek escaped her lips, legs messily clambering backwards as she tripped over the metal chair and tumbled to the floor.

Switch stood expressionless on the opposite side of the glass, feet planted firmly on the ground as he wiggled a mess of sand and dirt out from between his toes. A mighty, satisfied smirk overcame his mouth at Julianna's reaction, her trembling frame flattened against the floor as wild eyes connected once more with his.

"*Jesus*, Jules!" Wren exclaimed, falling to her wife's aide as she tore her quivering body from the floor. "What was that all about?"

"H-How d-did he–" Julianna stammered, shaking her head in disbelief as the criminal stood completely frozen beyond the glass, head cocked slightly to the side as he glared mockingly in her direction. "I-I d-didn't even s-see him m-move–"

"Stealthy little fucker, isn't he?" Wren teased. "Here, take a seat. You're shaking like a leaf."

Julianna collapsed onto the metal folding chair, the object abrasively groaning beneath her weight as she struggled to regulate her pulse, stare solely fixated on Switch's unblinking gaze as they seemed to enter some type of staring contest, just like the one she and her brothers would play as children.

"He's fascinating." Julianna boldly announced, admiring the madman's everchanging features as his tongue wormed its way from the comfort of his mouth, lapping at the indents of his scarred mouth, like some sort of wild animal. "Creepy as hell, but nevertheless fascinating."

Wren flatly frowned, toying with the dangling metal cuffs on her utility belt as she shrugged.

"I guess."

"No, really! I mean, just *look* at him, Wren! He's—he's *amazing*–" Julianna vented, shaking her head in disbelief as she released a shaky sigh.

"Amazingly psychotic." Wren countered. "Julie Bear, what is it with this guy? I mean, ever since you saw him on the news over the summer, you've been obsessed–"

"I'm not obsessed." Julianna spat, a scoff invading her features as she avoided Wren's stern stare and continued to watch him.

"Jules," Wren murmured, a palm meeting Julianna's shoulder as she exchanged her weight from either foot. "We moved here from South Dakota so you could work on his case. It's been nothing but *him him him* for months–"

"So?" Julianna spat, brushing Wren's hand off of her shoulder as she suddenly stood. "What's it matter? Just because I'm passionate about my job–"

"You're passionate about *him*."

Stale silence.

"You can tell me, Julie Bear." Wren cooed, her voice wavering. "I'm your wife. You can tell me."

Julianna sighed, avoiding Wren's reassuring stare as she met Switch's once more. The criminal was avidly pacing within the cubicle, presumably humming a tune beneath his breath as his lips curled into various shapes and sizes.

"I honestly don't know what it is, Wren." Julianna revealed. "I just feel drawn to him. Maybe we were lovers in a past life."

Wren's jaw fell, eyes welling up with tears as she profusely shook her head.

"Are you in love with him?"

Julianna did not reply. Instead, she merely toyed with her key ring, brushing a stray strand of brown from her eyes as she inched closer to the door.

"'Course not," she dryly countered. "You're my wife. I'm in love with *you*."

Wren blinked back tears, glancing rigidly in Switch's direction as she dug the toe of her boot against the ground. "I think you should go."

"Wren—"

"You need to go, Jules. I'll see you in the morning. On Christmas morning."

"Wren, don't be like this—"

"I'm serious, Julianna." Wren snipped, tone choppy and harsh. "You need to leave. I need to focus on my job."

Julianna simply nodded, audibly gulping as she took several steps backwards.

"Okay," she said, shyly waving goodbye to her wife. "Goodnight, Wren. I love you."

"Goodnight." Wren hissed, taking a seat on her chair once more as she laced her arms across her chest, imitating that of a pissed-off child.

Julianna yanked the door open, nearly colliding face-first with a profusion of blond as a sea of sparkling, blue eyes met hers.

"Shit," Nurse Briar exclaimed, clutching her heart in fear as her chest ached. "Uh, I'm sorry—"

Julianna ignored her stifled apology, assertively brushing past her shoulder as she filed from the cell block, abandoning an angry Wren and a puzzled Briar.

"Who was that?" Briar wondered, a fresh, drugstore razor and shaving cream held in her clutch as Wren fiddled her thumbs.

"My sorry excuse for a wife." Wren snipped, earning a distasteful, half-grin from the blond nurse as she claimed her ID from the breast pocket of her scrubs.

"I just need to shave Switch's face since I have the next two days off." Briar blandly explained, unlocking the cell door as a vibrant green light emerged, granting her access to Switch's "humble abode".

Wren stood to her feet, fingertips toying with her belt as she followed closely on Briar's heel.

"I'm coming in, too. For your protection."

Briar simply nodded, filing into the freezing cell as Switch released a sarcastic cackle.

"Lookie who we have *here*," he elatedly teased. "Here for some *fun* with *daddy*, hm?"

Wren's features contorted into a thick, ugly scoff; whereas Briar remained expressionless, clearly used to this particular strand of inappropriate banters as she thrust the razor and shaving cream up into the air.

"Just here to shave your face."

"Good." Switch mused, fingernails scratching at the sporadic, itchy patches of hair between the mess of scars on the half of his face. The hair grew in choppy patches, especially in comparison to the right side—which was considerably unscathed—and grew facial hair quite normally. "It's about time. I'm all *itchy*."

Wren awkwardly observed as the nurse routinely shaved Switch's face, cautiously applying mounds of fluffy, white shaving cream to his cheeks as she carefully removed the patches of hair from his face. The entire time, the madman glared at Wren—as if to openly mock her . . . as if he knew that her wife was utterly obsessed with him.

Ha Ha Ha, your wife is allll mine . . .

"Sit still, Switch." Briar hissed, steadying his giddy features with her fingers as heaps of the cream oozed between her digits. "I'm almost finished."

Wren stood silent and expressionless about a yard-or-so behind Briar's back, fingers persistently raveling and unraveling around the pink, sparkled handle of the pocket knife attached to her leather belt. Switch's stare met her fingers, gaze glued to the marvelous sight as he simply admired the concealed weapon, which clung loosely to Wren's clothing.

Something deep within the pits of his belly agonizingly churned at the sight of it, lips curling into an enthusiastic grin as Briar nearly nicked the flesh of his folded face, a scold slipping off of her lips as Wren met his objective stare.

"Keep your eyes to yourself, *freak*." The guard angrily spat, clearly taking out her feelings on him as Briar shot her a scolding glare.

"Hey," the nurse called, wiping the remainder of the shaving cream from Switch's face as his moist skin glistened beneath the harsh glow of the lights. "Don't call him that. It's inappropriate to refer to patients in that type of manner."

Wren threw her hands up in mock defense, side-stepping towards the door as she shot Switch an additional angry glare.

"Looks like you can handle this yourself, Missus Briar." Wren snidely snipped, easing her ID in between the plastic grooves of the keypad. "I'll be right outside."

The moment the door clipped closed on Wren's heel, Switch immediately spoke up.

"How is she?" He croaked, tracing the innards of his lips with his tongue. "My *Addy?*"

Briar released an exaggerated sigh, her bottom colliding with the floor as she sat cross-legged next to the notorious criminal.

"Bad." She said. "Very bad. Her hallucinations are worsening. The voices are louder. She's showing signs of depression."

Switch visibly frowned, glare meeting the ground as his fingers located a rogue piece of thread on the ankle of his rolled trousers. Curly brunette locks dipped into his line of sight, chin meeting the base of his neck as the illusion of multiple chins appeared.

"I'm scared for her." Briar admitted. "I don't know how she's going to be when I leave."

Switch remained deathly silent, looping the frayed strand between his fingers as he meticulously tugged at the material.

"I need you to listen to me, Switch." Briar lowly pressed, anxiously eyeing Wren on the opposite side of the soundproof glass as the guard dismissively picked at her palms.

"There's going to be a storm tonight. Really bad one, with lightning and thunder and everything."

Switch's stare met hers, curious orbs twinkling beneath the piercing glow of the lights as the woman directly beside him intently wet her lips.

"I've overheard Evers saying that the generator is faulty. If a storm is bad enough, it could completely kill the power." Briar briefly paused, turning the used razor over in her palm as she thickly swallowed. "I know that Adelaide told you my code. It's good for every single locked door in the building, especially the back door that leads out to the woods."

Switch's eyes significantly widened, absolutely appalled at Briar's rushed statement as she hurriedly continued. Wren was beginning to grow suspicious, fingers toying with her identification badge as she threatened to unlock the door once more.

"You guys have been extraordinarily careful so far, so I know it shouldn't be an issue if the opportunity arises." Briar pressed, pulse quickening as Wren unlocked the door.

"Switch." Briar pressed, meeting his stare as her heart nearly burst straight from her chest.

"Get her out."

With that, the blond woman stood to her feet, collecting the razor and aluminum can of shaving cream within her grasp as she spilled an abundance of lies in Wren's direction, going on and on about Switch's supposed "rash". The criminal, however, remained utterly stunned upon the floor, jaw agape in total shock as Briar slipped from the cell, abandoning the guard within his little cubicle with him.

"I really don't get it." Wren rigidly spoke, thrusting Switch from his momentary trance as he violently shook his head from side to side, as if to rid his mind of the puzzled thoughts.

"I don't get what's so *fascinating* about you."

The guard circled an exceedingly silent Switch, arms thoroughly crossed as she intently studied the interesting man at her feet, whose eyes were solely glued to her waist. Just as a disgusted scoff threatened to overcome her features, the toe of her left boot sloppily collided with the heel of her right, sending her tiny, timid frame to the floor with a dramatic *hmph*.

Almost as quickly as she'd fallen, the woman climbed to her feet, dusting off the knees of her slacks as Switch readjusted his form, hands buried beneath his bum as she raised a curious brow.

Instead of questioning his new stance, the woman merely spat onto the ground beside him before turning on her heel and exiting the transparent cell, a blatant vacancy present on her utility belt as the bright and sparkly switchblade lay absent.

As if on cue, Briar's voice interrupted Switch's thoughts, a single, confident statement repeating over and over and over and *over* . . .

Get her out.

XXXII

"If you bled, I bleed the same
If you're scared, I'm on my way."
–SYML, "Where's My Love"

"How's it healing?" Vern kindly wondered, placing Briar's neatly folded stack of t-shirts into a nearby box as the woman merely shrugged.

Her dainty fingers met the hem of her scrubs, gently lifting the material up from her sticky skin as a gorgeous assortment of vibrantly colored roses appeared, precisely plastered over the obscene branding that King Cici had left behind. The smooth surface was scarlet and angry—most likely due to the fact that the tattoo was only aged three days and her top persistently rubbed against that particular spot—but it was better than the healing process of the one buried beneath, which got infected a solid two times.

Thunder clapped overhead, violently shaking the paper-thin walls of her dead-end apartment as several framed photographs jiggled against the drywall. One photograph, in particular, was of Briar and her father, a man she hadn't seen in thirteen whole years. A man who dropped everything—job, wife, child—dropped it all with the simple snap of his fingers to move out to Italy and "see the world". Truth be told, she wouldn't mind it much if the thunder managed to knock that photograph off of the wall . . .

"You don't have to be here, U." Briar said, tucking several sloppily folded shirts into a nearby box, with the words *fancy shirts* scribbled across the side in bold, black ink. "It's nearly eleven and it's Christmas Eve. Go home."

"Hey," Vern lightly scolded, stretching a strand of electrical tape over the softened flaps of a filled box as he discarded it off to the side. "I have nowhere better to be, darling. Besides, I think we should just call it a night. You don't need to be out of here 'til the first, anyways."

"Yeah," Briar breathed, mindlessly itching the tattoo over her shirt as the skin agonizingly crawled beneath her nails. "By the first I'll be homeless *and* jobless!"

"Bri," Vern scolded, tossing the roll of tape aside as an inky ball of fur audibly protested, persistent pleas slipping of the kitten's lips as the man approached his crumbling girlfriend. Boldly, he took her in his arms, lips placing soft, shy kisses along her clammy complexion as she curled into his warm chest.

"We'll make things work. You're moving up to the suburbs with me, so you'll get out of this run-down area. There's so many opportunities for you— *hell*—I'm sure you could get hired on the spot at the Sears tower if you're interested!"

"I'm not." She groaned, voice muffled by the fabric of his navy sweater as he simply sighed.

"Mercy Hospital?" He suggested, placing an additional kiss atop her hair. "Put that nursing degree to good use?"

Briar failed to reply, her fingers tediously toying with the neck of Vern's sweater as several black curls of chest hair slipped between her grasp.

"I dropped the ball, Vern." She softly spoke, tearing out of his hold as she keenly avoided his bewildered glare, quivering digits lacing around a stack of severely faded denim jeans as she placed them into a nearby box.

"On what, babe?" He cooed, stepping towards the standoff-ish woman as she continued to mindlessly pack up her things, violent bouts of thunder constantly vibrating the patchily painted drywall as framed photos rattled once more.

"On Addy!" Briar despicably cried, a pair of agonizingly tight, ripped jeans slipping through her weakened grasp as the material fluttered to the floor in a dismissive heap. "I had the chance, Vern—I *had* it! I should've told her what I'd done with Switch back in October. I'm a *coward*–"

"You are *not.*" Vern boldly clipped, claiming her frantic figure in his arms once more as his lips met her clammy temple. "She doesn't need to know, Bri. It happened months ago, before her and him were even a thing. It wouldn't make any sense to randomly bring it up now."

"Still," Briar sobbed, messy mascara sliding down the slopes of her cheeks as she assertively brushed the makeup away with the back of her palm. "She trusts me with her life, and I've deceived her. I've let her down."

"I doubt she feels that way, sweetheart." Vern whispered, brushing a sopping strand of blond from Briar's eyes as her dark eyelashes briskly fluttered.

The pair stood in a stale silence for several moments, thinning torsos swaying from side to side as occasional, sealed, wet lips met in a multitude of shy pecks. Vern whispered sweet nothings against her flushed flesh, threading his bony fingers through her knotted hair as he tore the extremely stretched-out hair tie from her hair. Wavy, blond locks framed Briar's heart-shaped face in thick sheets, several irritable strands claiming her matted eyelashes as salty, wet tears claimed the hair. Almost instantly, the man cradling her ever-so-gently within his arms had managed to brush the bothersome mops of dyed hair from her eyes, revealing a sparkling sea of blue as he generously grinned.

"Wow," he mused, mouth curling into a hearty, toothy grin as the pad of his calloused thumb caressed her scarlet cheek. "Look at you."

"What d'you mean?" Briar murmured, wiping a fallen tear from her prominent cheekbone as the liquid oozed among the rigid edges of her fingerprints. "I'm sure I look like a hot mess."

"You're right about the *hot* part," Vern grinned, brushing away an additional fallen tear. "However, I'm not so sure about the *mess* part. Maybe just a hot babe? Or a hot nurse? Or a *hot–*"

Briar vivaciously giggled, forehead colliding with the ball of his chin as her nostrils flared. Weakened arms laced tightly around his torso, effortlessly squeezing as the pair stood in a warm, comforting embrace for what seemed like an eternity—that was, until Vern's mobile phone bitterly buzzed within the claustrophobic pocket of his jeans.

A chirpy Styx approached Briar, intently rubbing along the clothed flesh of her legs as the animal audibly purred, as if requesting to be held. The woman willingly complied, falling to her knees as several stiff bones vehemently cracked—earning a puzzled glare from the wide-pupiled kitten as she scooped up the warm ball of fur within her arms.

The inky-haired man sighed, greedy fingers dipping into the depths of the tight pocket as he fished the aging cell phone from the material. The object persistently vibrated within his palm, Elliot Greenwald's nettlesome name displayed across the foggy screen as Vern audibly groaned.

"Maybe I should just leave it go to voicemail." He dryly suggested, curling his arm back towards the vacant pocket as Briar snatched his wrist, nearly dropping the cat in the process as razor-edged nails dug into her bicep.

"Wait!" She called, pulse rapidly quickening as an additional rumble of thunder emerged from directly outside the curtain-covered windows. "Greenwald *never* calls you, especially when he's at work. Something might be wrong!"

Vern raised a suspicious brow, stubby fingernail easing beneath the flap of his flip phone as he pressed the cold plastic object to his ear.

"Hello?" He grumbled, voice low and choppy, bushy brows knit together in vexation. A thick, pulsating knot claimed Briar's windpipe, chest violently heaving as Vern's complexion clearly paled. Little Styx, however, seemed overly content—completely oblivious to the horrors and hells of reality as she drifted off into a peaceful, purring slumber within Briar's sturdy arms.

"Vern?" She whispered, stroking her palm along the kitten's smooth coat.

"Y-Yeah," the man croaked, fingers slick with sweat as the phone nearly tumbled from his hold. "We'll be there as soon as we can. Weather's really bad, might take us a few."

Briar gulped, immediately placing the irritated animal back onto the floor as her hands met her hair; aggressively tugging it away from her eyes as she attempted to string the thick mane back up into a ponytail. The aging rubber of the elastic band, however, seemed to have the opposite idea—suddenly snapping against her knuckles as she openly winced.

"Power's out at Stillwater." Vern breathed, slipping the phone back into his front pocket as he retrieved a sparkling set of keys from the nearby coffee table. "All of the cells are probably unlocked. Patients are running rampant. It's only Greenwald and Wren on guard and Blake's stuffed up in her office, probably oblivious to the situation."

Briar nodded, audibly clearing her throat as she slipped her palm into his moist embrace, nearly tripping over the uneven laces of her Chuck Taylor's as the duo slipped from the confinement of her warm, cozy apartment and out into the brisk Chicago air. Freezing rain pelted their faces, a stale silence and jumbled thoughts consuming the pair as they rushed into Vern's Cadillac and began their trip towards a powerless and crumbling Stillwater Sanitarium only minutes North.

Switch's hands fell numb beneath the tough tissue of his ass, calloused fingers firmly curled around the textured, sparkling handle of Wren Tribeca's personalized switchblade as time ticked by.

The ginger-haired guard sat perched upon a rusted silver folding chair, several splotches of paint chipping off in various places as a brazen, crimson color appeared from beneath. Her fiercely freckled eyelids were droopy and threatening to permanently seal shut with every staggered blink, stubby fingers tugging at her frizzy locks as Switch sang pleasant tunes beneath his breath.

Violent gusts of wind howled against the massive concrete walls of the sanitarium, raging rolls of thunder vibrating the structure as Wren stirred in her seat. It was late—nearly eleven—and she was several hours overdue for a nap. Angrily, her belly outwardly groaned, audibly begging for some type of food intake as she released a vociferous sigh.

It was absolutely absurd that a guard had to stand watch up in maximum security at all times. Quite frankly, the use of video cameras would be extremely beneficial at times like these, especially on holidays like today. Besides, it's not like the guy could just punch his way through the multi-layered glass. But—it appeared that Dr. Evers was just too damn *cheap* . . . Or maybe, he just didn't give a damn at all.

Switch had somehow managed to slip his dirty feet into the pits of his unlaced leather boots while Wren had drifted off into daydream land—the glittering, concealed knife still buried beneath his bottom as his pulse quickened with every brief flicker of the bright, colorless lights.

The flickers coincided well with the barbaric booms of thunder—aging, fluorescent lightbulbs heavily blinking in protest as the power threatened to cut out at any given moment. The temperature within the translucent cell seemed to plummet several degrees, prompting harsh, prickly goosebumps to raid the exposed flesh of his inked forearms as the sleeves of his jumpsuit lay habitually rolled. Adelaide always loved it when he rolled up the sleeves—the bulging fabric uneven and sloppily creased, hooked intently behind the protruding flesh of his elbows. She liked it because she could clearly see the duo of "lollies" that claimed the inside of his right forearm, as she boldly admitted. He could almost—*almost* visualize the hearty, scarlet blush that would creep onto her sunken cheeks when he'd teased her about it, chapped bottom lip yanked between stained teeth as she avoided his piercing stare, as if she were in the presence of her middle school crush.

Wren's mind was currently occupied with bombarding thoughts of the beautiful, brunette Julianna—her Julie Bear. *What was darling little Jules up to at the moment?* The ginger knew quite well that Julianna was a raging insomniac, hardly sleeping more than five or six hours a night, at best. She had bottle of prescription pills on the nightstand, right next to a cartoon-riddled box of tissues and several half-empty plastic water bottles. For the most part, the pills remained untouched. Unswallowed. Unaltered. Figuratively forgotten, just like the lovely bond that she and Wren used to share before they packed their things and migrated to Chicago.

She was probably buried beneath the bunched material of their bubblegum pink duvet, reading glasses shoved up against the bulging skin of her brows as a pricey laptop computer claimed her knees. God, Wren could literally visualize it so clearly—Julianna's fingers gliding across the sticky keys, (she had a bad habit of eating sweets and then failing to wash the goo off of her hands), gaze unblinking, mouth agape in wonder. Vibrant photographs of a notorious criminal flashing across the screen as she read and reread articles upon articles about the psychotic murderer, as if she already hadn't studied every single little detail about his case already.

Irately, Wren stood to her feet, shoving the irksome thoughts from her skull as she restlessly paced the premises. Switch seemed unbothered; beady, black eyes curiously observing her every move as she vigorously paced the hall, fingernails picking anxiously at the severed skin on her palms as her eczema boorishly flared up.

"This is your fault!" She rigidly muttered, glaring at Switch through hooded lids as her palms met her hips. Wren froze before the crystal-clear glass, brows knit tightly together in extreme vexation as the man merely grinned. Ghastly lesions claimed nearly the entirety of the left portion of his otherwise handsome face, her stomach violently churning as she simply studied his unique physique. She *hated* him—*hated hated hated hated hated hated*–

"If it weren't for *you*," she dramatically continued, jabbing her finger against the slick glass as an additional roll of thunder shook the walls, buzzing lights defiantly flickering once more with an exaggerated *click*. "Jules and I would still be in our little honeymoon phase. Still in love. No arguing, no bickering, no jealousy–"

Switch glared amusingly in her direction, the curled edge of his thumb delicately tracing the curve of the weapon beneath his bum as Wren's lips contorted into exaggerated shapes. He, however, couldn't hear a damn word that the woman was saying beyond the thick, impenetrable glass, but he could only imagine that it was in reference to her darling little *Julie Bear.*

Detective Tribeca, as she'd introduced herself. Informally known as Julie Bear by her significant other: a short, stocky woman with a head full of red hair and the clear absence of a soul. Switch knew from the get-go that Julianna harbored some type of clashing feelings for him, simply from the way her body physically displayed it. The way her cheeks had flushed at the sight of him that very first day—lips parted in awe, brows raised in curiosity, palms vigorously rubbing together to rid the smooth surface of the profusion of sweat. The way she'd aggressively yanked her foot away from the vicinity of his, just mere *moments* after they'd touched beneath the table, as if she feared that her mother (hint: Wren) would catch her flirting with the man across the cold, metal surface. Unlike most, Julianna looked at him as if he were human. That, in itself, spoke volumes—and also verified that she concealed some extremely conflicting feelings for the man, whether or not intentional, or rational.

Alas, thunder struck once again, only this time, the deafening sonance brought along a little friend—a bright bolt of electrifying lightning. Almost instantly, the generator supplying power to Stillwater exaggeratedly erupted, emitting a shrill shriek as the big, bulky box spluttered one final time before deliberately dying.

Darkness immediately consumed the cell block, prompting a lengthy sigh to spill from Wren's lips as she tore her tiny frame from the edge of the glass cell. Her palm cradled the idle walkie-talkie clipped to her utility belt, assertively tearing the object from the leather as she applied pressure to the textured button with her thumb.

"Come in, Greenwald?" She huskily spoke, shifting her weight from either foot as widened eyes observed the pitch-black area. She couldn't even see the skin of her palm even if it were an inch away from her face.

Complete and total blackness. It was as if she'd fallen into the pits of a supermassive, galaxial black hole—tumbling deeper and deeper into the pits of nothingness, spiraling down the shaft of a silent, tenebrous void. A true, cataclysmic nightmare—staggered, heaving breaths catching in the crooked pipe of her throat as the air around her drastically thinned.

Thus, the emergency lights kicked in—a deep, vermilion shade. Evenly-spaced, intensified flickers. A light hum. Patterns that resembled an irregular heartbeat—*thumpity thump thump thumpity thump*—the red light fully (weakly) illuminating the cell block for an agonizing three seconds at a time before dissipating entirely, blackness swallowing up the premises once more.

"Greenwald, come in." Wren coaxed, beads of sweat trickling down her cheeks as she took several staggered steps backward. Surely, Switch's cell would still be tightly sealed—it *had* to be . . .

"Mayday." She defeatedly whispered, frantic glare settling upon the generously parted doorway of Switch's cell as the buzzing red lights extinguished once more. Rain furiously pelted the compact roof, imitating more of a series of ice chunks (hail, possibly?) as an abundance of fallen objects coated the ceiling directly above her. After all, she (they?) were on the very top floor of the sanitarium, and by the sheer sound of the weather outside, the woman was almost certain that the roof would completely concave, crushing them both without a second to spare.

Wren held the eerily silent radio to her ear, blinking back mortified tears as she swallowed a massive chunk of bile. Rigidly, she continued to stare at Switch's blatantly vacant cell, pulse agonizingly accelerating as sweating fingers tightened their hold on the cheap, plastic radio. Besides the persistent raps of the rain overhead and the low buzz of the flickering emergency lights, the remainder of the cell block remained reticent.

Cautiously, her free hand curled downwards, quivering fingers grazing the smooth leather of her belt as her index finger collided with the spot where her personalized switchblade lay. Almost instantly, her lips parted in angst; finger dipping deeply into the bare hole that replaced the once claimed spot as patchy arrays of goosebumps coated the flesh of her neck.

Realization hadn't truly set in until she felt someone breathing down her neck.

Not just any someone—in fact, he wasn't a "someone" at all. *No*—he was much more (less?) than that—a monster. A *freak*. A barbarous lunatic—an evil, psychotic criminal with a hideous, artificial facial deformity and greasy curls and black, beady eyes and—

Wren's acrimonious thoughts immediately vanished, a petite squeak emerging through generously parted lips as the keen blade met the clothed surface of her belly—the cold, teasing tip of his freckled nose gently colliding with the curve of her jaw as she suddenly swallowed her obscene cries. Greasy, unkempt ringlets torturously tickled the reptilian skin of her cheeks, exaggerated giggles vibrating along her flushed neck as the shiny new blade glimmered beneath the haunting red hue.

As if on cue, the emergency lights had vanished once more—enveloping the frozen pair in sheer darkness as Switch erupted into fits of hushed laughter. Joyous. Mocking. *Gleeful.* Wren winced as the tip of the blade simply sliced the material of her navy uniform, cold metal colliding with flushed flesh as she repugnantly gasped.

"A pretty *blade* for a pretty *girl*," Switch nasally teased, licking a bold stripe up the length of her clammy neck as she openly grimaced. The knife was uncomfortably tucked against her skin, not quite severing the flesh but mere moments away from doing some good, lasting damage.

"It must belong to ickle *Julie Bear.*" He purred, hot breaths fanning over her ear as his lacerated lips just barely grazed the raised flesh. He could physically feel her heart rapidly racing beneath the shy skin of her glistening neck, a deep shade of red illuminating the room once more as his nose flattened against the surface, reveling in the feel.

Wren stirred beneath his rough hold, salty tears cloaking her face as she weakly attempted to pry herself from Switch's exceedingly strong hold. In return, the very tip of the blade managed to sink below the first layer of skin—beads of bright crimson arising as the guard released a heightened cry.

"P-Please," she pitifully begged, earning a sarcastic cackle from the man pressed against her back. "Please, let me go. I'll let you free if you let me live."

"*Hmm,*" Switch teased, latching his arm around her upper torso as she violently thrashed. "That's a *great* offer—truly—but-*uh, y'see,* I've been cooped up in this Godforsaken place for *way* too long, buttercup. In *fact*,"

The man generously paused, audibly nipping at the torn tissue of his lips as Wren's lower belly slightly oozed. Suddenly, his mouth met her ear once more, causing the woman to naturally retaliate as an additional sob emerged from paling lips.

"I almost forgot how *amazing* it feels to hold a knife, let alone *plunge* it into someone's *skin–*"

"Oh God, please don't–"

"I just *love* how vibrantly colored *blood* is." Switch purred, swaying from side to side as he tightened his grip on the handle of the feminine blade. "Especially in comparison to *extremely* light skin tones."

"Think of Julianna! What would she do if I died, Switch?" Wren obscenely cried, her words slightly slurred and muffled by her exaggerated cries as the madman simply rolled his eyes.

"Oh puh-*lease*," he droned, extracting the knife from her stomach as she audibly sighed in relief, his opposite arm still latched firmly around her chest as he toyed with his lips once more. "She's probably touching herself to the thought of *me*, while you're *here*, under your *own knife,* sobbing over some woman who couldn't give a damn whether you *live* or *die*."

"That's not true," Wren spat, shaking her head from side to side as her vision went blurry; head severely swimming from the persistent flickers of the lights as her knees went numb. "You're lying."

"*Am* I?" Switch sang, struggling to stifle his chuckles. The haunting sonance sent violent shivers down the length of Wren's nearly numb spine, a thin track of clotting blood coating the leather of her belt as the small intusion on her belly continued to weakly bleed.

"Okay, *okay*," Switch dryly joked, adjusting his confident grip on the knife as Wren intently held her breath. "Lemme tell you something *real* then, hm?"

"O-Okay." The woman thickly stammered, fingers encircled around his lower arm, nails buried between the softness of his arm hair as his mouth met her ear, again.

Lowly, the man muttered a very clear phrase: "this is gonna *hurt*."

Before Wren could protest, he'd managed to plunge the blade into the supple skin of her stomach, dipping directly into her appendix as she released a cry.

Immediately, a familiar warmth coated Switch's curled fist, bright scarlet dipping between the grooves of his clamped fingers as he tightly twisted the blade within Wren's stomach, causing her to obscenely sob as the severed tip utterly destroyed the particular organ. Once he was completely satisfied, the man abruptly tore the blade from her bleeding body, her shaking hands cupping the surface as the identically hued lights partially illuminated her sunken cheeks.

Admittedly, the man wanted to stay—to repeatedly strike the woman and watch her life dwindle away, to watch her soul (or lack, thereof) leave her blank, ugly eyes and bask in the incredible feel of her magnificent blood—but no. Because within these chthonic walls, time and opportunities (especially of this nature) were exceedingly brief, and if he was going to succeed tonight, he had to act. Fast.

He left Wren in a sobbing, bleeding heap upon the dusty old floor, crimson lights sporadically lighting up her crippled frame as she attempted to pull her weak, quivering body up. Blood-splattered fingers swiped against the glass of Switch's empty cell, smears of crimson coating the surface, elegantly shimmering beneath the identically hued, stagnant lights as the liquid form of her life coated the ground.

The last thing she saw before her vision went black was the infamous Switch slipping from the cell block, shoulders hunched and brown curls astray.

Switch shuffled from max, right hand slick and slippery with Wren's blood as the emergency lights routinely dissipated, enveloping the skinny hallway in complete darkness as his free hand met the concrete wall, fingertips trailing along the surface as he skillfully navigated the premises. The nearby staircase was vacant, uneven steps dipping down towards Level 4 as he quickly descended, occasionally skipping over a step as heightened exhales spilled from his lips. Right now, he only had one consistent thought—*Addy Addy Addy Addy Addy Addy Addy.*

The weighty, steel door that typically secured his and Adelaide's cell block was partially ajar, heightened chatter enveloping his ears as the inmates within erupted into fits of chaos, audibly brainstorming what to do in such a peculiar situation. He could distinctly hear Cora's agitating tone, sarcastic snickers slipping off of her lips as she boldly announced that she was going to skip across the hall and take refuge in Nayeli's cell.

Bloody blade in hand, the man eased into the area, inelegantly tripping over the too-long laces of his unlaced leather boots as the dully illuminated space appeared—mahogany cell doors open, jumpsuit-clad individuals standing around in wonder as his eyes locked onto Adelaide's.

Almost instantly, time seemed to stand still. The vermilion shade dissipated, masking their relieved expressions as the madman swiftly approached the frozen woman within the dark. Her hair was a matted mess, parted directly down the center and significantly oily, as if she hadn't washed the lengthy mane in days. Deep, inky bags claimed the underneath of her bright, bug-like eyes—hazel hued and lively, so inviting and welcoming and overwhelmingly stunning. Soft, faded yellow bruises claimed her temples, courtesy of Dr. Blake's completely immoral and inhumane practices—oblong shaped and uneven in size, random specks of purple and black claiming the circular surfaces. The black and white striped suit clung to her frail body like a garbage bag, unproportionate and baggy, a clear result of her extreme malnourishment and stick-like figure. Nevertheless, the seemingly unattractive woman had managed to make Switch's heart skip several staggered beats.

The dull shade of deep red reappeared, displaying Adelaide's bewildered features once more as Switch rapidly approached her, palms flattening against the hollows of her cheeks as the dull, flat surface of the blade collided with the side of her face. Exaggerated shivers consumed her spine at the foreign feel, lips naturally parting in wonder as determined teeth promptly clattered and noses achingly collided—eyelids slipping closed as that familiar taste of *him* immediately flooded her senses. Her hands met his dry elbows, fingers mechanically toying with the bunched material of his uniform as his tongue swiped against hers, jaws generously parting as the criminal breathed life into her agile frame.

Smears of scarlet consumed her cheek, courtesy of the bloody knife non-threateningly plastered against the side of her face as the pads of Switch's thumbs intently massaged the protruding flesh of her bony complexion. Adelaide's left hand detached from his elbow, reaching upwards to claim his unruly mop of curls as she buried her fingers within his hair, nails grinding against his scalp as he audibly groaned against her mouth, his hold tightening on her face as he drew her closer.

Tepid torsos collided; the woman's right hand claiming the hem of his top as her fingers curled inward, claiming the fabric between a sturdy fist as his pale midriff appeared, courtesy of her cold, prying touch.

The surrounding inmates seemed to fade to black; time ticking leisurely by as the pair continued to obscenely swap spit, lips rubbed raw as teeth occasionally clamped down on the angry flesh, nipping and tugging.

Several onlookers gawked in their direction, clearly stunned as they contemplated leaving and granting the couple some privacy. However, the battered blade within Switch's clutch convinced them otherwise, and mainly all of them, (besides Cora, who had already left), stood awkwardly in place.

Waiting.

"Don't ever leave me again." Adelaide murmured, her tone severely choppy and uneven as Switch's tongue wormed its way into the pits of her mouth once more, a simplistic grunt vibrating against her swollen bottom lip as her brain begged for oxygen. However, she couldn't quite care to breathe, for she had him, and he was wildly more important than fresh air could ever be.

"We need'a get *going*, dollface." Switch whispered, nipping hungrily at her lips as she stifled a giggle. Nearby, several patients, (onlookers, mostly), exchanged conflicting glances. The consistent flickering of the emergency lights uprooted pure panic, eyes widened in wanton abandon as the three individuals debated whether or not to vacate the premises.

"Okay." Adelaide pouted, stealing one final sealed-lip kiss as her lips flushed a taunt crimson. Their eyes met once more, black orbs sparkling beneath the dull lights as the woman stole a glance at the bloody switchblade in Switch's clutch. Her lips parted in angst, words resurfacing like vomit as her hand met the flushed flesh of her cheek, fingers immediately becoming slick with blood.

Switch's mouth curled into an amused grin, partially pockmarked skin folding over itself as a distinct set of smile lines consumed the area of his mouth like a halo—*ha! As if the cold-blooded murderer could possibly have anything in common with an angel!*

"You've-*uh,* got a lil somethin' *riiiight* there." He teased, brushing his stained palm against the surface of her face as the scarlet tint smeared along her complexion. Bitterly, the man attempted to rid the lukewarm liquid from her innocent features, but to no avail. Wren's blood had managed to effectively stain both his hand *and* her cheek . . .

"Whoops." He throatily mused, earning a shy giggle from the woman as their hands met in a calming embrace, fingers securely entwined. "Let's get *outta* here, princess."

"Gladly." Adelaide spoke, twisting on her heel as involuntary shivers consumed her spine. It was evident now that the heater had collapsed along with the generator, and the temperature within these sequestered walls was plummeting by the minute. For once, the woman was considerably fortunate that the material of their ugly, unkempt jumpsuits was so damn thick.

Just as the pair reached the ajar door—the lights briefly extinguishing once more as Adelaide's chest ached—a thought dawned upon her.

"Shit," she announced, freezing suddenly in place as the rubber soles of her boots obnoxiously squeaked against the floor. Switch raised a curious brow, momentarily masked by the absence of light as the dainty doll darted back in the direction of her cell before boldly announcing a simplistic fact: "I almost forgot something!"

Switch released a staggered sigh, grip tightening around the salmon handle of the blade as the nearby inmates scurried out the open door, avoiding his patronizing gaze entirely as the cell block remained otherwise vacant; all except for the presence of himself and his Adelaide.

Shakily, the woman rummaged through the top drawer of her dresser, fingers lightly grazing the cover of the dilapidating novel as she yanked it from the basin and stuffed it underneath her armpit. She nearly jumped from her skin in fright when Switch's nose collided with the hollow of her throat, lips peppering hot, open-mouthed kisses along the surface of her pulsating neck as she slipped Emmett's engagement ring into the pits of her pant pocket. The object eased downward into the fabric, nuzzling comfortably between a particularly large ball of lint and a familiar king of hearts card, one that hadn't been removed since the day it was gifted, (all besides on laundry day, of course).

"Okay," she spoke, curving her skull downwards to meet Switch's mouth in a shy, rushed kiss. "I'm ready."

The lights revealed his features once more—only briefly, but for a long enough period of time to display a cheeky, toothy-grin, complimented with rows of yellowing teeth.

"Let's go raise some *hell,* buttercup."

With that, the man claimed her palm in his, opposite hand tightly clutching Wren's blade as the duo scurried from the security of the cell block. The woman glanced one final time in the direction of her previously occupied cell, gaze lingering on the sight of Oliver's sloppily structured hole as a plethora of soothing memories invaded her jumbled mind, along with the presence of some *very* eager voices.

Luckily, the broad, steel gates of Stillwater Sanitarium were already open, allowing Vern and Briar to enter the parking lot with minimal conflict as freezing droplets of rain persistently pelted the windshield.

Briar's stomach was painfully churning, seatbelt already unlatched as the tires rolled through mounds of ice, which crunched beneath nettlesome tires as the vehicle rapidly approached the parking spot in the very front, right up near the building.

Widened azure eyes met the dashboard, heart plummeting at the sight of the time as the rubber tires came to a screeching halt, idle vehicle crookedly placed between invisible chalky-white lines as the woman thickly swallowed.

12:01.

"Shit," Briar whispered, adjusting her posture on the leather seat. "Merry Christmas, Ulysses."

Vern thrust the Cadillac into park, calloused thumb colliding with the vibrant red button of his seatbelt as the noisy object slithered back into place beside the sealed door. Ebony eyes met an antsy set of wild, blue orbs; blue like the ocean—bright and lively and ever-flowing. She was undeniably gorgeous, and as Briar managed to latch her quivering fingers around the cool plastic of the door handle, Vern found himself spilling his innermost thoughts.

The proclamation emerged shy and wary, tone drastically uneven and raspy as the three syllables blended into one unidentifiable term: *"Iloveyou."*

Briar raised a puzzled brow, breaths dramatically thinning as she blinked several times, head shaking from side to side as she struggled to comprehend the wildly rushed statement that had effortlessly spilled from Vern's parted lips. His complexion had significantly paled; black eyes widened in panic as his palm met her knee.

"I-uh," he stammered, tearing the keys from the ignition as the rain continued to furiously pelt the metal roof. "I-I'm sorry—*God,* that was just absolutely horrific timing—"

The woman refused to let him finish. Instead, her lips met his. Briefly. Softly. Confidently and lovingly, inaudibly reassuring the sweet, tender man that his unalloyed declaration of love was entirely and unreservedly accepted.

"I love you, too." She spoke, confident gaze meeting his puzzled stare as the woman abrasively opened the door and literally leapt from the vehicle.

The rain immediately bled through the drastically thin material of her scrubs, soaking wet snow audibly crunching beneath the heels of her sneaker-clad feet as she rapidly approached the sealed double doors of the sanitarium. A wary Vern struggled to keep up, a weighty wince plastered across flushed features as the sleet severely stung, imitating a set of hot, white knives as the frozen rain swiftly soaked through his sweater. By the time he'd reached the entrance, Briar had already slipped inside; partially drenched blond hair framing her face as the duo slipped into a seemingly scarce black hole.

Briar froze, breaths emerging in staggered pants as the evidence of her hot exhale visibly emerged in the form of a thick cloud, wide eyes struggling to focus on the lobby as the blackness promptly disappeared, replaced by a dull, buzzing round of shy, red lights.

"The emergency lights," Vern breathed, panting slightly as the warm glow faded into black a mere three seconds following. "Thank God they kicked in. Could you imagine if this place was completely dark? It'd be a total and complete nightmare!"

"Do you have your flashlight?" Briar dryly wondered, inching towards the locked door as Vern invisibly nodded, fishing the dainty object from his jean pocket as he ignited a steady stream of white light.

"It's a small one." He said, directing the duo towards the inner entrance as Briar quickly typed Adelaide's inmate number onto the keypad. Luckily, the tiny light in the corner glowed a gleeful green, granting the pair access to the rest of the building as Vern raised a suspicious brow.

"Wait," he began, following closely on Briar's heel as muffled chaos emerged from above. Blended voices and tremendously exaggerated cries ricocheted off the walls, causing their blood to immediately run cold as Briar shot him a worried glance.

"How'd the keypad work if the power's out?" He inquired as they bombarded the staircase, skipping up the drastically misaligned concrete steps as the red emergency lights continued to faultily flicker.

"The exit doors are battery operated. Evers changes the batteries out every-so-often just in case an event like this occurs." Briar exhaustedly explained, nearly tripping over a particularly lopsided step as the man extended his arm outward, catching her tumbling frame just in the nick of time.

"That means the cell doors should be battery operated too, right?" The man wondered, the flashlight illuminating a bold sign beside the staircase, which read: LEVEL 2.

Briar audibly gulped, her apparent head shake invisible to Vern's eyes as the building reentered "abyss mode". However, her lack of response ensured that the man had been wrong—the cell doors, which contained some of the most violent, most dishonorable individuals—were *open.*

"Where to first?" Vern asked, slightly out of breath as Briar continued to climb the stairs, avoiding the second level of the institution.

"Addy's cell." She breathed, the toe of her shoe painfully colliding with the rounded edge of the step as she openly grimaced. "Need to make sure she's okay."

"What about max? Evers had to be smart enough to make those keypads battery operated—right?"

Once again, Briar failed to reply. Vern seemed to get the memo, as a boorish obscenity slipped off his lips, cluttered chatter constantly filling their ears as they ascended up to the fourth level.

"Sweetheart," Vern began as Briar trudged through the parted doorway of Adelaide's cell block. "If the cell doors are open, I highly doubt that she'll still be here—"

"I have to check, Vern!" The faux blond woman seethed, fingers curling into exasperated fists at her sides as she slipped into Adelaide's open, empty cell.

A hopeful gasp emerged from the nurse, palms cradling the frigid steel of the mahogany door as she filed into the area, the tiny, bright light from Vern's miniature flashlight revealing an interesting clue.

The very top drawer of Adelaide's tri-drawer dresser lay opened, articles of musty clothing thrown astray as her copy of *Sense and Sensibility* lay absent, along with the presence of the Newport cigarettes and her engagement ring.

Proudly, Briar's lips curled into a smile, palm flattening against the curve of her mouth as Vern released a questionable: "What's going on, Bri?"

The woman turned on her heel, watering eyes meeting the wildly confused man opposite her as Briar's heart swelled multiple sizes within her chest.

"He's gonna do it," she said, choking back relieved sobs. "He's gonna get her out of here."

Vern weakly grinned, offering his arm to the woman as they emerged from the cold, vacant area that Adelaide involuntarily called home for two years.

Two *fucking* years—over eight-hundred days of unrequested admittance. Of egregious pain and loneliness. Finally, after all this time, her Adelaide would finally get out of this dreadful hell, this sorry excuse for a mental institution. And how absolutely ironic was it that the most feared man in all of Chicago would be the one to set her free?

"Let's go," Vern urged, leading her through the arch of the door. "We need to make sure nothing gets in their way."

Just as the pair filed from the specific block, an undeviating round of moans and sporadic cries filled their ears, emerging from an additional block on the very same floor. The cell block where Nayeli Schmitt spent her days, along with a timid, aging Lloyd and Schizophrenic Sarah.

"What the fuck was that?" He wondered, eyes widened in curiosity as they slowly approached the opposite cell block. Briar's heart thickly hammered beneath her ribcage, hands tremendously shaking as they rounded the exceedingly black corner and entered through the nearly sealed door.

A sobbing Cora sat on her knees before them, thick tears claiming her rosy red cheeks as she loudly cried, bloody fingers entangled in Nayeli's ringlets as Briar's jaw fell.

Oozing, scarlet blood twinkled beneath the wicked red lights, a careless, uneven *X* carved onto the otherwise flawless flesh of her forehead as the liquid form of her life steadily seeped from the substantial wound along the length of her neck.

"Holy shit," Briar gawked, falling to her knees before the blubbering woman as she cradled a dead Nayeli in her arms. "What happened?"

"What the hell do you think?" Cora brashly exclaimed, tightening her hold on Nayeli's arms as she held the deceased woman closer to her heaving chest. "The wound on her face says it all! *His* mark! T-That freak and his little *bitch!*"

"Cora–"

"Don't even try to defend them!" The crying mess of woman seethed, bottom lip violently quivering as she stole an additional glance at the mangled woman within her arms. "They took her away from me! They didn't even *care!* H-He just laughed! A-And s-she just watched, like it was some kind of *show!* Like a movie!"

Briar flatly frowned, glancing warily over her shoulder to view a conflicted Vern as she stood to her feet once more.

"Stay with her." She calmly instructed, glancing once more at a steadily bleeding Nayeli Schmitt as the shaded blood pooled at their feet. "I need to find them."

"But what if something happens to you?" Vern interjected, avoiding Cora's blubbering form. "I'm not letting you wander about this place alone, especially with a bunch of mentally ill patients who are in distress."

"I have my phone in my pocket," Briar argued, side-stepping towards the door. "If anything happens, I'll call you immediately."

"No." Vern clipped, shining the harsh light directly into her eyes as the woman hastily blinked. "Last time you said that, you ended up getting raped by some psychopath. We aren't splitting up this time."

Wordlessly, the woman nodded, sympathetically smiling in Cora's distressed direction as the duo excused themselves from the cell block and hurried back down the staircase.

"Blake worked the night shift," Briar explained, slightly out of breath as she scaled the wall with the tips of her fingers. "Hopefully she's still in her office. She's probably hiding in there like the coward she is."

"Maybe." Vern murmured, palm gently cupping her lower back as they approached Dr. Blake's office. Luckily, they managed not to encounter any irate inmates on the way down, and the persistent flicker of the lights was beginning to give Briar a splitting headache.

"Why can't these damn lights just stay on?" She complained, lacing her fingers around the circular handle of Blake's office door as the warm object nuzzled against her palm. Instantly, she froze—breaths thinning as her stomach violently churned.

"What is it?" Her boyfriend anxiously wondered, glancing several times between the woman and the closed door as she simply gulped.

"The handle," she began. "It's warm."

". . . and?" Vern drawled, exchanging his weight from either foot as his clammy hand readjusted its grip on the slippery plastic flashlight.

"Someone went in here recently." Briar pointedly explained, twisting the handle clockwise as the latch audibly clicked.

"Or left." Vern countered, palm flattening against the small of her back as the door swung widely open, emergency lights routinely dissipating as the blackness devoured the office. Vern lazily held onto his flashlight, vibrant beam pointed directly downward as they shuffled further into the stagnant space, the thick scent of cigarette-smoke consuming their lungs as the vibrant red lights promptly reappeared.

A horrified shriek slipped off Briar's lips, knobby knees collapsing beneath her weight as she attempted to scurry backwards, ultimately failing. Her weakened legs buckled beneath her, sending her violently shaken frame directly to the ground as Vern's jaw lay ajar.

Doctor Lyra Blake lazily lounged in her ripped swivel chair, a steadily burning cigarette sat snug between statuette digits as a sopping wide *X* claimed her forehead. Red. Bloody. Gruesome. Magnified eyes open; torpid orbs glaring longingly in Briar's mortified direction as thin tracks of blood from the wound dipped down to meet her pierced ears. Sparkling, dangling earrings were smeared with crimson liquid, oozing droplets consistently dripping onto the fabric of her flowy purple top as Vern took a significant step backwards.

"Did you see her stomach?" He muttered, helping Briar off of the dusty floor as the woman's eyes effectively sealed, her brain desperately attempting to ward off the undeniably morbid visuals of a deceased Lyra Blake.

"No." Briar breathed, swallowing a mouthful of bile as she twisted sharply on her heel and headed towards the door. "We need to keep looking for them."

"Can't say she didn't deserve it." Vern announced, closing the door behind them as Briar physically shivered, desperately attempting to ward off the nauseated feeling in her belly as they started back down the halls in search of Adelaide and a clearly deranged Switch.

"Didn't say that." Briar said, snatching the flashlight from Vern's grasp as they headed towards the rec room.

"You don't think that Switch's going to do that to Adel—"

"VERN!" Briar wailed, delivering a sharp slap to his bicep as he tossed his hands into the air in surrender.

"I'm sorry!"

Briar led the way, nearly bursting into a sprint as they rapidly approached the rec room, hands clamping together to steady the flashlight as muffled voices filled their ears.

"Briar, I'm really sorry for even saying something as absurd as that out loud. I don't think he would, I genuinely think that he may actually admire her a lot." The woman blatantly ignored Vern's rushed speech, blaring beam of light settling upon the ripped fabric of a couch on the left half of the ginormous rec room as a middle-aged Lloyd sat still, bottom pressed into the mattress as the aging material molded around his frame.

"It's happening." He announced, realizing Briar's presence as three additional inmates littered the room, all bug-eyed and terrified as Vern whispered reassuring phrases in their timid directions.

"What is, Lloyd?" Briar cooed, slowly approaching the sofa as the room was consumed by darkness once again, prompting a fearful cry to emerge from one of the women as Vern attempted to calm her down.

"He's done it." Lloyd monotonically stated, staring into oblivion as Briar audibly gulped for the umpteenth time that night. "He's done it. Satan has sent for his son. This was his storm."

Vern's palm met Briar's back once more, equally shallow breaths intermixing as the older man continued with his apparent prophecy.

"Those who intervene will fall." He explained, as a matter-of-fact. "Algort. Blake. Greenwald. Jackson. McGregory. Schmitt. Tribeca."

"What do those names mean?" Vern questioned, shooting Briar a perplexed glare as she ran a shaking hand through her messy locks.

"Say the names again for me, Lloyd." She gingerly requested, palm flattening against the man's cheek as he remained frozen on the couch, the very same one that he'd consumed half of the stuffing from the cushions over time.

"Algort." He began, enunciating each individual syllable of the name as he generously paused.

"Nurse Lora's last name is Algort, isn't it?" Vern wondered aloud, but Lloyd refused to let him finish.

"Blake."

"Lyra," Briar gasped. "Lyra Blake's dead."

"Greenwald."

"I hope he's dead." Vern raged, an objective grin consuming his features at the mere thought of Elliot Greenwald with a bloody *X* slapped across his head.

"Jackson."

Vern and Briar exchanged glances, at a complete loss for that particular surname as they struggled to list off the patient's names in their head, but Lloyd only continued, disrupting their thoughts.

"McGregory."

"Nurse Angelica." Briar said, shifting her weight. "Her last name is McGregory."

"Schmitt."

Briar and Vern exchanged worried glances, simultaneously muttering a vexed: "Nayeli."

"Tribeca."

Vern raised a brow, clearly at a loss as Briar audibly gulped, *again.*

"That's the new guard." She began. "The lesbian. The one who's married to the detective at the CPD."

"Oh." Vern whispered, brows raised.

"Lloyd," Briar requested, attempting to meet his gaze. The man, however, continued to stare into nothingness; eyes blank, as if unseeing. Unfeeling. Unhearing.

"It's hopeless." Vern groaned, kicking a nearby pebble with the toe of his shoe as the vibrant, oblong object disappeared beneath within black abyss. "He's in some kind of trance."

"It's a list." Briar announced, tucking the messy chunks of blond behind her ears as she shined the flashlight in the direction of the worried patients on the opposite end of the room.

"Sweetie," Vern coaxed. "That much is obvious."

"No," Briar keenly interrupted, waving her glowing, red hand in the air as she led a curious Vern from the rec room, making a beeline towards the cafeteria. "I mean, it's like a prediction. A prophecy."

"I'm not following." The man murmured, attempting to calm down a nearby inmate as the young man violently cried.

"Vern," Briar pressed, stopping dead in her tracks as the man nearly ran full-force into her lanky frame. "Don't you get it?"

Brows quizzically raised, the man shook his head, palms caressing the in-between of a man named Novak's shoulders as he sniffled beside them, jumpsuit trousers weakly clinging to his thin, wide-set hips. He was muttering something about the Switch miraculously sparing him, or so Briar overheard . . .

"It's a hit list." Briar breathed.

Adelaide claimed Switch's hand in hers, quivering fingertips grazing against his sturdy hold as his persistent giggles enveloped the void. Her personalized copy of *Sense and Sensibility* lay snug beneath the pit of her arm, warm and cozy and comfy within her embrace as she carried a little piece of Emmett around with her.

Vivid visuals of a very dead Dr. Blake consistently raided her mind, gruesome recollections of a total sanguinary struggle—pleading cries and wholesome, desperate moans. She seemed to have expected some kind of assistance from Adelaide—*as if!*

And still, the mere thought of Blake's organs spilling from her torn belly and the bloody, gruesome *X* that stretched from her hairline to her brows was enough to make the lithe woman's stomach churn and her head spin.

"Switch," she croaked, palm flattening against her roiling stomach as she stumbled sideways, vision temporarily obscured by the momentary darkness as the giggling mess of man abruptly dropped her hand.

"What?" He snipped, eyeing the woman suspiciously as he rotated the notably bloody blade within his grasp, hands stained a bold crimson as the woman bent over a nearby corner.

"Give me a second," she croaked. "I need to puke."

Switch sighed, running a hand through his hair as the woman deliberately retched into the corner, prompting the man's nose to crinkle in disgust as his hold tightened around the knife.

"Whassa *matter?*" He mockingly purred, tossing the open blade into the pit of his other palm as the woman wiped her mouth with the back of her hand, violent shivers consuming her spine as she choked back hefty sobs.

"I don't like blood." She said, clearly referencing Switch's trio of murders within the past twenty minutes as the madman burst into deriding laughter; head tossed fleetingly back on his shoulders as his broad frame vigorously shook with amusement. Smears of crimson claimed his hands, whereas a majority of his suit remained surprisingly unscathed. Although he was clearly a psychopathic murderer—*just like they've been trying to tell you all this time, Addy! God, don't you listen?*—he was shockingly stealthy and overwhelmingly clean. He knew how to keep his kills un-messy and under control, and if he were wearing latex gloves, there probably wouldn't be any evidence of his crimes on his skin at all.

"You're *kidding!*" He boasted, knife-clad palm claiming his belly as he continued to laugh. "Then why the hell are you with me, dollface? *Hm?* Is it for the sex? Or the-*uh, stability?*"

Adelaide took a generous step backwards. Switch's scars gave off a rather eerie vibe beneath the red lights, and the only thing missing was *his* marking—a bold, bright *X* along the flesh of his forehead, the very same that claimed Dr. Blake's, Nayeli's, and whoever else he'd managed to kill when Adelaide wasn't with him.

"Aw, *pumpkin*," he teased, palm cradling her cheek as she fearfully shook beneath his hold. "Don't worry, I'm not gonna hurt'*cha.*"

Adelaide's pulse immediately quickened, her palms slick with sweat as Switch leaned forward, placing a generous, open-mouthed kiss upon her stagnant lips. She slightly hesitated, mouth running dry as his tongue lapped at her sealed lips, desperately begging for entrance.

"*C'mon,* sugar plum." Switch cooed, caressing the ball of her cheek with his stained, calloused thumb as she unwillingly melted within his embrace. "S'only *me.*"

Adelaide eventually obliged, lips generously parting as Switch's tongue wormed its way into her mouth. The woman openly sighed against his soothing lips, familiar, mutilated skin caressing the sharp edge of her jaw as he strayed from her swollen mouth to pepper feather-like smooches to the surrounding skin.

"There's plenty *more* where *that* came from." He assured the woman, planting a fat, wet kiss to the center of her forehead as his hand claimed hers once again. "We need to go. Time's running *out.*"

Adelaide briskly nodded, following closely on Switch's heel as the pair navigated the area. She had a general idea where the very back door was, the one which opened up to the woods, surrounded by tall, dark trees; which formed into fearsome figures, ones that actually mimicked something straight out of a nightmare.

"I think it's around this corner." She announced, accidentally clipping Switch's heel with the toe of her boot as he irritably groaned, directing the woman down an extremely unfamiliar path as the lights habitually diminished once again.

They scurried into a dark and dingy room, filled with miscellaneous olive-hued plastic crates and brown boxes, a sealed, steel door claiming the opposite wall as Adelaide eyed the keypad. Suddenly, the woman froze—a peculiar sonance invading her ears as she impulsively smiled. For a split second, the woman was almost certain that she'd heard Nurse Briar's voice calling for her. Brows raised as she glanced curiously over her shoulder, fingers interlaced with Switch's as she awaited the arrival of her best friend.

You know how this goes, Ad. They said, reminding Adelaide of how insanely idiotic she was.

I know. Adelaide defeatedly replied, following closely on Switch's heel as the lowly-hued lights extinguished, causing them to freeze in place until they arose once more. *I guess I just miss her. I want her to see us escape.*

Switch's nose blindly collided with Adelaide's temple, a cold, serrated knife slipping into her objective grasp as her lips parted in angst. The book still lay buried beneath her armpit, a constant reminder of Emmett's presence as her heart immediately swelled.

"Keep it." He said, placing a kiss to the pointed tip of her nose. "I'm *good* with my *hands*. You need it more than I do."

"Are we going to be split up?" Adelaide whispered, crimson tint illuminating Switch's features once more as he stared longingly into her hazel-hued eyes.

"I don't *know*." He honestly replied. "But, it's always *best* to prepare for the *worst*."

"And the worst is yet to come." A third voice interjected, causing Adelaide's blood to run cold. The flickering red lights revealed a giddy Elliot Greenwald, who was currently blocking the access to the exit door.

His left palm gently cradled a standard Glock-19, a sinister smirk etched across dry, cracked lips as he swayed his weight from either foot, index finger mindlessly toying with the idle trigger. The skin surrounding his nose was angry and multi-colored, splashes of yellows, blacks and purples cloaking the surface as his broken nose apparently struggled to heal.

"That was unwise of you to do, Switch. After all, you *did* name yourself after a *switchblade*, so I assume that they're your only shot at survival." Greenwald tittered, eyeing the bloody blade held loosely within Adelaide's grasp. "That bitch wouldn't hurt a *fly*, and you gave up your only real weapon."

The guard's crimson hair was a tousled mess, eyes wild and widened beneath the routine, exaggerated flickers of the red emergency lights. The sleeves of his navy uniform top were uncharacteristically rolled, hooked behind the tattooed flesh of his elbows as Adelaide glanced worriedly in Switch's direction.

"With all due respect, *sir,*" Switch confidently mocked, taking a generous step in Greenwald's direction as the guard tightened his hold on the handgun. "You should already be aware that I'm *very* good with my hands."

"You just got lucky with this one." Greenwald hissed through gritted teeth, motioning upwards at the sight of his ghastly, misshapen nose as Switch merely snickered—lowly. Sadistically. *Mockingly.*

"However," the crimson-haired man throatily began, fingering the smooth curve of the pistol's trigger. "I'm afraid your luck has just about run out."

Greenwald raised the gun, darkness consuming the tiny space once more as Adelaide impulsively squeezed her eyelids shut, fierce trembles overcoming her every limb as she physically shivered. However, that dreadful, long-awaited sound of the gun firing never seemed to arrive—instead, the sonance was replaced by something entirely divergent; a dramatic, exasperated *hmph,* as if the man had managed to stub his big toe against the sturdy wooden leg of a nearby table.

Hesitantly, her squeezed lids reopened, displaying an amusing image beneath the taunting red glow—an image of Switch—*her* Switch, her *Andrew*—with his arms laced confidently around Greenwald's neck.

The psychopath kept a wildly tenacious grip on Greenwald's grubby neck, the guard's free fingernails desperately digging into the pale flesh of Switch's exposed arm as he desperately pleaded for freedom. Instead, the criminal merely laughed—a direful, deep chuckle, one which reverberated through the room and consumed Adelaide wholly; sporadic, evenly-spaced goosebumps coating her skin as Greenwald attempted to claw his way out of Switch's aggressive hold.

Cheeks flushed a petrified cerise hue, gun still firmly laced between oily fingers as the cold metal consistently collided with the clothed surface of Switch's thigh. He, however, failed to flinch, hold tightening on Greenwald's neck as the tall guard sloppily attempted to peel the man from his windpipe.

"*Geroffa me!*" The redheaded man dryly pleaded, fury laced with his choppy tone as Switch continued to cackle, clearly enjoying Greenwald's pitiful struggle as the madman cheekily winked in Adelaide's stunned direction.

After torturously teasing the piece of shit formally known as Elliot

Greenwald, Switch ultimately shifted his grip, confidently yanking the guard's skull slightly sideways, emitting a ghastly *crack*. The unfamiliar noise reminded the withdrawn woman of cracking knuckles—the distinct sonance of stiff fingers popping beneath the warm cradle of the opposite palm. A horrified expression overcame her features at the crude comparison, gaze diverting from the situation at hand as her stomach violently churned once again, and vivid recollections of Blake's bloody organs raided her mind.

A sudden, bold burst of energy consumed Elliot's core immediately following the first dignified crack, adrenaline pumping through his veins as he attempted, yet again, to toss the Switch off of him, only to miserably fail. It was evident that the head case was considerably stronger than him. Defeatedly, the crimson-haired fella feebly tugged at Switch's arms, the frigid barrel of the inactive pistol slapping against his thigh as Switch released a roaring grunt, arms heartlessly tensing around Elliot's neck as he violently jerked.

Unfortunately for him, the sorry excuse for a man was a damn fighter, breathy cries slipping through cracked, paling lips as a series of rugged, raspy gasps emerged from his severely severed windpipe. Bulging eyes met a frozen Adelaide a mere two yards away, lips parted in preparation to speak as he obscenely wheezed, black dots raiding his vision as the low glow of the red lights properly illuminated the tiny area.

Switch impatiently lapped at his lips, a heightened grunt slipping off of his determined tongue as he took a considerably deep breath. Once again, his arms tightened around Elliot's throat, vigorously twisting as the guard's skull nearly rotated an entire three-hundred and sixty degrees on his neck, a deafening *CRACK* filling Adelaide's ears as she fearfully covered her eyes with her palms. Simultaneously, the very moment that haunting sonance emerged—an ear-splitting sound ricocheted off of the walls as the firearm discharged, courtesy of the violent spasm that consumed Elliot's limbs.

Greenwald fell limp within Switch's embrace, the criminal's arms unraveling from the dying guard's neck as the crimson-haired gentleman inelegantly tumbled to the floor, grip loosening on the gun as it audibly collided with the concrete. Defeatedly, the lanky man fell to Switch's feet—blank eyes wide. Empty. Cold. The orbs glossed over, chest faintly falling as he surely slipped into ventricular fibrillation, mouth agape in protest as one final, gasping breath emerged—staggered. Weighty. Ultimately accepting.

Unseeing eyes glaring in Switch's pleased direction as the man let out several exaggerated giggles, the toe of his boot confidently colliding with Greenwald's temple as he aggressively kicked his skull sideways.

"Piece of shit." Switch spat, kicking the dead man's face once more as the already broken nose audibly cracked beneath the weight of his boot. The sound of the bloody blade—as well as a paperback book—meeting the floor promptly tore the man from his momentary trance, giggles instantly ceasing as Adelaide's choppy tone enveloped the stale air.

"Andrew?" The woman breathed, shaking fingers colliding with her stinging skin as the surface immediately became slick with warm, oozing blood. Her eyes immediately widened at the horrific sight, pulse drastically accelerating as the room seemed to expeditiously spin.

Switch's eyes immediately widened at the sight of a bright, fluorescent spot, which had appeared upon the shoulder of her jumpsuit. His chest physically ached at the image, legs wobbling as he rapidly approached the frozen woman.

"Addy," he lazily pressed, mangled jaw parted in angst as his palms met her face. The flesh of her cheeks was wildly clammy, complexion significantly paling by the second as her heart violently thudded beneath his fingertips.

"I'm going to *carry* you, okay?" Switch collectively cooed, earning a staggered nod from the shocked woman beside him as she stared fleetingly at her bloodied palm. The skin was already flushed a shy crimson from the blade, but now her fingers were slick and dripping with a more vibrant hue—a bright red color, which dipped between her nails and slipped onto the dusty, concrete floor. Before approaching her, Switch's fingers curled around the fanned-out pages of her favorite book, ripping it from the ground as he stuffed the object beneath his arm.

Weakly, the woman nodded, simply sighing as the man scooped her up in his arms, holding her bridal style as he scurried around Greenwald's unmoving frame and approached the locked door.

"Four numbers, baby." Switch breathed, his tone choppy and hoarse as he steadied both his and Adelaide's weight against the wall, left leg hiking up to secure her limp weight as the curve of his knee jabbed against her lower back. Clearly uncomfortable, the woman grimaced, violent shakes consuming her dainty body as the blood continued to seep from the apparent wound beneath her jumpsuit.

"That's all that separates us from freedom. Four *fucking* numbers—your numbers, babe." The man reassuringly spilled, bloody, trembling fingertips grazing along the keypad as he quickly and efficiently entered Adelaide's inmate number. The door slightly hesitated, vibrant viridescent light failing to emerge as the man's breaths impossibly thinned and his heart immediately plummeted.

No no no no no no no no no–

Alas, seconds later, the lively green light emerged, an audible *click* signaling their acceptance as the back door of the sanitarium swung widely open.

Switch released a throaty cheer, hold tightening on Adelaide's weak form as he stepped over the threshold, carrying the woman as if he were carrying his bride. The thought alone was rather amusing, really—the fact that he'd stepped over the threshold of a doorway with her confidently cradled within his arms, her nose nuzzled into the warmth of his chest as she staggeringly sighed against the surface.

Switch tumbled from the unwelcoming embrace of the hellish asylum, easing out into the open world as freezing cold rain furiously pelted their skin, persistent rolls of thunder generously vibrating through their chests as the man fell to his knees against the frozen grass. The book tumbled from the safety of his arm, printed ink blending together upon the pages as the rain soaked the novel through-and-through.

"We *did* it, princess!" He exclaimed, tearing sopping wet strands of hair from Adelaide's eyes as her pupils significantly dilated. "We're *free*."

Adelaide gawkily admired her surroundings, partially blinded by the bothersome droplets of rain as Switch rapidly tore at the collar of her uniform, breaths emerging in heightened pants as he observed the wound.

"It looks like the bullet missed your Axillary artery by half an *inch*." The man explained, freezing fingers applying pressure to the gaping wound as the woman outwardly cried.

"H-How do you k-know—"

"Believe it or *not*," the criminal teased, winking suggestively in her direction as she lay within his arms. "I went to med school."

"Oh," Adelaide dryly sang, blinking back tears as her palm met his cheek. "Doctor Switch."

Switch smiled—a broad, toothy grin—one that made the folds of his face curl upwards in amusement as the woman daintily caressed the morbid scar beneath his eye with her fingers.

"Oh, *c'mon,*" he purred, tightly holding the thick fabric of her striped top against the wound in a weak attempt to slow the bleeding. "You can *say* it."

Adelaide's heart swelled, her thumb dipping into the innermost grooves of his mangled flesh as numbness overcame her every limb.

"Doctor Andrew." She breathed, smiling softly as the man's grin grew. "*My* Andrew."

Almost instantly, a painful scoff invaded her complexion, brows knit together in vexation as she curled upon his lap in sheer pain.

"It hurts." The woman cried, black dots occasionally raiding her vision as Switch worked diligently to stop the bleeding. The cold rain seemed to multiply the amount of blood, creating a dreadful mess of scarlet along her chest as his brows irritably strung together.

"I know, Addy. Just *relax*. You're *safe*, now. You're free and with *me*. I'll protect you." Switch wholeheartedly promised, mouth agape in concentration as the woman shoved his hands away from her shoulder.

"No." Adelaide murmured, blinking the blinding rain from her eyes as a comforting, cocoa stare met her gaze.

"No *what?*" Switch impatiently clipped, leaning forward to shield her eyes from the rain as she shuddered within his hold.

"You don't need to protect me anymore, Andrew." The weakened woman stated, still actively caressing his face with her stained palm as he shook his head in bewilderment. Drenched curls framed his hollow complexion, constant droplets slipping from the strands and showering her bleeding shoulder as she stirred within his steady grip.

"You've given me everything that I've wanted." She continued, her voice hoarse and shy as the man stared blankly back at her. "You gave me freedom. There's nothing more that you need to give me."

"Addy–"

"Andrew. Listen to me." Adelaide snipped, curling her fingers inward as her nails dug against his complexion. Unwillingly, the man remained deathly silent, stare unblinking as the woman stirred in immense pain within his arms.

"I'm in pain." She simply said. "A *lot* of pain. I can't do this anymore, baby. I can't."

Switch's lips parted in preparation to speak, but Adelaide's index finger abruptly met his mouth, silencing his speech as she uneasily continued.

"Please." Adelaide begged, choking back hefty sobs as she cradled his cheek within her palm. "Please, Andrew. Just take the pain away."

Switch's eyes widened, breaths emerging in dumbfounded intervals as Adelaide reassuringly stroked his face. Her opposite, shaking palm slipped into the depths of her trouser pocket, quivering digits curling around the thick plastic of the king of hearts card as she withdrew it from the pocket. Switch's eyes widened at the sight of it, a sly grin claiming his mouth as Adelaide weakly chuckled, holding the card as tightly as she could within her exceedingly weak grasp.

"A-Are you *sure* . . ?" Switch gaped, pulse automatically accelerating as his hands profusely shook.

Adelaide silently nodded, flattening her fingers against his parted lips as his warm breaths showered her skin. Although the icy rain was freezing against her flesh and the outside temperature was surely below thirty degrees, (and dropping), she felt exceptionally warm. Cozy. *Safe.*

"Are you *surely* sure—" Switch flatly teased, attempting to conceal his raging excitement as his fingers violently buzzed, physically begging to latch around Adelaide's throat and squeeze the life directly out of her. His head and his heart, however, seemed to lean the other way . . .

"Andrew." Adelaide scolded, growing weaker by the second as she suddenly was unable to feel the warmth of his lips beneath her fingers. In fact, she couldn't quite feel anything at all. "Please do this for me. For yourself."

Switch blinked several times, nodding curtly as he stroked the ball of her protruding cheekbone with his slick thumb, tongue intently toying with the drenched skin of his chin as their lips met in a rushed, passionate embrace. The kiss was cold and wet, sealed-lipped and full of emotion as Switch ran his fingers through Adelaide's matted hair, smearing streaks of crimson through her locks as she smiled against his mouth. In that moment, Adelaide realized that there was nowhere she'd rather be. Nowhere she'd rather die. Because she was in Andrew's arms—*her* Andrew, the beautiful, gorgeous Andrew Carter who had just a few loose nuts and bolts within that brilliant brain of his. Andrew Carter, who put her before himself for anything, even though they'd only known each other since September and hardly knew a damn thing about one another besides the basics. Truthfully, dying in Andrew Carter's arms was the only way she could see herself going out truly happy. Truly content.

"I'm gonna take it *away*." He softly assured, mirroring Adelaide's accepting nods as their lips briefly met once again. "I'll take all of your pain *away*."

Their stares interlocked, the tips of their noses arduously colliding as Switch released a weighty exhale before drawing his head back and positioning his bloodied fingers around the curve of her throat.

"Your body is gonna *fight* it," he skillfully explained, smooth, calloused thumb flattening against her jugular as she lightly nodded, blinking back blinding tears as her lips curled into an accepting smile.

"Just don't stop." She said, batches of butterflies brewing within the man's belly as he faintly nodded, bottom lop drawn between chattering teeth as euphoria overcame his every limb, fingers physically aching to just do it already . . . To seal the deal.

"Ready, princess?" Switch murmured, glare darkening at the sight of her bold, blatant nod as she smiled. Her inspiriting expression immediately generated an additional bunch of butterflies to irritably invade the pits of his virtually empty stomach, his hold gradually tightening around the supple skin of her neck as her lips instinctively parted.

"I'm gonna *take* it away," he grumbled, applying an ample amount of pressure to her windpipe as she gaudily gasped, hazel eyes bulging as her body stirred, attempting to fight him off. Her palms impulsively cupped his drenched forearms, dense grip softening as she forced her body to submiss.

His thumbs rotated to the carotid arteries on the sides of her neck, violently squeezing the vessels beneath her thumping throat as her racing heart gradually slipped into arrhythmia. Salty tears unwillingly coated her flushed cheeks, eyes remaining locked on Switch's stygian stare for the entire scenario as his forehead crinkled in concentration, hold significantly tightening once again as the woman undeniably slipped into cardiac arrest. The playing card still lay entwined between stained fingers, flattened against her chest as the card hovered her slowing heart. *King of your heart . . .*

"It's *alright*," Switch whispered, watching intently as Adelaide's eyelids slipped closed, strangled breaths emerging from chalky white lips as his grip remained consistent. "You're *free* now, my princess. In more ways than *one*."

The rain gingerly slowed, Adelaide's comforting pulse absent beneath the curve of his fingers as Switch blankly stared downwards at the dead woman within his arms. Conflicting voices raided his jumbled skull—desperately attempting to convince him that this was, in fact, what he'd wanted all along. Ever since the moment he first saw her in that damn porcelain tub—long, soapy mane flattened against her heart-shaped skull as wide, inquisitive eyes followed his every move. He'd wanted to put her out of her misery from the moment her untrimmed fingernails grazed his lacerated expression for the very first time, trembling digits curling through the generous, oblong hole present between their cells as skin collided with skin for the very first time. He'd always wanted this—but now that he had finally gotten it, the man realized that he actually hadn't wanted this after all.

Angry eyes collided with Adelaide's gray complexion, sporadic spurts of rain coating her peacefully sealed eyelids as he gently stroked her face with his thumb, the very same thumb that killed her . . .

Switch wasn't quite sure how long he'd remained in that exact position, only a mere seven feet outside of the wretched Stillwater Sanitarium, a limp Adelaide Lynch held securely in his arms as his knobby knees fell numb against the frozen grass. He wasn't quite sure how long he'd simply admired her, memorizing the features of her darling complexion as if he were attempting to store it in the deepest parts of his memory for an eternity. He studied the shape of her lips—which were usually a shy, soft pink, but now displayed a ghastly, unpigmented hue. Heart shaped and slightly parted, discolored teeth peeking through the petite slit of her agape mouth as his fingertips softly traced the sticky skin, uneven mounds of dry flesh slipping between his touch as he choked back enraged shouts.

Briar Cunningway and Ulysses Vern filed into the storage room, eyes simultaneously widening at the sight of a dead Greenwald laid slump in front of the open back door, an idle gun weakly laced within his grasp as a mess of dark, soaking wet curls came into view.

"Oh my God." Briar whispered, pulse quickening at the sight of Switch directly outside of Stillwater's back door as she broke into a sprint, swiftly approaching the man on his knees in the cold as Adelaide's limp frame came into view.

A horrified shout slipped off of Briar's tongue, gaze colliding with the bloody entrance wound on the woman's shoulder, most likely a result of the gun that laid within Greenwald's grubby clutch. A clammy palm met her lips, blinding tears significantly blurring her vision as Vern stopped short in his steps, stomach violently churning at the sight of a dead Adelaide.

Switch failed to acknowledge their presence, fingers still intently stroking the relaxed features of Adelaide's face as Briar fell to her knees beside him, shaken palms meeting Adelaide's chest as she loudly sobbed.

"We were so close." Switch muttered, tearing a stray strand of brown hair from Adelaide's cheek.

"It's o-okay," Briar stammered, caressing Adelaide's unmoving cheek as she obscenely cried. "You did it. You got her out. You freed her."

"But I couldn't *save* her."

Silence consumed the crowd, the beam of Vern's flashlight firmly focused on Adelaide's youthful complexion as Briar claimed Switch's hand in hers. A shaken sea of blue met a conflicting case of cocoa, the woman's bottom lip trembling as she urged the man to hand Adelaide over.

"You need to go." Briar said, causing a completely confounded expression to envelope Switch's sullen features as he neglected to hand over his girl.

"You didn't come this far to fail," the nurse confidently continued. "The police will be on their way any minute, I guarantee it. Don't worry about Addy, she'll be safe with me. I'll take good care of her. I promise."

Switch frowned, nodding agreeably in Briar's direction as he pressed one final kiss to Adelaide's forehead before handing her over, easing the weighty woman into the arms of a profusely crying Briar as the king of hearts card still sat firmly within the woman's grasp, hovering over her still heart.

"Run." Briar pressed, voice rigid and wary as Switch glanced objectively up in Vern's direction. The guard simply nodded, side-stepping to allow the criminal access to the nearby swarm of trees.

The man shakily climbed to his feet, frozen palms dusting off the patches of ice from his bottom as he nodded curtly in both Briar and Vern's directions before stealing an additional, lengthy glance at his Adelaide.

"Goodbye, *Adelaide*." He croaked, shoulders hunched as he sprinted towards the trees and disappeared into the night.

XXXIII

"Well I never pray,
But tonight I'm on my knees /
I need to hear some sounds that recognize the pain in me"
–The Verve, "Bitter Sweet Symphony"

The thirty-first of December, 2008.

8:03 AM.

The Grind House was uncommonly busy for a Wednesday morning, but the one single barista on duty assumed that the sporadic spurts of extra business was most likely due to the current holiday. It's a cute little coffee shop downtown, where the elegant, glass windows surrounding the entirety of the petite premises provided a clear, perfect view of Lake Michigan directly across the previously repaved street, establishing a lively, family-friendly atmosphere for all paying patrons.

The theme was mostly grayscale with a dash of bright, bubbly pink—seven circular, unpigmented tables littering the freshly swept wooden floors as printed copies of *The Chicago Tribune* littered every single surface of the comfortable café. On some tables, three-or-so copies of the newly printed newspaper littered the area, partially sipped coffees claiming the corners of the paper as the thin material fluttered from nearby movement.

A pair of wide, hazel eyes wistfully scanned the garish article that claimed the very front page—bold, inky letters strewn across the very top as she audibly gulped. Although she'd read the printed piece several times over, she couldn't help but skim the story one final time, vision momentarily blurred by the intrusion of fat, salty tears as she hastily blinked them away.

CALAMITY AT STILLWATER

On the twenty-fourth of December 2008 at 11:04 PM, a bolt of lightning struck the faulty generator of Stillwater Sanitarium, ultimately killing the power and leaving the entire building in shambles. All that remained was the sporadic, three-second flicker of dull, red lights—the institution's weak supply of emergency lighting. The authorities were not contacted until 12:43 AM, and the event generated eight casualties and ultimately, the escape of the infamous Switch.

Unlike standardized facilities, (which are strictly required to follow any and all regulations in reference to both patient and guard/nurse safety protocols), the cell doors were not battery operated, nor were the maximum-security cells—leaving every single cell unlocked and open the very second the power diminished. The owner of the institution—Doctor Jeremy Evers—was NOT present during this particular event and has chosen to opt out of any and all questioning.

Although the true nature of the chaotic events that unfolded within Stillwater's walls is still vastly unknown, eight bodies were identified, and the casualties are listed as follows:
Head Psychiatrist — Lyra Jeanne Blake (46).
Security Guards — Elliot Rob Greenwald (31), Wren Marie Tribeca (24).
Medical Staff — Lora Louise Algort (33), Angelica Mae McGregory (32), Chadwick Charles Jackson (27).
Patients — Nayeli Elizabeth Schmitt (22), Adelaide Rhea Lynch (24).

The surviving patients will be temporarily transferred to surrounding institutions pending investigation of Stillwater Sanitarium.

Citizens of Chicago must be aware that Switch is currently unaccounted for. A reward for the criminal stands at 1MIL. Be advised NOT to approach, for he will most likely be armed and is extremely dangerous and unpredictable.

The woman released a lengthy sigh, dropping the newspaper onto the table as her clammy palms met her flushed features. A slight, tempestuous twinge poked and prodded at her left temple, momentarily blurred vision refocusing on her surroundings as the occupied tables lowly chatted. Most of them discussed the events that had unfolded at Stillwater only six days prior, gazes glued to the freshly printed papers as her stomach violently churned.

She wanted so badly to just rip it to shreds—to dig her manicured nails into the softened paper and tear it up into itty-bitty pieces. However, destroying the newspaper wouldn't change a thing. What happened *still* happened, and until someone decides to invent a time machine and eagerly leap through the time space continuum and possibly prevent this atrocious event from ever occurring—Adelaide would remain dead.

Lazily, the brunette woman glanced over her shoulder to view the counter, where the barista carefully cleaned the surface of the multi-hued gray granite with a dampened cloth. The translucent pastry case was practically bare; courtesy of the abundance of hungry customers that managed to raid the café of nearly the entirety of its baked goods before nine in the morning.

With an exasperated sigh, the lonely girl stood to her feet, tugging the sleeves of her itchy sweater down the slopes of her goose bump infested arms as she approached the register. The woman opposite the cluttered counter strut a head full of thick, bushy locks—a clean mixture between red and brown as half of the stick-straight strands lay draped over her shoulders, whereas the remainder clung to a loose rubber band at the top of her skull. Her eyes were impossibly dark, some kind of charcoal-like color, but warm and comforting and inviting all at the same time. Her smooth, pink lips twisted into a bright, boastful smile—clammy hand flattening against the swollen flesh of her belly as she adjusted her lopsided olive apron.

"Good morning," she politely chirped, dismissively tossing the cerulean rag into a nearby sanitizer bucket as the brunette briskly nodded, smile matching the barista's in intensity. "What can I get started for you?"

"Er," the customer generously paused, thumbing through the wrinkled dollar bills buried within her leather wallet as she quickly counted the bundle of money. "Let me have a large cinnamon latte with soy milk and extra foam. Oh, and a plain bagel with cream cheese, please."

The pretty barista nodded, entering the order onto the register with the curve of her knuckle as the exhausted patron tore a twenty from the confinement of her expensive, name-brand wallet. Awkwardly, the customer eyed the barista's bulging belly, lips strung into a generous grin as she released a pleasant inquiry: "how far along are you?"

The barista told the customer her total—a white, toothy grin enveloping her complexion as she tore the twenty-dollar bill from the beautiful brunette's clutch. Gaily, she glanced downward to view the protruding baby bump, butterflies raiding her belly at the sight of it.

"Thirty-six weeks." She replied, handing the woman her change as the girl on the opposite half of the counter simply shook her head.

"Keep the change. Honestly." The obviously wealthy woman stated, tucking a stray strand of brown behind her quad-pierced ear. Inky black eyeliner cloaked her upper lids, curling into identical, precise wings. Her eyes were a gorgeous shade of green and gold, and although they were by far the most enticing shade of hazel the barista had ever seen—she couldn't help but notice the overwhelming essence of despair that clouded her orbs.

"Is it your first baby?" The customer gently wondered, fiddling with the sleeves of her sweater as the barista prepared her coffee.

"Second, technically." The woman replied, a sheer smile stretched across her mouth as she retrieved the half-empty carton of soy milk from the mini-fridge below the counter. The little bundle of joy within her belly assertively squirmed in response to her jarred movements. "My first would be six years old, but she was a stillborn."

"Oh," the customer gaped, intently watching the heavily pregnant woman make her coffee as she shifted her weight from either foot. "I'm dreadfully sorry—"

"No, no, it's okay. I'm not sure why I just randomly blurted that out to a stranger." The barista lowly replied, shaking her head in bewilderment as the harsh hum of the milk steamer interrupted their speech.

"Boy or girl?" The customer wondered, slightly raising the volume of her voice in order to clearly speak over the milk steamer as the barista filled the base of the decorative paper cup with cinnamon flavored syrup.

"A boy." The barista gleamed, positioning the cup beneath the spout of the espresso dispenser. "I'm naming him Lucky. Before you judge the name—this is my third pregnancy and it's a high-risk one, probably because I'm an old hag. But he'll be the only baby of mine to actually make it, so he'll be called Lucky."

The brunette sincerely smiled, lounging against the counter as her manicured fingers fumbled with the container full of paper-wrapped straws.

"I like that." She said, tearing a single straw from the circular container as she studied the ridges of the bright white paper along the length of the object. "There's no way you're much older than me, though. You look young."

The barista froze, a chuckle vibrating its way through her throat as the espresso machine roared to life, vigorously prepping the two shots of addicting liquid. The aging machine groaned and spluttered, audibly grinding the roasted beans as the barista slowly stirred the syrup within the cup.

"I'm thirty-five," the barista explained, stroking her bulbous belly as the shots staggeringly slipped from the spout, splattering the inner walls of the cup. "I know I still look fifteen, but I promise that I'm not. Although, sometimes I wish that I was."

"You look great." The brunette cheered, waving the straw through the air as she glanced warily over her pointed shoulder to view her abandoned chair. The newspaper remained exactly where she'd left it—lifeless. Forgotten. A skeleton of what she used to be before she'd gotten the dreadful news.

The barista filled the cup with the steamed soy, topping it off with an extra amount of foam as she snapped on a lid and slid it across the counter, directly into the customer's open palm.

"Thank you," the customer said, flattening her fingers against the warm cup as she thickly swallowed. "I don't think I caught your name, actually?"

"Oh! How rude of me, goodness." The flustered barista tossed her palms into the air, flipping a significant chunk of fallen hair behind her shoulder as she extended her arm to claim the customer's hand in hers. "Kennedy Carter."

The customer nodded curtly, claiming Kennedy's cold hand in hers as she firmly shook it, replying with: "Westlynn Harris."

Westlynn excused herself from the counter, taking a tiny sip from her steaming cup as the tepid coffee seared her top lip. Bitterly, she yanked the cup from her mouth, falling flatly onto her seat once more as her gaze refocused on the article. Adelaide's name stuck out like a sore thumb, her throat growing painfully dry as the tip of her forefinger met the printed ink, gently caressing the surface as if it were her twin sisters face.

Her free fingers fiddled with the base of her weighty coffee cup, deep, dramatic exhales slipping off of her lipstick-smeared lips as a palm met her bony shoulder. Instinctively, the lithe woman violently flinched, nearly knocking over her cinnamon soy latte as the barista—apparently named Kennedy—handed her a small brown paper bag.

"Sorry if I scared you," Kennedy cooed, placing the bag—which was warm to the touch due to the toasted bagel within—into Westlynn's wary clutch. "Is it okay if I sit with you for a minute? My doctor recommends having me take a break every twenty minutes to get off my feet."

"Of course." Westlynn murmured, motioning towards the vacant seat on the opposite end of the circular table as the pregnant woman waddled towards the chair. It was rather cute, really, the way she approached the seat—her obviously swollen feet sliding across the wooden floor as the soles audibly scraped along the surface. She reminded Westlynn of the cute little penguins that she'd seen every year at the zoo growing up.

Penguins were Adelaide's favorite animal.

Almost as quickly as the thought arose, it immediately vanished—stomach aggressively churning as she eased the bagel from the depths of the bag and peeled open the container of cream cheese.

"So," Westlynn began, meeting Kennedy's lively stare as she smeared an abundance of cream cheese onto her crunchy bagel. "How's the daddy feel about naming him Lucky?"

Kennedy sympathetically smiled, running a palm along the curve of her stomach as she averted her gaze towards the table, the harsh headline of *The Chicago Tribune* filling her vision as she audibly gulped.

"There isn't a daddy," she shortly stated, palm settling on the left portion of her belly, where Lucky persistently kicked; making his presence known to the outside world. "He's a sperm donor baby, actually. I'm getting up there in age and all I want is to have a baby, so here I am. I was married at the time I miscarried my daughter six years ago. We separated half a year later."

"I'm sorry." Westlynn muttered, at a complete loss for words as she slowly sipped her coffee.

"Don't be," Kennedy gleamed, readjusting the hem of her apron as she continued. "I never really found love after him. I guess I didn't want to, to be honest. I thought I'd be better off without him, but once he'd left and I'd finally come to my senses—I really realized how wrong I was."

A considerably lengthy pause arose, stagnant silence filling the void as the low, mindless chatter of the surrounding individuals enveloped their ears.

"I never dated anyone after him. Not one person. Of course, I hooked up with some guys—and a few girls—but I just couldn't see myself with anyone else. I tried to go back to him, but it was as if he'd fallen off the face of the Earth. Quite literally, actually. He was completely wiped from the system. Not even the Chicago PD could track him down, because apparently, he doesn't legally exist anymore." Kennedy confidently explained, the confession oozing from her mouth with complete certainty as she met Westlynn's distressed features. It felt amazing to finally tell someone all of this, regardless of the fact that she'd only met this woman a mere five minutes earlier. However, something strange stirred within Kennedy's belly around Westlynn Harris—as if she'd known the woman for an eternity. As if she was meant to hear everything that Kennedy had to say.

"How is that possible?" Westlynn inquired, her tone vastly muffled by a particularly large bite of bagel.

"I don't know." Kennedy honestly replied. "He had some connections to some *bad people,* so one of them must've wiped him out from the system. To the government, he's a complete ghost. For what reason, I'm not entirely certain."

"So, are you guys still legally married?" Westlynn wondered.

"Kind of hard to divorce someone who doesn't even exist, isn't it?" The barista dryly chuckled, continuing to toy with the extended flesh of her stomach as baby Lucky wedged his little foot against her palm.

"Yeah, I'd say so." Westlynn mused, eyes awkwardly meeting Adelaide's name once more as her chest violently ached. Kennedy's glare followed hers, settling upon the front-page news as she thickly swallowed.

"Crazy what happened at Stillwater, isn't it?"

Westlynn wordlessly nodded, dropping the uneaten half of the bagel onto the crumb-infested bag as she blinked back tears. She was supposed to visit Adelaide on the Eve of Christmas, but backed out last minute due to conflicting plans with Jasper's family. If only she could've known that was the last time she would've seen her sister . . .

"My sister died," Westlynn revealed, chest heaving. "She was one of the patients."

Kennedy's jaw fell, words momentarily eluding her as she simply shook her head. What could she possibly say to a woman who'd lost someone as significant as her sister?

"I'm so sorry, Westlynn." Kennedy whispered, fingers meeting the warm flesh of the brunette's palm as she reassuringly squeezed. "If you need anything at all, please don't hesitate to ask. I know we've just met, but there's a spark in you. I really admire that."

Westlynn bleakly nodded, vision clouded with heartbroken tears as she squeezed Kennedy's hand before abruptly dropping it. The barista excused herself moments later, returning to her designated spot behind the espresso bar as Westlynn wiped the tears from her eyes, careful not to smear the precisely applied eyeliner as she tore the newspaper from the table.

Hesitantly, she tore the paper open, weakly viewing the inner articles as a spirited *ding* emerged, courtesy of the little yellow bell atop the entrance door. Curiously, her gaze drifted over the top of the newspaper, immediately widening at the sight of a group of heavily armed masked men.

Several chaotic shouts erupted from the surrounding tables, desperate cries and agonizing pleas for help overcoming the once peaceful atmosphere as Kennedy immediately fell to the floor behind the bar. The sight of the assault rifles in the masked men's clutches was enough to make her want to projectile vomit all over the floor—but for her safety and the safety of her unborn child, she remained deathly silent, palm flattened against the curve of her swollen stomach is if to inaudibly assure the baby that everything was going to be all right.

Westlynn fearfully observed the scenario through hooded lids, just barely peeking over the rectangular edge of the thick newspaper as her hands profusely shook. The sextet of men was dressed in an abundance of black, very loaded and intimidating assault rifles wedged between their gloved clutch as several customers scrambled towards the safety of the inner walls. Ski masks concealed their appearances, a creepy comparison to the famous fictional character Jason from *Friday the Thirteenth*.

Thus, a seventh individual appeared—strutting through the parted front door with an overwhelming essence of confidence. A classy, charcoal suit cloaked his features, double-knotted, jet black Chuck Taylors peeking out from the ankles of the uneven slacks as a vibrant mahogany dress shirt claimed his torso, buttoned all the way up to the collar. All that was missing was a sleek tie to compliment the tasteful arrangement. His thick, unkempt brunette curls were a tangled mess, thrown astray by the harsh winds directly outside the front door as his inky, leather-gloved grasp met his features—

oddly unique and undeniably mortifying. The right portion of his face was smooth and silky, a profusion of soft, nearly translucent freckles littering the pale surface as his tiny pink tongue poked and prodded at the severed skin of his lower lip. The opposite half, however, lay mangled and destroyed—an abundance of dissimilar lacerations coating the surface as the curve of his thumb elegantly caressed the bumpy, uneven flesh beneath his eye.

"Good morning, ladies and *gents*," the infamous Switch enthusiastically cheered, thrusting his arms outwards as the sleeves of his coat hiked up the length of his arms. Within his gloved grasp lay a freshly sharpened switchblade, threateningly glimmering beneath the mixture of natural and artificial lighting within the café as he filed further into the premises. Kennedy's blood ran cold at the unnerving sonance of Switch's grueling voice, uncontrollable shivers claiming her spine as she choked back mortified cries. *What the hell was he doing here?*

"I hate to *interrupt*, but I'm lookin' for someone special. So-*uh*, don't *mind me*." The criminal generously paused, brows raised in wonder as he observed his surroundings. Sets of wide, fearful eyes met his haunting black orbs, fingers fidgeting around the blade of his knife as his minions paced the premises, teasingly shoving the barrels of their rifles in the customers faces as the frightened individuals released vociferous shouts.

Switch dug into the pocket of his classy slacks, withdrawing a crumpled photograph of the nefarious Christopher Carter as he smoothed out the kinks with the pads of his concealed fingers. His features contorted into that of immense disgust at the sight of his father, pink tongue darting out from the depths of his mouth as he intently gnawed on his lips. He rapidly approached the front right table, earning a fearful cry from the middle-aged woman and her ten-year-old daughter, who was red in the face and profusely sobbing.

Switch met the child's gaze, tightened features mockingly softening as the back of his hand met her scarlet cheek, gently stroking the surface as he mumbled a giddy: "Shhh, don't *cry*, sweetie pie."

Thus, he diverted his glare towards her mother, thrusting his arm outward to meet her distressed complexion as the photograph of his father invaded her senses, as well as the taunting blade buried behind the wrinkled paper.

"Recognize him?" Switch thickly spat, cocking his head to the side as the woman shook her head from side to side, cowering into her chair as the man enthusiastically rolled his eyes.

"Ugh." He groaned, straightening his hunched posture as he audibly cracked his back. "You're *no help.* "

The criminal rounded the café, shoving the photograph of Christopher (King Cici) under nearly everyone's noses as several staggered statements slipped off of his lips, statements like: *"have you seen this man?"* or *"any clue where I can find this sonofabitch?"*

Alas, he arrived at Westlynn's table, lips audibly smacking as the woman effectively hid behind the newspaper. She could literally *smell* him—some hint of sweet-smelling cologne—and the sheer proximity of him was enough to make her stomach twist into painful knots.

"Excuse me, *ma'am.*" Switch wildly giggled, tossing the creased photo onto the top of the table as the headline about Stillwater raided his vision. Almost instantly, his eyes focused on the professionally printed section, the one which contained Adelaide's name.

Hotly, the psychopath tightened his grip on the base of the blade, jaw irritably clenched as he spat out a vexed, "y'know, it's very *rude* to not look someone in the eye when they're *talking* to you, sweetheart."

With that, the blade collided with the edge of the paper, swiftly slicing through the center as the material fell into two evenly shredded sections, littering the floor in piles as Westlynn obscenely cried. Her palms met her eyes, shielding herself from Switch is if this were some type of bad dream, and closing her eyes would make him just go away . . .

"Now *now*," Switch huskily purred, tucking the blade further into the surface of his palm as his leather fingers met her wrists, assertively tearing her hands from her eyes as his mouth went dry.

His ruined complexion contorted into that of immense confusion, jaw ajar as warm, staggered breaths showered Westlynn's flinching features. He smelt of mint and cigarettes, a somewhat strange mixture that made the woman's toes curl within the confinement of her boots. Quickly, the man collected himself, tongue lapping at the innermost creases of his marred mouth as he exchanged his weight from either foot, thumbs gently massaging the inside of her wrists as unwanted goosebumps showered the skin.

"Well well well," he gleamed, admiring Westlynn's gorgeous features as his heart swelled twice its size within his chest. "Back from the *dead,* princess?" Westlynn raised a puzzled brow, lips parted in uncertainty as she struggled to formulate a proper reply.

"W-What?" Westlynn stammered, her accent thick and uneven as Switch's chest ached, vivid visuals of a presumably dead Adelaide raiding his mind as he contemplated claiming her flushed face and slamming their lips together, to breathe life right back into her.

Oh, darling, you have no idea how much I've missed you . . .

Suddenly, a harsh realization struck, causing Westlynn's stomach to churn as she released a staggered inquiry: "Do you think that I'm Adelaide?"

Switch failed to reply, his grip loosening on her wrists as bewilderment consumed his marred complexion. It was obvious that Adelaide had never told him about her twin sister.

"Adelaide was my identical twin sister." Westlynn shyly revealed, audibly gulping as she defiantly tore her arms from Switch's significantly weakened grasp. "You two knew each other? She told me that you didn't."

"Oh," Switch giddily mused, twisting the blade between his fingers as he intently studied Westlynn's face.

God, she looked *just* like her . . .

"We knew each other *very* well, sweetheart. Tell me, what's your *name?*"

"W-Westlynn."

Switch's lips curled upwards as he glanced over his shoulder, blatantly motioning at one of his own personal Jason's near the front corner of the café. The henchman nodded, rapidly approaching a shaken Westlynn and a cocky Switch as the man mumbled something entirely inaudible into the minion's ear.

Before Westlynn could protest, the armed man had slithered himself beneath her arm, yanking her frozen frame from the safety of the chair as she defiantly thrashed beneath his hold. In response, three other Jason's surrounded them, claiming her trembling arms and kicking legs as the woman profusely sobbed, spitting an array of obscenities in Switch's direction as he dismissively diverted his attention. Gloved fingers grazed the folded photograph of his wretched father, slipping the object back into the depths of his pant pocket before approaching the empty espresso bar mere feet away.

He walked with a slight skip in his step—right arm mechanically slapping against the outer flesh of his thigh as his thumb grazed the serrated edge of the blade, boastful butterflies consuming his belly as his rounded fist met the granite.

"Knock *knock*." He announced, fist colliding several times with the squeaky-clean surface as Kennedy cowered on the floor, just barely hidden from his sight.

"Where can a guy get some *coffee* 'round here?" The criminal taunted, running a hand through his curls as Westlynn continued to obnoxiously shout from the doorway, her limbs entangled in the arms of the mystery men as one of the Jason's stayed behind, slowly approaching his boss as his fingers fiddled with the idle trigger.

Defeatedly, Kennedy rose to her feet—knobby knees furiously wobbling as her palm flattened against her belly, as if to stable herself. Streaks of auburn hair dangled within her vision, quivering bottom lip extending outward to blow the bothersome strands away as her fearful gaze met his.

Suddenly, the room seemed to be spinning on an axel. She damn well knew those eyes—those soulless, black pits—and in all honesty, she wasn't quite sure if she'd ever see them again before this day. His paling lips descended into a pout, mouth parted in awe as he, too, had managed to completely freeze in place. Neither of them seemed to breathe—unblinking eyes simply admiring one another's aged complexions as Andrew's orbs drifted downwards to meet Kennedy's pregnant belly.

At the sight of it, the man clearly felt his heart lurch—thin breaths escaping through parted lips as the remaining minion lightly tugged at his sleeve.

"Boss," he breathed, shifting his weight from either foot as he glanced over his shoulder to see the other masked men aggressively shoving a sobbing Westlynn into the sleek black van. "The cops'll be here any minute. We need to split."

"Yeah." Switch lowly breathed, distinctly clearing his throat as his eyes met Kennedy's once more. There was so much to say, so many things that he wanted to spill to her—to shower her with—but instead, he bit his tongue, effectively masking a distressed sigh as he twisted his hunched frame and made a beeline towards the door, the spitting image of Jason sharp on his heels.

Kennedy stood stunned behind the counter, blinding tears clouding her vision as she choked back hefty shouts, clammy palm clamping over her mouth as she stifled her sobs. The remainder of her customers seemed to do the same, several of them obscenely crying to the police on their cell phones about the event as the remainder of the criminals filed from the café.

Switch's palms met the frame of the van door, lunging his weight into the vehicle as he slid past a frantic Westlynn, completely ignoring her heightened pleas as she tore at the ankles of his trousers, nails digging into the thick material as she nearly tore them from his legs.

"Ge-*zuuuus*," he drawled, assertively kicking her off of4 him as he settled into the back corner of the van, hand easing into the inner pocket of his overcoat as he retrieved a fresh pack of cigarettes. Jason's look-alike claimed Westlynn's arms, pinning them down so that she couldn't harm Switch. He then claimed a nearby set of shiny handcuffs, quickly latching them around her wrists as she attempted to nudge him off, but to no avail.

Switch slipped the cancer stick between his lips, palm curling around the fluorescent flame of his vibrant lavender lighter as the low, orange glow illuminated his features. The wildly claustrophobic scent of smoke and nicotine immediately consumed Westlynn's lungs, prompting her to loudly hack as she kicked at his shoe.

"What do you want with me?" She cried, ripping her shoulder from the masked man's hold as the minion simply sighed, hand meeting the rubbery material of his mask as he tore it from his face. Sweaty, jet-black strands of hair clung to the crinkled flesh of his forehead, dark eyes settling upon an extremely lax Switch as he dramatically inhaled the nicotine into his lungs.

"It's crazy how much she looks like Adelaide." The henchman stated, closely studying Westlynn's frantic features as the van took a corner a bit too sharply, sending the trio airborne as their bottoms abruptly collided once more with the plastic floor mats.

"*Wild,* innit?" Switch grumbled, tearing the steadily burning object from his mouth as he twisted it between gloved fingers.

"Y'know, *Verny*-boy," the theatrical bloke began, slyly eyeing a sweaty Vern as the former Stillwater guard fiddled with the loaded gun, ensuring that the safety was properly clicked in place as his black gaze met Switch's identically hued orbs. "I almost thought she *was* Addy-Bear for a second back *there*. Thought I was *losin'* it."

"I honestly thought the same, bud." Vern admitted, chuckling slightly as he met Westlynn's bewildered glare. "They aren't kidding when they call 'em identical."

414 // ALYSSA DICARLO

"I don't know what Adelaide did to the both of you for you to want to kidnap me, but I swear, I'm *nothing* like her." Westlynn shakily defended, her words rushed and hoarse as she steadily studied a surprisingly calm Switch, who lounged against the back doors of the van.

"Blah-blah-*blah*-blah-*blah*." Switch irritably growled, adjusting his posture as he crawled on all-fours towards a distressed Westlynn, who miserably attempted to back away, only to hit her head on the harsh plastic wall of the van.

"Look at me, sugar plum." He ordered, tearing the black gloves from his grasp as he dismissively handed his half-smoked cigarette over to the man named Vern, who, apparently, also knew Adelaide.

His bare fingers met her face—cold, calloused digits—as his thumb met her bottom lip. Slow, steady breaths showered her face, hot and pleasant, smelling strongly of nicotine versus the majority of mint that she'd detected earlier. He was studying her lips, pale pink lipstick smeared and messy, transferred to the flesh of her rounded chin, courtesy of his prying fingers.

Finally, she looked at him. Really, *truly* looked at him—wide, hazel eyes meeting a multitude of cocoa. Somewhere deep within those soft orbs, she saw a sliver of light. A sliver of hope.

She saw what Adelaide had seen all along.

"Oh, Westie-*lynn*," Switch grinned, habitually wetting his lips as the skin glistened beneath the weak lighting of the van, his grip tightening on her cheeks as he dug his nails into the surface.

"Daddy is going to have some *fun* with *you*."

epilogue

The second of January, 2009.

Waterlogged puddles consumed the pockmarked concrete of the road; practically fathomless, the bottom of the filled basins invisible to the naked eye. Several individuals fell victim to these miniature lagoons, distracted feet stumbling into the depths of the trap as the rainwater soaked through the ankles of their trousers, irritated groans toppling from parted lips.

Six *fucking* people showed up to the funeral of Adelaide Rhea Lynch on that day. Half of them arrived merely out of sympathy. Sympathy for the poor soul who'd arranged the entire event, a weeping woman with bountiful blond locks and stunning blue eyes, lanky limbs adorned with an elegant silk dress.

A plethora of pretty pink peonies and gorgeous orchids littered the premises of the funeral home, supplied from an unknown sender with considerably careless handwriting—a sender who couldn't even take the time to dot their i's or finish the circles on their o's, leaving them indistinguishable between the multitude of u's on the written note.

Family failed to show. Briar made sure to find out the wretched Alice Lynch's exact address, and she'd even expedited the letter all the way to Australia so that Alice would have time to find a considerably cheap flight. Briar never heard anything back.

Westlynn, Adelaide's identical twin sister, actually managed to reply, enthusiastically ensuring Briar that she'd be there through a neatly written letter, her penmanship loopy, bright and bold. But as the rain slowed and the aging funeral director with a thick white mustache and tiny green eyes urged Briar to come inside—*it's time, Miss Cunningway*—realization truly struck: Westlynn wouldn't be attending Adelaide's funeral, either.

Slightly smudged winged eyeliner claimed Briar's upper lids, salty, sorrowful tears seeping from her red-rimmed orbs as she woefully wept. Mascara consumed her rounded cheeks; webbed and thick, like a spider had swiftly constructed its home and abandoned it almost immediately. Left it for something better. Someone better. The six guests had promptly left following the service, blank expressions plastered across their complexions, and yet, not a single tear was shed from the lot of them. In fact, the number of tears that had emerged from Briar's eyelids was enough to compensate for the lack thereof.

And as the sobbing heap of woman lay collapsed over the closed metal casket—*ironically named Briar Rose; a lilac purple with a pink interior and gorgeous, faux gold trim along the exterior creases*—she swore that she could almost hear the delightful cadence of Adelaide's voice. Diffident and overwrought, the mousy tone laced with a thick, comely accent; blatantly Australian. Plentifully perfect.

The elegant and somewhat pricey jet-black gown that claimed her daunt limbs was severely creased and wrinkled, a majority of the fabric wrapped around one bony ankle. Adelaide lay beneath the shiny sealed tomb; resembling that of a life-like doll. Her once straggly, ashen locks were perfectly parted and carefully curled, daintily cupping her bountiful breasts. A foundation that matched her skin tone had effectively concealed the vibrant violet bruises that claimed her neck, little circles that cleanly resembled the shape of Switch's fingers. The fingers that stole Adelaide's very last breath (per her dying request, Briar had come to learn). The bullet wound from Elliot Greenwald's gun was wrapped and hidden, concealed by the sleeve of a pretty pink dress. Adelaide looked healthier in death than she had in the last two years she'd been alive.

"Sweetheart," Vern cooed, rubbing circles in between Briar's extended shoulder blades as she profusely wept against the rounded surface of the casket. Her manicured nails dug into the painted metal as his lips met her hair. His limbs were adored with a striking stygian suit, cuffed slightly at the ankles, sparkling dress shoes glimmering gleefully beneath the low lighting of the funeral home. His hair was a tousled mess, several strands sticking outward in an unappealing fashion as he attempted to flatten the locks back to the surface of his skull, but to no avail. Apparently, they had a mind of their own.

"I m-miss her so m-much, U." Briar cried, stumbling over her words as she buried her face against the chilly surface of the casket, chest inordinately heaving as the man continued to mindlessly etch miscellaneous drawings against her clothed flesh.

"I know."

Mustache man had excused himself from the area moments prior, allowing Briar some time to mourn over Adelaide before they lowered her into the ground for good. Vern figured the elderly man (possibly in his late-sixties, evident by the deep, ghastly crow's feet that claimed the edges of his eyes) had found the buffet table in the opposite room, where a multitude of hot food claimed a six-foot-long folding table. For the most part, the food remained untouched.

"I wish I could bring h-him back," Briar murmured, wiping away the pitiful streaks of smeared mascara from her rosy red cheek as Vern glanced curiously in her direction.

"Bring who back, baby girl?" He cooed, tangling his slender digits within her knotted hair as the beautiful blond strands lay draped over one shoulder, the tight-knit curls sticky and stiff between his fingers.

"Greenwald." She verified, features contorting into that of immense disgust as her hands balled into fists upon the sealed casket. "I wish I could bring him back so I could kill him myself. Kill him for what he did. Make him pay."

Vern laced his arms around a trembling Briar, whispering a series of sweet nothings against her hair as he held her close. Today felt like an event straight out of a dream—out of a nightmare. Ulysses Vern wished nothing more than to be able to take his darling Briar's pain away, to absorb it through her skin and bask in it. For her, he'd do absolutely anything.

"I love you," he spoke, pressing a locked lipped kiss to her forehead as his fingers tediously tore a bothersome curl from her lashes. "I wish I could take your pain away."

"I wouldn't wish this pain upon anyone," Briar replied, tugging out of his comforting hold as her hands met the cold casket once more. "Especially you."

"I wouldn't care," he clipped, taking a generous step forward as his hands, too, met the rounded edge of the elegant casket, pulse erratically thumping beneath his heaving chest as Briar blatantly avoided his gaze. "I'd die for you, Briar."

Their stares hurriedly met, fresh tears prickling in her eyes as their fingers interlaced upon the surface of Adelaide's tomb. Just as the woman's lips parted in preparation to speak, a voice emerged from beyond the doorway several yards back. Deep. Guttural. Hoarse, yet phlegmatic—so much so that she could vividly visualize the partially marred complexion that it belonged to.

"Am I too *late?*"

Briar spun around on her heel, eyes widened with wonder as her heart skipped several elongated beats. And yet, just as she'd suspected, there he stood—ungloved hands tucked away within the roomy pockets of his black slacks, loose and ill-fitting, as if he'd snagged them off some beefy bloke with a set of thunder thighs. The cuffs of the slacks were sloppy and folded, gently kissing the white laces of his faded black Chuck Taylors (*ha! Chuck Taylors! Totally fucking typical*). The coat of the tuxedo ensemble was absent, and his torso was claimed by a silky-smooth dress shirt, ironed and sleek, with evenly spaced horizontal dashes along the surface. A personable pink tie completed the look, bright and lively. Utterly unimpaired. Looking completely debonair in his attire, as if he simply knew how handsome he was, how unbelievably *gorgeous* . . .

The horrifyingly familiar fraternal bunch of gaudy, healed scars claimed the left half of his face, per usual, his perfect pink lips curling upwards into a cheeky grin. Those tremendously curly brunette and lengthy locks teased his cheeks, (well, the pieces that managed to slip from the confinement of the pale rubber band, that is) as most of the hair remained in a neat, tight bun near the base of his skull. He looked absolutely stunning. Stunningly sad, that is.

"Switch." Briar squeaked, cupping her palms over her painted lips as she broke into a sprint, nearly tripping over the fabric of her dress as she scaled the commodious room. Switch gradually removed his clammy palms from the depths of his pockets, feet shifting upon the carpet as he adjusted his stance. Before he could utter a snarky remark, Briar had, quite literally, thrown herself at him—latching her slender arms so tight around his neck that she'd nearly managed to knock the wind right out of him. Hesitantly, his arms curled around her trembling torso, brows inexplicably raised as he shot Vern a questionable glare. At this, Vern merely shrugged.

"Good to-*uh,* see you *too,* pumpkin." Switch teased as Briar eventually unlatched her arms, sparkling eyes admiring the hunched man before her as she nodded.

"I'm so glad you came." She said, stumbling over her words as she wiped her fresh tears away with mascara-stained fingers. "Do you want to see her?"

Switch visibly stiffened, a guttural gasp catching in his throat as his beady black gaze fell upon Adelaide's closed casket. His stomach agonizingly churned at the sight of it, and for once, the man felt as if he were completely numb.

"I see you guys got the flowers." He dismissed, inching slowly towards Adelaide's casket as a genuine grin claimed Briar's lips.

"Oh, Switch," she breathed, walking side-by-side with him as they approached a frozen Vern and a hidden Adelaide. "You sent those? They're absolutely stunning. Addy would love them."

Switch simply grunted in reply, shaking fingers gliding along the oblong edge of the casket as his fingertips collided with the cool metal casing. His empty glare cautiously met Vern's, lips curling into shy smile as he ushered a low greeting.

"Afternoon, Vern."

"Hey, boss." Vern coolly replied, nodding curtly in the Switch's direction as he met Briar's side, right arm instinctively twisting around her waist as he held her close.

"You can open it." Briar uneasily chirped, tucking her hair behind her ear as she cautiously approached the beautiful lilac casket. Switch's stare met hers, mouth ajar as staggered breaths slipped off his tongue. Wordlessly, the duo unanimously unlatched the gorgeous brass latches, slowly lifting the lid as Adelaide's pale unmoving form came into view, and Switch nearly choked on his own spit.

Briar audibly whined at the sight of the dashing dead girl, locking the lid into place as Switch's fingers curled around the edge, knuckles flushing a ghastly white as if he'd dipped them into a fresh can of oily white paint. She laid upon a comfortable sheet of fluffy pink lining, bubbly and bright like the eyes that lay beneath her sealed lids. Her palms were neatly folded across her chest, Emmett's engagement ring snug around her finger, shiny and silver and sparkling.

"Fuck," Switch murmured, fingers unlatching from the side of the casket as his hand dipped into the elegant box, fingertips tickling the shy skin of Adelaide's blush-splattered cheeks as he swallowed an additional mound of bile. "She looks so beautiful."

Briar's palm met the in-between of his shoulders, patting twice in reassurance as she stepped back.

"I'll give you a moment alone with her." She whispered, choking back an additional round of sobs as she glanced fleetingly in Adelaide's direction. Seeing her lifeless within that fancy, expensive box was almost too much to bear for the woman in her mid-thirties.

With that, Briar slipped her hand into Vern's, and the duo vacated the stuffy room, the persistent clicks of her inch-and-a-half tall heels ricocheting off the wooden walls as Switch gently caressed the ball of Adelaide's cheek. His thumb traced cautious circles along the surface, breaths emerging in thin, evenly spaced pants as his brows knit together in vexation. The flesh of her throat was utterly flawless, free of any struggle—any evidence. Irately, the man's slender fingers met the skin, lightly rubbing away at the very same spot where his thumbs only recently laid. Sure enough, after enough persistent rubbing, an essence of boorish, unappealing purple bruises raided his vision—brash and even, perfectly circular and symmetrical. A petite whine caught in the pipe of his throat, quivering thumb intently colliding with the surface of the larger bruise as the finger perfectly aligned with the unattractive mark.

"What've you done?" He gruffly droned, applying an ample amount of pressure to the violent violet flesh as the spongy skin dipped beneath his hold. Unfortunately, there was no struggle. No gasps for air or widened, bulging eyes.

Of course there wasn't, dumbass. She's fucking dead.

Switch promptly removed his touch, ebbing eyes diverting from the undeniably morbid sight of Adelaide's dolled-up appearance as his gaze migrated to the covered entrance wound from Elliot Greenwald's bullet. For a moment, the man debated whether or not to peel the sleeve of her periwinkle pink dress from that very spot, so as to reveal the wound that ultimately catapulted her into her acceptance of death—but instead, he remained frozen. Numb. Unfeeling, unthinking—as if the tide had washed over him and sucked up every last bit of sanity that remained within his dwindling mind.

After all, *he* was the sole reason for her untimely demise.

He'd attempted to banish the thoughts of that night from his mind on multiple occasions. A night full of martyrdom and sin and bloodlust, of desire and hurt. The memories haunted him like a substantially sized and undeniably unyielding storm cloud, one which followed his every step and consistently down poured over his head. Every inch of Adelaide's sweet, innocent body was a harsh reminder of the hellish reality in which Andrew Carter lived and breathed every single damn day.

A bouquet of peonies cradled the head of her casket, in full bloom as the madman assertively tore a single flower from the stack, trembling digits overturning the lovely object within his clutch as his opposite hand claimed Adelaide's frigid fingers. With a thumping heart and wide eyes, Switch eased the green stem between stick-like digits, placing the flower within Adelaide's hold as he released a hefty breath.

Thus, a small hand met his hunched shoulder once more, the shy breaths of a distraught Briar invading his ringing ears as she slipped something into his hand.

"Here," was what she said, her tone small and collective as the man's glare met the wistful object within his palm. "I think she'd like this to be with her, too. If you're okay with it."

Bleakly, Switch nodded, swallowing a mouthful of bile as he reached down into the casket once more, delicately prying Adelaide's fingers apart as he wedged the materialistic object between her unmoving digits. Boldly, Briar's hands met his, assisting him in positioning Adelaide's hand over her heart as the creased card hovered the unanimated organ. A cheerful cartoon king claimed the surface of the card, the laminated paper slightly crinkled—courtesy of the freezing cold rain from that dreadful night.

Why don't-cha stick him in your pocket.

Switch frowned, the vivid visuals of a measly Adelaide raiding his vision as he clearly recollected the scenario of that very day when he'd given her that card—when he'd given her his heart.

That way I can always be with you.

Together, Briar and Switch lowered the lid once more, Adelaide's body disappearing from view as they latched the box closed for good. Neither of them spoke, nor did a quiet, uneasy Vern who hovered the doorway. The white mustached man entered the room once more.

"Are we ready for the burial?"

Watching Adelaide be lowered into the ground was almost too much for Briar to handle. In fact, she'd managed to crumble completely—lithe limbs vibrating in sloppy spurts of loud cries as her lover, Vern, held her nice and close. Her tears drenched the white of his tie a muted grey, courtesy of her ever-running mascara as Switch stood silent beside them.

His legs were generously parted, clammy hands buried deeply within the depths of his trouser pockets as the tip of his forefinger fiddled with a softened pack of Newport cigarettes. Before his imprisoned days, Andrew was a slut for Camels, but ever since the deranged man had been locked up within the suffocating, sequestered walls of Stillwater Sanitarium—he found himself craving the warm, familiar taste of Newport cigarettes. Because maybe, just maybe, if he smoked enough of them, they'd end up tasting just like Adelaide.

Her headstone was gorgeous and marble; an aesthetic, snowy white with sporadic specks of gray, accompanied by her full legal name, etched in bold, black ink. It was obvious that Briar spent a nice pretty penny on ensuring that Adelaide had the absolute best service and burial that she could ever have, because in reality, if the incredibly dismal Alice Lynch had been in charge of it all, she probably would've just chucked Adelaide's lifeless body into a ditch somewhere and called it a day.

Due to Adelaide's position in the cemetery, it was quite evident that Briar had managed to get in touch with a sad, aging woman with thick-rimmed spectacles and a mouthful of faux teeth—Carla DuPré. The woman's husband had left a mere six months after their only child's unanticipated death, complaining of "brash, emotional trauma" before shacking up with a leggy blond who caked on her makeup and was barely over the legal age. Luckily, after Carla's son Emmett's death, the woman had managed to snag an abundantly roomy plot for her only son to lay to rest, one which cradled a multitude of gorgeous eastern redbuds and had a perfect view of Chicago's skyline. Adelaide's resting spot lay parallel to her late fiancé's, as if they were some type of elderly married couple who'd lived and died together like life and society had intended, not a couple of kids who had met their demise at exceedingly young ages.

The cemetery was old and decrepit, but it was one of the nicer ones that held some of Chicago's finest deceased citizens. It was located on the edge of the city, just hovering the Burnham Harbor, and contained a multitude of old, cracked stones—some stained, some broken, all courtesy of the wonted wear-and-tear of the land. Apparently, the gargantuan plot of land had been dedicated to a man by the name of Arthur Winnipeg—*Winnipeg Park, fancy that*—and they'd even established these eerie, wrought iron gates—which were absolutely littered with bird shit, such a tragedy—accessorized with nice and sharp, pointed spikes along the top.

The funeral director (Mustache Man) kept stealing quirky, side-eyed glances in Switch's direction, stare solemnly studying the messy mange of curly brown locks atop his skull as he awkwardly avoided the gruesome bunch of selcouth scars that marred the left portion of his complexion. He looked frighteningly familiar, like some type of eldritch omen, or the face of a heinous villain out of a child's nightmares. Mustache man was half-expecting a flock of inky crows to land on the guy's shoulder at any waking moment to solidify his suspicions, but was left somewhat disappointed.

Thereby, Adelaide was laid to rest beside her darling beau. Lovely, lilac casket perfectly placed within the cautiously carved hole, an elegant headstone hovering above her head as a group of semi-silent men in stained, denim overalls hobbled over to begin filling her grave with damp dirt, being overly cautious around Emmett's resting place.

Briar's palm managed to rid her nostrils of the oozing clear snot, bloodshot eyes focusing on a rigid Switch as he tore a single cancer stick from his half-empty pack and eased it between partially parted lips. Vern was busy thanking the funeral director for his time, warm hand claiming the elderly mans as he offered a sincere smile in his direction. Mustache Man, however, couldn't seem to quit glancing in Switch's direction, little lips formed into a pout at the mere sight of him.

"That was brutal." Briar whispered, her tone choppy and dry as she inexplicably cleared her throat. Switch, however, failed to reply—palms cupped around a vibrant orange lighter as he lit the cigarette with ease. There was a pleasant breeze throughout the outskirts of Chicago, utterly atypical but nevertheless welcomed. The dazzling dewy grass was wet beneath their feet, audibly crunching with every miniscule movement as Switch began to pace. Thick, fluffy clouds obscured the sun's presence, enveloping the entirety of the creepy, old cemetery with a warm, yellow glow as the greasy-haired man took a long, lingering drag off of his cigarette.

"Glad it stopped raining," Briar animatedly added, grazing her sweaty palms along the length of her dress in a weak attempt to dry them. "It's been raining for like, eight days straight."

Had it even stopped raining since Adelaide died?

"Ge-*zuuuus*," Switch droned, voice muffled by the entity between his lips. "Chatty fuckin' *Cathy* over here. Does she ever shut up, Verny boy?"

"Nope." Vern mused, inching his arm around Briar's bony shoulders as she bitterly shoved him off.

"Sorry for trying to be social." She snipped, arms crossed like a tantrumatic child. "And positive. Uplifting. Happy—"

"News flash, *tater tot*," Switch bitterly clipped, tearing the cigarette from his chapped lips. Briar flinched at the sight of his ominous, beady black gaze—defined jawline tightened in vexation as he spilled a plethora of proclamations. "There ain't nothin' happy about today. Our Addy bear—*my* Addy bear—is *dead*. She *ain't* comin' back, and there isn't a damn thing we can do about it. The world is a goddamn negative place, Bri-Bri—a fucking *shit* show. We don't *get* to be happy. Not now, not ever. Until you learn to accept that, you'll just be stuck in your little fantasy land, frolicking about and eating candy canes and lollipops—"

Switch tediously trailed off, stuffing the burning object back between his lips as Briar stood stunned, jaw agape in mortification as realization sunk in. He was right—fuck, he always was.

"I'm—"

"Bri," Vern scolded, claiming her wrist between cold fingers as she impulsively flinched. "Don't."

Alas, silence consumed them. Stagnant and maladroit—like a weighty, winter cloud, smothering them with irrational ire. Goosebumps consumed the exposed flesh of Briar's arms, coating the surface like a set of slimy scales, ones that would usually consume the length of a squirmy snake.

"Switch," she heartily began, inching towards the persistently pacing man as he twirled the cigarette between long, lanky fingers. His silhouette looked marvelous against the pink painted sky, hunched form perfectly placed between the blurry buildings in the distance as he dismissively kicked a rock aside with the toe of his sneaker. "Why don't you come Uptown to have dinner with Vern and I? We could get Chinese takeout, I've been craving it for weeks now. Plus, you could see our place, I'm all moved in and I've started decorating it nice."

"That's a generous offer," Switch muttered before tossing his unwanted cigarette into the nearby water. "I'm just not in the mood for cat tonight, I'm afraid."

Briar's brows etched together in uncertainty, smeared lipstick-riddled lips parted as the criminal continued to monotonically speak.

"However," he said, lapping at his dry lips like a dog as his warm, cocoa-hued stare met hers. "Your boy-toy and I have some business to tend to, so I'll be needing to-*er, borrow* him, if you don't mind. Well, it doesn't really matter if you do mind, I suppose. Either way, he's coming with *me.*"

At this, Vern raised an inquisitive brow. "Everything alright, boss?"

"Just *peachy,* bud." Switch grinned, a Cheshire-cat smirk that nearly kissed the discoloration beneath his tired eyes. Briar laid stunned opposite him, mouth still ajar as Switch clamped a warm, sturdy palm atop her shoulder before patting down several times.

"Until we meet again, lovebug." He dryly teased, winking seductively in Briar's direction before withdrawing his touch and sauntering towards the nearby carpark.

"I'll call you." Vern lightly offered with the simplistic nod of his head, lips puckered to place a fat kiss upon Briar's lips before he, too, drifted toward Switch's crookedly parked vehicle.

Briar hadn't expected any type of thanks from the wanted criminal for what she'd done—for allowing him to escape completely unscathed—but the least he could do was come over for supper, she figured. However, when it came to the Switch, nothing was simple. He was, by far, the most complex man she'd ever had the pleasure to meet, and possibly, could consider as her friend. Maybe.

With a thickly churning belly, the woman weakly watched as the two men clambered into a sparkling sleek vehicle, a muted gray color, with windows tinted so dark that it was surely over the legal limit (not that Switch abided by any laws, of course). A 2007 Maserati Quattroporte, most likely stolen, but nevertheless, comely for the bloke's clearly expensive taste. So, the woman smiled—a broad, toothy grin, accented with an occasional giggle as she, too, headed into the direction of her idle vehicle in preparation for departure, glancing one final time in the direction of Adelaide's now fully-filled grave as her heart skipped several beats.

"So," Vern started, easing into the pleasantly warm and gloriously scented vehicle as Switch tossed the smashed carton of cigarettes onto the dashboard with an enthusiastic grunt. "What's the sitch?"

Switch shot him a scolding glance before adjusting his posture against the smooth leather, fingers dipping into the fabric of his knotted tie as he loosened it slightly.

"I've got a lead."

"No fucking way," Vern gawked, running a hand through his disheveled locks. "Tell!"

Switch cleared his throat, glancing awkwardly out the window to view a giddy Briar as she clambered into her own vehicle several spaces down. "Word on the block is that my old man's been hangin' around Hancock Tower. No clue what his business is there, but it's a start."

"Absolutely," Vern breathed. "So, should we head on over there? Pay the bastard a little surprise visit?"

"On a Friday afternoon? Nah," Switch clipped, shoving the key into the ignition as the engine roared to life. "No *no no,* I've got someone else to tend to for now."

The duo fell silent as Switch peeled the Maserati from the parking space, side-eyeing a rigid Ulysses as he wet his lips.

"She-*uh,* doesn't *know,* right?"

Vern gulped. "No."

"Good." Switch purred, gnawing on his bottom lip. "Little Westie-*lynn* will be our *little secret.*"

acknowledgements

For starters, I'd like to thank my parents. From the very first story I wrote (a short paragraph about SpongeBob when I seven years old), they've been *so* unbelievably supportive. I remember printing my little stories out and hanging them around my room, and my mom ended up buying me a binder with laminated place holders to put them into. I still have that binder today, and it's an amazing reminder of where it all began. Where *this* all began. Now, fourteen years later, I've put a solid 100-plus ideas onto paper. Some, of which, never quite went anywhere. Until this one, of course.

To my best friend Mona, who stuck by my side through this entire journey and listened to my late-night rants and wild ideas. Thank you for providing endless support and helping me through all of my bumps in the road with this tale. Your encouragement and dedication helped shape this book into what it is today. Thank you for being my first reader, a listener, and most importantly, a friend.

To my loving husband, my *endless* support system. Tyler, your beautiful arrays of love and support have driven me to be the best that I can be, regardless of the copious number of roadblocks I've encountered in life. I could never thank you enough for encouraging me to better myself and my writing.

To my late best friend Cassidy, who would've been cheering me on from the get-go and definitely would've been the first to read this. You were always so supportive with my writing, regardless of the quality. In fact, no matter what, you supported me through everything. Everything I do is for you.

To Cheyenne—a reader. A listener. An editor. A friend. Thank you for reading this novel not only once, but *twice* in its eternity. For being my second set of eyes and an undevoted ear. I don't think I could ever express my gratitude.

And for you—the person holding this book in their hands. The person who read *Catatonic* from cover to cover—thank you. Thank you so much for supporting me on this journey. Words could never convey how truly thankful I am for your support. Thank you for giving me and my work a chance.